Acknowledgements

Once again I am indebted to my editor, Jerry Ziegler, who kept me on track writing this novel while he waited patiently for the story to evolve. And to my good friends and accomplices in writing, Carole Lexa Schaefer and Kyp Bisagna, for their advice and for chuckling in such a heartening way as I read passages of this book to them. Louise, too, when she was able to join us. I would also like to thank Don Smith and Elizabeth Powell, for being so accommodating about tailoring their artwork to suit my needs, and Mary Ann Wisman for her proof reading prowess. A big shout out to Lisa Pierce, for pre-ordering *Borrowed Ground* for her book club, which kept me moving towards the finish line, and to the members of said book club for their 'first reader' insights, which were invaluable. Thanks also to John Leach for answering my questions about Muchelney Pottery and for allowing me to use his real name. And finally to the people that love and support me in my writing: my wonderful husband, Stephen, who reads and re-reads everything I write; our children, Reed, Annie and Esther; my mother, Vera; sister, Sandra; and all the friends who buy, read and spread the word of my books – thank you.

Cover Art:

Original cover art by Don Smith;
Graphic design by Jon-Paul Verfaillie.

Interior Art:

Original drawings by Elizabeth Powell.

for Esther,
who was there.
~ with love ~

Winter

Chapter 1

"Hey, Joe, d'you want me to go get ice for the champagne? You're putting it in coolers, right?"

Joe was upstairs and had just found the bow tie he'd been looking for when he heard Sonny calling up to him. He scooted out of the bedroom, bow tie in one hand and a length of red ribbon in the other, and looked down from the top of the stairs to see his best friend standing at the bottom, his right foot three steps up, his knee poking out from under his shorts.

"No, you know what I'm going to do," Joe replied as he raced down the stairs, bobbing out of the way of his neighbor, Laura, who was on her way up carrying a silver fir bough and a staple gun. At 35, Joe was agile and fit, with a muscular upper body from years of wedging clay and a head of dark, untamed hair. His large, square frame glasses slid down his nose when he bounced on the landing in front of his friend, and Joe pushed them back up before continuing. "I'm going to drive up Sauk Mountain later today," he told Sonny, "and fill the back of the truck with snow. Then I'll park it over by the pottery studio and push the champagne bottles into the snow to keep them cold."

"That'll work," agreed Sonny. "Who are those for?" he asked, nodding at the items in Joe's hands.

Joe looked down at the bow tie and the ribbon. "The dogs."

"The dogs?""

"Yeah. So they'll look smart for the wedding." He turned as the front door opened and a blast of chilly December air blew into the house. It was Jimmy, Laura's husband, coming in with a double armload of thick, dark green fir boughs that filled the entryway to the little house in the mountains with their woodsy scent.

"Hey, Joe?" Jimmy called out, craning his face around the boughs. "Do you want me to move all those pruned limbs that are on the ground out front?"

"The ones under the King David apple tree? Yeah, if you would."

"Where d'you want me to put them?"

"Maybe in a wheelbarrow? That way I can take them up to my new kiln and burn them in the first firing."

"Roger that," said the tall Texan. He and Laura were also artists and had quickly become friends with the potter when they moved into the neighborhood. "And where do these boughs go?"

"Up here," Laura called out from above them. All three men looked up at the sound of her voice. The wall to the right of the stairs was covered in unfinished sheetrock and Laura had taken it upon herself to paint the names Joe and Lucy in sloping red letters on a large heart made out of brown craft paper and pin it in the middle of the wall. Now she was stapling fir boughs around the edges of the heart.

Joe shifted away from the bottom of the stairs to let Jimmy go past. He led Sonny around the Christmas tree set up in the crook of the stairwell and when his arm brushed against the needles on the branches they were both treated to an extra hit of the tree's evergreen scent. Joe let his lungs fill with the tangy aroma before bending over to toss a chunk of firewood into the woodstove. "What are you wearing?" he asked Sonny.

"What? For the wedding?"

"Uh huh."

"A tweed jacket that I got from the Goodwill and long pants."

"No shorts, huh?"

Sonny gave him a crooked smile. "Nah. I figured if I wore shorts, I wouldn't have a pocket for the rings." He walked around Joe and sat down on the faded red couch, folding one leg to prop the ankle on the other knee and running his hand over the golden coating of hair on his shin.

Joe crossed his living room in three strides, opened the sliding glass door and whistled for Max and Maggie. He nodded and smiled at Dave and Mario, two of his other upriver neighbors, who were tying a blue tarp between the cherry tree and the vine maples. They'd told him they wanted to barbeque salmon outside on Webers for the wedding feast and since the weather forecast was for rain, Joe had them string a tarp up alongside the house to act as an awning.

The dogs ran over from the woods behind Joe's studio, bounded up onto the back porch and trotted into the house. Joe let Maggie, his aging Chesapeake-mix, go past but he blocked Max with his knees. The brindle-coated dog looked up at his master, wondering what was up. Joe bent over and wound the bow tie in his hand around the thick fur on the dog's neck. Max sat patiently, letting him do it, while Maggie lay down by the woodstove.

"Did you get yourself a suit?" Sonny asked from behind Joe.

"Yep, a suit *and* a tie. Which I'll probably never wear again." Having clipped the two ends of the bow tie together, Joe stood up straight and pushed his fingers through his mop of brown hair. He liked wearing what he always wore - faded blue jeans, black suspenders over a t-shirt and wool shirts - but he also liked getting dressed up for the right occasion. And marrying his sweetheart, Lucy, definitely counted as the right occasion. He bent forward again and centered the black bow on the tie at the back of Max's head, making something of a cummerbund between the white of the dog's head and a long brown patch over his body. Then he turned to

Maggie. "Okay, your turn," he told her.

Magnolia looked doleful as Joe approached her with the ribbon but she lay still while he began the process of tying it around her neck. The house buzzed with wedding preparations; Jimmy and Laura talked on the stairs over the staccato shots of the staple gun while Dave and Mario could be heard calling instructions to each other outside in the yard. The radio played jazz and the new chunk of fir firewood snapped loudly in the woodstove.

The front door opened again in the background and a female voice sang out, "Yoo hoo."

"Hi, Katie," Laura called out from the stairs.

"Oh hi, Laura. Hi, Jimmy. That looks great!" came Katie's reply.

"We're over here," Joe yelled as he pushed his index fingers through the loops on the red ribbon and pulled them into a bow. He straightened back up and turned in time to see Katie pop her wool-capped head furtively around the Christmas tree. Katie was only five feet tall so bending to peek around the tree made her even shorter. "Is Lucy here?" she whispered with exaggerated theatricality.

"No. She went down to the airport to pick up her brother."

"Great!" Katie rounded the tree to stand in the living room and squeezed her shoulders together excitedly. "The ladies are getting together tonight to arrange flowers for the wedding..."

"Yeah and drink all my tequila, right?" griped Sonny.

"No, we're doing the flowers at my house instead of yours this time because Lucy and her brother are staying with you tonight. Remember?"

"Apparently not," laughed Joe. He adjusted the loops he'd made in the bow of the red ribbon around Maggie's neck to make it even puffier. "How's that look?" he asked.

"Oh, Maggie," crooned Katie, bending over immediately to pet the beautiful brown dog. "Are you going to be the flower child?"

"No, Maddie's our flower child," Joe corrected.

"That's right! Of course." Katie turned her head left and right, looking around the room. "Is she here?"

"No, she's down at my house with Jimmy and Laura's daughter, entertaining Sarah," Sonny explained.

"Knowing your wife, she's entertaining *them*," said Joe.

Sonny's wife, Sarah, was renowned for her ability to teach young children and the joy she put into learning ranked her "best teacher ever" in most kids' eyes.

Katie straightened up again. "I can't stay long because I have to go pick out flowers and buy coals for the Webers..."

"I have coals," Jimmy called out from the stairs.

"Enough?" Katie called back.

"Three bags."

Katie nodded her head vigorously. "That's enough." She called up above her again. "Great. Thanks." Then she looked at Joe. "I came to find out what color the combs are that Lucy's wearing in her hair for the wedding."

"Red. That's how come I gave Maggie a red ribbon."

"Okay good. We'll use red ribbon on the men's boutonnieres then."

"And I should use red ribbon to tie boughs along the railing on the stairs?" called out Laura.

"Sure," Joe called back.

"Don't you look handsome!" Katie told Max, scratching his head as she walked back around the Christmas tree. She stopped and looked up at the top of the 8-foot tree. "Is this for our ornaments?" she asked.

"Whose idea was that?" Jimmy asked.

"What? The ornaments?" Joe moved towards the kitchen sink to rinse off his hands and looked across the entryway of the house at Jimmy standing on the stairs. "That was Pete's. He's in charge of the party and he figured because we're getting married in December, it would be fun to have people bring Christmas tree ornaments as a party favor."

"They'll make great memories for you and Lucy every time you decorate your Christmas tree," Laura said.

"Okay, see you tomorrow, Joe," Katie sang out as she opened the front door. She looked up at Laura. "Are you coming over to my house to do flowers tonight?"

"You bet. Especially if Sonny's wife brings the tequila."

They both grinned over at Sonny but he was standing with his back to them, staring out the kitchen window. Katie slipped away, Laura turned her attention once more to the boughs and Sonny pointed in the direction he was staring. "What's that thing glinting?" he asked.

Joe looked up and turned his head towards the window. "Over by Daisy the cow's old loafing shed next door? I have no idea."

"But you know what I'm talking about?"

Joe swung around and grabbed the towel off the cook stove, drying his hands on it as he continued to look out the window. "Sure I do. I've seen whatever it is catching the light for days now. I just can't figure out what it is." He threaded the towel back over the handle to the stove and braced Sonny. "Wanna help me move the pots out of the shop so the kids can use it as a play room tomorrow?"

"Sure," nodded Sonny distractedly.

He couldn't take his eyes off whatever was glinting at him from next door.

*****

Hilda Hess lowered the binoculars and shifted her slight frame from one foot to another. It really was agitating having to stand out in the cold under the green metal roof of the loafing shed to see what Connors was up to at his place, but she feared if she went back to the little cabin she lived in across the pasture, she wouldn't have an adequate view. Plus the man from the County still hadn't shown up and she certainly didn't want to miss that. He'd assured her he would pay the pottery shop a visit during business hours today and it was, what? – she shook her left arm, exposing her watch from underneath her raincoat, then looked down at it – almost 11:00 am. Her thin lips pressed tightly together as she pushed her gray curls away from her forehead. Why wasn't Connors in his studio as usual?

A brown, Ford escort pulled into the driveway of the pottery shop and Hilda lifted the binoculars back up to her eyes. She watched as a woman she didn't recognize, a woman with a tight ginger braid that circled her head, climbed out of the drivers' seat and walked around to the trunk. This was a pattern that Hilda had seen repeated a number of times this morning and she wondered, as she watched the woman reach her hands forward and lean down into the trunk, what was going to be carried into the Connors' house this time? The wind picked up suddenly and Hilda shivered, tightening the green and brown, hand-knit scarf around her neck as she watched the woman back out of the trunk, stand upright and turn to face Connors' house. That's when Hilda saw the cake. A three tiered, white icing covered, wedding cake.

Of course! Connors was getting married. That's why he wasn't at work today! Hilda had heard talk of the coming wedding, in the post office, the café, the grocery store, but she didn't know exactly when it was supposed to happen because she hadn't been invited. Which suited her just fine because she felt like her own wedding plans were on hold because of Connors, so she had no inclination to go and help him celebrate his. Especially not if she had to bring a potluck dish, which is how weddings always seemed to be in the Upper Skagit.

She shifted the binoculars back to the guys that had set up a blue tarp on one side of the house. Now they were arranging Webers underneath it. Hilda's mood soured slightly as she realized that she'd probably be missing out on some good, Skagit River salmon by not going to this wedding. Salmon followed by cake.

Her knees popped as she bent first one then the other, trying to ease the stiffness out of them. She decided she'd had enough. She dropped the binoculars into the pocket of her raincoat and, using the trees for cover, angled back over towards her house. Maybe she'd eat her lunch sitting in a chair by her kitchen window so she could watch Connors' driveway for the arrival of the County inspector. Picturing the guy pulling in lifted Hilda's spirits once more and she found the corners of her mouth turning up as she walked in her pink flowered rain boots through the wet grass towards her house. To think that he might just be showing up on Joe Connors' wedding day. How poetic.

*****

The first thing Lucy noticed when she pulled into the driveway after coming back from the airport, were the long, feathery plumes of greenery tied around the railings on either side of the front steps. Then, when she opened the front door, she was struck by the incredible aroma permeating the house. It was as if someone had taken the essence of forest and breathed it in through the log walls. It was enchanting.

Her green eyes lit up with wonder as she looked from the tree to the boughs on the stairs to the heart on the wall with her name on it. She pushed her thick, strawberry blonde hair away from her face as she called out, "Who did all this?"

The dogs raced around the corner from the living room to greet her, their rear ends swaying the lower branches of the Christmas tree.

"Did all what?" Joe called back.

"Hung all the greenery?" Lucy petted the dogs, then nipped around the tree to find Joe and Sonny at either end of the couch, lifting it up off the floor.

"Laura mostly," Joe grunted. "Move out of the way now."

"Where are you going with that?" The words lilted up and down with her English accent.

"Into the shop. So the kids can use it tomorrow."

The two men rounded the corner of the stairwell and Joe caught site of Colin, Lucy's brother, standing patiently by the front door, playing with Max and Maggie. "Heeeey, Colin," he beamed, lowering his end of the couch to the floor again. "You made it! How was the journey?"

"Not bad," replied Colin his English accent even more pronounced than Lucy's. "Except they don't let you drive very fast on the motorway here, do they?"

Sonny chuckled. "This ain't Europe," he said, setting his end of the couch down on the floor now too. "They won't let you go 100 miles an hour here."

"My brother drives 100 miles an hour wherever he is," Lucy added.

"Even on those tiny streets in England," agreed Joe, who'd spent a white knuckle 20 minutes as a passenger in Colin's Jaguar the first time he'd gone to England with Lucy.

"You get a lot of tickets?" asked Sonny.

Colin, who was over 6-feet tall like Sonny, with a tidy, businessman's cut of his thick, chestnut hair, pinched his lips together in mock peeve under his moustache. "Just a few," he admitted.

Joe reached out his right hand. "Good to see you!" he said, and the two men shook vigorously. "This is my brother, Sonny," Joe went on, with his hand outstretched in Sonny's direction.

"Your brother? So you must have flown in from New York?" Colin asked as he shook Sonny's hand.

"No, he's not my bio-brother...." explained Joe.

"Just someone he's known long enough to make carry the heavy end of the couch."

Joe laughed.

"You need some help with that?" offered Colin.

"Nah, you're dressed way too smart for schlepping furniture around."

"Oh I was going to suggest Lucy help," quipped Colin.

"Ha, ha," Lucy scoffed.

"I hope you brought something to change into," Joe said,

looking more closely at Colin's elegant pants and his teal blue, Marks and Spencers' sweater. Or pullover, as the Brits would call it. Joe knew all about Marks and Spencers, the big department store in England that sold good quality clothing, because his soon-to-be in-laws had already given him many cotton shirts to go hiking in from that store.

"I have a suit for the wedding, yes."

"I was thinking change down, not up. You know, into something more heavy duty. For the woods."

Colin looked at his sister. "Are we going into the woods?"

Lucy gave a happy shrug. "What do I know?" she laughed. "When I left this morning the house looked completely different so I haven't a clue what's going on." She turned back to Joe. "Except your brother and his son are arriving later, right?"

Joe nodded. "Around 5:00 this afternoon."

"Good. So I have time to show Colin around."

"Well I want to take him up Sauk before it gets dark," cautioned Joe. "What time is it now?"

"2:30," said Lucy, after a quick glance at her watch. "When do you want to leave?"

"Right after I get this couch in the shop." Lucy frowned. "Hey, it gets dark at 4:30 and it'll take us 45 minutes to get up to the snow."

"Snow?" questioned Colin.

"Yeah," said Joe, bending over to pick up the couch again. That's when he noticed Colin's shoes. "I hope you've got something other than those to wear!"

Lucy's brother looked down at his narrow-toed, black, patent leather shoes. "Why? What's wrong with these?"

"You'll slip off the mountain in those things! And it's a long way down from the top of Sauk, beh-lieve me!"

"I've got some boots down at the house that might fit him," Sonny put in as he hefted the couch back up into the air along with Joe.

"Are they a large size?" Colin asked, opening the front door for them.

"Of course they are!" snorted Joe. "Have you seen how tall Sonny is? He'd be falling over all the time if he had small feet!" He followed Sonny out the front door and cut around to his left so that now he'd be the one backing up, across the porch to the pottery shop. "Hey, and the wedding cake arrived," Joe told Lucy, who'd moved to stand next to her brother.

Her mouth dropped open. "Wedding cake?!"

Joe winked at her. "You forgot about that, didn't you? Good job I didn't. It's in the pantry if you want to see it."

Lucy danced around Colin, threw open the door to the pantry and slipped inside. She heard a catch in her breath. There it was, sitting on the freezer; tiers of cascading pale blue and lavender flowers on lacey circles of white, trimmed at the bottom with cuttings of sword fern.

"You like it?" Joe asked, coming into the pantry behind her and slipping his arms around her waist. He pulled her close to him and tucked his face up against hers, feeling her soft curls against his cheek.

"It's lovely," she replied. "Who made it?"

"Twyla."

Lucy pictured the ginger-haired baker she'd first met making doughnuts over at the Barter Faire in Eastern Washington.

"She had to drive for 7 hours to bring it to us because the Pass was closed."

"Oh my!" Lucy swiveled in Joe's arms and he leaned forward and kissed her. The two walls to the outside in the pantry were log walls with no windows and Joe had pulled the door closed behind him, so the tiny space was semi-dark and very private. After all the comings and goings of the previous few days it felt good to have a moment alone.

"You doing okay?" he asked when they finally pulled apart.

"Mmmm," she replied. "Thank you, for thinking of the cake."

"Thank you for marrying me."

Colin coughed outside the door. "Lucy, Sonny wants to take me down to his house to get those boots."

Joe opened the door to the pantry. "Great," he said, moving out to stand next to Colin, with Lucy behind him. "I'll follow you down in my truck and we'll head up the mountain from there. You coming?" he asked Lucy.

She shook her head no and looked past him, out the front door, at a blue Jeep pulling into the driveway. Joe followed her gaze as the dogs leapt up on the front porch, barking in tandem. "I think that's Rachel with my wedding dress," Lucy explained. "So you should definitely leave."

Joe didn't need any more prompting than that. "Okay, Colin," he said. "I'll get a shovel and meet you down at Sonny's house."

*****

Ten minutes later they were bumping up Sauk Mountain Road in Joe's three-quarter ton Chevy pick-up, with Sonny trying to point out the Skagit River below to Colin even though it was veiled by a soft fog suspended in the sky. Joe scoured the clear cuts along his side of the steeply curving road for signs of wildlife as he drove higher and higher up the mountain, headed for the small glacier at 4,500 feet where the snow never melted. As they climbed, the surface of the road went from a dusting of white snow to an accumulation and, at about the 6-mile mark, 1,000 feet from their destination, the truck barreled into 8 inches of snow and shimmied its resistance to going any further. Joe took the Chevy out of gear, stepped on the emergency brake, and jumped out of the truck to lock the hubs and engage the 4-wheel drive. He swung back into the driver's seat, shifted into low range and tried to ease the truck further up the road. But the snow was slick and the rear wheels slid to the left, propelling the front of the truck precariously close to edge of the road. Sonny, who had been peppering Colin with questions about rugby, lifted his chin and peeked over the hood of the truck, as if trying to determine the depth of the drop. "We gonna leave it here then?" he asked Joe.

"It's not that deep," was all Joe said in reply. He put the truck in reverse and tried easing her back but the tires spun and the front end nosed even further to the right. Sonny wound down his window and stuck his head out. "How close are we?" Joe asked.

"Close enough," replied Sonny.

Joe stepped on the emergency brake, switched off the engine and threw open his door. "Okay, let's dig her out," he instructed then jumped out his side, turned around and climbed back up onto the frame of the door. He reached over and grabbed a snow shovel from under the bungee cords that were holding it to the headache rack. Sonny had his shovel in the vehicle with him so he just rolled out his side, and used the shovel like a ski pole to balance himself as he pushed through the snow to the rear of the truck. He began immediately to dig the snow away from the tire on his side and throw it into the bed of the truck.

"I think this stuff's too wet to take back with us," said Joe, once he got to the driver's side rear tire.

"So what are you saying? I shouldn't throw it in the back of the truck."

Joe looked at what was already in the truck bed. He shrugged. "I guess. But once we've dug Nelly out I'm gonna try to get her further up this road so we can get some of the good stuff."

"You're not worried you'll get stuck and you'll be late getting back."

"Nah! I've had this old girl in worse than this. We'll be fine."

Sonny chucked his head to one side and went back to shoveling. It was quiet so high up the mountain, and for a while all the men could hear were the shushing sounds of the shovels slicing through the snow and the thonk of it landing in the truck bed. "How come Colin's not helping?" Sonny asked after a while.

"He's sleeping."

"Sleeping?!"

"He did just take a 9-hour flight…."

"I wasn't sleeping," came Colin's voice and both men looked up to see him standing behind Sonny, looking bleary eyed. "I was enjoying the view."

Joe looked out at the dense fog. "What view?"

A small smile flickered at the sides of Colin's mouth. "The view of the inside of my eyelids."

"Ha!" bleated Joe.

"Is there a shovel that I can use?" asked the Englishman.

"There's another one tied to the headache rack but we're almost done here," replied Joe.

"The headache rack?" asked Colin.

Joe nodded towards the criss-cross, black metal shield directly behind the back window of the cab. "That thing there," he said.

"And why do they call it a headache rack?"

"Because it stops a piece of firewood from coming through that window and giving you a headache," explained Joe.

Colin tipped his head to one side as if he found this very interesting. Then he looked perplexed. "And why are you throwing the snow into the back of your lorry?"

"So we can take it home."

"Why?"

"So I can use it to chill the champagne at the wedding party."

"They don't sell ice in your shops?"

"Yeah they do," Sonny chimed in as he lifted the last of the snow from around the tire and tossed it into the truck. He stuck the shovel down into the snow on the road and leaned on it, his cheeks ruddy from exertion. "But this is free."

"Plus I got thirty bottles of champagne," said Joe, throwing the last of the snow from under his tire into the truck. "That'ud be a lot of ice."

"Only thirty?!" Colin sounded aghast.

"Hey, we're not all stockbrokers," Joe shot back. Then he

smiled. Lucy had told him how much Colin liked to tease and now he was experiencing it first hand. “Okay let’s get the front tires,” he said and they all moved forward to the outer edge of the road.

Colin watched as Sonny tossed a shovelful of snow over the side of the road. “I don’t think I heard that land,” he said, sounding queasy.

Joe stopped shoveling and stepped forward to look over the side. “What’d’I tell you? That’s straight down. Take a look.”

Colin put his hand on his stomach. “No, no I’ll take your word for it.”

“You were just 30,000 feet up in the air!” said Joe, going back to his shoveling. “You can’t be scared of a drop off in the mountains.”

“It’s not the drop off I’m scared of,” explained Colin in a calm, very precise way. “It’s your driving.”

Joe let out a raucous laugh. “You can walk if you prefer.”

“I would. But these boots leak.”

“They do?” asked Sonny, surprised.

“Well my feet are wet so I assume they do.”

“Huh. Maybe that’s why I stopped wearing them.”

Colin clucked his tongue against the roof of his mouth and rolled his eyes.

“I still think you’re better off in the boots than in those useless businessmen’s shoes from London,” declared Joe.

“Hey, we’re not all lumberjacks,” reasoned Colin.

“Touché,” laughed Joe

By now they had all the snow removed from under the front tires. “Okay,” said Joe, “let’s try this again.” He threw his shovel into the bed of the pick-up as Colin and Sonny climbed back in on their side, then he opened the driver’s door, grabbed the steering wheel, pulled himself up and bounced back into the seat. He started the engine and turned the heater up full blast, blowing on his hands to take the icy sting out of them. He put the truck in low gear and eased down on the gas pedal. The wheels scuffed against the gravel then bunny jumped forward and for one nerve wracking moment it looked like they were going over the side. All three men braced backwards reflexively, eyes wide, but Joe had spun the steering wheel left and as he pushed harder on the gas pedal the pick-up gained traction and curved to the left before rolling uphill. He turned and grinned at Colin. "That's what we call a sphincter special," he said.

"Except I don't think Sonny's is working," Colin whispered.

"Nah, that's just last night's beans," Sonny put in and casually rolled down the window an inch on his side.

The truck climbed closer to their destination, pushing easily through the deeper snowdrifts with the help of the four-wheel drive, but as they came around the final corner, they were stopped by a Subaru station wagon plugging the middle of the road. Joe thought about it for a couple of seconds and then decided there was enough room on the uphill side to get around the Subaru. He put the truck in low gear again and eased it up to the left but just as he began to nose past the stranded vehicle, Joe felt the tires on the truck begin to spin. They spun and then they sank down, just a little, into the snow. He put it in reverse, to go back around the Subaru, but again the tires spun and sank down into the snow. Joe opened his door and looked down. The snow was even deeper here than over the rest of the road, probably from the trees dumping their load from above. And from the build up of compact snow and ice in the ditch alongside the road. He sighed; they were definitely stuck this time. He turned off the engine and looked at Colin and Sonny. "I guess we're getting our snow here," he announced.

"And then what are we gonna do?" asked Sonny.

"Hope that somebody comes along that can pull us out."

*****

It was getting on to 4:00 in the afternoon and Hilda was sorting through the junk drawer in the cabinet next to her kitchen sink just to keep herself busy. She'd picked at her lunch – leftover noodles from a meal she'd had at a Thai restaurant and a few seeds from a not-very-juicy pomegranate – so that she could focus on the driveway next door but the man from the County hadn't shown up. Hilda packed away her lunch dishes feeling a tension headache between her eyebrows. She set about vacuum cleaning her kitchen and living room, both of which had windows that looked out towards the adjacent property. Then, because she was looking through them, she decided to clean the windows. That's when she saw Connors take off in his pick-up truck! Now what would happen if the County inspector showed up now?!

Hilda spent the next 20 minutes on hold to the County, only to be told, when she finally got through to a human being, that Rosencrans, the inspector she'd been dealing with, wasn't in the office. Where he was this person didn't know. Or wouldn't tell her.

Frustrated, Hilda called Gus, her gentleman friend in Hawaii, and complained to him for almost an hour about this turn of events, all the while keeping her eyes on the driveway next door. Gus took her mind off it by encouraging her to describe for him exactly how she planned to develop the land between her house and the neighboring property. She felt her anxiety lessen. But then Gus brought up how much money the development would make, which was one of Hilda's favorite subjects but she found herself flinching at his speculation because what if he got the idea that he was somehow entitled to this money too?!

Hilda became vague and suitably memory-impaired for her 70 years of age before hanging up the phone with a promise to call Gus back with news of whether the County inspector ever made an appearance or not. Then she turned her attention to sorting through her junk drawer, a task that raised her blood pressure all over again because what else was she supposed to do with this stuff except leave it in this drawer? But she had to occupy herself until 5:00 pm, preferably in a way that allowed her to keep watch on the neighboring property, otherwise she'd get itchy to call the County -

again!

She picked up a walkie-talkie that didn't work, but which one day she thought she might get to work, and was wondering where it could live other than in the junk drawer when a movement in the driveway next door registered in her peripheral vision. She grabbed her binoculars and peered through them to spy Lucy, heading towards her Pinto, carrying a long, light-colored dress covered in the plastic used by dry cleaners. Her wedding dress probably, Hilda thought with a sneer of bitterness. She watched the young English woman flick her long, blond curls over her shoulder as she leaned forward to put the dress in the back of her car. She closed the door and looked down at her watch. Hilda saw her glance back up at the house, biting her lower lip, as if worried about something. Then Lucy turned away, took a few steps forward and stood, with her hands on her hips, looking up the highway in the direction that Joe Connors had driven. She looked down at her watch again, then back up at the house and finally lifted her arms up at her sides and let them slap down onto her hips in a gesture of resignation.

As Hilda watched Lucy climb into her Pinto and drive away, she wondered with a certain sense of malice, whether Joe Connors might miss the County inspector's visit AND his wedding?

*****

Joe, Sonny and Colin dug snow and dumped it in the pick-up for a steady 20 minutes until there was a block that spanned the width of the Chevy, went to the top of the bed and 3 feet in towards the cab. "That should hold a few bottles of champagne," Joe remarked, slipping his glasses off and wiping the steam that had gathered on them onto a bandana. He was beginning to get nervous about being late back – after all his promises to Lucy – but there was nothing he could do about it. There was just no way they could dig the truck out, or push it for that matter. They had to wait for help. Fortunately neither Sonny nor Colin seemed perturbed by their situation. They'd carried on a amiable banter while digging and throwing, on subjects ranging from the British pension scheme to gun rights in the US. Now that the job was done they walked, their feet 'post-holing' up and down in the deep snow, around the Subaru to stand at the edge of the road and gaze at the mountain peaks poking up above the fog line like islands in the mist.

"That's what we call a Zen view," said Joe, but Colin and Sonny were lost in the otherworldliness of it all so Joe let himself fall into companionable silence alongside them.

A sudden swish to their left made them all turn to see the branch of a cedar tree see-sawing up and down as a bald eagle moved away from it, his wide, brown wings making a gentle thrum, thrum, thrum as he climbed steadily upwards in the sky. The bird reached the misty space opposite the three men and spun full circle, exposing his entire wingspan vertically like an elegant fan in the sky. He followed this with a high-speed plunge towards a second bald eagle that had also come from the cedar tree. He looped underneath and around the second eagle, and the two birds began flying together, wheeling and soaring, spinning and gliding, like partners on an ice skating rink. Then they were gone, swooping down to the valley below, their white tail feathers leaving the suggestion of an imprint on the mist behind them.

Colin looked at Joe. "I think you should take that as a sign."

"A sign?"

"Yes. Of a happy marriage."

Joe grimaced. "I'd go for a sign that I'll even *get* to the marriage at this point."

"Sorry. Sorry. Am I in your way?" came a harried voice to their left.

All three men turned to see an older fellow snowshoeing his way down the road in their direction. He was short and fit, wearing tightfitting Gore-Tex with a wool scarf, wool hat and fingerless wool gloves and he was waving his arms around in the air as if they might not be able to see him. "I left my car there because I wasn't sure she'd make it any further in the snow but I didn't think I might block anyone this far up. I apologize. I truly apologize." Without looking down he deftly unzipped the fanny pack he had around his waist and pulled out some keys. "I'll get my Subaru out of your way post haste."

"I don't s'pose you could pull us out while you're at it?" Joe called up.

The man stopped, looking a little taken aback. "Do you have a rope?"

"I do."

He resumed his snowshoeing. "Then yes, of course, of course. I have a hitch."

Colin snorted from behind Joe. "I should have you ask for a sign about some of my stocks and shares," he said.

Joe laughed.

Sonny looked skeptically at the Subaru in the middle of the road. "You think his car's up to it?"

Joe made a *phuff* sound of derision and flapped his hand in the air. "Piece of cake."

*****

Lucy lifted her dress out of the Pinto glad that it was covered by plastic because it had started to rain. What had her French friend, Délphine, told her? Mariage pluvieux, mariage heureux; rainy marriage, happy marriage. She draped the bottom of the dress over her left arm, to keep it from dragging across the ground, and started up the rock-lined path towards Sonny and Sarah's house. She could see little Maddie, watching her through the big picture window in the living room, her rosy cheeks cupped in her little hands as she leaned her elbows on the window sill.

Lucy walked left around the gambrel-roofed house and climbed the back step to go in through the kitchen door. She slipped off her shoes in the tiny mudroom. Maddie was on the other side of the door, having run over to greet her. “Can I see your wedding dress?” Joe’s six-year old asked.

Lucy nodded yes. “Let me take it into the bedroom and I’ll get it out.”

“It’s a sunroom, not a bedroom,” Maddie corrected as she skipped along beside Lucy, who walked around the woodstove and into the little glass-walled room off the kitchen.

“But I’m using it as a bedroom right now,” Lucy explained. She hung the dress from the top of a narrow shelf unit holding an assortment of seashells, black kukui nut beads and colorful hula dolls from Sonny and Sarah’s vacations in Hawaii.

Lucy lifted the plastic up over the dress and freed it from the hanger. It was a simple design; scoop neck, cinched waist and sleeves that billowed at the top then narrowed. Lucy lifted one of the sleeves, the satiny, ivory-colored fabric soft against the palm of her hand, and ran her fingers over the tiny pearl buttons sewn along the outer edge. She hadn’t wanted a wedding dress originally but then Rachel had offered to make her one as a gift and Lucy had chosen this style because the actress in her liked the suggestion of Shakespearean times in the sleeves. She felt a sudden burst of tenderness for this little community that she was striving to be a part of, for the help they had given so freely, so generously, towards her wedding. Things she hadn’t even thought about. Like the cake. And flowers! They’d just taken it upon themselves to make it all come together.

“Pretty,” sighed Maddie from behind her.

Lucy smiled and looked down at the little girl. “You think so?”

Maddie nodded an energetic yes, up and down, up and down, her flame red curls bouncing with each nod.

“Are you excited about the wedding?” Lucy asked.

Maddie looked up, as if she were thinking about her answer, then asked, “When’s Uncle Paul coming?”

Lucy didn’t mind her lack of reply but it did make her wonder what this little girl really thought about her daddy marrying a woman who wasn't her mother. She glanced at her watch; it was 4:20 already. "Pretty soon," she told Maddie, hoping that Joe was back at the house already in case Paul arrived early.

Maddie clapped her hands in joy.

"I'm glad you're looking forward to seeing your uncle."

"And cousin Jakey," Maddie informed her.

"I made a big spaghetti dinner for us all to eat." Lucy lifted Maddie up into her arms and began to walk her back into the kitchen. "Although I don't know why I did that. Jakey's mum's Italian. I bet she makes the best spaghetti."

"And what's for dessert?"

"Ice cream," announced Lucy. "But only if you finish your dinner."

Maddie rolled her eyes. "O-kay," she agreed reluctantly.

*****

The driver of the Subaru was called Windsor and he was also a potter. From Wisconsin, he told Joe as they got the rope and began tying it to the back of the truck; but he had a son living in Seattle and had come out to visit him and decided to go snowshoeing on Sauk Mountain. "I saw your place on my way by," he acknowledged, once he found out that Joe was the owner of the double gable house on the highway with a sign indicating it was a pottery. "I would have pulled in but the sign said closed. What kind of kiln do you have?"

"A wood-firing kiln."

"No kidding? Me too."

Joe grunted, too busy struggling to make a knot in the rope with his cold, wet hands to take this comment further but Windsor didn't seem to mind. He squatted down beside the truck and took off his snowshoes, then unlocked the Subaru and threw the snowshoes in the back seat. "Your place looked charming by the way," he remarked, taking the other end of the rope around the front of the Subaru to tie it to the hitch. "But it's a long way up in the mountains.

How far do you have to drive to sell your pots?"

"No, no, I don't do that. Not if I can help it," Joe explained, coming out from under the tailgate of his truck. "I figured if I had to schlepp my pots all over the countryside, I'd never make a living as a potter. So I built a little shop right onto my house."

"How's that working out for you?" Windsor asked.

"Well, you know, there's times it's tough. Like wintertime," Joe admitted, holding his right hand out to the snow all around them. "But I only built the house a couple of years ago so I figure it's early days."

Windsor cocked his head to one side from his crouch in front of the Subaru and exacerbated the wrinkles in his face with a frown. "For some reason I got the impression that house had been there a long time."

"Me too," agreed Colin. He and Sonny were leaning on the hood of the truck, waiting for the tow to get set up. "All those wood shingles on it give it an aged quality."

"Well I wanted to make it look like it belonged in this environment," explained Joe.

"Like a tree house," Windsor reflected.

"Brilliant!" said Colin, snapping his fingers and pointing into the air. "That's exactly what it looks like."

"I take it you're not from around here," said Windsor, turning to face the Englishman. But Sonny was between them and as Windsor stood up his eyes bugged at the sight of Sonny's bare legs below his shorts. He opened his mouth, as if to say something, then closed it just as quickly.

"No, I'm from England," Colin replied. "My sister's marrying Joe here so I came out for their wedding."

The potter from Wisconsin lit up with enthusiastic surprise as he looked at Joe again. "You're getting married?!"

"Yep. That's how come my shop was closed today."

"Well, good for you," he nodded. "Good for *you*!" Then he did a double-take from the truck to the Subaru and back to the truck. "That probably means I'm holding you up, doesn't it?"

"Just a little."

Windsor scrabbled his way back to the driver's side door of the Subaru again, both arms flapping as he did so. "Enough said," he declared.

"You want us to push?" asked Sonny.

"I don't think she'll need it," Joe answered, meaning the truck.

"Just put it in gear and don't spin your tires," Windsor called out from the driver's seat before slamming the door.

But Joe knew what he had to do. He pulled himself into the truck on the passenger side and slid across the bench seat to sit behind the steering wheel. He heard Windsor start the Subaru and watched him begin to drift backwards down the road. He started the truck and the heater blared its presence, drowning out all other sounds. Joe leaned forward, turned it down and put the truck into reverse. Almost immediately he felt a gentle jolt and the truck began rolling backwards, gliding easily over the snow as Windsor kept the length of rope tight. And then the truck was on the road again.

Joe stepped on the emergency brake, took the vehicle out of gear and looked up to see Sonny and Colin sloshing their way towards him in the tracks left by Windsor's Subaru. He threw open his door. "I'll get the rope while you guys get back in," he called out and jumped down into the snow again. He hustled around the back and untied his end of the rope as Windsor did the same on the Subaru. Once it was free, Joe wound the rope from his hand to his elbow and back a few times until he'd made a long, loose coil, which he looped over the end of the wood racks on his truck. "Thanks for the help," he told Windsor who'd come up to shake his hand goodbye.

"Oh you're welcome. I'm just sorry I blocked your way."

"Are you going to stop by the house on your way back to Seattle?"

Windsor shook his head no. "I think you've got enough to cope with today without me stopping by."

Joe grinned sheepishly. "Yeah, you're probably right. What time is it anyway?"

"I don't know," said Windsor, with a contented smile. "I'm on vacation."

"Ha! Well I'm guessing it's after 4:00 because the light's going." Joe nodded at the trees above them, which looked so much sharper in the flattening light of dusk.

"Could be," said Windsor, who was already moving back towards his Subaru. "But I don't need to know. You do though." He smiled back at Joe and waved his right hand goodbye above his head.

Joe received the comment like a lightning bolt and charged towards the cab of the truck. "Here's hoping that Windsor isn't too slow getting down the mountain," he told Sonny and Colin as he did a 6-point turn to get his truck facing downhill.

"Do you want me to race him?" asked Colin. "I can get up to 100 in this thing, can't I?"

"Are you nuts?!"

Colin turned to Joe, poker-faced. "My sister asked me not to mention that until after the wedding."

Joe howled. "Lucy never told me you were such a joker."

"Who said I'm joking?"

But when they came around the next corner, they found Windsor tucked into a wide spot, up against a gate to a private logging road, watching for them to come by.

"Ah, he's a good man," said Joe, honking his thanks as Sonny rolled down his window and waved.

Joe took them down the mountain at a steady pace, keeping constant watch out for wildlife in the trees alongside the road, and then picked up speed on the highway as he headed home. They had just come around the corner and started down the final hill towards his property when Joe glimpsed a white vehicle parked in his driveway. "Maybe my brother got here already," he thought out loud. "Do you see Lucy's Pinto?" he asked Sonny.

Sonny narrowed his eyes, peering at the driveway in the distance. “Uh uh, no.” He paused. “Your brother would be in a rental car, right?”

Joe nodded, seeing what he suspected Sonny was seeing.

“Yeah, that’s not a rental car. Not with those orange lights on top of it.”

“You’re right,” said Joe as they got close enough for him to start braking. “That’s a government rig.”

“How can you tell?” asked Colin.

“The license plates,” answered Joe. “See the XMT alongside the letters on the plate? That means it’s exempt from paying road tax. Because it’s a government rig.”

“Do the police have those kind of license plates?”

“Yup,” said Joe and Sonny in unison.

“Makes spotting them that much easier, doesn’t it? I’d never have to pay a speeding ticket again.”

“Dream on,” said Joe.

“Maybe it’s the highway department,” said Sonny, his eyes still on the vehicle in Joe’s driveway.

But Joe had seen the green, blue and white, mountain image of the County Logo on the driver’s side door and his stomach sank. “Shit,” he grumbled. “It’s someone from the County.”

He rolled in alongside the white, Chevrolet station wagon, expecting whoever was in it to jump out and accost him. But he waited, once his truck had rattled to a stop, and nothing changed.

“Maybe it’s empty,” he said to Colin. He leaned forward across the steering wheel, and glanced in the vehicle next to them, then flashed Colin a look of disappointment.

“No such luck?” asked the Englishman.

“Nope,” said Joe. “The driver’s in there. But he’s looking through a pair of binoculars at my neighbor’s property.”

“Maybe it’s your neighbor he’s here for,” offered Colin.

Joe opened his mouth to reply but noticed Sonny looking up the hill towards the loafing shed again. And this time, Joe knew what the glinting from that area signified; a pair of binoculars, trained on him.

"No, I suspect he's here for me," he replied with a sigh of resignation. "And I suspect I know who sent him here. The only part I don't know is..........why?" He threw open his door, tugging one side of his mouth ruefully into his cheek. "But I suspect I'm gonna find out."

Chapter 2

Joe hurried around the back of the County vehicle while Maggie and Max barked at him from inside the house. He'd left his hat propped on the gun rack in his truck and it was raining, in addition to which he was very aware that he needed to get Colin down to Sonny's house so he could change out of the wet socks before dinner with the extended family, so he was hoping this wouldn't take too long.

He came up alongside the driver's side door but stopped short when he noticed that the guy sitting inside the rig had a pair of binoculars up to his eyes and was completely engrossed in watching something in the pasture opposite. The man had curly, graying hair that covered his neck in the back, and a short, matching beard. His mouth was open and his tongue rolled up to rest against his top teeth as if he were really enjoying what he was seeing. Joe glanced at the pasture, curious; but he was more curious about the clipboard in the guy's lap, propped against the steering wheel. It had some kind of official document on it and Joe tipped his head to the left and edged forward, trying to read the words. He figured if it was something he didn't want to deal with, he could slip back into the truck and drive off before the guy even knew he'd been there. But the County official must have caught sight of the movement in his peripheral vision because he suddenly lowered the binoculars and turned towards Joe with an excited smile. Rolling down the window he whispered, "I think you have an adult Cooper's hawk sitting over there in the vine maples."

"Is that right?" Joe whispered back, squinting at the vine maples beyond the tangle of desiccated blackberry bushes along his fence line.

"Here, use these," said the driver, handing Joe his binoculars. "I take them everywhere. Just in case."

There was silence as Joe tracked down the sleek hawk with the blue-gray wing feathers and cap. "He's not very big."

"No. And see how rounded his wing feathers are? That's an advantage when it comes to hunting. The Cooper's hawk is kind of like the ninja of hawks, they're so stealthy."

"Beautiful coloring," muttered Joe, "His chest feathers look almost rose-toned." He stared at the bird a few seconds longer then handed the man back his binoculars. "Thanks," he said. "Is that what you came to show me?"

"I wish," said the County employee, looking for something on the seat beside him. "Because I really don't want to be here."

"Hey, I won't tell if you don't," Joe suggested, half an eye on the hawk still in the vine maple.

But the man ignored his suggestion. Instead, he found what he was looking for and passed it through the open window to Joe. It was a business card. "I'm Paul Rosencrans," he said, "and your neighbor – a Ms. Hess - has been calling and faxing me every day for a month to come pay you a visit."

"So it *is* something to do with Hilda the Horrible," Joe said.

Rosencrans looked down at his paperwork. "Yeah, she didn't give her middle name."

Joe chuckled; at least the guy had a sense of humor. Hilda Hess had a reputation as an indomitable enemy when it came to neighborhood strife and ever since she'd finished her fight with the neighbors on the other side of her, Joe noticed she'd been taking an interest in him. "What's she saying I'm doing?" He bent forward and openly tried to read the document on the clipboard.

Rosencrans covered it a little with his left hand. "She has a number of complaints most of which are not really my place to investigate. Plus, I can see without getting out of my truck," he went on, making a point to keep his eyes down on the clipboard, "that they're without basis. *But*," he added quickly, "the reason *I'm* here is because she claims this area is not zoned for a business." He looked at Joe. "It's zoned rural residential."

Joe shot upright, throwing his hands into the air. "I've got a special use permit!"

"Yes you do," agreed Rosencrans, flipping through the pages on the clipboard. He was obviously looking for something and as soon as he got to it, he held it between his thumb and forefinger, half showing it to Joe. "I've got a copy of it right here."

Two sport motorcycles buzzed loudly into the conversation, zooming up the highway at full throttle. Both men turned towards the intrusion and when they turned back, they were treated to the sight of the Cooper's hawk spreading his steely blue wings wide and leaping into the air. They watched, transfixed, as the hawk glided through the pasture then used his long tail feathers like a rudder to flick left and right through the narrow openings in the trees and disappear into the woods.

Rosencrans flashed a smile at Joe. "I could watch that all day," he said.

Joe nodded at the paperwork in front of Rosencrans. "That's my permit?" he asked.

"Uh-huh."

"Good. 'Cause I doubt I could find my copy. I got it when I first moved here…"

"1976," said Rosencrans, reading the date off the form.

"Yeah, but mine probably burned up in my house fire. But that means I'm good, right?"

"We-lll," equivocated Rosencrans. He was peering at the fine print on the bottom of the permit. "It says that you're not supposed to make retail sales." He looked up at Joe again. "Are you making retail sales?"

Joe stalled. He'd built his house alongside the highway with a separate space in it specifically for selling his pottery, completely forgetting the proviso that had been added to his special use permit 12 years back. "That depends," he equivocated. "Can I make wholesale sales?"

Rosencrans looked down at the permit again. "No," he said. "According to this permit you can't make any kind of sales."

"Yeah, but that's only because when I got that permit, you guys at the County didn't understand the nature of a home-based business." He jabbed his forefinger in the air in the general direction of the permit. "You thought I was gonna turn it into some kind of Giftmart up here. Plus I remember asking the Commissioners – or whoever it was that gave me the permit......yeah, I think it was the Commissioners - I remember asking if someone drove into my driveway offering to give me money for my pots, would I have to turn them away? And they said no, no, I could make the sale."

"Unfortunately they didn't write that on your permit."

Joe took one step back and slapped a hand to his chest, like he'd been shot in the heart. "So what are you saying? That I can't sell my pottery here anymore?!"

Rosencrans waved a hand for calm. "Hopefully it won't come to that." He shuffled through the paperwork on the clipboard again and pulled a sheet free, holding it out to Joe. "What you have to do is apply for an amendment to your special use permit."

Joe snatched the sheet. "How much is that gonna cost?"

"I think it's about three hundred and fifty dollars."

"THREE HUNDRED AND FIFTY DOLLARS?! Are you *kidding* me? The permit itself only cost twenty-five bucks!"

Rosencrans offered a small, deprecating smile. "That was 12 years ago."

Joe growled and looked down at the document. The rain had progressed from a soft drizzle to big wet drops, which were making inky blobs on the white paper. "Environmental impact statement?!" he scoffed, smacking the document with his free hand. "You going to give me grief about my kiln now?"

"No no. No no," stated Rosencrans and this time he did sound reassuring. "You've already got the right to make pottery because of your special use permit. We're only concerned with sales so the environmental impact statement is about the impact of your business on highway traffic."

Joe glanced at the highway again and laughed. The road was deserted. "Yeah, cause they're all beating a path to my door, can't you tell?"

Rosencrans looked out at the highway too and nodded. "It is quiet around here," he agreed.

The rain was coming down steadily now and Joe lifted the paper in his hand and held it over his head, like a tent. "So what happens next?" he asked, his mouth tight because he was asking under duress.

Rosencrans kept his friendly manner as he explained, "Next you have to come down to the County offices and pick up the forms for the amendment to your special use permit. It's quite the stack, I'm afraid..."

"Why do I have to come down?" argued Joe. "If I'm not being able to make sales I won't have the money for gas. Why can't you mail them up to me."

"We can do that," nodded Rosencrans. "Yes, we can definitely do that if it's more convenient."

"What's more convenient is you guys leaving me alone but I'm guessing that's not an option."

"Not when I'm getting calls two and three times a day from your neighbor, no." He was looking down at the paperwork on his lap but sneaked a furtive glance Joe's way from under his thick, gray and white eyebrows. "Did you do something to make her mad?"

Joe pressed his tongue against the back of his upper teeth and made a squeaky, sucking sound. "Could be something to do with the septic tank."

"The septic tank?"

"Yeah." His eyes bounced from the fence line to his neighbor's house in the distance. "I guess she doesn't like that I shit on her land."

*****

In the quiet of the truck Colin tipped his chin up to see over the hood. "What are they doing?" he asked no one in particular, even though Sonny was sitting right next to him. Colin was watching Joe push through the long, wet grass to the property line, Rosencrans picking his way behind him.

Sonny made a rumble of discontent in the back of his throat. "Looks like this guy from the County has come to talk to Joe about his septic tank."

"Is there a problem?"

"With the septic tank? Yeah. Joe's had nothing but problems with his septic tank ever since he bought this property."

"Because?"

"Because Burns – that's his old neighbor, the guy that sold him this property, made it look like the septic tank was on Joe's side of the fence but it wasn't."

Colin stared out the windshield at Joe and Rosencrans, his brow creased in obvious confusion. "I thought you said they were talking about Joe's septic tank?"

"I'm guessing they are. By the way Joe's pointing over the fence it sure looks like it."

"But what you just said implies that Joe doesn't own a septic tank."

"He owns it all right, 'cause he's got a court order saying so. It's just not on his property."

Colin turned his face towards Sonny, his gingery moustache crumpled on his puckered upper lip, his eyes glassy and narrow as he cogitated this information. Then he snapped to. "Right!" he said and maneuvered his legs awkwardly over the gear stick, pushing down on the bench seat with his fists as he eased his bottom closer to the driver's side door.

"Where you going?" Sonny asked.

"To tell this bloke from the County to bugger off. It's none of his business."

"No-o, you don't wanna do that," warned Sonny.

Colin already had a hold of the door handle. "Why not?"

Sonny looked out the windshield at the animated way Joe was explaining the problem to the guy from the County and winced. "It's raining," he said.

"Is it?!" Colin marveled, peering through the windshield like this was a brand new concept. "I hadn't noticed." A big, mischievous smile opened on his face as Sonny rolled his eyes in exasperation. Colin pushed open the truck door and stepped out, looking up at the soft drops of water coming down from sky. When he turned back to Sonny, he quipped, "It's a bit wet out here," then closed the door and made his way over to join Joe.

*****

Minutes later Pete pulled into the driveway in his VW bus. He'd spent the last three days in Seattle, sleeping in the VW while he worked in the city, then he'd picked up Sol, as a favor to Joe and Lucy, to bring him up for their wedding. After which, he beat feet as fast as he could to his cabin in the Upper Skagit.

"What's going on over there?" Sol asked. He'd quasi-adopted Joe and Lucy since becoming a patron of the pottery shop and could tell by Joe's body language that something was amiss.

Pete parked next to the Ford Escort. "Don't know," he said, looking at the three men over by the fence. "That's a County rig next to you so I'm guessing those two guys with Joe are County employees."

Sol had seen the County logo too. "Humph!" he grunted. He pushed his false teeth forward in his mouth as he tried to detect the details of the conversation from afar.

Pete lifted a toothpick from the edge of the open ashtray between the front seats and slipped it into the side of his mouth.

They watched the scene in front of them in silence for a few seconds then, without discussing it, opened their doors and walked around the front of the VW to meet up. They were an incongruous pair; both blue eyed and white haired but Sol a head taller with short, thick hair, sweatpants and sneakers to Pete's long ponytail, Birkenstocks and rolled up jeans. They crossed the grass without talking, Pete looking laid back now that he was in the mountains again and Sol with a glint in his eye that said nobody had better be messing with his favorite potter.

"Maybe it would just be easier for you to buy it off her," Rosencrans was saying, the suggestion of a laugh slipping out around the words.

Joe felt his head wanting to spin 360 degrees, like a cartoon character. He stepped back, both arms levitating into the air. "I don't *have* to!" he argued.

Colin interceded. "Excuse me. Excuse me." There was a managerial edge to his voice. "But I believe – " He rolled his forehead up as he looked at Joe. " – and correct me if I'm wrong – " He looked back at Rosencrans. "But I believe he's *already* paid for it."

"Twice!" bellowed Joe. Rosencrans widened his eyes, like how could this be. "Once when I bought this property," Joe explained, sticking his thumb up as a counter. Then he gunned out his index finger to join it. "And again when I had to defend it in court!"

"Are you getting grief over your septic tank again?" Pete asked, now that he'd come up alongside them.

"See, see!" Colin reiterated, a hand flapped out in Pete's direction as he looked at Rosencrans. "*Your* septic tank! Everyone knows this septic tank belongs to Joe."

"Of course it does," added Sol. "What use would anyone else have with a septic tank in this location?"

Four pairs of eyes turned towards Sol, the logic of what he'd just said hitting them square in the face. They turned back to stare at the wide expanse of nothing between where they stood and the neighbor's house in the distance. Nothing but green pasture, rolling up and down with the contours of the land, and a large cedar tree, all dark green and brown, at the mid-way point, its branches arched in a gesture of grace.

"Nobody would get a permit to build this close to the property line," Pete informed them.

"And he would know," Joe told Rosencrans. "Because he's on the County Planning Commission."

Rosencrans smiled across at Pete and Joe decided it was time to make some introductions, for Colin's benefit. "These are my friends, Pete and Sol," he told his soon-to-be brother-in-law.

"You must be Lucy's brother from England," said Pete with a big smile for the Englishman.

"I am, yes. And I'm sorry, I'm very pleased to meet you, of course, and I don't mean to be rude but," Colin flashed them a hasty smile as he spliced his hands through the air in front of Rosencrans. "We have a bit of a problem here."

"Have at it," Pete chuckled good-naturedly, popping the toothpick back in his mouth.

The three Americans looked at Rosencrans like he was in for it now and Joe saw his eyes go someplace far away, as if following the Cooper's hawk out into the forest. The rain had stopped and the air on their faces was colder as twilight brought evening into the valley.

Colin came at Rosencrans from another direction, like a terrier, nipping at his heels. "Do you need Mr. Connors to go and get his legal paperwork proving ownership of this septic tank? Because he can do that."

"I wasn't saying that the septic tank didn't belong to Joe," said Rosencrans.

"Actually, I think you were."

"That's what I heard." agreed Sol.

"Me too," Pete added.

Joe just smiled, figuring if he kept his mouth shut, his friends would run circles around this guy and might make him dizzy enough that he'd retreat to his office without completing his mission.

But Rosencrans held his ground. "No," he said, stretching the word out like he was talking to a naughty child. "I was only suggesting that Mr. Connors purchase the land his septic tank is on so his neighbor would leave him alone."

"You don't know Hilda the Horrible," came Sonny's voice from behind them. They all turned to see Joe's lifelong buddy tramping through the wet grass towards them, his upper body leaning noticeably to one side like he needed his spine realigned.

"That's her name?!" exclaimed Colin.

Pete and Joe nodded.

"Sounds charming!"

"What's her problem anyway?' Pete asked Rosencrans. "She bought the land knowing Joe's septic tank was here."

"Well now that I see the location of the septic tank, I think I know what it is. Ms. Hess has submitted a plan to the county to subdivide her property..." Rosencrans spun around as he said this, to stand with his back to the other men, facing the property line. He lifted his right hand and made a sweeping motion from the highway towards the woods in the distance, as he continued. "...and her drawings have a road, running right along this fence line to access the subdivisions."

When he turned back around, Joe, Colin, Sonny, Pete and Sol were all gaping at him. Suddenly they had nothing to say.

*****

Hilda couldn't figure it out. The guys at the property line looked like they were intermittently having a good time, then getting angry with each other. What in the world was going on? Why hadn't the County employee just put a lock on the pottery shop door?! She'd focused the binoculars on Connors for a while but when she saw him grinning like a Cheshire cat, she got so irate she had to lay the binoculars back down on the kitchen table. Then she took a quick break from her spying activities to throw some more maple rounds into the woodstove in her kitchen. When she got back to her seat at the table and lifted the binoculars again, she saw long-haired Pete, that hippie-looking friend of Connors that she'd flirted with when he first came to the Upper Skagit, strolling across the grass towards the group at the fence. He had that air about him that galled her, like he thought he was God's gift to women, and every time she had the misfortune to be around him, which was unavoidable in this small community, she found herself wanting to tuck her right hand into her pocket so she wouldn't slap him in the face with it. Hilda sniffed and leaned back in the chair again. Maybe she felt like that about Pete because he'd been so rude in his rejection of her. He didn't need to be, not from her point of view. She was a grown woman, after all, and knew that not every flirtation led to a tryst. Then, to see him turning up again and again at Connors' house as their friendship grew, and to find out that he was on the Planning Commission and she might actually have to be nice to him if she wanted her subdivision to go through, well that just reinforced her dislike of him.

She rolled her shoulders as the warmth of the woodstove reached her brittle bones. The kitchen wasn't as fancy as her living room, where she had a gas heater, but she enjoyed the ambiance created by her woodstove. After all the angst waiting on the County had given her today, she'd be feeling pretty miserable but for that radiant heat.

Hilda lifted the binoculars again and saw another guy coming up to the fence alongside Pete. A guy she hadn't seen before. The quiet of the tiny kitchen suddenly seemed louder as Hilda held her breath, staring at the lean, good-looking, older man. Then, to her amazement, he lifted his face and stared right across the pasture at her, with a look so piercing she nearly dropped the binoculars. She felt her heart flutter and heat rise from her neck up across her face. She looked around, wondering if she ought to close the drafts on the woodstove, then giggled as she realized the heat she was feeling was inside her. Apparently the new guy across the fence had stirred a little something. Not that she'd go there, of course, not now that she was with Gus.

Hilda slid further forward on her chair, put the binoculars back up to her eyes and watched the white-haired man stare across the pasture at her house. The conversation around him seemed to be very involved yet his gaze never moved from her kitchen window. He was chewing on something white but that didn't interrupt his eyes. They seemed to be staring right through her. She sat up and pulled down on her thin sweater to accentuate her slim torso, then realized that this was ridiculous. There was no way he could see her. Although she wouldn't mind....

The man suddenly shot his head to his right, towards the County official, who was motioning with his arm from the highway towards the back corner of her shared property line with Connors. Even in the fading light, she could see the shock on the new guy's face. Then his mouth dropped open. She ran the binoculars slowly over the faces of the other men around Rosencrans. Their mouths were open too. Hilda leaned forward, a smug expression on her face. Things were finally getting interesting.

*****

"A subdivision??" everyone said at the same time.

"And she's gonna put a road next to my place?!"

Rosencrans nodded. “That’s the plan.”

Pete shook his head. “She can’t put a road over a septic tank....”

“I’m guessing she knows that...”

Something that had been nagging at Joe suddenly made sense. “*That’s* why she tried to sell it to me!” His mind wandered back to early fall when he was out in the driveway, saying goodbye to a customer. He’d just placed a bag of pottery in the back seat of the customer’s vehicle when he noticed something moving behind the blackberries, on the other side of the fence. He looked a little harder as he straightened up, thinking it might be a deer, and realized it was Hilda, arranging something on the ground. Maybe planting something, he thought. Joe waited for the customer to drive away before strolling over to the fence to investigate further. He stood for a moment, watching his neighbor place river rocks in a deliberate line on the ground alongside his septic tank, then he asked, “Whatcha doing?”

Hilda must have known he was there because she didn’t jump at his voice and she didn’t bother looking at him. “Laying out an area of land around your septic tank that you can buy from me.”

“Why would I buy my septic tank when I already own it?”

“You don’t own the land that it’s on.”

“Don’t need to. I have all the rights to use it.”

He watched her place the last rock from her pile at the end of a rectangle she’d created around his septic tank then she stood up, in her blue and white polka dot dress, and made a flourish with her hands at her sides, palms up like a child explaining something. “This is what I’ll sell you,” she said, “for ten thousand dollars.”

Joe had laughed.

Now, he pulled his eyes back from the thicket of blackberries along the fence line to focus on Rosencrans again, and wondered if he was paying for that laughter today. He heard Sonny say, “Yeah, but she didn’t try to sell him his drainfield.”

“Exactly right.” Joe looked at Rosencrans, to make sure he was following, and pointed west. “The drainfield for my septic tank extends about 50 feet in that direction."

The County Inspector shook his head and little droplets of rainwater spat off his curls in all directions. "You can't use a drainfield with a road on top of it."

Joe stared across the fence, into the gathering dark, imagining headlights filling the void as people returned to their homes. "I wouldn't mind buying a wider swath of land, to protect my septic tank drainfield *and* my privacy. The only thing is..." He pulled one side of his mouth into his cheek. "I don't have any money."

"That's not a problem," Colin said, with a dismissive flap of his hand.

"Rich brothers-in-laws," grinned Joe. "We like those."

"Rich *maybe* brother-in-laws. If you can't provide my sister with a toilet she can flush, I might not give her away to you tomorrow."

""You're getting married tomorrow?" asked Rosencrans, a certain delight in his voice. Then he quickly turned to Colin with a defensive hand in the air. "I'm not here about the septic tank."

Colin tipped his head to one side. "No? Then why are we bloody well standing out here when we could be inside, warming up my wet feet."

"They still wet?' Sonny asked, looking down at Colin's feet.

The Englishman lowered his brow and gave Sonny a scathing look from under his eyebrows.

"I don't remember those boots leaking for me," explained Sonny as they picked their way across the grass towards Joe's front porch.

"I think I'll join you," Sol said from behind them.

"Me too," agreed Pete, veering away from the group towards his VW.

"Where are you going?" asked Joe.

"To get the bottle of wine I bought for tonight's dinner."

"I hope it's a big bottle," Colin called out from the front steps.

"It's all right. I've got some strawberry wine from the Barter

Faire if we need more," said Joe. He looked around for Rosencrans but when he realized the County official wasn't alongside him, the potter did a double take towards the fence. Rosencrans was still there, standing in the dark, peering out at the pasture. "You coming?"

"I think I heard a barn owl....."

"Yeah. I heard that too last night."

"I've never seen one though.."

"Well come on inside. I have a book of birds..."

Rosencrans turned around and began walking towards Joe. "Oh I know what it looks like," he said. "I've just never seen one." He got to the Ford escort and began to open the driver's side door.

"You not coming in for some wine?"

Rosencrans checked his watch. "I'd better not." He laughed a soft laugh. "Wouldn't want to upset the neighbors."

"Too late for that," joked Joe.

Rosencrans climbed in his vehicle. "I'll send you the paperwork."

"Only if you really want to."

*****

Lucy threw a look into the white Ford Escort as she passed it at the end of the driveway but couldn't really see the driver, and she missed the logo on the outside of the vehicle because her eyes had already moved on to the house in front of her. The beautiful, fairytale-looking house that Joe had built, which from tomorrow on, she would call home. She stopped in the middle of the driveway and stared up at the peaks of the double gable roof. When she met Joe, four years ago, in the summer of 1984, he was in the process of building the house but didn't have the roof on. When she came back to visit him again, the following summer, she was enchanted by the slopes and angles of the roof. How the peaks reached forward in the sky, like proud eagles' beaks: how the squares of rich brown cedar shakes, layered on the steeply sloping sides, made it look like a gingerbread house.

Her eyes drifted down to the small, mullioned windows arranged in triangles underneath the peaks, and she watched the amber glow from inside dance behind them. It was a very inviting house and Lucy often heard customers say that it drew them in from the highway. Joe's creativity had not only built a house that was charming and looked like it belonged in this densely forested valley of the Pacific Northwest, but his business acumen had built a house that would help sell his pottery. Now, together, they were going to turn this house into a home.

Lucy sat for a moment, enjoying the quiet inside her car. She was excited and nervous about this life she had chosen, but not about marrying Joe. That she felt completely calm about. After being scared for so long, she welcomed the calm. Of course, she knew it was going to be tough, chasing her own dreams so far away from the city, and she already sensed that she and Joe would have struggles over making a living from his pottery. But their togetherness, that felt right.

Headlights pulled into the driveway behind her, stealing Lucy away from her reverie. Time to make dinner for the relatives, she thought. She gently touched the gas and turned the steering wheel to the left, easing around the corner to park next to Joe's Chevy.

Chapter 3

Joe spent the night sleeping in the loft of his studio. His older brother, Paul, and nephew, Jake, were sleeping in his bedroom while his sister and her husband slept in the small, second bedroom that was Maddie's when she came to visit. Joe didn't mind being over in the studio. This was where he'd lived when he was building his house and he'd had kind of a restless night, because of the visit from the County, so was glad he wasn't over in the house disturbing everyone. Man, he'd screwed up big time when he'd bought this property, yet his plan had seemed so together when he'd come up with it. "Think of it," he'd told Erica, his first wife – or practice wife, as he liked to call her now that he was marrying Lucy. "If we don't have to make payments then we won't feel pressured to sell the pottery, which is good. We'll just have to make what little we need for utilities and gas money. And if we grow a garden we won't even need that much for food."

They'd looked at one piece of property for their future pottery business up by the Canadian border and walked away because the owner didn't want to be cashed out. He wanted payments. And the thought of payments just made Joe nervous. He knew his income would be irregular if he and Erica were to live the artist's life and he didn't want to be in a place where he might not be able to make a payment and maybe end up losing everything they'd worked for. So they were looking for someone to take their cash. And, boy, did they find the person for that.

Yet Clarence Burns had seemed like a sweet old fellow when they'd met him. He was short, maybe five foot five, and skinny; the runt of the litter. He wore cowboy boots and a ten-gallon hat like a kid playing dress up and spoke through barely moving lips, as if someone had punched him in the mouth. But Erica and Joe loved his tar-heel drawl and the powerful way he marched across the uneven, brushy terrain on the five acre piece he wanted to sell them.

It was a damp, overcast day in October but Burns led them over ground covered in thick layers of burnt orange maple leaves and through, underneath and around trees and vines boasting countless shades of green.

"There's two 'n' a half acres goes up that way," he muttered, when they stopped at a creek towards the back of the property. "That you can't do much more'n use fer growin' trees."

Joe and Erica gazed up at the dense forest of sweeping cedars and tall Douglas firs, at the maples and alders wrapped in thick coats of furry moss. They wanted to linger but Burns was already marching down alongside the creek, leading them to a corner of the property that stopped at the highway. From there they tromped along the highway easement, Joe picturing the ease of access for his future pottery customers, and ended at the narrow driveway Burns had punched in to help sell this piece of land. He pointed forward. "There's yer concrete slab," he said, meaning the 20-foot wide by 50-foot long rectangle of concrete on the ground ahead of them.

They moved forward as one and stepped onto the slab of concrete. "I was thanking someone could use this fer a mobile home. Or a house," said Burns, his arms out at the side of him to suggest a space above the concrete. He moved to one end of the concrete. "An' here's the 'lectricity." He opened a workbox and pulling out a drill motor, lifted a blue tarp lying on the concrete and plugged the drill motor into the end of an extension cord. It started right up. He nodded at Joe and Erica, then turned and spat a big gob of tobacco juice onto the grass at the end of the concrete and pointed uphill. "The 'lectrical box is over there, next to the spigot for the water line coming down from the crick."

"That would be our water source?" asked Joe.

Burns unplugged the drill motor and returned it to the workbox. "Ye-ap. The D.O.T. put that water line in so's all the houses down that road opposite," he swiveled around and pointed at the street on the other side of the highway, "could get their drankin' water from the crick."

"D.O.T. did that?"

"Uh huh." He let the lid of the workbox bang shut and his tiny eyes narrowed to slits in his leathery face. "They cut up my land when they put in this highway," he said, with a terse nod towards the highway in front of them, "and left them families without potable water. I'd been takin' care of 'em with a gravity feed pipe down from the crick an' I told the highway department, you wanna split up my land, you'd better take care of these folks' water." He nodded, satisfied. "They did. We get to use it too 'cuz I wasn't gonna give 'em access to the crick if I couldn't be on the waterline."

"And you still own the acreage on the other side of the highway?"

Burns spat down onto the grass again. "Nope. Weren't no good to me all cut up like that so I sold it."

"How many acres do you own on this side?" Erica asked.

Burns let his eyes cut towards her and there was a hint of suspicion in them. It was a look that Joe attributed to Burns being maybe wary of negotiating with women but, at that point, he didn't know the mendacity of the man. "Twenty eight," snapped Burns, "once I sell this five." He stepped off the concrete slab and took a half a dozen steps out towards the pasture. He pointed down at the ground in front of his feet. "Septic's right here," he said. "Poured it same time I poured the slab." Then he walked forward another half a dozen steps. "Ev'rythang you see from here to the tree line in the distance is my land. I would'a kept this five acres too, only I need to pay off my ex." Joe and Erica had moved to stand beside him and he turned to Joe with a terse look. "We're divorced."

There wasn't much Joe could say to that so instead he asked, "And where's the property line on this side?"

Burns took one more step forward, so he was out in front of Joe and Erica, and pointed his index finger uphill to the right. "See that pink ribbon?" Joe squinted into the distance; he thought he saw something pink hiding from the rain under the brush. "It comes down from there to about where we're standin' and then down to that apple tree." Now Burns had his left arm extended too, pointing at the King David apple tree in the grass down by the highway easement. "There's survey ribbon down there too."

This time Joe saw the fence-post that had been driven into the ground on the pasture side of the apple tree, a short length of pink survey ribbon tied around the top. He turned to Erica. "What do you think?"

She shrugged and he could tell she wasn't smitten. He was right there with her. The property had a lot of what they needed to start their home and pottery business, with the foundation already poured for a building, power, water and septic, but it just wasn't that appealing in the rain. Or maybe it was the way the light was fading so late in the afternoon.

"Can we pitch a tent?" he asked Burns. "Spend the night so we can look at the property again tomorrow?"

Burns agreed and the rest was history. Joe and Erica fell in love with the land the minute they saw Sauk Mountain towering over it the next morning. They went with their cash and counted out exactly what the old fellow was asking for it. They didn't even negotiate the price; they just paid for it.

Joe fell asleep thinking of what an idiot he'd been. Burns must have seen them coming: two naïve hippies from back East. They'd left him their money, taken the deed to the property and driven back to Ohio to pick up their belongings. It wasn't until they got back to the Skagit that they found out just exactly what this sweet old fellow was really like.

The next morning, Joe was woken by the sound of Maggie's tail thump, thump, thumping on the floor of the studio. Darn! He'd overslept. Must have been all that tossing and turning before he got to sleep. He slipped his glasses on and peered at the little alarm clock he'd brought over from the house; it was 6 am. His internal alarm had not failed after all.

He sat up in his sleeping bag, pushed his fingers into his thick, brown hair and moved it back away from his face, adding a vigorous wake up scratch on both sides of his scalp in the process. It was cold in the studio, since he hadn't taken the time to relight the fire in the woodstove when he'd stumbled over to bed last night, and there was a yeasty tang to the air from the clay. He slipped his t-shirt back on and sat for a moment, willing himself to pull his legs out of the warm sleeping bag. Now he could hear both dogs moving around downstairs, their claws clicking on the wood floor. "I'm coming, I'm coming," he muttered before forcing his legs out into the cold and snatching on his jeans. He fumbled around in the dark for his socks as the dogs made yawing sounds, playing bite-the-other's-open-mouth. The lambs' wool socks he'd traded pottery for with a lady at church felt incredibly soft, and they warmed his spirits as he pulled them onto his feet. He leaned back over the sleeping bag and grabbed his wool shirt, pushing his arms into it as he stood up.

The dogs had turned their mouth play into full-bodied jostling and he heard one of them bounce against a box of finished pots he'd put on the floor when he and Sonny had emptied the shop of pottery yesterday. "Cut that out!" he grumbled. The jostling stopped and he heard them both slump down on the floor, knowing they couldn't get into trouble that way. Joe buttoned the top two buttons of his shirt as he stuffed his feet into his sneakers then threw one leg over the top of the ladder stairs to descend into the studio.

He could see the dogs watching him as he stumbled over to the light switch by the door but they knew better than to move until they got the command. Joe turned on the lights and then the radio sitting on the shelf above his clay mixer. He paused, to hear what was being discussed on the news. The Congressional Committee's report on Iran-Contra – again! Hadn't they gone over this enough already! He turned the volume down two levels and bent to tie the laces on his sneakers. The dogs were still in place, their heads twisted around to watch his every move. He finished his laces, stood back up, brushed off his knees and looked at them. "Ready?" he asked. They looked back at him, their eyes saying, "that's not the command." Joe took two steps to the right, grabbed the handle on the barn door to the studio and looked back over his shoulder at the eager dogs. "Okay!" he announced. They leapt up as he rolled the door open and scooted outside at high speed.

*****

Hilda woke early, as usual, and reflected on yesterday's happenings as she drank her cup of warm water. Last night, after watching Connors get agitated in front of the County Compliance Officer, she decided she would celebrate by starting a cleanse this morning so she didn't want to shock her system by filling it with caffeine. She was looking out her kitchen window, wondering if his wedding had taken place last night or not, when the phone rang. She glanced across at the time on her microwave; 6:20 am. It must be Janet.

She picked up the black, rotary phone almost without looking at it. "Yes?" she said.

"Hi Hilda, it's Janet."

"Mmmm hmmm."

"Are you going to the wedding at the pottery today?

Hilda had been preparing herself for yet another story about goats giving birth in the middle of the night, or goats climbing into the duck coop or goats tripping Janet or whatever the latest goat story might be so she was a little taken aback by the question. Especially since it provided her with the information that no, Connors did not get married last evening because he was getting married today. Very interesting. "I haven't decided yet," she answered as if she were totally in the know. "I was just looking for the invitation to remind myself what time it starts."

"The wedding is at 12:15...."

"That's right," said Hilda asif she were grateful for the reminder but she'd known all along.

"But I was only invited to the party – not the actual ceremony – well I don't know either of them very well so that makes total sense to me...."

Hilda let Janet ramble on as her eyes narrowed, wondering how the County had stopped Connors from doing business. Did the guy hang some kind of public notice on the door to his shop and out on the telephone pole at the end of his driveway? Of course, she would have preferred a length of yellow tape across Connors' driveway, stopping access altogether; something that read, Caution: Incorrect Zoning: Do Not Cross, but she knew *that* would never happen. She could call on Monday and ask what kind of Cease and Desist order he'd used but she'd rather know now, so if she caught Connors violating it, she could turn him in. But how would she find out? She could ask Janet to look for her but that might prompt questions and Hilda was not one to take people into her confidence. Especially not people like Janet. No, better that she find a reason to be close enough to the property line that she might actually be able to *see* a notice pinned to the door.

"I'm not going to show up till sometime after 3:00 so I can take care of my animals before it gets dark...." Hilda heard Janet saying as she contemplated what kind of activity might put her on the property line, preferable *at* the time of Connors' wedding making a loud noise. She usually mowed the lawn to disturb his social time but she couldn't mow the lawn in December. "...and of course I was banking on the goats to eat all those blackberries growing against the duck coop but now it looks like I might have to cut them down myself…"

That's it! thought Hilda. She could use the pretext of cutting down all those pesky blackberry bushes growing on the property line. And she could use that new chain saw Gus bought her to do it. "That's a *great* idea!" she said out loud.

"Oh. You think so?" said Janet, sounding like Hilda's reaction had surprised her a little but in a good way. "I was hoping it would work out but I wasn't sure if you were going to the actual wedding beforehand."

"No," said Hilda, making herself come back to the conversation. "No. I can't because Gus is calling me from Hawaii at noon."

"Perfect! Then we can go to the party together."

"No, I started a cleanse last night so I don't want to go to the party because I don't want to be tempted to eat anything."

"Then why did you say…"

"But I think it's a *great* idea that you go," Hilda said, hoping she was covering whatever faux pas she may have made. Then she changed tactics to get rid of Janet so she could go and plot the details of her plan. "What is that bleating sound? Did you let the goats in your garage again?"

"Oh no!" wailed Janet, "they'd better not be in my apples!" And she hung up without saying goodbye.

Hilda put the phone back down on the kitchen table. First she'd read the instructions for the chain saw, then she'd figure out her wardrobe for this event.

*****

It was still dark out and drippy with rain. Joe followed the dogs to water a tree then grabbed a couple of pieces of firewood from the wood shed closest to the studio. He didn't really need to build a fire since he wouldn't be working in the studio today and it wasn't cold enough to freeze his clay, but his brother and sister had both expressed an interest in seeing his workspace so he decided he may as well take the chill off the air.

When he walked back inside the studio, he heard the radio commentator announcing a review of *Good Morning, Vietnam*. This he wanted to hear. He dumped the firewood on the floor in front of the woodstove and spun around to turn up the radio. If the movie sounded any good, he'd ask Lucy to go see it. Date night. Sometime after the wedding, when things went back to normal.

If they went back to normal, he thought, his mind harkening back to his conversation with Rosencrans. He bent down in front of the woodstove, opened the door and placed a wedge of Doug fir inside. A part of him was miffed that he'd allowed himself to get spooked the night before his wedding. Fortunately he'd held back from mentioning it to Lucy. Didn't need her worrying about how they were going to make a living the night before she said, "I do."

His mind switched gears as he picked up a length of cedar and spliced a thin strip off one side, listening to the reviewer share his opinion of *Good Morning, Vietnam*. The wood split easily, making a clean, tearing sound as the axe moved from top to bottom. Joe repeated the process twice more, then lifted the three, wafer thin strips of cedar and snapped them with his fingers into shorter lengths. He found a piece of pitch wood on the hearth, lit it and held it under the cedar until the pieces caught fire. He watched the flames leap into action as he laughed at Robin Williams doing his slick shtick, then waited until the fire was well underway before he placed another hunk of fir at an angle across the first. He watched the fire grow as he listened all the way through the review, then he closed the door on the firebox.

It was 6:20 am according to the reporter on the radio. Maybe he'd go measure for the length of pipe he needed to hold the doors to his new kiln before going back down to the house. He grabbed a tape measure, switched off the light in the studio, stepped outside and took a right towards the new kiln shed. He looked for the dogs but they were off somewhere, probably patrolling the perimeter for their daily smell-check. Joe hustled forward in the shadowy morning sky and turned on a work light in the new kiln shed. Then he trotted up a six-foot ladder he had set up, and hooked the metal tongue on the end of his tape measure over a 2 x 12 beam he'd nailed to the rafters. Once he got it well hooked, he backed down the ladder, letting the tape roll open, bent over and folded the final measure down onto the concrete floor. Ten-foot, he said to himself. That's what he'd thought.

He stood back up and shook the tape so the tongue on the beam came loose. The inches disappeared rapidly as the tape slid and thwanged back into its metal housing. Joe dragged the ladder across the concrete floor to measure for the upper chamber but his brother, Paul, stepped out of the dark alongside the kiln shed and moved towards him. "Whacha got going here?" he asked, interested.

"Oh hi," said Joe, pleased to see him. "You're up already?"

"Jet lag."

"That's right. You're 3 hours ahead of here."

"Jake's still sleeping but the rest of us are up."

"Did you get coffee?"

Paul shook his head no. "We couldn't find the coffee maker."

"It's right on the kitchen counter!" said Joe, surprised Paul hadn't seen it. When his brother didn't show any signs of recognition, Joe added, "Made of clay?"

"Ah," sighed Paul. "That would have been our first mistake." He smiled at his younger brother then tipped his head down to look at the series of 3 platforms in front of them. They were stepped up, a foot to 18 inches at each level, and measured about 4 feet wide by 5 feet long. Except the highest one on the right. That was closer to 8 feet long. "What's going to be here?"

"My new kiln," Joe declared with a certain pride. "These are the floors. The lowest one, on the left, is for the firebox, then the one in front of me is for the first chamber, and that one," he said, pointing to the longest one, "is for second chamber and the chimney."

Paul scratched a fingernail over the material. "Is this concrete?" he asked.

"No. It's a castable, refractory clay. To stand the high temperature of the firing."

"And you cast it into cement blocks?" Joe's older brother, who was built like their father in his younger years, tall, wide-shouldered and athletic, tipped himself way over to one side, peering at the foundation under the floors. The dogs had wandered into the kiln shed after completing their morning ablutions and now Max padded up to Paul, curious, and sniffed his left ear. Paul tipped himself back upright immediately and almost side-swiped Joe in the process.

"Watch it," said Joe, putting a hand on his brother's arm.

Paul stepped back. "Sorry. I just wasn't expecting to get a wet ear."

Both men laughed.

Joe went back to Paul's question. "I built a form on top of the cement blocks and then cast it. And the intake and exit drafts," he continued, pointing to the short, perforated, brick walls that looked like castle turrets on the left and right of each platform. "Those I built out of a mixture of brick and castable."

Paul tickled his dark mustache as he thought. "So what's next?"

"I have to cast the chambers."

"How are you going to do that?"

The kiln shed had a concrete floor and a sheet metal roof but no walls and daylight was beginning to filter in slowly. Joe pointed at a wooden form sitting on the floor at the far end of the shed. It looked like a vault made out of plywood; solid in the front and back, with an arched center, 3 foot wide, created from curved Masonite. The front end had an additional 6-inch aura of plywood, like the brim on a bonnet. "That's the form I built," said Joe. "I'll sit that on top of the intake and exit walls, nail a length of 1 x 6 between the front and back shadow arch on both sides and fill the trough it creates full of castable."

Joe's brother had his own construction business in Upstate New

York and knew all about building forms for concrete. He looked closely at the front and back then his brow creased. "Back shadow arch?" he queried.

Joe indicated two more, free standing, plywood arches leaning against a post. He walked around the kiln floor to the back and pointed down to a 2 x 4 brace. "I'm going to set those floating arches on these braces, one at the back of each floor, cleat them in place and add diagonal braces at the back for stability."

"That's how you'll trap the castable for the back wall?"

"Uh huh."

"Will the back walls and side walls be continuous?"

"That's the theory. I've never tried casting the back wall at the same time as the arch but I'm hoping," - he crossed his fingers and made an X with his arms in front of his chest – "*hoping* that it'll come out as one piece. It's a big source of heat loss, to pour them separately, and I'd rather avoid that in this kiln if I can."

Paul held one hand out horizontal in from of him, palm down, parallel to his chest. "So you'll keep nailing up 1 x 6s and adding layers of castable," his hand stepped up in the air as he said the words, "till you get to the top -." He stopped, peering at the curvature to the Masonite at the top of the arch. "Then what're you gonna to do?"

"Well it's castable *clay*, so I'm hoping I can kind of, like, mold it over the top of the arch and it'll stay." Joe shrugged. "But I'll find out. I've always made my own castable before, from recycled and salvaged materials. This'll be the first time I'll be using brand new."

Paul thought for a second. "Where does one buy castable clay? From your clay supplier?"

"No, I got it from a firebrick supply house that was going out of business in Seattle. I bought all the insulating firebricks for the doors from the same place, plus kiln shelves. Then the owner offered to order me some castable refractory even though he was going out of business. He told me this stuff is great. It's the same kind of material they use to build the NASA space shuttles..."

"Hopefully not the same as the stuff that broke off the Challenger last year."

"Yeah, no, that was the tile on the outside."

Paul nodded and they both stood silent, eyes glazed, remembering the horror of the Space Shuttle Challenger exploding on take-off. Around them the only sounds were the beads of moisture dripping from the trees as the soft rain kept up its steady rhythm.

Then Maggie yawned and snapped Joe out of his reverie. "Anyway," he said, "the castable we bought is not the quality of the stuff they use at NASA." He looked over his glasses at his brother. "Our budget wouldn't run to that quality."

"How do you determine its quality?"

"By how insulating it is. The guy told me – Vladimir Uren, is his name..."

"That's a mouthful."

"You're telling me. Nice guy though. He told me the distributor said if you made a wall 3 inches thick with this refractory, you could get up to 3,000 degrees on the inside and it would only be 250 degrees on the outside."

"I didn't know you got up to 3,000 degrees in your kiln."

"I don't. I only go up to 2,200. And I'm making an arch wall that's going to be closer to 6 inches thick, but still. If it works..."

Joe's brother walked slowly around the plywood arch. "You gonna use this form to cast both chambers?"

"Yep. That's the plan."

"And when you're done, you'll take the 1 x 6 boards off the outside of the walls, remove the shadow back wall and then what? Walk this arch out of the inside?"

Joe hustled over to the front wall of the form and pointed to a square hole in the middle of it. "See this? That's a manhole. Once the castable sets up I'll climb inside the manhole and knock loose the blocks I used to set the form on top of the flues and if I'm lucky, the form'll drop down to the floor and I can walk it out."

"The castable clay won't stick to the plywood?"

"I'll put tarpaper between the two so it shouldn't, no."

"Why don't you just build a second form and let this burn in place when you fire the kiln?"

"You seen the price of plywood?"

Paul laughed. "There is that."

"I am gonna do that with the firebox though."

"What shape will that be?"

"That'll be another arch," Joe said, nodding his head up and down like this was something Paul might have imagined. "Only quite a bit smaller than the two chambers." He heard a noise in the distance and swiveled towards the sound. It seemed like it was coming from the other side of the pasture. He listened a moment. Was that a chain saw? "What time is it?" he asked his brother.

"I've no idea," said Paul, shaking his head and holding out his arms to show no watch. "I'm still on East Coast time."

Joe looked outside the kiln shed; the light quality suggested it was approaching 7:00 am.

His brother drew Joe's attention back to the kiln. "Why two chambers?" he asked. "And why the 12 inch lift between the floors?"

"Because heat rises."

"Ahhhh."

"Right? So the flames come from the firebox into the first chamber through this flue," – Joe's hand swept from the lowest floor up to the first perforated brick wall on the second floor – "then they follow the line of the arch up, across the top and down, before heading into the upper chamber via the second flue, all the time being pulled along by the draft of the chimney."

Paul watched Joe's hand move through the air as if across the two humps on a camel's back. "So when the chambers sit side by side," he said. "They'll look like the famous golden arches. Except listing."

Joe laughed. "Ha! Yeah. Except listing. I like that."

"The chimney's going to be how tall?"

"18 feet."

Paul nodded his head up and down, impressed. "This thing's gonna be huge."

"About 70 cubic feet. That's what I calculated."

"And how many pots will it hold?"

"That I don't know. Not yet. But I'll find out."

The dogs leapt up suddenly, barking, and both men turned to see them sprint down towards the house. "Here comes somebody, I imagine," said Joe. He looked up at his older brother. "Maybe it's time for that coffee."

*****

Lucy was standing in the little sunroom on the back of Sonny and Sarah's house where she'd spent the night, watching Sarah walk her brother around her property. Sarah loved working outside in her yard when she wasn't teaching and not only did she have a green thumb and could make pretty much anything grow, she also enjoyed putting ornaments and bric-a-brac amid the plants, to tell a story. She and Colin were both holding onto cups of coffee and walking a few feet in one direction then stopping, at which point Sarah would use her free hand to make swirls and angles and contours in the air, presumably describing the evolution of what they were seeing in front of them, and Colin would raise his eyebrows, make a little oh of interest with his mouth and nod. Sarah had made them French toast for breakfast, which Lucy and Colin knew as 'eggy bread' in England and always ate with a coating of ketchup. Lucy had eaten French toast with maple syrup many times since coming to the United States but she enjoyed watching her brother look at it like he wasn't sure, then dive in and devour it. It made sense that he was now following Sarah obediently around her garden.

It was raining again. A fine soft rain that laced moss covered maples with delicate skeins of moisture and darkened the tips of Doug fir needles like brush strokes of mascara. Lucy looked up at the sky; it wasn't dark with rain clouds but rather fluffy with white mist that floated across the landscape like a gauzy veil. Very atmospheric for a wedding, she thought to herself. She wanted to be disappointed that it was raining on her wedding day but she couldn't because inside herself it felt like a sunny day in Hawaii.

"You nervous?" Skye said as she came into the room behind her. Lucy turned to look at her friend. In one hand she was holding two palm-sized, tortoise-shell combs, and in the other some loose red ribbon, and two mini-arrangements of red roses pinned with ivory-colored beads.

"Not at all," said Lucy. Skye sat down on the bed and laid out the hair combs and ribbons. Lucy dropped down on the bed opposite her, eager to put her thoughts into words. "If anything," she went on, her body leaning towards Skye, her hands in the air in front of her, adding visual references to her explanation. "I feel as if someone's handed me a memory that's edged with elation and wrapped in a tissue-paper thin layer of bliss and I want to put it somewhere safe, so I won't lose it. That way, if anything ever changes, I can find it and remember how carefully it was given to me and not be bitter that the picture the memory came from is not the same anymore."

Skye began to weave the red ribbon around the top and between the teeth of the comb. "You think that's possible?"

"I do, yes." Lucy traced the tiny rainbows of color falling across Skye's hands up to a beveled, teardrop glass bead hanging in the window. "I remember this TV interview I saw once with Priscilla Presley - you know, Elvis's ex-wife?" Skye looked up at Lucy like she couldn't believe her ears. Lucy laughed. "No, it was really good. The interviewer kept on about all the pills Elvis took and all the women he chased and how their marriage had lasted such a short time, given the length of their courtship, and it was obvious that he was trying to push Priscilla into saying how much she regretted the whole thing. But he couldn't. Because every time he pushed her she laughed, this beautiful, tinkly laugh that came from someplace deep inside her that said she couldn't look back on her relationship with

Elvis with anything other than joy. Because she loved him." Skye ended the weave and cut the ribbon matching lengths at each end of the comb. Lucy handed her one of the flower arrangements and a pin. "That's how I want to be if things go south between Joe and me. I want to remember how good it felt now, not listen to the naysayers."

"When did you get to be such a romantic?" Skye asked, a smile in her voice.

"When Joe turned on the love switch in my heart."

They both fell silent as Skye focused on attaching the flowers to the outside edge of the comb without pinning herself in the process. The room was intimately quiet, with occasional bursts of joyous giggles filtering through the walls from Maddie, who was watching cartoons in the living room. Skye finished the first comb and held it up for Lucy to see. "Can I try it on?" she asked.

"Go right ahead."

Lucy took the comb, slid off the bed and walked out of the little room into the kitchen. She turned immediately to face the big mirror on the wall between the living room and the sunroom, the woodstove behind her, Skye now out of sight. She lifted the comb and used the teeth to pull her thick curls away from one side of her face. She pushed it into place and turned her face away to glimpse the finished product.

"What are you and Joe gonna do about this problem with the County?" asked Sonny from behind her.

Lucy spun, still in her internal sweet place, and found him leaning against the arched opening between the kitchen and living room. "What problem with the County?"

Sonny cut his eyes away from hers then brought them back, slowly, furtively, like he was about to drop a bombshell. "Joe didn't tell you?"

Lucy wasn't going to let him spoil her mood by suggesting that Joe was holding something back from her. "He probably did," she answered and chuckled, as if at a private joke. "I just haven't been paying all that much attention these last few days." She kept her face neutral, to reassure him. "Why don't you fill me in?"

Before he could answer the outside door to the kitchen opened and Sarah marched in, a mix of buoyancy and business. Colin followed more sedately. Sonny turned towards them. "Nah, I should probably let Joe do that."

One look from Sarah suggested she'd summed up the situation immediately. "Let Joe do what?" she rapped out as she set her coffee cup down on the counter.

"Sonny was just going to fill me in on a problem we apparently have with the County," Lucy replied.

Colin stood more than a foot taller than Sarah and gave Sonny his pinched look, lips pressed tightly together, eyes glaring, over the top of her head. "I thought we agreed not to talk about this until after the wedding?" he said.

Sonny became instantly evasive. "Oh no, I didn't..... Is that what we?.....I thought Joe......"

"Well you're going to have to tell me now," Lucy interrupted.

"It's nothing to worry about," her brother said from across the room. "Just some chap from your County government. I didn't particularly like what he had to say but he said it pretty nicely." He shrugged as he slipped off his shoes by the door. "I told Joe just to ignore it."

Sonny growled, deep in his throat. "That ain't gonna work."

Lucy was used to Sonny's gloomy outlook. "What exactly did you suggest he ignore?" she asked her brother.

But Maddie had heard Sarah's voice and was skipping into the kitchen, her hands clapping in rhythm to her feet, her voice sing-songing, "Is it wedding hair time?"

"That sounds like a great idea," said Sarah.

"Don't worry," Colin said across to his sister, as the women took their places around her. "I'll fill you in later."

*****

Some of the guests started arriving about an hour before the wedding. These were the die-hard locals, who knew that wherever there was to be a party, help would be needed for set up and take down. They pulled in to be greeted by Pete, wearing jeans with a turn up at the bottom, a clean white shirt, a red waistcoat, black jacket and a cowboy hat over his white hair, which was tied back in a ponytail. The hat was so he wouldn't get his hair wet and when Joe asked him about it he said he planned to lose it for the actual wedding. Pete was sending the cars away from the front of the house up the highway easement to park in the grassy quarter acre at the back of the property that Joe called the playground.

At first Joe balked at the idea of so many cars parking in his playground. "It's raining!" he told Pete. "They'll tear it up with their tires."

"So where do you want me to have them park?"

"What's wrong with out front?"

"For one thing your front yard is not big enough for all the cars, which means most of them will end up on parking out on the highway and you know you don't want the State Patrol to drive by and see a bunch of cars parked on the shoulder of Highway 20. Plus Lucy's going to be the last to arrive – do you really want her hustling down the highway from wherever your brother can park the Pinto?"

Joe's head rocked on his shoulders. "Okay no, you've got a point there. But make sure you warn them not to head into the playground too fast."

"You got it."

Vehicle after vehicle cruised sedately up past Joe's rose garden and the copse of conifers blocking his studio from the highway, to turn in alongside the creek to the quarter acre that a violent windstorm ten years previously had denuded of trees. Joe had considered replanting that area but since the land was mostly flat, he decided it would make a great space for parties and the odd game of volleyball. So he'd planted grass and dubbed it the playground.

The cars and trucks pulled in cleanly, and guests in flowing dresses and scarves, in jeans and tidy checked shirts, in patchwork skirts and knitted tops climbed out of their vehicles then leaned back in to pull out their potluck dishes and colorfully wrapped wedding gifts. None of them seemed affected by the light rain. They chatted, laughed, stood and discussed what kind of Christmas tree ornament they'd brought, then fell in step beside each other to pick their way across the grass, and meander down past the dome house and duck coop, bob under the overhanging cedar tree to emerge at the chicken coop and Joe's garden before reaching the house. They stopped some more, to talk to the people starting the coals in the Webers, and then they set to work.

The wedding was supposed to take place under the cherry tree alongside the house but even if the minister, bride and groom could stay dry under the tree, which was doubtful, none of the seats for the guests would be spared a soaking. And as much as the locals wanted to see Joe marry his sweetheart they didn't want to get their butts wet doing it. They put their heads together and formulated a plan B. The biggest room in Joe's house was his 20 foot by 30 foot bedroom. It had dormers in the front, which would make a perfect alcove for a wedding, and a view out to Sauk Mountain in the back and if they took out the few pieces of furniture he had in there, the guests would have plenty of room to witness the vows. And that would allow the downstairs of the house to be set up for the reception.

Everyone set to work. Laura had made a big heart out of cedar boughs and ivory ribbons to hang on the side of the house but now she carried it upstairs to surround the mullioned windows under the dormers. Others emptied the room of furniture then carried in lawn chairs and set them up for the guests.

Downstairs, Sarah and Skye set a long plank of old growth cedar on saw horses, covered it with two white tablecloths and left it to fill with pastries and bread, fruits and vegetables, pastas, meats, grains and desserts, while they set up the wedding cake on a small table next to the Christmas tree. Katie organized the drinks and glasses to be on one counter in the kitchen and the musicians had their keyboard, bass guitar and microphone in the space between the living room and kitchen.

Joe kept stepping in to help only to be shunted out of the way time and again so he could stay calm and focused. He finally stepped out onto the front porch to be with Maddie, who had her basket of flower petals ready but was more interested in meeting and greeting the children that were arriving for the wedding. "Come with me," she told them, "we have a whole big room to ourselves with a piñata and everything."

"Don't get your dress dirty," Joe warned as she skipped the newcomers into his pottery shop.

"I know, daddy," Maddie replied, touching the flower in the band holding her red hair away from her face. "Lucy told me already." Immediately her attention got diverted and she laughed at the neighbor children, leaping up to try to touch the piñata as they went into the shop. Joe's heart melted at the sight of the big dimples in her cheeks and the way her eyes lit up. She looked like a little pixie in the pink and white dress that hung from her shoulders with no cinch at the waist so when she turned, the bottom billowed out like dancers round a May pole.

Laura arrived with her children carrying a big tray of vegetables. She looked very arty in a black coat from the sixties with silver and white fur trim. Her generous lips were painted bright red and she smiled broadly at Joe as she sailed past. "Is my husband here, taking photographs already?'

Joe nodded. "Last I saw Jimmy he was taking photos of the food on the table."

"Well tell him to take one of our children when you see him. Before they get sticky from eating wedding cake."

She disappeared into the house just as a chain saw roared into action somewhere close by. Joe's head shot around to the right and there was Hilda, on the other side of the property line, her head down as she concentrated on whatever she was cutting up. He hoped it might be those obnoxious blackberries that Clarence Burns had piled up and encouraged to grow on top of his septic tank. But he suspected what she was really doing was trying to mess with his good time.

He stared across at her, feeling his breathing settle out again as his anger dissipated. She wasn't wearing much for protective clothing from what he could see. She was likely to get hurt in that mess of thorns, especially if she hit a piece of vine maple. He lifted his head and nodded at Dave and Shana across the driveway, thinking Hilda would get whatever she deserved for for trying to ruin his wedding day.

*****

Lucy and her brother had a quiet moment together after the others left for Joe's house. They spent much of that time apart, Lucy putting on her wedding dress as Colin changed into his suit upstairs. It wasn't until Lucy added the red-ribboned comb to her hair, using the mirror in the living room to see, that she heard Colin coming down the stairs behind her.

The stairs were made of thick, reddish-brown planks of cedar and she noticed that Colin was moving very slowly, pausing on each tread as he descended. At first Lucy thought it was because the steps were much more ladder-like than stair-like, notched, as they were, between two steep logs. That was because they had to function but not be too intrusive in this room that housed the large woodstove and had been a kitchen, living room and dining room at one time. But when Colin's head appeared in the mirror above his elegant dark suit, white dress shirt and a blue and black paisley tie, Lucy could see that he was looking at everything around him, one slow step at a time. She wondered what he thought of the log walls with their white stucco chinking, the masonry chimney with a dragon painted up the length of it, the tendrils of green hanging down from plants in the loft and the tiny lights hung around the log archway leading into the more modern-looking addition.

Sonny and Sarah's home was like many that belonged to Joe's hippie peers in the Upper Skagit in that it had started small, made from wood salvaged from the property it was built on, and then grew, both in size and modern conveniences. It was charming, in its mismatched kind of way, and definitely rustic, but it didn't look like the centuries-old, timber-frame houses in England.

Lucy turned her face to the right and double-checked that the tiny roses in her comb were not being covered by any of her hair. She needn't have worried. Sarah had straightened her usual mess of honey-colored curls by blow-drying it, bobbing the bottom around her neck and shoulder blades. The comb easily held one side of the straightened locks up off her face. She looked down at her wedding dress. It was a little loose on her slender figure but it was graceful and uncomplicated and it made her smile. How kind Rachel had been to make this for her. Lucy leaned forward and ran her finger under the lower lashes of her right eye, to take off a little smudge from her eyeliner. She glanced up at the clock on the wall beside the mirror; ten minutes till wedding bells.

"They have a nice place here, don't they?" her brother said from the bottom step.

Lucy thought about this for a moment. Sonny and Sarah's house was homey and welcoming but it wasn't nearly the kind of high-end home that she thought impressed her brother. His statement suggested that maybe he was more like her than she knew, admiring the same things that had first drawn her to this community. Things like building styles suggestive of making use of what was available, then dressing it up creatively rather than throwing money at it. And if the owner-builder couldn't do the creative part, somebody else in the community could, which often led to eclecticism in the finish but gave an overall effect of hand-crafted. Of course, Colin couldn't know how non-transactional all this community help was, something that Lucy loved about the Upper Skagit, but maybe he could feel it? It wasn't called the Magic Skagit for no reason, after all; maybe the magic was in the indiscernible appeal of lifestyle over largesse.

"Yes," she said finally in response to his statement. "It's lovely."

"You look very nice," Colin told her.

"So do you," she said. "You'll probably be the best dressed man at the wedding."

"Except for Joe."

"Oh, I expect he'll be in his usual jeans and suspenders."

"Suspenders?!"

Lucy corrected herself quickly, remembering that suspenders in England meant the things used to hold up ladies' stockings. "Braces," she said and Colin's eyebrows lifted from the dive they had made above his nose. Lucy laughed. "Don't worry, I'm not marrying that kind of man."

"Just one that's wearing jeans to his wedding."

"I was kidding," Lucy said.

Colin did a slow eye roll, like he'd known all along, then he tipped his head to one side. "Is it time for us to go?"

He made it sound like a practical question but the tenderness in his eyes told Lucy that he was thinking of something other than the clock; was she ready to go and marry Joe? The thought started an explosion of bubbles in the center of her stomach, like she might lift off and float if she weren't holding onto something.

"I should say so," she replied.

*****

Hilda could see Joe standing on his porch watching her. She hoped she was disturbing his good time with the sound of her chain saw. She had three chain saws but this one had the noisiest muffler, spluttering and growling and roaring as she cut. She only hoped she had enough gas in it to run it through the wedding ceremony. She'd've preferred to start work right on the dot of 1:30 but she knew that would look suspicious so she'd timed it to arrive in a way that suggested she'd been out here working for a while and that's why she was making noise throughout the ceremony. After all, she hadn't been invited to the wedding; why should she know what was happening at the Connors' house? She revved the chain saw and began cutting through the blackberry vines hanging over the septic tank. This was *her* property and she was going to reclaim it no matter what! Even if she had to cut the tight line to the drainfield so the septic tank began backing up into Connors' bathtub. That might make him move it!

She heard laughter and greetings from the people milling around Connors' house, bringing their offerings for the festivities. She glanced up once then decided she didn't want to see all the happy faces. It had been a long time since Hilda had been invited to an event like this. Not that it bothered her. She didn't need to go and have a good time with these people to enjoy life. She had her boyfriend to warm her. And besides, even though that food smelled good, she shouldn't be eating it. She wanted to stay slim for her own wedding. She yelped as a blackberry vine caught at the thick tights she was wearing under her mini skirt, then yelped again when another seemed to spring up her skirt and clutch at her behind. She shook, trying to rid herself of the pincer-like grip of the vines but that just snarled them more around her. It was as if she'd walked into a swarm of bees. The vibrations of the chain saw weren't helping anything either, almost walking her towards the thorny brambles. Hilda looked down to see some clinging dangerously to the front of her jacket and across the width of her skirt. Then one seemed to leap out of nowhere and scratch her across the face. She squealed.

"You okay over there?" came a voice from the other side of the thicket.

Hilda had her eyes squeezed shut against the pain and frustration of the situation but the sound of the voice made her pop them open. And who should she see but that Pete, looking suave with his long, white ponytail and red waistcoat. She was tearing up a little from the sting of all the scratches, so she couldn't determine if that was amusement she saw twinkling in his startling blue eyes. She wasn't going to give him the satisfaction of thinking she was beaten.

"I'm fine!" she yelled over the noise of the chain saw and pumped out a quick smile to go with it. She lifted a gloved hand, to primp her hair back into place, and completely lost control of the saw. The weight and movement of the operating chain saw dragged her forward, deeper into the blackberry thicket as she tried to regain control of it.

"Hey, watch out for that vine maple," she heard Pete yell, just as she got both hands back on the saw and felt it cut through something meatier than blackberries. Then - *POW!* - something hit her square in the nose and blood poured from both nostrils down onto her arms.

Pete wanted to help Hilda but there was no way he was going to attempt climbing over the rusty sheet metal that acted as a fence between the two properties, especially with the line of barbed wire on the top. "You need to turn off that chain saw," he yelled at Hilda, who had been stunned into rigidity, her eyes crossed in disbelief.

His voice snapped Hilda back to the present and she almost lifted a hand off the chain saw again, to swipe at the blood pouring out of her nose. But she caught herself and switched it off, looking down at it in consternation. She couldn't believe that this small an instrument could create such havoc so quickly.

She pushed her lips up despondently as she stared down at the mess of blood and vines across the front of her new, pale blue fleece jacket. She wanted to hurl the chain saw way far away from her to punish it, but her fight with the blackberries and the smack to her nose had sapped her of any strength she might have to do justice to such an action. So she took her anger out the only way she knew how.

She looked past Pete towards Connors and yelled, "This is *your* fault!"

Pete balked immediately. "What did *I* do?" Then he realized that her crossed eyes were making it seem that she was looking at him when really she was looking past him, at Joe. He spun around, fearful that Joe would be upset on his wedding day, and was pleased to see that the potter had his back to them, and was fully engaged in conversation with Jimmy.

Pete turned back to Hilda to see she wasn't looking his way anymore. She was busy extricating herself slowly, painfully from the brambles that had her in their grip. He opened his mouth to offer help, then thought better of it.

Instead, he discreetly left her to it and went back to the more pleasant task of directing incoming wedding guests towards the best place to park.

*****

Joe heard a clicking sound to his left and turned to see a Nikon camera in his face. He smiled and the camera clicked again. "That's better," said his neighbor, Jimmy, lowering the lens. Jimmy was a little bit beatnik and a little bit rodeo, walking tall in his washed out 501s and cowboy boots. "You were looking kinda grim there for a man about to get married."

"Hilda," Joe said, pointing, without looking, back towards the fence.

"Of course," said Jimmy, puckering his upper lip like he'd smelt something bad. "There's no way she'd leave you alone to enjoy this day."

Hilda had embroiled Jimmy and Laura in a complicated lawsuit after they bought the property adjacent to hers so they were no strangers to her vindictiveness.

"She always seems to find something loud to do right along the property line when we have company," Joe complained.

Jimmy put the camera up to his eye again and took photos over Joe's shoulder, presumably of Hilda in action with her chain saw. "How did your septic tank end up not on your property again?" he asked as he snapped away.

Joe could hear yelping and Pete's voice, presumably trying to mitigate Hilda's activities, but he wasn't going to turn around and give her the satisfaction of seeing that she'd disturbed him. "When Erica and I got back from Ohio," he answered, getting very involved in his explanation. "We found that the property line had magically moved, and instead of the whole concrete slab Burns had promised us, only half of it was on our side of the line. The half without any of the improvements."

"No kidding! How did that made any sense?!"

"I know!" Joe threw his arms out at his sides, to emphasize his concurrence. "Why put in a concrete slab big enough for a mobile home and then cut it in half?"

There was a short, sharp scream over the noise of the chain saw and the look of shock and amazement on Jimmy's face told Joe something major had gone down. He wanted to turn around but when he saw that Jimmy was now trying to hide his camera while taking a photograph, he sensed he should keep talking and not pay any attention. "I mean, what use would half a concrete slab be to anyone living out here?"

"In the city maybe," mumbled Jimmy, still trying to get an angle on whatever he was photographing.

"Exactly!" agreed Joe.

The chain saw noise stopped suddenly and Jimmy stood upright again and looked at Joe like he'd never taken his eyes off him. "But didn't you get a court order saying the septic tank was yours?"

"Oh sure. But that didn't stop Burns from trying to deny us access to it. And now that he's gone, Hilda the Horrible seems to have decided she needs to take up where he left off."

As Joe made the statement he thought he heard Hilda yelling something in the background but he couldn't read anything on Jimmy's face to suggest he was right. Instead, his lanky, New Age neighbor leaned in a little closer and said, his voice low, "If it's any consolation, she's gone and given herself a nasty knock on the nose with her chain saw activities."

Joe howled – Ha! Ha! Ha! – not caring whether Hilda heard him or not. "Did she get herself smacked by some vine maple?"

"I don't know what got her exactly." Jimmy tapped his camera meaningfully. "But I'm pretty sure I'm in possession of a couple of good shots of her bleeding from both barrels."

Joe laughed some more. "Ain't Karma a bitch," he said, thoroughly impressed with the turn of events.

"It sure is," agreed Jimmy. "And you know what I tell Laura is the best revenge?"

Joe shook his head, no.

"To live a happy life." Jimmy motioned towards the front door with his free hand. "So why don't you come inside and stand next to your best man, because I think you're about to start down that path, my friend."

*****

When Colin and Lucy pulled into the driveway at the pottery, the only living creatures along the property line were some black cap chickadees, with soft yellow bellies and smart gray wing feathers, feasting on a string of popcorn that someone had hung in the silver fir tree. The sky in the background was fluffy white with a thin layer of powder blue angled across the top of Jackman Ridge. Rain fell in tiny drops, like silvery sugar granules, on the windshield. As Colin swung the Pinto into the front yard, the birds took off in an explosion of tiny flutterings that mirrored the butterflies Lucy could feel in her stomach.

She looked up at the house and saw Pete, standing on the porch in his black tuxedo jacket, the red rose in his boutonniere matching his red waistcoat. He was holding an umbrella. Lucy felt like a queen as he trotted down the to the car with it and opened the door for her, Jimmy in the background on the porch, snapping her photograph. Colin came around from the other side of the vehicle and Pete handed him the umbrella then reached forward with his hands to relieve Lucy of her bouquet so she could step out of the Pinto unencumbered. Lucy wistfully gave him the bouquet that Skye had placed in her hands this morning, a diamond shaped swag of red roses and pink carnations set against dark green, winter leaves, interspersed with sprigs of white baby's breath. She gathered satiny folds of her long dress in one hand and, watching where she put her feet so she didn't step in a puddle, unfolded herself from the Pinto to stand underneath the umbrella. She stepped forward and Pete closed the door behind her, smiled as he handed her back her bouquet, then scooted up to the porch and inside the house, leaving her to have a moment alone with Colin.

She glanced up at her brother but Colin was staring at the house, lost in thought. She followed his gaze, wondering what he was seeing that had so captured his attention. Was it the vertical log work that intrigued him or the deep brown cedar shingles covering everything around the logs? Or, she wondered, was this little house in the mountains all too different for him to get his mind around?

She looked up at him again and noticed that his head was nodding, very slightly, almost imperceptibly. He must have felt her eyes on him because he turned after a moment and folded his right arm at the elbow, ready for her to take. "I'm proud of you," he said, "for making a life for yourself in another country. It's something I've always wanted to do but I've never had the courage."

Lucy blinked in surprise; these were the last words she expected to hear him say. Especially since she'd always assumed that it took more courage to stay around family than it did to run away. But she slipped her hand into the crook of his arm and let his kind words fill her, like the sweet scent of the roses in her bridal bouquet, as he walked her up the driveway towards her wedding and her new home.

Chapter 4

"So here's what we'll do," Lucy announced. She was standing on a plank stretched across cement blocks at the upper end of the second chamber of the new kiln, her feet slightly apart, pushing down on insulating, castable clay with a length of metal fence post. "Rodding" Joe called it. Rodding the castable to make sure it was smooth and not full of air pockets between the main arch and the length of 1 by 6 that he'd nailed on the outside to hold it in place until it dried.

Lucy's jeans, wool shirt and the orange work gloves Joe had given her were splattered with the murky material, plus parts of her face, where she pushed her hair away with the back of her wrist, but she was enjoying this particular task in the building of the new kiln. "I'll write a letter explaining the situation and send it to all your customers...."

"Our customers," corrected Joe, as he emptied another bag of castable into the concrete mixer.

"Our customers, and ask them either to turn up to the public hearing or send letters of support about your right to make retail sales."

"Our right," he corrected again.

He turned on the mixer, drowning out further conversation and Lucy put her shoulder into rodding the one section he'd just poured. The gray, castable clay was darker than concrete and thicker. It reminded Lucy of handfuls of wet sand on a beach. It could be pushed around easily but it was gritty enough that it didn't want to tumble into an open hole and fill it. That's why she had to encourage it. Once she finished this layer, she'd rod castable on the other side of the arch while Joe nailed up another 1 by 6 on this side. They'd already poured the arch for the first chamber so the round robin they'd established had found its groove.

"Yeah, I like that idea," agreed Joe after he turned off the concrete mixer. He flipped the barrel up and castable slid out of the mixer down onto the cement floor of the kiln shed. "I'm more worried about how we're gonna come up with the three hundred and fifty bucks for the fee though." He began shoveling castable into a 5-gallon pail. "We still need to buy the blocks for the chimney on this kiln."

"I already have that money set on one side," said Lucy as she jumped down from her plank, went around the back of the kiln, and climbed half way up a ladder on the backside. This half of the arch was harder to access because it sat too close to the wall of the first chamber to extend a plank between them.

Joe climbed a few steps up a ladder on the front side of the kiln, the bucket of castable hoisted up close to his shoulder. Before he poured it into the trough between them he looked at her. "What, the money for the fee?"

"No, the money for the chimney blocks."

"Oh." Joe tipped the gritty slush down into the arch form. "Good deal," he shouted. He headed back down the ladder with his empty bucket as Lucy leaned forward and speared the castable with the metal rod. He grabbed a 1 by 6 and climbed up onto the plank. "But we still need the steel pipe for the kiln doors."

Lucy stopped rodding and sighed. "Yes. I'm hoping someone

will need a cord of firewood this weekend."

Joe hammered twice on one of the nails holding the 1 by 6 on the shadow arch. "Why?"

"Cash flow. You know, to put towards the pipe."

"Except I need a new chain for my saw."

"Okay I could put *some* of the money from it towards the pipe." She looked across the top of the form and flashed him a cheeky smile. His eyes locked onto hers as he smiled back and for a moment there was nothing in the world except the two of them, making a connection in their own private zone.

Lucy hopped off the ladder, walked around to the front and climbed up the ladder there to rod from that side. She pushed her hair off her face with her gloved hand again. The temperature around them was well above freezing and felt damp, the trees shimmering moisture from an overnight rainfall. She thought about taking off the wool shirt Joe had leant her to wear for the project but that would mean interrupting their groove. "It'll all work out," she said when she heard him jump down off the plank.

"I guess I'm just having a hard time thinking about handing over three hundred and fifty dollars to the County. For a stupid amendment to a permit I already have!"

"Well there's no escaping that," she said. "But I wouldn't worry. We'll make it back when you fire this new kiln." Her words came out sounding labored as she leaned further towards the center of the arched wall. She felt his hands on her hips.

"Need some help there?" he chuckled.

She pulled the metal rod out one last time and straightened up. "Stop it," she chided. "Or we'll never get this finished."

He let go of her and went back to shoveling. "Only married a week and already you're rejecting me."

"Has it only been a week?" She turned and watched him scoop up more castable with the shovel and drop it into the bucket. "It feels longer because we've packed so much into this week."

"Well isn't that that how we wanted it?" asked Joe.

"What do you mean?"

Joe sank the tip of the shovel down into the pile of castable and looked up at her, wiping the sweat off his forehead with the sleeve of his jacket. "The wedding. We wanted it to be a small blip in the regular routine of our lives, like a moment on a radar screen, so it wouldn't feel like some kind of fairy tale. It's proving to have worked."

"True," said Lucy. She pondered the image of the radar as she looked out at the ground between the kiln shed and the garden, dark, muddy and rutted from driving across it in the truck. Some of the ruts had thin streams of purple, pink and blue rainwater in them and Lucy let her eyes swim in the colors as she felt her body decompress gently from physical exertion. "Only it hasn't ending up feeling like a blip. It feels more like all the elements of our lives have coalesced to form this one, moment of iridescence that will hopefully last."

"Like a pearl," said Joe.

Lucy nodded, her eyes still on the rainwater; yes, that was it. "Like a pearl," she agreed.

*****

She and Joe had stayed at the wedding party until about 5 pm, when the snow in the back of Joe's pick up was full of holes instead of champagne. They'd taken their leave to spend their wedding night in a cabin at a local resort further up the highway so the wedding guests could party at their house as long as they wanted. And they wanted. According to everyone, but especially Pete, people had a fabulous time dancing to the local band.

When Joe and Lucy returned home on Sunday, they discovered their guests had even cleaned up after themselves. All the furniture had been put back in the house and the kitchen returned to normal. Not that normal was anything fancy, not with the sheetrock walls and wood floors still needing to be finished and all the trim work put in, but at least their relatives had been able to have breakfast without stumbling through piles of soiled paper plates and plastic glasses.

"Who did all this?" Lucy asked, walking into the house, eyes wide at the reorganization and tidiness of everything.

"I didn't catch everyone's name," her brother-in-law, Paul, told her. He was sitting on the couch across from the woodstove, the Sunday newspaper spread out around him. "But a bunch of your neighbors got the majority of the clean up done before they left last night. Then Sonny and Sarah came over this morning with Maddie – before Margaret left - and got the rest of it. Any Sonny lit us a fire," he said, pointing at the woodstove. He looked at his brother. "You've got a great community here."

Joe nodded. He couldn't disagree. There was coffee too, by the smell in the house. He lifted one of his mugs down from a nail above the counter in the kitchen. "So where is Maddie?"

"She and Jake went outside to play in the woods armed with a couple of squirt guns."

"Squirt guns? Today??" He glanced out through the sliding glass door. "Well I guess it's not raining."

"That's what they said," chuckled Paul. "Too bad it couldn't have been like this yesterday."

"I don't think the rain deterred anyone from having a good time," Joe remarked as he walked his mug over to the coffee pot on the woodstove.

"True."

"Should we take advantage of the kids being occupied to bring the boxes of pots back down from the studio?" Lucy asked Joe.

"Maybe after I've had some coffee." He threw a look over at the kitchen. "And cake," he added. "Do you know where they might have put the wedding cake?" he asked his brother before slurping on his hot coffee.

"In their mouths, I think," Paul said, lifting his shoulders and smiling. "I don't know for sure but it looked pretty decimated when I went to get a piece."

"Oh well. It was good while it lasted."

"It was very good," Lucy agreed. She'd had a piece out of the lemon layer but didn't get to taste either the chocolate and or the carrot cake layers. But she imagined they were equally tasty.

"Why would you put your pots back in your shop if you can't sell from there anymore?" Paul asked.

Joe was walking towards him, to sit down on the couch next to him and read the paper, but the question made him stop, surprised. "Who told you that?"

"Sonny."

"Hmmmm," hummed Joe. A high-pitched squeal rang in from outside and Joe glanced through the glass in the sliding glass door to see his daughter racing between the garden and the studio. He smiled, drank another slug of coffee, stepped towards the couch and sat down next to his brother. He set his mug down on the arm of the couch.

"But that's not what the guy from the County said," he went on. "He didn't say I *couldn't* sell my pots from the shop anymore. Just that I wasn't *supposed* to sell my pots from the shop."

"Technicalities," grinned Paul. "Nice."

Joe looked at the cedar tongue-and-groove ceiling above him and narrowed his eyes trying to remember. "I don't know, maybe he didn't even say that." He shrugged, to indicate how unbothered he was by what the guy had said. "I just have to jump through some hoops to change my special use permit, is all. But I'm going to keep selling my pots here until they tell me I can't."

Somebody screamed outside and the brothers turned towards the sound. Maddie's red curls bobbed into view off the end of the back porch, then the rest of her appeared, little legs clambering up the steps as fast as they could. She bounced on the porch, scooted in the sliding glass door and rammed it shut behind her, keeping her eyes fixed on whatever – or whoever - was chasing her.

"Hey, hey, hey, slow down," Joe told her, lidding his coffee cup with his left hand.

"I *can't*, daddy! Jake's filling a bucket of water and he said he's gonna dump it on me!!!" Maddie was running up and down on her tippy toes, her rosy cheeks full of playing outside.

Joe sprang off the couch and headed for the kitchen. "Quick, let's fill one in the sink here and sneak out the front door," he said. "Then we can come around from behind Jake and get him before he gets you."

"Game on!" cheered Paul and bounced up from the couch to join in.

*****

The Monday after Joe and Lucy's wedding, Hilda was leaning up against the counter in the foyer of the Concrete Post Office, staring down at one of the letters she'd received. She recognized the handwriting on the envelope as soon as she'd pulled it out of her post office box and had glanced around her to make sure she was alone in the foyer. It was from the investigator she'd hired three years ago and it was the first she'd heard from him in a very long time. Well, ever since he tried to force her to pay him the balance they'd agreed on before he took on her job, even though he hadn't completed it.

She wondered if this was another begging letter or if, by some small chance, it was news. Good news she might prefer to read it at home, so she could start plotting with no one around to see her. Bad news, well, that wouldn't be any different than what the investigator had told her previously, and she had since given up so why stir everything up again now? She looked at the letter and couldn't make up her mind. But she also couldn't stop looking at it.

The thing that galled Hilda was that she'd been got. She'd taken up with Clarence five years previous, just after her divorce from her second husband, and she was convinced, at the time, that she'd made a step up. Clarence owned thirty acres of prime real estate in the Upper Skagit and had talked at length about the money they could make subdividing and building houses on it. The market had changed, he told her, and people were looking to move out of the city and into the country. What better place than the Upper Skagit? It was perfect; rural yet accessible. Heck, people could live here and drive down to the city to work every day if that's what it took. And with all the Californians moving up to Seattle with more money than they ever dreamed, they'd be paying top dollar for the real estate down in the city, giving Seattleites looking to escape the city, *plenty* of money to spend on real estate up here. It was a perfect set up. All they had to do was cut the land into sellable portions and they could make thousands.

The only problem was, Clarence didn't have the money to sink into subdividing the land; Hilda did. She'd forced her ex into selling all the property he owned and had walked away with a large settlement. But, she told Clarence, she wasn't about to invest her money into his property without her name on the deed. And since she had no inclination to marry again, she didn't imagine her name would ever go on the deed.

But no, she was wrong, he told her. If she wanted to invest in the project he would transfer title and put it in her name exclusively. It was the perfect partnership; he'd give the land, she'd give the money and they'd both be laughing all the way to the bank. What could go wrong?

Hilda believed him. He seemed like such a sweet guy. And he was very convincing. He'd shown her the short plats fees, the county fees, the estimated architect fees for the future buildings, and she'd handed over the first amount of money. He'd come back with the deed to his property in her name and then shown her the fees for the perk tests, the road building and the plans to put in one well that would take care of all the lots. She winced a little at the amount but he showed her how he'd already surveyed out a five-acre parcel on the north boundary line of his property, around that washroom he'd built for campers to use. Since he and Hilda were onto a different plan than his camping resort plan, he could sell those five acres to someone who could build a home around that washroom. And he'd put the proceeds from that sale into the development project.

It all sounded very plausible, and after Clarence carried through and sold that section of land to Jimmy and Laura Lee from Kentucky, Hilda handed over the balance of what they needed for the road building, perk tests and well. Half the settlement from her divorce went into the subdivision plan but she was twenty-eight acres richer, with plans to make five times the amount she'd gotten from her divorce. She didn't quite understand how cutting five acres off the thirty would leave her with twenty-eight but Clarence assured her it was just the way it shook out once the surveyors had finished their job. Then he disappeared. Completely. She went down valley to run errands one day and came home to find the RV they had bought together gone, and all of Clarence's gear with it.

Hilda went to the County and discovered there was no short plat filed with them, no architects had been approached and there was no road builder. Admittedly she was holding the deed to twenty-eight acres but she also came to discover that Burns had defrauded Jimmy and Laura Lee by selling them land that belonged to the State of Washington. Hilda found herself in the middle of a huge lawsuit between the State and the Lees since she owned the deed to the land the Lees *thought* they had bought from Burns. It didn't matter than she hadn't sold this land to them; it just mattered that her name was on the deed. And she couldn't even claim that maybe they had misunderstood and it was their fault that they were building their house around an improvement on the State's land because their lawyers had found Connors. And Connors was willing to testify to being defrauded previously by Burns *over the very same issue*; the location of a property line!

Hilda had been got good. She discovered there was nothing she could do about it except give over part of her land to the State, so they could build a road to access their timber, and give another portion, plus a settlement, to Jimmy and Laura. She ended up with a meager fifteen acres and she wasn't about to yield *any* of it to Connors for his septic tank! As far as she was concerned, he could put in another. Or pay her what she wanted for it.

She looked at the letter once more, still debating whether to open it or not, then slipped it at the bottom of the pile in her left hand. Underneath she discovered a letter from the County; *this* she had been hoping for! Behind her, the door to the foyer squeaked open and she froze, immediately regretting having vacillated over going back out to the car with her mail. She hoped this wasn't anyone she knew. She was wearing dark glasses to cover her black eyes but the damage to her nose from the vine maple was still plenty visible and she didn't want to have to answer questions about it. She crouched over her mail as she heard a male voice say, "You remember that tractor commercial where I had to find a farm shop in a high school for the filming?"

"Oh yes. Didn't you take some photographs of a school in Mount Vernon for it?"

Hilda ducked down further, recognizing Lucy's British accent. Darn!! She certainly didn't want to be seen by *her*! She listened as the conversation behind her continued, trying to figure out the identity of the other person. "…and it was a national commercial so they got paid the big bucks….," the male voice said. Hilda scanned her information bank and decided this must be Pete, talking about his job as a locations scout for the movie industry. "… turns out the teachers had been wanting a remodel of the farm shop for a long time but there was no money in the budget…"

Hilda heard keys jangling as the conversation continued, like one of them was going to open a post office box. She chomped down on her jaw. She wanted them to move forward into the little Post Office so she could skedaddle out to her vehicle but apparently neither of them had any business to do there today. Or maybe one of them did but not the other so they were having their conversation out here, effectively trapping her. "….the teachers were so pleased I recommended their shop for the shoot…,"

"They probably made the money they needed for the remodel from that commercial."

"Exactly right. So when I told them about building the doors for Joe's new kiln..."

New kiln? New *kiln*?! Hilda said in her brain. How could that be? She had specifically talked to the County about closing down Connors' pottery business so why would he be building a new kiln? That didn't make any sense at all. She tuned into the conversation more astutely now, hoping she'd heard wrong.

"And not just use of the shop," Pete was saying. Hilda heard the door to a post office box slam shut and keys jangle again. "They're giving me access to all their welding materials and equipment...."

He rattled on and Hilda momentarily doubted that she'd determined the right person. Could Pete be a welder as well as a locations scout? She lifted her eyes from her mail, without moving her head, and tried to see the man's reflection in the wall of windows in front of her.

"Well Joe's thrilled that you came up with this plan because it's always been very time-consuming for him to brick and unbrick the opening to his kiln."

"It'll be trip down memory lane for me, 'cause that's how I paid my way through school."

"Being a welder. I know. Joe told me."

"And now that we have the space to build these doors....."

"All we need is the steel." There was a moment of quiet then Hilda heard Lucy add, "Hopefully there's not a time constraint on using the farm shop?"

"Oh no. Not at all."

"Good. Because we're still waiting on the castable to pour the arches..."

Hilda felt heat steaming out of her ears, nose and mouth. Doors? Arches?! How big was the kiln going to be? She'd only seen one arch on the kiln Connors was using back when she was trying to be friendly with him and now he was graduating to something with multiple arches? What was this, light industry? The County had better do something, and fast! She held her breath, realizing that the conversation behind her had stopped, and listened anxiously to the footsteps coming towards her.

"Here, let me get that for you," she heard Pete say. "Where's that going?"

"New York," came Lucy's voice again, closer, almost directly behind Hilda. "We made a few sales this weekend, to some of our out-of-state wedding guests."

"Even though you had the shop torn apart for the kids?"

"Uh huh. We didn't want to sell any of them pottery but you know how people are."

"They do love Joe's work."

The door to the inner section of the Post Office swung open behind Hilda and she heard a sound like rapping of knuckles on cardboard. "And hopefully this will help towards the cost of the steel for the kiln doors," said Lucy. A couple more footsteps moving away from Hilda then Lucy's voice, raised to talk back through the doorway. "That or the cement blocks for the chimney."

"See you later," Pete called back. He must have let go of the door behind Lucy because Hilda heard it bang shut, then the scuffing of his Birkenstocks over the linoleum tile floor, heading towards the outer door. "Bye, Hilda," he called back as the outer door squeaked open. "Hope your nose is okay." And then the sound of the door closing behind him.

The gall of that man, Hilda thought, letting her shoulders relax as she lifted her chin defiantly. Her nose was none of his business! Especially not if he was in on helping Connors build a new kiln. And where was the County in all this?! They were supposed to be closing Connors' business down, not encouraging him to grow it. Her eyes narrowed; had Connors bought a permit to build this new kiln? She'd be sure to find *that* out. She looked back down at the letter in her hand from the County. This had better say something good, she thought. Then she hurried towards the outside before Lucy could try to bring up her nose too.

*****

"I just saw Lucy in the Post Office," Pete said as he walked into the pottery shop. There were boxes of pottery stacked against one wall and Joe was lowering a thick round of varnished, old growth cedar onto a tree stump that he'd turned into a table bottom.

"Check that this is centered, would you?" he grunted.

Pete bobbed down, eyeing the bottom of the cedar round as it landed on the 2 by 4s notched into the top of the stump. He signaled Joe yes with a thumb in the air. "I thought you guys were taking Maddie back to Seattle today?"

"Nope," said Joe as let go of the wood. He immediately spun around, lifted a pitcher out of one of the boxes, tossed it lightly, confidently, into his other hand and placed it on the fir tabletop. "Tomorrow. We're taking Maddie to the zoo for a couple of hours then, after we drop her off with her mom, Lucy wants us to go by Immigration to get the forms for her green card."

"They can't mail those to you?"

"Sure they can." Joe picked up a large, shallow salad bowl and reached across the table to put it on the opposite side from the pitcher. "But they said it was quicker if we went and picked them up from their office in Seattle and since we want to go to Lucy's folks' place in England in May, we decided quicker was better." Joe started to move around the tiny shop, carrying individual pieces of pottery from the boxes and making decisions about where to place them on the rustic display tables and cedar slab counter tops. He tended to prefer fewer pieces on display than more, so customers could get a feel for whether they liked his work or not when they first entered the gallery.

Pete lifted his right leg and perched awkwardly on the bar stool in the corner. "Well like I told Lucy, I found out this morning that we can weld the frames for your kiln doors down in that farm shop I scouted."

Joe stopped moving and looked over at Pete, stoked. "Hot dog!

So now all we have to do is find someplace to cut the steel...."

"No, we can cut it there."

"We can?"

Pete leaned forward on the stool, like he was going to share a secret with Joe. "They've got power hack saws..."

"That they're willing to let us use?"

"Damn straight. So not only can we cut the steel there, we can make angle cuts and miter anything we need to miter."

"Oh man, this is de-luxe!"

"Right?" The dogs started barking on the front porch and Pete turned his head towards them, interrupted by the sound.

"Is that Lucy pulling in?" Joe asked, as he hung coffee cups on nails in the live edge of another round of old growth fir.

Pete stretched his neck up and peered out one of the multi-paned windows of the shop. "No. It's a Sheriff's vehicle...."

Joe stopped, holding a mug in mid-air. "A Sheriff's vehicle?" He hung the mug on a nail and looked across at his friend. "Pulling in here?"

Pete nodded, his eyes still on the window, his head lifted to see out. "Uh huh. And parking by the looks. Looks like a female Deputy."

Joe strode across the room, and pulled open the door, Pete right behind him. The dogs were both barking up at the driver in the dark green Ford Explorer but, as fierce as they sounded, the Deputy slid out of the vehicle and bent over to pet them both. "Hi there," Joe called down to her as she straightened back up. The dogs wandered away from her to sniff the tires.

"Hi," said the young woman, an attractive, heavyset girl in the twenties with shiny, shoulder length blonde hair. She walked towards him, her puffy green jacket and pants making swishing sounds as she moved. "I'm Deputy Porteous and I'm here because," she stopped at the bottom of the porch steps, fumbling with the button on the top pocket of her jacket with her left hand as she looked up at Joe and Pete. "Hang on, I'm getting there," she said.

When she glanced down at the pocket, Joe stole a look at Pete – what's this about? – then watched as she pulled out a small, red, spiral bound notebook.

"I'm here because your neighbor -," Deputy Porteous flipped to a page in the notebook. "- Hilda Hess –,"

Joe groaned.

"- complained that you, Mr. Connors." She stopped and looked up at Joe. "You are Mr. Connors, right?"

"That depends. What's Hilda saying I did?"

Deputy Porteous laughed, revealing a beautiful wide smile and small dimples in her full cheeks. "Well actually I was just being polite. I know you're Mr. Connors because I've visited your pottery shop before."

"You have?"

"Uh huh. Your girlfriend – the one with the English accent – she helped me."

"Wife."

"What's that?"

"Wife. Lucy's my wife now."

Porteous smiled again. "Well congratulations." She looked back down at her notebook. "Okay, so Ms. Hess complained that you hit her in the face with a piece of vine maple on Saturday."

Joe and Pete both jumped at the same time.

"I was getting married on Saturday!"

"He wasn't anywhere *near* her!"

But the young Deputy, held a mitigating hand up in the air; she wasn't finished.

"That was what our dispatcher wrote down from her phone call but when I paid Hilda Hess a visit earlier today she claimed she'd never actually said *you* hit her but that the debris on your septic tank hit her and so she wanted to lodge a complaint."

Joe sat down on the top step, dumbfounded. "You came out for that?!"

Deputy Porteous didn't show offense. Instead her big, gray eyes looked amused as she kept a straight face and answered, "No. I came out because she'd made it sound like an assault and we have to respond to assaults but once I got here and she changed," – the Deputy hesitated, obviously rethinking her choice of words – "clarified her story, I told her that it was a civil matter and so not something the Sheriff's office could help her with. I just thought you might want a heads up on what she's doing over there."

"I appreciate that," said Joe.

Joe turned and looked at Pete; they had a friend here. He leaned forward, as if sharing a secret with the Deputy. "You know what's crazy?" There was something in this young woman's Irish eyes that suggested not only did she know crazy, but she knew that *Hilda* was crazy. "The septic tanks belongs to me but it's not on my land. So the brush that "assaulted her" on Saturday" – he made quotation marks in the air as he said the words – "is her responsibility, not mine."

"Do you know how it came to "assault" her?" Deputy Porteous made similar quotation marks with her fingers in the air.

"She was messing around with a chain-saw, something she'd no business doing by the sounds of it. I didn't see it but there were people here for my wedding that did. One even got a photo, so I've got evidence if she tries to push it. Anyway, she obviously wasn't paying attention to the vine maple and it bit her. Vine maple's like that. How bad is she hurt?"

Porteous twisted her lips, like she was thinking of the best way to answer this. When she replied, her head was nodding up and down, as if to underscore the importance what she was saying. "She has a nasty bruise on the bridge of her nose."

Joe rocked backwards, face tipped up, knees rising into the air. "Haw! Haw! Haw!" he bellowed.

Pete chuckled and Deputy Porteous turned her face away but not before Joe had recovered from his outburst and caught the hint of a smile at the edge of her mouth. When she turned back to look at him again, he noticed she was po-faced. "My advice," said the Deputy.

"Stay well back from Ms. Hess. She's gunning for you."

Joe snorted derisively. "Tell her to bring a lunch!"

"Is that an official warning?" asked Pete.

Deputy Porteous lifted her left arm and glanced at her watch. "Can't be. I'm now off duty. Consider it a tip."

"What time is it anyway?" Joe asked her.

"Just after four."

Joe turned and looked up at Pete. "And you said you saw Lucy in the Post Office?"

"Uh huh. I saw Hilda too but she made a point of not looking at me." He tipped his chin towards Porteous. "Must have been that nasty bruise on her nose."

Joe laughed again and looked past Deputy Porteous. The light was flattening out around them, darkening the green in the trees and slowly silhouetting their shapes against the sky. Intermittently a vehicle would race past on the highway behind the Deputy but in between, there was nothing but tranquility filling the air around him. Joe took a moment to let that restful peace wash over him, like a bath tub full of warm water, then he blinked his attention back on Porteous. He caught her coming off a smile at Pete that was so charming, he almost turned to see his friend's reaction. But he didn't.

"So tell me this," he said to the young Deputy. "Did you wait to come see me so you could be off duty when you gave me the warning?"

"Tip," Porteous corrected. Then her face seemed to process his question. "What d'you mean?"

"Well you said you saw Hilda earlier today but you're only just now getting here..."

Porteous grinned guiltily and Joe smiled up at Pete, only to find his friend's eyes glued on the Deputy. Porteous pointed into the air above Pete's shoulder. "I timed it so I could visit your shop once I got off work. You are still open, I hope?"

Joe made a regretful sucking sound in one side of his mouth. "I was hoping to make it up to the dump before it closed, to clean up from the wedding."

"I can take care of her," Pete offered.

Joe looked at his friend, then back at the Deputy. There was definitely some chemistry here that didn't have anything to do with pottery. He pushed himself to a stand and stepped back up onto the porch, the light from the shop throwing warm beams of yellow out into the accumulating darkness. "Sure. If you don't mind," he said.

"Thanks!" said Deputy Porteous, with a smile for both the men. She trotted up the steps and swished her way into the shop like she wanted to get there before anyone changed their mind.

Once she had her back to him, Joe tapped the fourth finger of his left hand at Pete - she's married.

Pete smirked and jerked one shoulder up – so?

Joe filled the front yard with laughter.

*****

Lucy lifted a milk crate and placed it upside down on the plank, her mind going back over all that they'd accomplished this past week. From taking Maddie back to her mother and starting on the paperwork for the amendment to their special use permit *and* her permanent residency, to reorganizing the shop and driving down to Seattle a second time, to pick up the castable refractory clay; they had certainly kept hopping. Business as usual. Not that she minded. There was something so eminently satisfying about doing what you wanted to do with your life, despite the financial hardships and the worrying over whether you'd ever make it work. Of course, she tended to worry more than Joe, who moved forward with such conviction. She wasn't sure whether it was conviction that he'd make this pottery business work or conviction that this was what he *had* to do with his life, but every step he took was towards his goal of being a studio potter. And now he had her beside him, moving towards that goal, too.

Lucy stepped back to let Joe pass in front of her, up onto the plank and the milk crate to dump the next load of castable down into the arch form. For her, of course, the pottery was a day job that she was willing to work to support her theatrical dreams, like Joe cutting firewood and doing occasional building projects to support his pottery. She smiled to herself, feeling her skin begin to cool in the December air; maybe she was a little *too* optimistic to think that one financially strapped creative endeavor could underwrite another, but she didn't care. She liked her day job. She liked the challenge of taking something that was kind of working but not completely and trying to turn it into a success. Joe made beautiful pottery; all she had to do was find ways to get people to discover it.

She leaned back again, as Joe jumped down off the plank, and then climbed up to rod what he'd just poured while he crossed the kiln shed to refill the bucket. She lifted the metal fence post high above her shoulder, then sank it down into the wet castable. Maybe she should have used something taller than a milk crate, she thought. She was standing on her toes to get an angle over the 1 x 6., since they were nearing the top of the arch and the form was leaning in, following the curve.

"You got enough room up there?" Joe asked, noticing her dilemma.

"I think so," she said. Out of the corner of her eye she saw the dogs racing down the hill from the dome house, their mouths open, venting great puffs of warm steam into the air around them. "How will you know when this has set up if you can't see it from either side?"

"Where it's exposed at the top will tell me enough. To get the forms off at least," said Joe. The shovel scraped across the concrete floor as he filled it for the last time from this batch. "From what I've read, and what Vlad told me," he said, as he dumped the shovel full into the bucket. "It won't harden completely until I fire the kiln. Then the heat will react with some property in the refractory and cause it to set up." Max and Maggie trotted into the kiln shed and sniffed the floor on their way over to the boss. "What have you two been up to?" Joe asked. Both dogs ignored him, continuing their investigation of the smells on the concrete, while Joe waited for Lucy to finish rodding the back wall on that side. "You ready?" he asked when she turned towards him.

"Uh huh." Lucy climbed down and sat on the plank, prompting both dogs to come and nuzzle up to her. She slipped off her gloves and petted them, as Joe hefted the bucket of castable onto his shoulder before climbing the ladder.

"It doesn't really matter when it sets up though, does it?" said Lucy, thinking about all the steps they had still to finish before the kiln would be ready to use.

"It does to me," Joe argued, then tipped the castable down into the form, causing both dogs to jump at the gravely noise. "I want this thing done, so I can fire it."

Lucy wanted that too because Joe had already declared his last firing in the old kiln and they didn't have much left in the shop for the upcoming holiday season. Between the bills, the fee for the amendment to the special use permit and the fee for her green card application, things were going to be tight. Plus she was banking on a new batch of pots for the second annual pottery party in Seattle the weekend after next.

She opened her mouth to ask when he thought the first firing might be in this new kiln, then clamped it closed just as quickly. They might only have been married a week but that was long enough for Lucy to know that the one thing Joe didn't like, was being pushed.

Chapter 5

"So are you guys gonna take a honeymoon?" Sonny was standing in the bed of Joe's pick up truck and caught the round of firewood mid-question. He twisted at the waist, dumped the round on a row and twisted back in time to catch the next one.

"That's the plan."

"Where?"

Joe twisted away from Sonny and grabbed another round of wood, then back towards him and tossed it. "My folks want to throw us a party in Saratoga 'cause they couldn't make it out to the wedding."

"A party for the family?"

"With the cousins."

"And the neighbors?"

"Everyone they can fit into their house."

"Sounds like a good time."

Their movements were perfectly synchronized, punctuating the dialogue with the rhythm of away-stack-grab, back-toss-catch, making the wood fly from the ground to the truck. "We'll go there first. Then Lucy's folks want a chance to celebrate since they didn't make it either."

"So you're going to England?"

"We're going to England."

"Oh." Sonny shifted forward in the bed to start a new row. "When?"

"Probably sometime in May. After Tulip Festival. So we can make the money for the tickets."

"Didn't you get money for your wedding?"

"Some, yeah."

"But not enough?"

"Nope."

"Oh."

It was Sunday morning and Joe and Sonny were up in the snow on Middle Finney Ridge, having cut and split a cord of firewood from a log left on a landing. It was beautiful, clear grain, old growth fir that split like cutting through butter and promised lots of snap, crackle and pop as it burned. Joe hated to sell it, hated even to cut it for firewood, but that was the designation the Department of Natural Resources had given it and he needed the money. So when the call came in first thing from someone needing firewood *right now* - "I just put my last piece of wood in the stove!" the person wailed - Joe started to gear up. Sonny was visiting at the time and didn't have anything on his plate for the morning so he offered to tag along. Joe was not about to turn down that offer. He knew it would go fast with Sonny along. So he passed him some gloves, a mall and some wedges and they hopped in the Chevy. Joe was eager to get back to building the chimney on his kiln, because then the whole thing would be done. Except for hanging the doors over the chambers. Turn, stack, grab/turn, toss, catch. "We'll figure it out," said Joe.

"How long will you stay?"

"In England?"

"Yup."

"I don't know. Lucy's talking about taking me over to France."

"France?!"

"Yeah. She has some good friends in Bordeaux that want to 'sniff' me out. Make sure I'm good enough for her."

"Oh. They're kind of too late. You're married now."

They had four rows in the bed of the truck now and not much left on the ground. Sonny held up a finger for Joe to wait while he adjusted the position of some of the wedges on the top of the last full row. Some of the fir still had snow on the bark and the moisture added another dimension to its naturally clean, tangy aroma. Once Sonny finished rearranging, he turned back to Joe and they picked up the rhythm instantly.

"Could be fun though, going to France."

"Maybe. Depends on whether I need a visa or not."

"I didn't think Americans needed a visa to go to France."

"Didn't used to. But Lucy thinks they've changed the rules because we make the French get a visa to come here."

"Damn straight."

Joe laughed. They paused again, so Sonny could climb down out of the bed and load the final, half-row from the ground, then fell back into synch. Turn, toss, catch, load, turn.

"Is Lucy gonna become a US citizen?"

"I'm guessing. But she has to get her green card first."

"Oh."

"Yeah, she got the paperwork but that's another big fee we have to come up with."

"How much?"

"I think it's $150 to file and then she has to pay 50 bucks for a physical."

"Why's she need a physical?"

"They want to make sure she doesn't have any diseases."

"Like what?"

"Tuberculosis. AIDS."

"Oh." Sonny shifted around the tailgate to the other end. Joe held onto the wood in his hands.

"She has to get an AIDS test," Joe told him.

"We can say no to someone with AIDS?" Sonny held out his hands and Joe threw the wood.

They turned away from each other. "Apparently."

"Oh."

A final turn grab, toss, catch, stack and the truck was full. Now Joe and Sonny paused for real, to take in the view of Mount Baker. It had been misted over when they arrived but now the mist had lifted, leaving just a smoke-ring shaped cloud hanging in the air over the flat top of the snow-covered peak. It looked very otherworldly. Joe and Sonny stared off at it, their breath making plumes of steam in the air in front of them. Then, without discussing it, Joe picked up the chain saw and peavey while Sonny grabbed the mall and wedges. Sonny kicked through what was left of the snow around the truck to get to the cab while Joe hefted himself up on the tailgate one last time, and sank the bar of the saw and the hook of the peavey down between the rows of wood. He leapt down, spat on the ground and squelched through the slush to get to the driver's side door. Once there he stopped, and unconsciously turned back to take in the view one more time.

"It's almost a sin to sell it," said Sonny from the other side of the cab.

Joe turned back and gazed at the glorious load of orangey-pink wood in the truck. "Should we just take it back to our places and split it."

"Nah," said Sonny. "You need the money."

With that, they both bounced up onto their sides of the bench seat and Joe turned on their engine. "Okay, Nellie," he said to the truck. "Take us to the customer."

*****

Fortunately the firewood customer paid not only for the cord being delivered but also for a second one to be delivered in "a week or so."

"Now we definitely have enough for the pipe for the kiln doors," Lucy said when Joe put the money on the kitchen table.

His feet were wet from standing in the snow for so long and he walked over to the rocking chair by the woodstove, sat down and began to take off his boots. "What about the fee for the amendment to our special use permit."

"Will you stop worrying about that," Lucy told him. She finished chopping up some onions and threw them in a sizzling frying pan on the stove.

"What're you making," Joe said over his shoulder, drawn by the aroma of the onions frying.

"Shepherd's pie," said Lucy, moving the onions around with a fork in the hot oil. "There was no deadline on when we had to file the paperwork," she went on, returning to the subject. "So we'll do it when we can afford to do it. And if I get this commercial I'm auditioning for in Seattle tomorrow, we'll use that money to pay the County."

"But what about the money for your green card?"

Lucy got the meat out of the fridge to add to the onions. She looked across at him. "Use the money to pay for the doors," she insisted. "Then you can get this new kiln finished and fire it up before the pottery party in Seattle the weekend after next."

"I wouldn't count on me being able to fire the new kiln by then," Joe countered quickly. "Because I'm not sure Pete will be able to make the doors anytime soon."

*****

But Joe was wrong. When he talked to Pete about it up in the sauna that evening, Pete's immediate reply was, "You wanna build them tomorrow?"

Joe looked across the dimly lit interior of the sauna. He was sitting towards the front of the top bench, close to the stove, and Pete was leaning against the slatted backrest in the far corner where the sweat came on slower. “Are you serious?!”

“As a heart attack,” quipped Pete. “No, why wouldn’t I be?”

“Well can we use the farm shop on a school day?”

“Tomorrow’s a teacher in-session day so there won’t be any students. But we can get in.”

“How do you know that?”

“The shop teacher sent me a list of days when the kids wouldn’t be there, in case we had to work a weekday, and I’ve had my eye on it, waiting for you to give me the go.”

“You’re not working on that movie sequel this week?”

“Nope. That got postponed again. Too much snow up at Mount Baker.”

“Yeah, there was quite a bit up on Finney today, where we were cutting firewood.”

Pete was sitting across from the window in the sauna and he nodded towards it. “It’s snowing here now, too.”

“Is it?’ Joe looked past the three candles flickering on the outside sill of the window and saw the big flakes of snow. “Said in today’s paper that the temperature’s supposed to go up then down again.”

“Yeah, I doubt this will stick.”

“Well then sure, I’m game to build these doors tomorrow if you are. How long d’you think it will take us to weld them?”

“Couple of hours.”

“Oh.” This surprised Joe. The heat from the stove was coming on strong now and he let his shoulders roll forward to relax into it. “So we might be done by noon then?”

“Probably. Why? D’you have plans for the afternoon?”

“No, not at all. I was just thinking I’d like to get them back here and off my truck before it gets dark.”

There was a long pause as both men decompressed further in the radiant heat, then Pete added, “The steel and recycling center opens at 8:00. Should I come over at 7:00 and we’ll go down in your truck?”

"Sounds like a plan."

*****

Hilda saw them go by in the Chevy when she walked down to get her newspaper from its box out by the highway the next morning. Then, when she turned around to head back up to her house, she saw Lucy follow them in the Pinto. Hilda thought about this as she trotted back up her driveway. Both of them leaving so early in the morning could mean they were gone for the day, which would make it a good time to do what she'd been plotting since she'd found out that the County wouldn't be closing Connors down in the short term. It had snowed overnight but it was only a light dusting and the temperature wasn't low enough to have frozen the ground.

Her mind churned this possibility as she wandered back into her house, slipped out of her ankle high muck boots just inside the front door and dropped the newspaper on the kitchen table. She walked over and turned the coffee pot on, then backtracked to the table and picked up her binoculars. She stood for a long moment staring through the binoculars as the coffee pot bubbled and spat behind her. The small space was warming up from the fire she'd built in the wood stove and Hilda lifted her right foot and scratched the back of her left shin as she moved the binoculars slowly over Connors' front yard and porch. She couldn't see the dogs, another indication that Connors and his wife were gone for a while. She looked at the clock on the microwave and decided to give it an hour, and if they hadn't returned by then, she'd chance it.

*****

Joe pulled into the high school parking lot, his truck weighted down by 12 long pieces of right-angled steel. "Drive around back," Pete instructed, pointing to the left of the main building in front of them. "That's where the farm shop is. If the teacher's not in there we can always come back here and have the people in the office track him down."

Joe put the truck in second gear and lugged it slowly through the mostly empty parking lot, down past the football field to a big, brick building with a blue metal roof that had three garage doors and one regular door. A tan, Ford 250 pick-up was angled across two parking spots, the only evidence that someone was in the building. In every other way the premises looked and felt deserted without the presence of children. Joe idled his truck as they looked around, deciding what to do.

"Park in front of one of the garage doors," Pete said after a moment, pointing across Joe, "'Cause I'm pretty sure Stan Stanley'll have you back the truck into the building if he's there."

Joe looked at Pete, eyebrows raised. "That's his name, this teacher? Stan Stanley?"

"Uh huh. And don't rib him about it either. He gets a lot of that from the kids. They call him Mr. St-St-St-Stanley."

"Kids can be so mean."

Joe swung the Chevy around to the left, then put it in reverse and backed up to the building. "Close enough," he pronounced once his tailgate looked to be a few inches from the garage door. He switched off the engine and grabbed his orange work gloves off the bench seat.

"Let's do this," said Pete.

*****

They rolled out of the truck and sauntered over to the door, both of them tucking their gloves behind one side of the suspenders on their chests. Joe stepped back and let Pete be the one to twist the gold knob on the door and push it open.

The smooth, mellow sound of an alto saxophone, backed by percussion, burst from the space and filled the air around them in greeting. "Sounds like Artie Shaw," whispered Joe, his fingers automatically snapping to the rhythm. "I like this already,"

Pete led him inside and they both stopped by the entryway, to look around the space. The interior was large, the size of an eight car garage, with workbenches along the inside walls and welders, drill presses and tools Joe was unfamiliar with, scattered about the floor. But there was also a lot of empty space, presumably for whatever equipment needed to be worked on. He noticed how shadowy, unlit, the shop was, and how the big band sound of Rose Room echoed off the walls. He imagined the sound would be very different when there were teenagers in there, working on various projects.

Towards the back of the building there was a rectangular, walled-in area with light-filled windows and a door. It looked like a small office. Joe turned to Pete, who nodded that this was the way to go, and they both drifted towards it as what sounded like a fleet of saxophones came in to harmonize with Artie Shaw. Joe's head bopped up and down with the beat as they approached the office at the back and, as they got closer, he saw a man bent over a desk, drawing something. Or drafting something. He was holding a ruler and using it to measure and draw lines. Joe's eye fell on the coffee cup next to the man's right hand. It was one of his.

Pete rapped on a windowpane in the door with the knuckle of his forefinger as the trumpets, tubas, bass and drums came in with the saxophones and lifted the music, note by note, towards a grand finale. "Hi, Stan," he called out.

The man's head shot up, surprised, then his face broke into a smile. He let go of the ruler, dropped his pencil on the paper and stood up. He was short, blocky and bald, with a burgeoning belly and a wide, dimpled smile. "Heeeey, Pete," he called out over the music. "Good to see you!" He came around the desk to shake his hand.

"You too. I hope we're not disturbing you."

"No, not at all. I was just having fun, designing the new space." He looked at Joe. "Are you the potter?"

"I am, yes." Joe stretched his right hand forward. "Joe."

"Stan Stanley." He grinned and added, "But you can call me Stan."

They all laughed.

"So, are you here to build those doors?' Stan asked, looking from Joe to Pete then back again.

"If that works for you."

"Sure, no problem." He moved swiftly between them as the music switched to Benny Goodman and his orchestra playing "Sometimes I'm Happy." Joe recognized these big band sounds from his dad's collection. Stanley continued on out the door to his office, leaving Joe and Pete to spin on their heels and follow him at a trot.

"I'll turn the lights on for you and get you set up with a welder." He retraced their steps, his shoulders back, his belly thrust out in front of him, high and happy, like a dog with his tail. "You should probably back your truck in to be close to the hoist," he said pointing at the big lift contraption in the center of the rafters above them. "I imagine you'll need that to lift the kiln doors onto your truck, right?"

Joe and Pete looked at each other like they hadn't thought of this, then nodded their heads enthusiastically. "Sounds like a great idea!" said Joe.

Stanley reached the light switches on the wall by the door and flicked three of them up, causing the overhead fluorescents to blink to life as Benny Goodman trilled on his clarinet. "You familiar with the new wire feed welders?" he asked Pete.

Pete shook his head no. "It's been 30 plus years since I've welded."

"All right. I'll set you up with a stick welder." Stan Stanley turned and looked at Joe. "Behind which door?"

"Do I win a prize?"

Stanley's mouth spread into an amused smile while he simultaneously shook his head no. "Your truck," he explained. "It's parked behind which door?"

Joe pointed at the middle one. Stanley pushed another switch on the wall and the garage door began washboarding its way up the wall. "Back your truck in and I'll get the welder."

Joe bent low and scooted under the rising door. He yanked open the door to his truck and bounced into the driver's seat, switching on the engine as he watched Pete walk behind him to the center of the room, rolling his hand in the air to indicate he could come back. Joe put the truck in reverse and drifted back slowly, until he saw Pete's gloved palm pointing straight up in the air. He killed the engine, stepped on the emergency brake and hopped out, pulling on his gloves as he walked around to join his friend.

Stan Stanley came from the back pushing a red Lincoln welder on wheels. "This should do you," he said, bringing it to a stop alongside Pete. He thrust a bunch of welding rods into his hand.

"Can I pay you for those?" Joe asked.

"No, no, it's fine," said the teacher. "Just let me know if you need more." He pointed to his office. "I'd better get back to my design plans and grading papers while I don't have hormonal teenagers around." He strutted away, yelling back, "I'll turn the music down."

"Don't," Pete and Joe shouted together.

"Okay then." He grinned at them. "I won't." He disappeared back into his office and closed the door behind him.

*****

Joe didn't waste any time. He reached into the bed of the pick-up, grabbed one of the lengths of steel, and pulled it towards him. Pete placed the welding rods in the corner of the bed of the truck and automatically grabbed the other end of the steel as it slid out. Following Joe's lead, they each took a half a dozen steps towards the welder and lowered it onto the floor.

"How d'you get that working for you?" Pete asked as they moved back towards the truck.

"What?"

"People always helping you out financially by giving you

stuff?"

"Ah come on, it doesn't *always* happen."

"Seems it happens a lot more to you than it does to me."

Joe shrugged as he pulled another length of steel towards him. "I don't know. Maybe 'cause I don't care that much about money. I'm pretty sure I give it away just as often as it comes back to me."

Pete leaned forward and grabbed the end of the steel and they stepped sideways again to lay it on the pile. "Yeah, but that's the thing...."

"What's the thing?"

"I give money away to help people too but I never see it coming back my way."

They lowered the steel to the floor again and then walked back to the truck.

"That's 'cause you think it's on a sprint," said Joe as he grabbed a third length and pulled it towards him.

"What?!"

"The money. You know, traveling in a straight line, back and forth."

"What?!" Pete said again.

Joe tipped his chin up to indicate that Pete should lift the steel. Pete obliged, despite his confusion, and Joe went on. "But it's not. At least, in my mind it's not. Money's on a relay. So you slap it into the next person's hand, they pass it off to somebody after them, and on and on until it comes full circle back to you."

"O-kay," said Pete, obviously not convinced. "But what if it doesn't come full circle?"

"Why wouldn't it?" They put the third piece of steel down as the music switched to In the Mood and Joe caught up with Pete to look directly into his face as he asked, "You don't think most things follow the movement of earth?"

Pete looked skeptical.

Joe hoisted a fourth piece of steel into the air and slid it out. "I do," he said. "Especially money, 'cause that's all it's good for, is circulating. So my guess is that as long as it doesn't get fumbled in one of the hand offs, it *has* to come full circle."

"What do you mean, fumbled?"

"Like if you attach strings to it, preventing it from moving on."

"I never attach strings to the money I give away," argued Pete, "but I still don't see it coming back to me."

"Well maybe you don't attach strings on how you want the money spent," said Joe as they lowered the steel to the floor. "But if you're expecting it to come back to you, that's a kind of string. Don't you think?

They stepped back to the truck, and Joe slid the fifth length of steel out without even thinking about it.

"Yeah, but whoever I give the money to doesn't know I'm expecting it to come back," said Pete, reaching for his end.

"But the universe does. And if it's trying to move your gift around the world and it feels you pulling back on it- metaphorically speaking - then maybe it lets go, and your money drops into neverneverland. Which is how come it doesn't come back to you."

Pete still didn't look convinced. "Anything's possible, I guess," he muttered.

They both stopped, mid-bend, at the sound of a telephone ringing, loudly, through an overhead intercom. The jazz was lowered swiftly to background volume and then the ringing stopped. Joe glanced over at the office and saw that Stan was talking on the phone. He and Pete let go of the steel and moved back to the truck. "You know what I think?" said the potter.

"No. What do you think?"

"I think the money probably does come back to you. You're just not feeling the hand off."

"You're talking about the relay again now, right?"

"Uh huh."

This time they each grabbed two of the shorter lengths of steel to carry over to the welder. "The thing is," Pete said, letting his pieces drop with noisy clangs onto the cement floor. "If money's on some kind of circular relay then that suggests I don't get to hold onto it."

"Exactly right."

"Then how do I get ahead?"

"You don't. But you don't get behind either," said Joe. He marched back to the truck and pulled the last length of steel towards him. "You just keep on moving it, around and around."

Pete stared at him, blue eyes narrowed, like he was wondering if he was being teased.

"Think about it," said Joe, sure of his reasoning.

Pete pulled both sides of his mouth down and nodded, like maybe there was truth to this. He grabbed the other end of the steel and they finished what they'd started.

"Okay," said Joe, looking down at the pile on the floor, arms at his sides. "Now what do we do?"

*****

Hilda waited exactly an hour, sipping her coffee and nibbling on a slice of whole wheat toast, and when neither of the Connors' vehicles reappeared in the driveway at the pottery, she dressed in what she considered work appropriate clothes – leggings, a turtle neck, her down jacket and boots – stuffed a wash cloth in her pocket and tramped across the pasture with a shovel, an axe, and a handsaw. There had been a little snowfall overnight but most of it hadn't stuck and the ground felt soft under Hilda's feet. According to the radio weather, however, the temperature was supposed to drop some more and by the looks at the puffy bluish clouds moving across the front of Sauk Mountain, there was going to be a whole lot more snow by tonight. Hilda was glad she was doing the digging now and not when there might be a few inches of snow packed on top of ground that was in the process of freezing solid.

She reached the other side of the pasture and set the axe and the saw down on the ground. She knew roughly where to dig because her ex, Clarence, had dumped a bunch of blackberry vines and rusty old sheet metal on and around Connors' septic tank drainfield. Of course that meant she had to maneuver under a bunch of debris but she also hoped that digging underneath it would provide her with a certain amount of cover. She gave a furtive glance out towards the highway, pulled on her yellow work gloves, picked a spot and began digging.

Five holes and two hours later, Hilda's shovel hit something hard. She bent over and pushed the dirt away with her gloved hands, dug a little more and scratched the rest of the dirt away. She was sure this was it. It looked exactly the way Gus had described it to her. She levitated to a stand, giddy with excitement, and stumbled across the grass to retrieve the rest of her tools. She was hot from all the digging and hadn't noticed how cold the morning had become. But she didn't care. She picked up the small saw and the axe, took them over and set them down next to the hole in the ground. A truck growling down the highway made her spin around, nervous. But it wasn't Connors. She pushed up the sleeve of her jacket and looked at her watch. It was just after 11:00 in the morning and the sun emerged from between the clouds, making the day seem full of possibilities. Hilda smirked, proud of how little time it had taken her to unearth this stupid thing. She put her hand in her pocket and felt the washcloth. She slipped her fingers behind it and pulled out a bandana, which she folded at a diagonal in the air in front of her to make a triangle. She pulled it towards her so it hung down over her nose, and knotted the long ends together at the back of her head. Then she set to work.

*****

Joe and Pete pulled into the driveway at the pottery with two massive steel frames, five and a half feet wide across the bottom narrowing to two and a half feet wide at the top, propped in the back of the truck. Each frame was rectangular in the bottom for two and a half feet, then had sides which tapered, at a 70-degree angle, to meet the shorter length at the top. This would accommodate the narrowing of the arch in the chambers of the kiln, Pete explained, as he welded the sides on the frame. He added two horizontal lengths of steel across the width of each frame. One door was hinged on the left and the other on the right, so the doors would open out from the center and not block access to either chamber. Pete welded the hinges onto pipe that was set in wide flanges at both ends and would run from the kiln shed floor to the roof to anchor the doors. Finally he added an 8-inch length of steel to the opposing sides, "to act as a door handles."

"That's great," said Joe. "I can wind a length of heavy chain from the handle to the beam under the roof to unweight the door so it doesn't buckle the pipe over time."

It had taken them two hours to do the welding, as Pete had predicted, then they'd stopped for an early lunch on the way home, which Joe paid for – "See, you got a little payback" - and now it was time for the hard part.

"Have you thought how we're gonna do this?" Pete asked, as Joe backed the Chevy up the driveway towards the new kiln shed. It was almost exactly noon and the December sun, playing peek-a-boo with the clouds, was glinting on the fresh, shiny white snow on Jackman ridge.

"I've thought about it," said Joe, easing past the garden and the old kiln, then spinning the steering wheel to back up to the new kiln shed. "Doesn't mean I know how we're gonna do it."

Once the rear tires touched the edge of the concrete floor, Joe turned off the truck and stepped on the emergency brake. He didn't want old Nellie rocking around too much as they fought physics to heft the frames down off her bed. He looked at Pete who looked at him and they both nodded – let's do this.

"I'll just walk over to the house and let the dogs out," said Joe.

"And I'll try to think up a plan."

*****

Hilda was just about to walk back across the pasture to complete the job when she saw Connors' truck pulling into the driveway. Her heart leapt in her chest at the thought that he would climb out and immediately smell something amiss. She tucked herself in behind the trees along the driveway then snuck back into her house for protection. She ran to her binoculars and trained them on Connors's front yard. The blue Chevy turned in facing the blackberries and her house then began backing up. Before she knew it, it had disappeared behind the pottery shop.

Hilda waited, fifteen, twenty minutes, to let her heart beat slow down, then went back out again. She slipped through the trees and across the pasture, darting behind the big cedar tree before slipping into the old loafing shed to snoop on Connors. It was much colder than it had been earlier, even though the sun was out, and she wished she had the work gloves that she'd left lying next to the holes she'd dug. She tugged on the sides of her wool hat to cover her ears, then slipped her hands into the pockets of her down jacket and squeezed them open and closed a few times, to warm them up. She pulled her right hand back out and lifted the binoculars she'd hung around her neck. She trained them on Connors' property. She could see the truck clearly, facing towards her with two pieces of pipe sticking out, at an angle, over the top of the cab. What was *in* the truck and beyond it she didn't know because she couldn't see. She knew Connors was there, though, because she could hear him conferring loudly with his friend, Pete, even though she couldn't make out the words. She bobbed to the right, trying desperately to see what was going on, and caught sight of the dogs, sniffing the ground between the truck and the Connors' studio. As she watched, one of them, the husky, brindle and white one that looked like he was part pit-bull, lifted his head and seemed to look directly at her. Hilda felt fear flood her torso and decided she'd better fill that hole in the ground quickly, before Connors – and his dogs – found it.

*****

Joe knew that Pete would prefer to stand and discuss the best way to get the frames out of the truck and in place but he thought the more they talked about it, the more they might talk themselves out of it. And he just wanted to get it over with. He started untying the rope that was holding the frames in the back of the truck as he gave directions on how this would go. "Let's walk the top frame this way," he said, pointing into the kiln shed, "until the flange at the bottom of the pipe hits the cement floor. Then we can use that as leverage to lift the rest of the frame vertical."

"And the frame with the shorter length of pipe went in second, right?" Pete asked.

"Correct. So it's coming out first," said Joe. "We're aiming for the first chamber."

They both pulled themselves up into the bed of the truck, on opposite sides, and without discussing it further, wrapped their leather work-gloved hands around the top frame, bent at the knees and lifted the heavy steel up a couple of inches. "You got it?" grunted Joe.

"Uh huh."

They inched towards the rear tires, until they heard the flange hit the concrete. Then they rested the top of the pipe on the cab so the frame was suspended over the bed. "Okay, now my vote is we push it," said Joe, "till we think we've got enough of the main frame on the tailgate that we can slowly lift it and move it into position against the chamber."

"How close do we need to get it?"

Joe pointed at two insulating firebricks that he'd taped in the top and bottom of the frame. "Close enough that both these bricks touch up against the cast arch."

"Okay," said Pete.

They lifted the steel just slightly and pushed it, with a loud scraping sound, across the concrete floor, until the main frame was over the tailgate of the truck. It went fast. Both men straightened up and gave a nod – that was easy – then jumped down from the truck. They looked up at the pitch of the roof. Then Joe pointed towards the mouth of the first chamber. "First that way a few feet, then we stand it upright and wrestle the top onto the beam. Okay?"

Pete gave one strong nod – yes.

They unweighted both sides of the frame again and let the flange slide in towards the kiln after which it became obvious what they had to do. They both stepped their feet back from the door and leaned their shoulders in to push and heave and lift the massive framework up to vertical. Once the bottom flange was flat against the floor and the weight was no longer an issue, they pulled and scraped and hammered on the pipe with a wrench until it moved enough for the top flange to catch snug against the beam under the roof.

Their heads popped up at the same time and they looked at each other, smiling around their labored breathing.

"That wasn't so bad," said Pete.

"Uh uh," agreed Joe. "You ready to do it again?"

In the distance the dogs were barking, Maggie slow, deep, repetitive and Max louder and scarier above her. Joe realized he'd been hearing that for some time but muted, behind the sound of his hammering on the pipe. His head was naturally drawn towards the direction of their barking, even though his mind was still on the project at hand.

He found himself looking outside the kiln shed and saw that it was snowing. Big downy flakes that were floating down to rest on the ground around them. He walked out past the truck, enjoying the cold against his overheated face, and ignored the dogs barking in the distance as he turned back to face the kiln shed, trying to gauge the height of the pipe sticking out over the cab of the truck against the entry edge to the roof. He was pretty sure he couldn't back the truck up any further without hitting the roof with the pipe. Maybe after they lowered the frame onto the tailgate. He strode back into the kiln shed and slipped his hand around the wood rack, ready to pull himself up.

“Think you have a customer?” Pete asked, nodding towards the sound of the dogs.

“Don’t know,” said Joe. He stepped up into the truck.

Pete wiped his nose on a bandana and looked up at the top of the door they’d already installed. “You don’t want to C clamp that top flange before we move the second frame?”

Joe followed his gaze up to the flange on the beam. “Nah. I’m pretty sure that’s not going anywhere.”

Pete stuffed the bandana in the back pocket of his jeans as he nodded his assent and then hauled himself up into the truck bed. Someone held down a car horn - once, twice - in the distance. “You’re sure you don’t want to go get that?” said Pete, bending his knees to lift again.

“Uh uh,” grunted Joe, feeling the muscles in his arms flex as he hefted the second frame up a few inches. “Shop’s closed.”

*****

Lyle Pfeiffer braked a little harder than he intended when he turned into the driveway and his wife bounced forward in her seat. “The sign says closed,” he told her.

“They said that as long as we could see the potter’s truck and his dogs somewhere in the front yard, we should pull in no matter what the sign says.” Ingeborg explained. “And now that it’s snowing I don’t think we should turn back before we investigate thoroughly.”

“Do you see his truck?”

Ingeborg Pfeiffer was peering around the grounds in front of the double gabled house. “No, but the dogs are right there,” she said, pointing off to the left. “Barking at that thicket of blackberries.”

“Barking at blackberries?” questioned Lyle. “Why would they be barking at blackberries?”

"Well I expect there's something in the blackberries. Like a squirrel or something. Maybe if you pulled forward we could see whatever it is."

Lyle did as advised and pulled their blue Ford up past the sign and around to the left, to park alongside the dogs. Ingeborg sat high and forward in the front passenger seat, trying to locate the object of the dogs' interest. "See anything?' asked Lyle.

"No, but whatever it is they don't like it. Their tails aren't wagging," Ingeborg replied.

Lyle cast an all-knowing eye on his wife. "One of them doesn't have a tail."

"Well you know what I mean," she insisted. Ingeborg was elegant, stately even, but her riposte was very matter-of-fact. "Both times we've come here the white-headed one has been very animated in the rear."

"You mean he shakes his butt?"

"To indicate he's happy, yes," Ingeborg shot back. "And neither of them are happy today. See," - she pointed through the side window at the dogs - "their hackles are up."

Lyle peered across his wife to see. "What's on the one dog's head?" he asked.

Both canines suddenly lost interest in what they were barking at and turned towards the vehicle that had pulled in the driveway.

Ingeborg peered down at Max through the passenger side window as he trotted over with Maggie to sniff the tires. "It looks like a snowman," she said.

"A snowman?!"

"Well that's what it looks like from here. But he's turned away from me right now, headed for the back tire. Hang on a minute." She swiveled her face towards the back of the vehicle. "Okay, now he's turning around." There was a moment of silence while Ingeborg watched the dogs, then she announced, "Yep, it's definitely a snowman. In magic marker by the looks of it."

"Really?!"

"I seem to remember the potter's girlfriend – what's her name again?"

"Lucy. And I think she may be his wife now."

"Oh that's right. She did say they were getting married. Anyway, I remember Lucy telling us at the Tulip Festival, that the potter liked to draw on that dog's forehead."

"Funny guy, huh?"

"No. It had something to do with people being scared of this dog even though he's a good dog because he *looks* mean."

"Sounds mean too."

"But if the potter draws on him," Ingeborg went on without pause, "It amuses people. So then they laugh instead of being scared of the dog. Oh wait," she said, interrupting herself. "They're on their way around the back of the van so you should be able to see the snowman yourself pretty soon."

Lyle flipped his eyes to his side mirror and the inside of the vehicle became hushed as he waiting for the dogs to appear. When they did, he opened his mouth and let out a loud guffaw. "HA!"

"See, it works," said Ingeborg.

"What works?"

"The drawing. Now you just think he looks funny."

"Well he does," said Lyle. He took a hold of the door handle on his side. "Shall we go see what they were barking at?"

"You go first," said Ingeborg, causing Lyle to look at her in surprise. "You're meatier than me," she explained.

Lyle's eyebrows popped up. "And my wife's a funny lady, it seems."

Ingeborg's tongue curled to her upper lip in merriment.

They both climbed out of the van and Ingeborg pulled the collar on her light purple parka up around her neck to protect against the cold of the mountain air. The dogs greeted them with enthusiastic nuzzling and wagging then Max broke away and trotted across the driveway to pick up a foot-long wedge of wet wood. He brought it back to Lyle and dropped it on one shiny black shoe, looking up at him hopefully. Lyle was in his fifties and built like a tough guy, average height, square-shouldered, thick eyebrows and strong jaw, but the softness in his eyes told the real story. He warmed to Max's plea immediately. "You want me to throw that for you?"

Max looked down at his stick then back up at Lyle, who bent, grabbed the wood by the thin end and tossed it underhand before rising to a complete stand again. The wet wood didn't lift very far into the air, sailing just a short distance before it tumbled down to land on top of the patch of blackberries.

Max, not realizing the stick was lodged on top of the blackberries, barreled his blocky body deep into the tangled, thorny thicket and disappeared out of sight. The desiccated winter vines snapped loudly as he ploughed further into them and then somebody let out an unexpected, high-pitched squeal. "That must have been what they were barking at," Ingeborg muttered under arched eyebrows to her husband.

"No, get away! You get. GET!!" screeched a voice and a woman in a brown, knit bobble hat over gray curly hair rose up on the other side of the blackberries. She was wearing a black and brown checked bandana over her nose, like a highwayman, and holding what looked like a shovel.

Lyle's mouth dropped open at the sight of her, then he caught himself and stepped forward to come to her assistance. "I'm sorry if the dog's bothering you," he called across the brambles. "It's my fault because I tossed a stick for him."

Hilda had been keeping a low profile behind the blackberry bushes while she filled in the hole over her vandalism job and she'd got it two thirds full when Connors's pesky dogs started barking at her from the other side of the fence. At first she was terrified that Connors was down at the front of the house with them, but she heard loud clanging noises from up by the studio, like someone was hammering on a metal pipe, and prayed that it was the potter and his friend. She got the main hole covered and was going to leave it at that when it occurred to her she should cover some of her botched attempts, too. She got two filled and was about to start on the third when the dogs suddenly quit their barking.

Relief came in such a wave that she sank to the ground and sat, hands resting on her knees, allowing herself to be mesmerized by the falling snow. She might have sat there longer if she hadn't been jolted out of her reveries by the sudden arrival of voices on the other side of the blackberries. She held her breath, listening; was that Connors? Now what should she do?! She couldn't make a run for it because she'd likely slip in the wet snow and he'd see her. Her heart was slamming against the wall of her chest, causing her throat to constrict with panic, and she reached, unconsciously, for the shovel on the ground beside her. Maybe she could crawl under the blackberries and wait him out. But as soon as she thought this she heard snapping sounds behind her and swung around to see the bulky, white-headed dog, frenziedly moving towards her. Hilda screamed and leapt to her feet, the shovel out in front of her like a weapon.

Somebody spoke to her – a man she didn't recognize. And there was a woman behind him. Hilda yanked the bandana down from her nose, pointed at the dog and shrieked, "Get him away from me!"

"He won't hurt you," said Lyle.

The reassurance in the man's tone caused Hilda to stop and take stock of the fact that this wasn't Connors. Relief replaced panic and quickly switched to indignity. She swiped her gray curls away from her forehead with her gloved hand. "These dogs are a menace!"

"We've only met them twice but both times they've been very friendly," Ingeborg said, her voice gently soothing.

Hilda was wearing a puffy brown jacket with narrow black sleeves, which made her torso look wildly bigger than her skinny arms and legs. She'd chosen it against the cold but the way this woman was eyeing her made her suddenly self-conscious. She lifted the shovel up in front of her and declared, "I'll hit him with this if he gets any closer."

"I don't think there's any need for that," said Lyle. He took a few steps across the driveway and up onto the concrete slab alongside the pottery, hoping to make eye contact with the dog so he could call him back. But the blackberries were shaking vigorously, an indication that Max was continuing to search within the vines while the stick was still teetering on top of the whole mess. Lyle sighed; this was likely to take a while. He looked across at Hilda and that's when he noticed the series of holes in the ground around her. And an acrid, fetid smell that made him wrinkle his face in displeasure.

"What *is* she wearing?!" his wife whispered from behind him, having followed him onto the concrete slab. Ingeborg could now see the brown and black knit leggings that completed Hilda's outfit. "She looks like a bee!"

"Forget what she's wearing," Lyle muttered, turning to look at his wife. "What's she *doing*?!"

"Ugh and what's that *smell*?" exclaimed Ingeborg, her face taking on a look of displeasure to match Lyle's.

"Exactly." He swiveled back to face Hilda, lifting his head a little higher to see if he couldn't make out what the holes in the ground were all about. Hilda immediately took a wide-legged stance in front of her handiwork, hoping to block it from his view. "What are you digging there?" Lyle asked, his voice steady, non-threatening.

"What's that to do with you?!" huffed Hilda. "I don't even know you."

"Oh I'm sorry. I'm Judge Pfeiffer," said Lyle, deliberately using his title so that she would know exactly who was in front of her. "And this is my wife –"

But Hilda didn't let him finish. "This is *my* property!"

Lyle was surprised. "So close to the pottery?"

"And that's the problem," Hilda snapped. "But I'm *not* letting him get away with it. I didn't do anything wrong!"

Lyle had had way too many people come before him arguing that they 'didn't do anything wrong' not to get a sense of when they were lying to him, and this woman was definitely lying to him. About what, he didn't know but he suspected it had something to do with those holes in the ground.

"Come on," said Ingeborg, tugging on his arm from behind. "Let's go find the potter. I'm getting cold, standing out here in the snow, and I'm not enjoying that smell one bit."

Lyle opened his mouth to ask where she thought they might find the potter when Max reappeared in front of him with the hunk of wet wood in his mouth. "You found it!" the judge declared, prompting the dog to drop it on his foot again, then look up at him hopefully. Lyle obliged by retrieving the stick and lifting his arm to throw it. He looked around, thinking maybe he'd avoid the blackberries this time, and noticed that they were alone again.

"Where'd that woman go?" he asked his wife.

But Ingeborg was gone too, around in front of the house and pottery shop. "I heard a noise," she called back to him when he turned around to find her. She indicated where by pointing up the path towards the studio.

Lyle heard a distant clanging sound and looked down at Max. "I guess we're going for a walk," he told the pup. He stepped down off the concrete slab and walked around to the front of the house, tossing the stick ahead of him for Max to chase. He inhaled a big, welcome lungful of untainted mountain air, then followed his wife and the big brown dog up the path towards the hammering.

*****

Down in Seattle, Lucy ran a thumb over the letter lying across her lap. She'd been expecting this for some time but, fortunately, she was married now, so it wasn't much of an issue. At least, she hoped that's the way they were going to see it. A gust of apprehension blew through her stomach and made her hands feel clammy. Of course, they could always throw her out of the country.

She snapped her head up, choosing not to focus on that thought, and stared at the three helpers in their windows behind the counter, willing them to say her number next. A man walked away from one window and Lucy sat up a little straighter. “Number 32,” said the woman at that window. Lucy’s shoulders slumped back down. She looked at the white ticket in her left hand even though she knew the number on it because she’d already checked it a million times.

“What number do you have?” said the woman sitting to her left.

Lucy turned and looked at her. She was an older woman, maybe in her sixties, shaped like a Russian nesting doll, with no neck and a girth that expanded gently from her ears down to her feet. Except Lucy couldn’t see her feet but she imagined the bottom half of this lady followed the line of the top half. “45,” Lucy replied, showing her the ticket in her left hand.

“You’re lucky,” said the woman, then held up her own ticket. “I’ve got number 60.” She tipped her head down and peered at Lucy over her wire rim spectacles, small, soft blue eyes that were easy to look at, like a calm sea at twilight. “It’s going to be a long afternoon for me,” she sighed and they both wrinkled their noses in displeasure.

There was an awkward pause then the woman nodded at the letter under Lucy’s hands. “Are you here to change the name on your card?”

“I beg your pardon?” Lucy didn’t understand the question.

The woman smiled. “I just wondered why you were here,” she explained. “You’re too young to be collecting Social Security so I thought maybe it was for a name change.” Lucy still didn’t get it and the woman nodded down at her hands again. “I saw your wedding ring.”

“Oh.” Lucy smiled at the woman now. She was generally uncomfortable making small talk with people when she was on a mission but this woman’s voice was gently encouraging, like you could talk to her about anything. “No, actually I came to get a real Social Security number.”

“A ‘real’ one?”

"Well the one I've been using isn't real," whispered Lucy. She stretched both sides of her mouth down like she was in trouble then whispered again. "It's a dummy."

The woman thought about this for a moment then her eyes got wider. She leaned right, as if to bump Lucy's shoulder with her own. "Are you telling me you're one of those illegal aliens?"

Lucy glanced around the room, concerned that they might be overheard, but everyone was busy looking down at their hands or the floor or staring intently at the interactions happening at the counter. She leaned left, almost touching the woman's shoulder, and confessed, "I suppose I am a bit, yes."

"Oh how exciting," squeaked her neighbor. "I've never met an illegal alien before." She pulled back and stared hard at Lucy. "You don't look at all like what I expected."

"Why? Because my skin is white?"

"That," nodded the woman. "And you have no antenna."

Lucy chuckled. This woman was all right.

"No," said her neighbor, after pulling her purse further up her legs to rest against her tummy. "I suppose I just picture illegal aliens as people with great need. You know, people escaping economic hardship or threats to their freedom. You don't look like someone in that situation to me."

Lucy felt her shoulders lift and drop, a tiny shrug. "Escape doesn't have to be for poverty or incarceration," she said, thinking about the concept as the words came out of her mouth. "Escape can be about a feeling, like something's missing or unfulfilled. Or, in the case of a family, escape can be about a pattern." She let her eyes drift out into a void in the hushed, neutral toned room.

"A pattern you don't want to repeat but you're not sure you can fully see it so you step back to get a better perspective. Like looking at art in a museum. And you keep stepping back, hoping to gain some understanding of the uneasiness this pattern creates inside you, and before you know it, you've backed into a country you weren't born to and have no intention of staying in, until someone puts an arm around your shoulder and encourages you to stop and look at the pattern from a different angle. And there's something about the light they shine on it that makes the shapes and the colors and the repetition of the pattern less jarring. So you stay." Lucy turned and looked directly into the woman's enrapt face. "That's what my husband did for me," she said. "He made me stop moving and look."

"And is the pattern more acceptable to you now that you can see it from here?"

Lucy thought about this for a moment. "I don't know," she said. She tipped her head to one side, thinking some more, then turned to the woman, the start of a smile curling the edges of her mouth. "I haven't had time to tell."

The woman reached her right hand forward and tapped lovingly on Lucy's knee. "Well, I hope they give you a 'real' Social Security number so you can stay and figure it out."

"Me too," agreed Lucy.

"Number 33," said the man at the middle window. Like a reflex, both women checked their tickets, then sighed.

"What does a not real Social Security number look like?" asked the woman. "I'm just curious. I've never seen one."

"Oh." Lucy unfolded the letter she had on her lap and showed it to her neighbor, pointing at the nine digit Student Identification Number she'd been given at NYU. The one a lawyer for the Metropolitan Opera had said was a valid Social Security number when she got her first job in Manhattan.

The woman's eyebrows shot up. "They're going to want to change that number, I'm sure."

"Why?"

"Well it's a 900 number!"

Lucy looked down at her student ID number as if for the first time. She'd never made that connection. She looked back at the woman and held her thumb and pinkie up to her right ear, like she was talking into a telephone. "1-900-ILLEGAL," she suggested.

And they both giggled like a pair of schoolgirls.

*****

Joe was up close to the top of his eight-foot ladder, next to the kiln's chimney, hammering on the pipe for the second door. Pete was down on the floor, looking up, watching to see if the flange at the top was moving across the 2 x 12 beam as Joe hammered. They were trying to maneuver it into the right place on the beam for the door to be level.

Joe was hot, sweaty and tired but he gritted his teeth and smashed on the pipe one, two, three more times until he felt the flange skid a little to the left. "How's that?" he shouted, looking down at Pete. His glasses slid down his nose and he quickly nudged them back up before they could fall off. He ought to make time to see the eye doctor, he thought. Get them adjusted before they really did fall off someplace.

Voices were drifting up the hill towards the kiln shed but Joe ignored them, holding his breath as he watched Pete peer at the level sitting on one of the horizontal cross bars on the frame. Pete stepped back, looked up at Joe and stuck one thumb up in the air.

"Hot dog!" Joe yelled down to him. "Finally!" He saw the dogs running towards the kiln shed from the garden, their breath cloudy on the air in front of them. "Swing it closed, would you," he told Pete. "See if the bricks touch."

Pete obliged and Joe leaned over, anxious. When he saw the top brick touch the outside of the chamber, he threw his head back and whooped his delight into the air.

"Have you got a permit for this thing?" barked a deep, gravely voice as Joe trotted back down the ladder.

He stopped at the bottom, bent over to pick up his drill motor and glanced past the dogs to see who had joined them. "Hey!" he yelled as he straightened back up. "If it isn't the judge and his wife."

Lyle and Ingeborg stepped further in at Joe's welcome. "You haven't got this thing fired up yet?" teased Lyle.

"I'm working on it." Joe used the drill motor to point as he spoke. "I'm about to bolt down the final piece of the structure then I'll fill these door frames with insulated firebricks and it should be ready to go. This is my friend, Pete, by the way."

Lyle nodded and reached a hand out to shake with Pete. "I'm Lyle and this is my wife, Ingeborg." Pete's eyes had that faraway look of someone trying to remember something. "Ye-es," said Lyle, long and slow. "I may have been that judge."

Pete smirked as he nodded. "The traffic ticket."

Lyle tipped his head towards Joe. "A hazard of the job. People recognizing me from court."

"Yeah, but at least you're on the right side of the bench. Us," he added, with a grin in Pete's direction, "not so much."

They all laughed then stopped, as the dogs chased down towards the house again, barking loudly.

"I thought I had the sign closed," said Joe. He dropped down to one knee next to the bottom flange.

"You did," Ingeborg confessed. She looked dutifully sheepish as she added, "We were hoping to do some Christmas shopping."

"Well, sure," Joe agreed, slipping a drill bit on the end of the motor. "Just let me get this pipe secured."

"Could be that your dogs are barking at your neighbor again," said Lyle.

Joe was leaning forward, ready to drill a hole in the concrete, but Lyle's comment caused him to stop and lean back again. He looked up, his face wary. "My neighbor?" he probed.

"Yes. She's digging alongside your property."

"I think she must have been planting something," added Ingeborg, "Because there was a strong smell of fertilizer."

Joe flexed his lips back, teeth clenched, and sucked in air noisily.

"Your septic system," Pete growled.

"Sure sounds like it."

"She said she was on her property," Ingeborg indicated,

obviously trying to reassure the potter.

"I'm sure she is," Joe and Pete chimed together.

"Then how can it be your septic system?"

Joe thought about how to answer this. He didn't know these people very well and consequently didn't want to drag them into the saga of his septic tank but one of them *was* a judge. His eyes narrowed as he contemplated this. It might be helpful to have a judge in situ while Hilda was up to whatever she was up to. "Well, the court declared it mine," he said, leaning forward again. "And I have the paperwork to prove it."

He took his time positioning the drill bit over the hole in the flange, hoping that Lyle would rise to the bait. Out of the corner of his eye he saw the judge's patent leather shoes start to move across the concrete floor towards the outside of the kiln shed again.

"Maybe we should wait for you down by the house," said Lyle and Joe looked up to see him standing with his right arm held up, folded at the elbow, ready for his wife to take.

"You gonna give my neighbor the stink eye?" Joe asked him.

The judge nodded solemnly. "I'm gonna give your neighbor the *legal* stink eye."

Chapter 6

Lucy talked to the woman with the soft blue eyes for another hour before she heard her number called and then she almost levitated from her seat. She was anxious to get this over with. She grabbed her purse from between her feet and stuffed it under her arm as she hurried across the flat, scuffed-shiny carpet towards the center window, where a middle-aged assistant with reading glasses hanging around her neck, was waiting for her. A small rectangular nameplate on the woman's right breast introduced her as Mila Zolopf and Lucy wondered if Mila had immigrated to the US and, if so, whether she'd ever done anything illegal in the process.

Even though Mila wasn't looking at her, Lucy smiled as she gingerly slipped the letter she'd received under the window. "I came to get a Social Security number," she said. Better to assume she could, she rationalized, than ramble on about what she'd done up to now. Mila Zolopf said nothing. Instead she opened the folded letter, pushed her reading glasses onto her nose and read. Lucy waited, watching for a reaction, but saw nothing. The woman's eyes moved left to right, left to right, swiftly down to the bottom of the letter, then flitted back up to the top. There they stopped and fixed on something. Lucy held her breath, exacerbating the hammering of her heart, which seemed to pick up speed when she saw Mila Zolopf slowly shake her head from side to side. "I can't believe anyone ever took this number from you!" Mila said, with just the suggestion of an accent. "It's obviously a dummy."

Lucy worried that if she opened her mouth, the heavy drum roll coming from her chest would deafen the people sitting quietly, waiting for their numbers to come up, so she held her tongue.

"The fact that it starts with 900 makes it a dummy," explained Ms. Zolopf.

The partitions on either side of the window isolated them perfectly and Lucy felt sure that the silence she was unable to break was communicating every guilty deed she had ever committed to this woman who was presently in charge of her future, but she still couldn't bring herself to speak. Because speaking would involve trying to talk her way out of this situation and she was pretty sure that would just insult her interviewer.

Mila Zolopf let out a short, tired sigh as she dropped Lucy's letter to the right of her counter. "You know, you could be fined $10,000 for this," she said, still looking at the letter. But Lucy heard the finality in her tone, like it was a parting shot, and started to decompress. They were onto the next thing. Sure enough, Ms. Zolopf removed her glasses, looked at Lucy and reached forward with her hands, palms up. "Did you bring a copy of your marriage certificate?" she asked.

Lucy dug immediately into her purse. "Yes. It's right here."

Zolopf stood up and withdrew a form from a pigeonhole in a stack of them behind her. She sat back down, and pulled the marriage certificate towards her that Lucy had slipped under the window. Mila Zolopf picked up a pen and bounced it on the counter in front of her, clicking the nib on. "All right," she said, with a level of neutrality in her tone that said she wasn't invested in this interview. "I'll get your information and you should have your new Social Security card in about a week."

Now Lucy felt chatty again. "Where are you from?" she asked.

*****

Ingeborg had a vase out in front of her on the 8-foot long cedar counter in the pottery shop. It was a square vase, slab made rather than wheel thrown, about 16 inches tall, made out of bronzed stoneware clay. Joe had carved a beautiful red tiger lily up one side, spreading its pointed petals and broad leaves around the clay to partially decorate the other three sides. A braid of unglazed clay, flashed gold by the wood ash in Joe's kiln, finished the lip and Ingeborg had a thumb and a forefinger resting gently underneath that braid as she turned the vase around, slowly, studying it.

"Do you like it or not?" Lyle asked from behind her. He had found it in one of the wooden crates under the counter and had lifted it out, intrigued by the shape.

"I love it," said Ingeborg, and turned another side around to face her.

Lyle looked at the vase then up at his wife's face. She was thoroughly immersed in her contemplation of the object so he backed up and walked over to the bay windows overlooking the highway. He stood, feet slightly apart, hands clasped behind his back, watching the snow fall outside through one of the small panes of glass in the window. It was quiet in the little shop and he watched the snow land like powdered sugar on the fringed boughs of the big fir tree next to the driveway. Pretty soon the highway would be covered with it. Yet he had no inclination to move.

"I hope the potter's not too much longer," he said, as if from inside a trance. "The snow's coming down pretty hard now."

"Hmmmm?" muttered Ingeborg. Then he heard her exclaim from behind him, "Oh my! It's really snowing now!"

Lyle snapped out of his reverie and turned back to his wife. "Are you thinking of that for a gift?" he said, his right arm extended to indicate the vase.

Ingeborg shook her head no, then nodded with her nose towards four mugs further along the counter. "I chose those mugs for our gift needs. I just think this vase would look lovely on our dining room table."

"Sure," said Lyle. "It would really go with that watercolor I painted of the red barn over by the tulip fields."

"That's what I was thinking."

"So get it then."

"The only thing is," mused Ingeborg, turning the vase round once more.

Before she could finish her statement, the door to the shop swung open, a strip of bells on a red ribbon jangling as it did so, and Joe entered the shop.

*****

"Do you know this vase leans?" Ingeborg said to the young potter, her fingers holding onto the top of the vase in case it fell over.

"Yep," Joe asserted. "And pretty soon it's going to twist too."

"Twist?" Lyle's interest was piqued. He pushed his lips up as he tried to picture a tall square vase twisting.

"Not that one, of course," Joe clarified. "The next one I make like that."

Ingeborg was still staring at the vase, enjoying it, and Lyle was nodding behind her.

"How'd you do with my neighbor?" Joe asked. "Was it her the dogs were barking at?"

"No, no," said Lyle with a shake of his head. Joe thought he was going to go on to explain but his wife beat him to it.

"Somebody was tying down a tarp over whatever they'd got in their pick-up truck," she said, pointing out the window towards the highway. "Probably to protect it from the snow. Your dogs were letting him know they'd seen him."

"That's what they're paid for," stated Joe and perched his left buttock on the bar stool to the left of the door. Lucy had rearranged the shop after their wedding so that they could sit close to where the actual sales and wrapping took place. Then she'd put a wooden box with a colorful sign on it ~ Bargain Basement ~ where the stool used be, over by the mugs. Now they a place for the 'seconds.' Joe was cautious about selling his rejects but it was either sell them or turn them into gravel in the driveway. Since selling them had a chance of making him a little income – "and making some purchaser very happy," argued Lucy - then why not?

"But I saw your neighbor before," Lyle put in. Then nodded at his wife. "We both did. And she was looking very suspicious. So if you need any witnesses..."

The door jingled open again and Pete put his head in. "I'm heading back down to my place."

"D'you need a ride?"

"No, I'll walk."

"Could we drop you off somewhere when we leave?" asked Ingeborg, her hand still on the vase.

"Thanks, but it's not that far," said Pete, "and I'd enjoy the walk. Nice meeting you though." He pulled the door closed behind him as Lyle and Ingeborg called out, "You too."

Joe watched him slip on a broad brimmed cowboy hat and trot down the front steps. He would probably be glad to get home, get a fire going in his woodstove, Joe thought. Which reminded him of his own woodstove. He hoped there was still a bed of coals in there for him to stir up when he went inside.

"Are you going to get it?" he heard Lyle ask.

"I am, yes," replied Ingeborg as Joe turned around to face them again. She laid her left hand flat on top of the four mugs she had set on the counter next to her. "These too, if you don't mind."

"I don't see why I would," said Joe. He walked around the display tables in the center of the shop, and picked up the four mugs by crooking two fingers on each hand inside them.

"I'm assuming if your friend left that you managed to attach the doors on your kiln?' said Lyle as he followed Joe back across the room to the counter to the left of the door. Joe had bags and newspaper set under the counter and began wrapping the mugs for the judge and his wife. Ingeborg carefully carried over the tall square vase.

"We did," said Joe. "And now I just need to fill them full of firebricks."

"When do you plan on doing that?' asked the judge. He was very interested in the process of making a piece of pottery since he'd toyed with the idea of making ceramics himself.

"Today, if I can. Depends on whether there's enough daylight left. What time is it now?"

Ingeborg pushed the sleeve of her parka up and glanced at the watch on her wrist. "It's almost two," she said.

"Oh! Plenty of time," said Joe. "I might even have time to make myself a cup of coffee."

"Where's your - ?" Ingeborg caught herself. "Where's Lucy?"

"My wife? She went to Seattle to get some paperwork stuff done and then she has an audition this afternoon."

"Oh good, for an acting job?" asked Ingeborg. "We were hoping to see her on stage."

"This one's for a TV commercial. But I think she's been talking to the director of drama at the community college about an acting and co-directing job for next fall," Joe explained. He had all the mugs wrapped and in a grocery sack now and opened his hands to suggest he was ready for the vase Ingeborg was holding. She made no move to give it to him so he started totaling the sale on a little calculator instead.

"I hope there's a way for us to find out when it's on," said Ingeborg, "because we'd like to come."

"How much do we owe you?" whispered Lyle, leaning in to Joe like he wanted to keep it a secret.

Joe showed him the total on the little calculator as he said to Ingeborg, "It'll be in the newspaper, I'm sure. But, if you want, you could sign in the guest book and that way Lucy will let you know directly."

"You have a guest book?" Ingeborg relinquished the vase to Joe as she stepped around him to find the guest book.

The vase was warm, from being cradled against Ingeborg's chest, and Joe took that as a sure sign that it was meant to go home with her. He pulled out some more newspaper from under the counter.

"And is this how much we owe you?" asked Ingeborg, pointing at the calculator next to the guest book with the pen she'd picked up.

Joe nodded, wondering if he'd blown it by letting her see the total. He glanced at Lyle but the judge seemed unconcerned.

"I'll write you a check as soon as I finish signing the guest book," Ingeborg told Joe. "Maybe you have some pottery events you can let me know about?"

"Will you wife spend the night in Seattle then?" Lyle asked as he looked out the window at the snow falling.

"I hope not," said Joe. "I hope she's on her way home already."

*****

Lucy stepped through the revolving door of the Federal building out onto 2nd Avenue in downtown Seattle and was immediately accosted by the cold. She was carrying a brown, legal sized envelope with all her paperwork in it and she clamped it between her legs so she could zip up the forest green down jacket that Joe had bought her last Christmas.

"Excuse me," said a skinny, young lawyer-type with a briefcase, whose direct passage along the street had been interrupted by Lucy's standstill.

"Sorry," said Lucy and immediately scooted herself back and to the right, away from the revolving glass door and out of the main foot traffic.

She pulled the zipper up as high as it would go, lifting her head when it reached up under her chin. That's when she noticed the tiny flakes of snow coming down from the sky, crisscrossing in the air in an elaborate dance as they got caught on the breeze coming in from the Puget Sound. No wonder it was so cold, Lucy thought to herself. She lifted the envelope and tucked it under her left arm, freeing her hands so she could stuff them into the pockets of her jacket. Then she turned and hightailed it down the street.

Tipping her face down, to protect it from the cold more than from the tiny beads of ice-cold moisture that amounted to snow, Lucy threaded her way swiftly through the afternoon pedestrians to get to the zebra crossing on the corner. She pushed the button for the walk sign and, without thinking about it, stared at the three lanes of traffic racing down the street towards her. She watched them whizz past her line of vision without slowing and when she'd had enough, she blinked her eyes away and let them drift to the tiny Christmas lights laced among the branches of the spindly cottonwood trees lining the pavement on the other side of the street.

That's when she noticed the snow again, landing alongside the lights and adding to their twinkle. It was really very pretty although she would much rather have been safely home to admire it. Lucy was not very practiced at driving in the snow coming from the south east of England. In fact, she'd hardly ever *walked* in the snow in her hometown of Southend when she was a child, let alone driven in it.

She let her eyes blur as she thought back to the one time she could remember playing in the snow in Southend. It was Christmas Eve and she and her little sister, Gillian, had gone to Midnight Mass with their father. When they stepped out of the church after the service, the ground was covered in billowy white snow and she and Gilly squealed in delight as they ran and skipped and scuffed their way through it. Their father walked along behind them, smiling at their delight, and the only sound echoing through the streets was the sound of their laughter.

Traffic slowed on the busy street in front of Lucy and brought her back to the present. Oh well, she thought, there was a first time for everything. She glanced at her watch; it was just 2 pm. Her audition was at 2:30 and hopefully she'd be out of there and on her way back home before rush hour traffic hit the freeway.

*****

Hilda hid behind the blackberries until she heard the Pfeiffers' voices get fainter then she peeked around the vines to check. Her heart was pumping hard in her chest, she was so scared to face them a second time, especially now that she knew one of them was a *judge*. But they were gone. And it looked like they'd taken those damned dogs with them.

Hilda didn't waste any time. She didn't even bother to get back up and use the shovel to fill the last two holes she'd made in the ground, preferring to scratch and claw at the rapidly chilling dirt with her gloved fingers to move it into place. When that stopped being effective, she circled the ground on her knees and shoved the dirt with the heel of her hands on top of the holes. A hot cauldron of anger, deep inside her stomach, fueled her determination to keep going despite her rising fatigue and frustration: anger at Connors for putting her in this position in the first place instead of just paying for his septic tank; anger at his dogs for giving away her position; anger at that meddlesome judge and his wife.

Finally Hilda got the holes covered and pushed herself upright with the last of her will power. She stood for a moment, feeling pins and needles in her knees and legs from being on the ground for so long, then trudged over to the mess of sheet metal and blackberries. A bead of sweat trickled down between her eyes and Hilda swiped at it with the back of her gloved hand, only to feel some residue on the glove scratch into her nose. Her eyes automatically moistened and Hilda thought she was going to cry so she held her breath till she'd fought back the urge. Then she grabbed a gnarly, rusty length of sheet metal and tugged on it testily to get it out of the pile. It surprised her by sliding out so easily she stumbled over backwards and landed flat out on the ground, half the sheet metal on top of her. She let out a small howl of anguish, head tipped back, eyes scrunched closed. When she opened them, she gasped at the myriad of tiny snowflakes, floating down from the sky to land on top of her. They felt so soft and cool as they dropped onto her face and neck, mitigating the heat broiling out from within her and making her want to stay in place and succumb to a burial in white. Like a bride married to the ground, protecting what was hers. Her breathing slowed and her body relaxed as the image of herself, martyred by a property line dispute, grew in poetic beauty.

Hilda would have lain there for a long time only a vehicle with no muffler growled into her reverie and rekindled her irritation with her situation. She snorted loudly, pushed the sheet metal off her belly and legs and sat back up. She clambered back onto her feet and walked out five more pieces of sheet metal, dumping them, this way and that, over the mole holes she'd made in the ground. It began to resemble the tip it had been before she'd started digging.

She lifted her shovel and scooped up some of the loose, dead blackberry vines, like hay on a pitchfork, and dragged them over to dump on top of the sheet metal. She repeated this half a dozen times before deciding that enough was enough. With the snow coming down the way it was, her tracks would surely get covered and the ground would freeze. Her chances of getting caught were diminishing rapidly. Satisfied, she picked up the rest of her gear and staggered across the pasture to call Gus.

*****

Joe looked up at the sky as the Pfeiffers picked their way across the driveway, arms interlocked to prevent themselves from slipping on the patchy surface slurry. The snow was coming down pretty steady now, he thought. Wouldn't be long before the highway was covered. The snowplows would get right on it though. They were good about that in the Upper Skagit. Not like down in Seattle, where there didn't even have snowplows. But then, Joe reasoned, it didn't snow much in Seattle.

He thought about Lucy, down in the city, and how much she didn't want to drive in the snow. The thought torqued the pit of his stomach like a wrench on a lug nut. The cold was seeping under his skin, reminding him that he was tired after manhandling the kiln doors into place and in need of a sugar hit. Maybe he'd take care of that with coffee and some cookies. His eyes dropped to the length of highway he could see from his front porch and he noticed that it was wet but still mostly clear of snow. Which probably meant it wasn't snowing down in Seattle. Joe waved to Ingeborg who was waving to him and then spun around to go into his house.

The first thing he noticed was how warm it felt inside; the benefits of slow burning maple, he smiled to himself. He turned to close the door behind him and caught the pleading look in both dogs' eyes.

"You wanna come in?" he asked, then stood back as Max and Maggie raced past him. He let the front door slam closed, slipped off his wool jacket and rested it on the back of a kitchen chair as he looked up at the clock on the wall. It was after 2:00 already. He thought Lucy's audition was sometime around now. A commercial would be good, he thought, especially if it went national. That paid the big bucks. Hopefully she got her paperwork sorted out with Social Security so she could *take* the commercial if they offered it to her.

He walked around to the woodstove and dropped to one knee alongside the dogs, who were already making themselves comfortable in front of the hearth. He opened the door to the stove and a wave of heat wafted out, prickling the skin on his face and neck. He pulled a poker out of the ornate, Turkish copper pot on the hearth, and smacked what was left of the hunk of maple he'd thrown in earlier three, four times. Tiny sparks spat this way and that inside the firebox as the wood broke apart. Joe let the poker clang back into the copper pot, then he grabbed another piece of maple from the wood box next to the hearth and tossed it in on top of the blackened residues.

A lively discussion about Gorbachev's recent visit to the US was taking place on the radio as Joe latched the door closed but when he stood back up and reached for the ceramic coffee pot he'd left on top of the woodstove to keep his coffee warm, he heard the discussion get interrupted by a warning to drivers of the snow slowing traffic on the freeway through Seattle and Everett. He picked up the coffee pot and walked it into the kitchen, pausing by the sink to look at how much snow had accumulating on Hilda's pasture already. That reminded him – he slid the coffee pot onto the counter, flipped his palms around and pushed up on the edge of the sink with the heels of his hands to see out towards his septic tank. He hovered there for a long moment, balancing on the edge of the sink, his eyes drifting this way and that over the terrain. He couldn't see any holes in the ground. If he was to be honest, it looked like it always looked, covered in blackberries, derelict barbed wire and random lengths of rusty sheet metal. He lowered his feet back down to the floor, moved his mug next to the coffee pot and poured himself some of the steaming, dark brew. He overfilled the mug and crouched over to sip some off the top, welcoming the jolt on the back of his palate. He stood back up and reached around the coffee pot to take the lid off the porcelain cookie jar he'd made. He'd put red and light blue slip under a clear glaze on the jar, hoping for a kind of aurora borealis effect, but the red had dulled to a brown and the clear glaze had run like a thief, sticking the bottom of the pot to the kiln shelf so it chipped when he lifted it up. If there was one thing his fourteen years of being a potter had taught him, it was that he had to let go of the finished product. Too often it didn't come out nearly the way he pictured it when he made it. But at least he got to make it.

He chewed absently on the ginger snap he'd pulled out of the jar, thinking about what to do next as he stared at the never-ending dashes of snow pouring from the sky. He really wanted to go set the firebricks in the new kiln doors but he was pretty sure it had to be above freezing to make the fireclay slurry he needed for the mortar. He swallowed his mouthful of sweet and spicy then took another glug of coffee. It definitely wasn't above freezing right now. He bit down on the cookie again and thought about the fire he'd lit in the studio earlier, to keep his clay from freezing. Maybe he could make the slurry there. He took another swig of coffee, unfocusing his eyes as he contemplated this idea. The mortar was bound to fail in the long-term anyway, because of the intense heat on one side and cold on the other during firings; all he needed it to do for now was level the firebricks as he secured them in the door frames. He blinked back to reality, crunched down on the remaining piece of ginger snap, then filled his mouth with the last of the coffee. He held the hot liquid on his palate for a moment, to cleanse it, then swallowed hard and set the empty mug down with a clatter in the sink.

He strode over to retrieve his wool jacket from the chair as Max moaned softly, stretching out in front of the hearth. Maggie was coiled into a tight ball on top of her blanket between the couch and the woodstove. The stove itself was a simple, matte black box, made by a local welder, but Lucy had been talking to Joe about investing in something more decorative when they could afford it. A woodstove with a glass pane in the front so they could see the flames. He liked that idea.

He slipped his arms back into his wool jacket and hesitated, wondering if he should walk out onto the front porch and see if he could detect what Hilda had been doing with that shovel the judge talked about. But then, there was only so much daylight left to start on the firebricks in the kiln doors. Yeah, he thought, as he picked up a broad brimmed, dark brown, felt hat from its hook on the stairs, time to go back to work.

*****

It was dark before Lucy left the freeway at Cook Road and

started towards Highway 20. Snow blew towards her windshield in a kind of kaleidoscopic swirl and she realized her head was tipped slightly to the right as she stared into it.

She snapped her eyes away and focused on the white line at the side of the road, the way Pete had taught her when they'd shared the journey down to Seattle in his VW bus, so he could scout locations and she could go to auditions. Her mind leapfrogged to today's audition. She was pretty sure she hadn't got the part. Mostly because all the other women waiting to audition were dark haired and older than her. Maybe she should have paid better attention to the casting description before booking herself an audition. But the casting director had been really nice, telling her how well she took direction. She doubted that would change the outcome though.

It was probably just as well, thought Lucy. She needed to get her green card paperwork together and fill out the forms for the special use permit. Plus send out a letter to all the customers that had signed Joe's guest book so far. She had a lot on her plate in the short term.

Plus, she had no camera experience so she wasn't sure how she'd feel about acting in that context. It might not have the same appeal for her as theatre. She tipped her head slightly again, looking at the snow. There was something very magnetic about feeling an audience move through a speech. Like she had her hand outstretched and they were stepping towards it, powerless to refuse, if she used just the right tone, the right inflection. Or, more accurately, if she believed what she was saying enough to make them believe it too. That was what acting was really all about; telling lies that she believed. And you had to have someone listen to those lies to tell them well.

It was too bad she'd ended up living so far from all the professional theatres, she thought, as she watched the pinprick red tail lights that she'd been following disappear around a bend in the road. She flipped her eyes back to the white line. Theatre had been a wonderful guide for her life so far but the road to her goals wasn't quite as linear as she'd once perceived it. Now she either had to embrace the curves and the turn offs, or ignore them, and risk missing out on something that might have been worth the side trip.

Like children. She'd been adamant that she never wanted to follow that particular path and become a mother, but Maddie was making her rethink her resistance. Merely contemplating it, however, was presenting her with hurdles. Roadblocks really, because Joe was sure he didn't want to go down that path again. He claimed it was because children were too expensive and he couldn't afford the one he already had, but Lucy knew it was more about him being scared than being too broke.

Scared she would take any baby he might have with her away from him, just like Maddie had been taken from him for almost three years, in the bitterness of his break up with Erica. That three-year hiatus from the tiny, perfect creation that was beyond anything he'd ever made before, scarred his heart badly and made it tender to the touch when the subject of fatherhood came up. So Lucy knew she had to tread gently if she wanted to follow that particular bend in her road to its end point.

She turned the cassette player on, to switch off her thoughts, and Patsy Cline sang out. *"Oh I'll be walk-ing, after mid-night..."* Lucy hated country music but she loved Patsy Cline. She drove past the Lyman fire station and continued on under the railroad trestle in Hamilton, hoping there would be some cars ahead of her when she came around the bend in the road. That way, she could piggyback on their taillights, instead of having to follow the white line the rest of the way home. A log truck was turning left into the log yard, across the highway in front of her on the other side of the railroad trestle and Lucy had to slow to let him complete his turn.

She glimpsed the road, stretching into the distance after the log truck had gone by, dark and bare, despite the thick flakes of snow coming down steadily from the sky. She pushed down on her accelerator, creeping up from 50 to 55 to almost 60 mph, eager to get home before conditions worsened. She'd driven a little in the snow since moving to the Skagit but not enough to really know what she was dealing with. In fact, she was beginning to think that people were making a fuss over nothing because it wasn't that hard if she kept her eyes on the road.

She pushed past the worm barn on her right, a paranoid light illuminating the yellow, board and batten siding behind the flurrying snow, and glimpsed a series of taillights at the far end of the long, slow curve in the road. This was good.

Her headlights picked up the line of snow that started at the near end of the bend in the highway then covered it all the way to the taillights but Lucy thought nothing of it. She sailed into the snow, at almost 60 mph, and felt the rear of the Pinto fishtail left and right across the slippery surface. She screamed a little, her foot off the gas, as Patsy sang out, "*...see a weeping willow..*" scared this was going to be the end for her.

But the Pinto settled down quickly, at the moderated speed, and Lucy felt it drop back into the grooves in the snow on the highway, made by the other drivers. She turned the music down, her heart still pumping, and clutched the steering wheel tight with both hands.

Now she knew what all the fuss was about!

Chapter 7

At five forty-five the next morning, Joe's eyes popped open, fifteen minutes before his alarm was due to go off. He bolted upright, panicked that Lucy hadn't made it home last night. Max bounced to a stand alongside his bed as soon as Joe moved and he could hear Maggie downstairs, her nails click clicking across the plywood floor towards the front door to be let out. He swiveled around to look at Lucy's side of the bed. There she was, all tucked up in the blankets, way off in lala-land.

Of course she'd made it home because they'd had dinner together. He pushed the heels of his hands into his eyes and ground them, left and right, to wake up; that had been *some* dream! Now that he could focus he watched her breathing softly, her tangle of long, blonde hair spread across the pillow. Then he noticed how much of the quilt was cocooned around her and how little on his side of the bed. It wasn't the dream that had woken him up so early after all, he thought. He'd been cold!

He reached over to the bedside table and picked up his glasses, propping them on his nose before he pushed his fingers through his hair to get it back off his face. He yawned, swung his legs out of bed and hit the floor, ready to start the day. He lifted his jeans off the chair by his bed and padded, barefoot, over to the shelves he'd built at the end of the closet. He reached into the middle one and pulled out the top t-shirt. He slapped that on the jeans over his left arm and reached into the higher shelf for socks and underwear. He walked out the bedroom door, pulling it closed behind him so Lucy could sleep on. That was one thing they did not have in common. It had been many years since he'd been able to sleep in.

Max bunny-hopped down the first half dozen stairs, his back arched to protect himself from tumbling, but then he stretched out and ran the last few at high speed. Joe followed more sedately, stopping at the bottom to let both dogs out the front door. It was still dark out but his eyes could see the layer of snow glittering on the ground in front of the house. It didn't look too deep, maybe only three inches but if the gust of bitingly cold air that had blown in the house when he opened the door was anything to go by, it was going to stick around for a while.

He made his way into the bathroom, flicking the light switch on as he went through the door, and immediately scanned the floor when the smell of poop assailed him. Max sometimes came down in the night and made a mistake on the floor of the bathroom, but Joe couldn't find any evidence that that had been the case last night. Maybe it was something in the laundry bin making that smell. He laid his clothes on the counter around the deep purple bathroom sink that he'd made, turned the faucets on in the bathtub, to warm up for the shower, and then sat down on the toilet.

When he finished, he closed the lid, flushed and shifted right to climb into the tub for his shower. But as soon as he had one leg raised, ready to step over the edge of the tub, he saw it. Unmistakable brown water, frothing up through the drain hole and mixing with the water coming out of the faucets that wasn't going anywhere, except in the tub, since someone had obviously plugged the tight line to the septic tank. *That's* where the smell was coming from!

"GODDAMMIT!" he yelled, every part of him now fully awake and boiling with fury. This is what Hilda had been up to when the judge came upon her yesterday.

He snatched his jeans off the counter and stuffed his legs into them, hopping about the floor as he did so in his impatience to get them on.

"Are you all right?" Lucy called down from the top of the stairs. She had bolted awake when he yelled and was worried he'd hurt himself somehow.

Joe pushed his head through his t-shirt and put his glasses back on, turned off the water and stomped out of the bathroom.

"What's the matter?" asked Lucy.

"That goddamn Hilda cut the tight line to our septic tank so we've got shit backing up in the bathtub," Joe snapped, stepping into his muck boots at the bottom of the stairs.

Lucy grimaced at the thought of shit in her bath water but didn't quite know what to say. He sounded so angry and now that he had his boots on, he was reaching for his wool jacket like he was definitely going outside. She was worried he was going to march right over to Hilda's house and vent, something that would involve a lot of uninterruptible yelling and cursing, and that twittering Hilda would be likely to call the cops if he raised his voice and swore at her. "What are you going to do?" she asked.

"I'm going to fix the fucking thing!" He clumped across to the table against the wall between the pantry and the bathroom and grabbed a wool hat out of the basket on top of it. "We can't use it if I don't fix it," he added, pulling the hat down over his hair and ears.

"Can I help?"

"Nah, it'll take me a while to locate the tight line," he said, some of the steam gone from his tone as he started to plan the mission in his mind. "No point both of us freezing our asses off, standing out in the cold."

Lucy was already chilly standing at the top of the stairs with her dressing gown slung loosely around her shoulders; she wasn't averse to pulling on her jeans and going out to dig with him, especially if it meant she didn't have to share her shower with effluent. She pushed her arms into the thin, cotton dressing gown, and tied it around her waist.

Yesterday evening, over dinner, Joe said something about the judge seeing Hilda acting fishy out by the septic tank. "If she did cut the tight line," Lucy said, thinking out loud as she walked down two steps then dropped to sit at the top of the stairs. "You should be able to find the holes she made."

"Here's hoping," said Joe, unconvinced. He slipped into the pantry where he found his Petzi Zoom headlamp. He positioned the battery pack on the back of his head and pulled the band over and around his head and so the light would be in the center of his forehead. It was going to be complicated enough finding the tight line; he wasn't about to do it in the dark.

"I'm going to get a shovel," he said, emerging from the pantry and looking up at Lucy as he pointed towards the back of the house. "Stoke the stove, would you? And feed the dogs."

"Of course." She stood up and headed down the stairs, hoping to kiss him before he went out into the cold. But Joe was already half way across the living room.

"I'll put the kettle on for some tea, too," she called out.

*****

Hilda sat at the kitchen table, chewing abstractedly on a piece of whole-wheat toast, her right hand resting gently on her father's old Ithaca shotgun. In front of her, propped up against a jar of apple butter, some of which she was enjoying on her toast, was an article that Gus had sent her about the effects of bird shot. It was still dark out, with a hint of a crescent moon providing just enough light that she could see the snow shimmering on the driveway in front of her house, but nothing beyond that. But then she hadn't expected anything this early in the morning. She had her binoculars handy, just in case. In the meantime she was glad to have an unhurried moment to enjoy the warmth of her woodstove and a light breakfast. Her fingers ran gently over the dark walnut stock on the shotgun. Yes, she was very glad for this moment.

*****

Joe crunched across the snow on his back porch, down the steps and up the path towards the old metal loafing shed. He felt the cold pierce immediately through his wool jacket and wished he had a down coat like the kind he used to wear as a kid in Upstate New York. Well there was nothing for it now. Hopefully he'd warm up once he got digging.

The dogs chased around from the front of the house to catch up with him, their breath steaming the air ahead of them. Joe glimpsed a sliver of ivory in the sky lighting the leaves on the big maple tree in the front of his property. For a moon so small it sure shined a lot of light on the ground. Maybe it would illuminate his digging activities too. His eyes pulled back to the loafing shed a few steps away. Something about it looked decidedly askew and Joe couldn't tell if it was an optical illusion created by the precariously balanced snow on the steep shed roof or the fact that age was catching up with the building and bringing about its slow collapse. It had been the only building on the five acres when Joe bought the property, 14 years ago now, and it hadn't been new then. He couldn't wait for the day when he could build a garage-cum-woodshed-cum-storage space for his garden tools. Although when that day might come with all the projects he had in line first and the fees he had to pay to this, that and the other government entity, he didn't know.

He leaned into the shed and grabbed a shovel and a rock bar, turned around and trudged across the snow towards his property line with Hilda. He moved quickly, as protection against the cold and because he wanted to get this damn business over with, but with no tread on the bottom of his muck boots, he found himself sliding on the slick surface of the icy snow more than he wanted. The dogs danced around him, like this was great fun, but Joe was not amused. He resorted to sticking the tip of the heavy metal pry bar into the snow every second step, like a ski pole, to keep himself from slipping again. He certainly wasn't going to fall if he could help it.

Partway there he realized he should have brought something to cut the blackberries with, dammit. He thought about turning back but his feet kept moving him forward, towards the three, silver fir saplings that he'd planted a few years back to mark the boundary of his property. They looked like father, mother and baby tree by their heights, and today, the crisp, white snow shouldering their branches gave them a decidedly regal bearing. Joe's septic tank lid was directly behind the tallest one, on the right, so he guessed the tight line going from the house into the tank would be west of his concrete slab. He took two steps forward, up onto the concrete slab, pushed down on the barbed wire fence with his pry bar, and hiked himself up over to the other side.

*****

Upstairs in the bedroom, Lucy pulled on jeans and a t-shirt and reached for a cream, Aran pullover her mother had knitted when she was younger. Lucy marveled at the fact that for all the years she'd owned this pullover, it never seemed to age or become too small. Her mother must have knitted it for her to grow into, Lucy thought as she walked out of the bedroom, running her hand over the elaborate, raised ropes and crisscrossing cables in the pattern. That definitely sounded like something her mother would do.

She pulled it down over her head and slipped both arms into it as she walked around the stairwell to look out the window over her writing desk and make sure Joe was all right. He'd bought her a $20 typewriter in a pawnshop when she told him she wanted to get more serious about her writing, and set it on a long slab of deep, reddish-brown fir that he'd salvaged. Sitting at this makeshift writing desk with the tree's growth rings naturally pin-striping the surface, Lucy could see all the way out from the property line, across Hilda's pasture to Jackman Ridge. Today, even in the pre-dawn dark, she could see that vista was covered in snow. She put her hands under her hair and flicked it out of the turtleneck collar of the pullover as she stood at the window, looking down at Joe, who was looking down at the ground. The light from the lamp he was wearing around his forehead moved in a slow arc, left, right, left, as Joe edged forward gingerly. Lucy watched the snow glint and sparkle under the light like a disco mirror party ball.

She watched, transfixed, her eyes moving with the light beam over the snow-covered piles of debris she was so used to seeing on that side of the fence. Joe stopped once he got past them all and Lucy let her gaze travel over to Hilda's house in the distance. The fir trees lining Hilda's driveway masked part of the house but Lucy was pretty sure she could see a light on in the kitchen. She made a face: Hilda was probably sitting there, gleefully watching Joe suffer in the cold. She looked back down at Joe just as he swung around to retrace his steps and Lucy wasn't sure if it was the way the light hit the piles or if she'd noticed this before and it had taken a moment for it to register, but something wasn't right. She looked at the piles one more time, then back at Hilda's house. No, something was definitely not right!

*****

Joe tramped forward, around the mini igloos of snow covering what he knew to be the blackberries, sheet metal and barbed wire on this side of the fence. His headlamp ran a spotlight this way and that as he tried to find signs of digging, but it was no good. The snow had neutralized the entire area and there was no chance he'd see down to where Hilda had dug without digging himself.

The dogs had come the long way around, up through a hole in the fence beyond the garden to join him, and in the vast quiet of the snow covered river valley so early in the morning Joe could hear them snuffling the ground next to him. He wondered if their snuffling could lead him to Hilda's trail then jumped when Max lifted his head and let out one, quick, ear-piercing bark. Joe looked up to see Lucy standing at the end of the front porch, looking over at him.

"What?" he snapped.

"Shine your torch on that area there, behind you," she said, pointing.

"What? Where?" He swiveled around as he spoke and the beam from his headlamp hit one of the snow piles.

"Yes, there. There!" she cried out, her finger still out in front of her. "Something's off there."

"What d'you mean?"

"I can see that area when I'm at my desk and I'm sure that bump wasn't there before," Lucy said. She clamped her hands around her upper arms against the cold. In her haste to get outside, she'd forgotten to put on a coat, and as warm as her knitted pullover was, it was no match for the freezing temperature.

"You mean this?" said Joe, sinking the tip of the shovel into the snow pile. He heard it hit metal.

"Yes!"

Joe pulled back on the shovel, striping away enough snow to expose the sheet metal. Then he stabbed lower down the pile with the pry bar and it sank into loosely piled brush. He dropped the shovel and pushed the pry bar further in.

"Go back inside," he encouraged Lucy. "You'll freeze out here."

"Let me just see if I helped," she replied, hunkering down into her shoulders as she started to shiver.

But Joe didn't hear her. He'd already turned his attention to pushing down on his end of the pry bar to lift up the other end. The pile broke apart easily, scattering the snow on the top of it and toppling the sheet metal to the ground. Joe dropped the pry bar. He grabbed a hold of the sheet metal and walked it further in on Hilda's property, where he let it drop to the ground. It was just trash, that he could have dumped any place he wanted; trash that had been blocking access to his septic tank, which he had every right to work on. But still. He didn't want to give Hilda the impression that he was trying to rip her place apart.

He tromped back to where the metal had been, strumming his fingers inside his gloves to keep them from going numb with cold. In the half-light he could see the short stack of dead brambles that had been under the sheet metal. He lifted them easily to one side and when he looked down at the exposed ground, a bolt of anger lit right though him. "*SON*-of-a......!" he snapped.

"Did you find something?" Lucy called out.

"Looks like it!" He hit the pile of freshly dug dirt with the tip of the shovel but it just bounced off the surface with a gravelly twang so he dropped the shovel, picked up the pry bar again, lifted it high in the air between both hands, then rammed it down into the center of the frozen earth. It made a clean hole not half an inch deep but he could see the circle of white, which gave him something to aim for. As he lifted the pry bar again he glanced over at Lucy, to tell her she really didn't have to wait through this, but she was gone. Good, he thought. He didn't need her out here shivering in the shit with him.

The beam from his headlamp spotlit the hole as Joe plunged the pry bar back down, feeling it sink deeper. He did it a third, fourth, fifth time until he got it about 4 inches down, then he began rocking the pry bar left, right, pushing and pulling forward, back, forcing the earth to break around the hole.

It broke apart in big clumps and Joe dropped the pry bar, leaned down and grabbed at them with his gloved hands, chucking whatever came loose behind him to get it out of the way. Right underneath the chunks of frozen dirt, his glove touched soil that felt soft, loose, and he leapt back up to his feet and picked up the shovel again. He sank the tip down into exposed dirt, stepped on it and scooped it out, letting it slide back off the shovel on one side of the hole. He kept going, working quickly, efficiently, partly to beat the cold but also to get this done before full daylight so as not to antagonize Hilda.

From what he'd heard, Hilda the Horrible was not pleasant when she felt antagonized and no amount of legal paperwork was likely to change that.

*****

At 6:00 am, Hilda finished her breakfast and trotted down the narrow hallway in her cabin to her bedroom to get dressed. She'd taken a nice, long, hot bath yesterday evening, after all that digging, so she didn't need to shower, and it was still early enough and dark enough that she didn't figure Connors would be out, trying to find the leak in his septic system yet. It was chilly in her bedroom, so far away from the woodstove, and that was good. Hilda decided it would encourage her to dress for the cold so if she had to go out later and confront Connors, that would be a plus.

She pulled a pair of flannel-lined jeans out of her closet, slipped them on and then carefully folded up the leg bottoms so the flannel would show. It was red, purple and pink gingham and she rather liked how it dressed up the jeans. She picked out a pair of heavy, red, wool socks that she'd knitted herself and pulled those over her feet, then stood, staring down at her sweater drawer. Should she wear a purple or a red sweater to go with the gingham?

A dog yipped off in the distance and Hilda snapped out of her stare. She didn't have time to make a fashion choice, she decided. Not today. Not with Connors always looking to circumvent her rights as a property owner. She snatched up the purple sweater, and a pink and white bandana to tie around her neck. That ought to do it, she thought.

She trotted back to the kitchen and slipped another small fir round into her woodstove. She didn't have a very big firebox in this stove so she'd have to stoke it often today, to keep the cabin warm and the pipes from freezing. She turned around, prepared to sit down at the kitchen table and watch the sun come up when she saw the light beam circling over by the property line.

He was out there! He was out there!! She wanted to run right out the door and over to him, tell him to get off her property, but she needed to gear up. What to do first? Boots, she thought. Pull on her boots. Then the jean jacket she'd bought with the flannel lining. And she should probably grab a hat and gloves too. She needed to be able to hold her own against him. She looked down at the kitchen table and smiled. Oh, she'd be able to hold her own all right.

*****

Joe expanded the size and depth of the hole, as daylight chased him with its pre-dawn glow. A school bus rolled by slowly on the snow-coated highway, heading up to Marblemount to pick up kids for school in Concrete. Joe would have waved at the driver but he was suddenly aware, now that he was about two feet down, that as fast as removed the dirt, the hole filled up with water. Cold, brown, fetid water that was rising rapidly up the sides of his muck boots.

He bent forward, trying not to inhale the acrid aroma, and repositioned the light from his headlamp in an attempt to pinpoint the pipe. Specifically where it was leaking, so he'd know what he was dealing with, but the water was way too brown. Even if he waited until the sun was fully up, he doubted he'd be able to see the pipe in this muck hole. He growled low in his throat, his teeth clenched tightly together; he was going to have to feel for the pipe. He lifted the shovel out of the dirt and tossed it to one side of the hole. Quickly, without giving himself time to think, he plunged his gloved hand down into the water. It was so cold it stung, even through the glove, and he fought the urge to yank his hand right back out as he moved it this way and that, under the surface, hoping to hit the tight line to his septic tank.

When his fingers failed to make contact with anything tangible he plunged his arm down further, feeling the water rise up past the top of the glove and soak into the sleeve of his wool shirt; that's when he felt something hard. He tipped even further to the right, his arm now up to his elbow in the brown water and gripped his whole hand around the smooth surface of what had to be the plastic pipe. He crab walked in the hole about two inches and let his hand slide down the length of what he'd exposed until, sure enough, it came to a break.

"Dammit!" he cursed. He ran his numbing digits over the exposed end; it felt smooth, not jagged, like it had been cut with a saw. But where was the other end? He swished his hand left and right and – bam! - hit the side of it against the second piece of pipe. Joe stood up immediately, and shook off his cold, wet hand. Hilda must have sawn the pipe in half and then hit one end of it with something hard, like an axe head or a hammer, dislocating it away from its coupling so wastewater from the house couldn't go out to the septic tank. He imagined if he fumbled around down in the water further, he'd find a rag or something that she must have stuffed in the exposed end, forcing the waste water to back up into his bathtub. She must not have stuffed it hard enough, he thought, because he probably dislodged it with his digging.

He could have reached back into the water and manhandled the dislodged pipe back into alignment with the other piece, enabling some of his waste water to travel to the septic tank but he was shivering in his thin t-shirt under his wool shirt and daylight had arrived. He'd come back when he'd gone to the hardware store in town and bought a sleeve to go over the break in the pipe.

He went to pull his left foot out of the wet mud so he could step back up onto the ground, when he heard a screech coming from the direction of Hilda's house. He peered in that direction, turning the light off in his headlamp as he did so, and saw Hilda, flailing her way towards him. He was sure there were words somewhere in all her screeching, but they were drowned out by an eastbound snowplow thunderously scraping the snow off the highway. Joe's eyes flicked towards the snowplow as his mind skidded the question of what he should do. He wanted nothing more than to head back inside and get out of this wet wool shirt but without confronting Hilda about the damage she'd done to his tight line, she could do worse. Especially exposed the way it was now. He looked back at her, deciding there was nothing for it but to wait.

And then he saw what she had in her hand.

Chapter 8

Lucy was pouring hot water from the kettle into the teapot when she heard some kind of caterwauling outside that caused her to look out the window in the kitchen. She saw Hilda bearing down on Joe, one arm raised like a battle cry, the other arm struggling to hold onto – oh no! was that a gun? Lucy slammed the kettle back down onto the kitchen stove and ran from the kitchen to the stairwell.

The dogs leapt up from their spots by the woodstove and chased around to join her, not knowing what was going on but caught up in the speed of her movements like they thought whatever it was she was up to, they needed to go along too. Lucy shoved her feet into the oversized Sorel boots Pete had given her for Christmas last year and snatched a wool jacket off its hook on the stairs. She pushed one arm into a sleeve hole and grabbed the door handle while she was still flailing with the other when a loud explosion rocked her world. The dogs tipped their heads back and howled in response, as panic gripped Lucy's chest making it hard to breathe.

"Oh no, oh no, oh NO!" she cried, snatching again and again on the door handle, trying to get it to open. Her brain finally kicked in gear, and told her to tug the sleeve on her jacket up if she wanted to get a grip on the handle. Seconds later, she had the door open and was around it, the dogs tearing past her, racing across the porch and down the side steps, as Lucy ran, ran....

*****

Joe's mouth dropped open as he watched Hilda coming at him, the shotgun in her right hand swinging perilously left and right and up and down. He was hyped up enough that she was marching towards him with a firearm, but her lack of control over what looked like a classic, slide action shotgun, was rocketing his blood pressure sky high. He only wished his body would rocket right along with it because the cold, wet mud had a suction hold on his muck-booted feet, making a hasty escape impossible. The only thing he could do was stand his ground. Or keep standing down in the ground. Whatever.

He wasn't doing anything wrong so he was going to assume that Hilda would see reason when he explained what he was up to. The only thing that made him nervous about that scenario was that *she* had caused the damage to his septic tank so it was unlikely that she didn't already know what he was up to. And the way she was swatting at the air with her left hand, sign language for "get the hell away," suggested she was not in favor of what he was doing and was prepared to defend her point.

He picked up the shovel, flipped it upside down and, with a crisp swish, pierced the snow with the handle, holding the blade out in front of him, American Gothic-like. He could only make out intermittent words from Hilda's tinny screech, "...told ....never ....step ....MY ....call .....arrest ...," but he heard enough to know he was in trouble.

"Calm down. Calm DOWN," he yelled as she got close enough that he could decipher a string of words.

"....no right to be over here when I've told you...." At which point what he said must have reached her ears because she suddenly stopped her squawking, made eye contact and slapped the barrel of the shotgun into her left hand, implying she was ready to use the damn thing.

Joe's sphincter muscle tightened.

"Don't you tell *me* to calm down!" balked Hilda, charging the last few feet towards him. But the increased speed played havoc with her footing and her legs scissored out in front of her and kicked up and before Joe knew it she was toppling backwards.

He lunged, desperately hoping to grab the gun before it could land on top of her and then – BOOM! – it went off and Joe fell forward, his feet stuck in the mud behind him, the shovel slamming down ahead of him, right on top of Hilda's prostrate body.

*****

Lucy rushed at the fence, wanting to leap it like a hurdle, the one sport she'd been good at in high school, but the ground was way too slippery for leaping. The dogs raced up the property line, headed for the break in the fence and for one second, Lucy thought about following them. But all she wanted was to *be* on the other side with Joe, because she'd glimpsed him from the front porch, slumped over on the ground, Hilda prostrate a few feet away, the shotgun and shovel on top of her, and she had no idea what any of that meant.

Her hands were shaking when she shoved the barbed wire down and arced her right leg over it, and even though she could feel that she'd pierced the palms of both hands and scratched up her thigh, she wasn't going to let that distract her from her mission. Her right foot hopping on the snow, she tugged her left over the wire to follow and fell sideways, with an ungainly thump, to the ground. A flash of pain jolted her right hip and buttock but she rolled onto her stomach and pushed herself back to a stand without pause, the icy snow feeling good against the punctures in her hands. To her right she was aware of the dogs panting down towards her but she wasn't going to wait for them. She needed to get to Joe. She set to, her eyes on the ground to be sure of her footing, her right side throbbing with a pain that was radiating from her bum.

"I'm okay, I'm okay," she heard Joe call out and she lifted her eyes to see him standing upright in the hole in the ground. The relief was so intense she felt her face break into a smile. Then she saw Hilda lift herself to a sit, blood running from a wound in her head down the length of her face. Lucy's gut tightened with fear.

What had Joe done??

*****

The dogs came tearing down the hill towards him and collided to a stop once the smell coming out of the hole hit them. They set about sniffing the perimeter with alacrity as Joe glanced around and saw Lucy sliding this way and that towards him. He yelled out that he was okay hoping she'd slow down. He didn't need her falling on her butt and breaking something. One injured person in this mess was enough.

He looked across at Hilda again. The blood running down her face was an ominous sign but it didn't look like it was coming from a gunshot wound. He guessed that she'd hit herself in the head with the shotgun when it fell on her. Maybe even knocked herself out a little because she was gazing around blearily, like she didn't understand where she was. He peered, trying to find the source of the blood, then saw Hilda tentatively touch a small gash on her forehead. She winced, lowered her hand back down in front of her and stared, mouth agape, at the blood on her fingertips. Joe glanced up at Lucy who had arrived next to him, her face fraught with anxiety. He opened his mouth to tell her not to worry, that head wounds just bleed a lot, when Hilda jumped in ahead of him.

"You....*you*....!" she spat.

"Now, Hilda, don't get..."

"...you....... *hit* me with a shovel!!" she went on, like she couldn't believe this had happened to her.

"Like hell I did!" Joe shouted back, amazed that she would even think something like that. "You came running at me..."

"And you smacked me to the ground with *this*!!" She thrust the shovel up into the air like it was evidence.

"No! No!"

"You *assaulted* me!!!"

"You fired a weapon!!!"

"Oh no you *don't*!" screeched Hilda, letting the shovel fall to the ground with an icy clang. The dogs both jumped then veered away, down towards the apple tree growing out in front of Joe and Lucy's property. Hilda struggled to a stand, both hands on the shotgun. "Don't you try saying it was self-defense."

"I wasn't going to because I *didn't* hit you with the shovel!" Joe balked as Hilda stumbled, trying to get her balance on the slick snow. She must have tried to counterweight her unsteady legs by tensing her arms because Joe heard the unmistakable shucking sound as she inadvertently pumped the slide action on the well-preserved Ithaca shotgun, ejecting the spent cartridge case. At least he thought it was inadvertent but he wasn't taking any chances. He pushed on the ground with his fists and yanked his feet out of the wet mud to climb up next to Lucy. Unfortunately one of his boots stayed stuck in the mud so he found himself hobbling on a sock and a boot.

"Then why is my blood on the tip of it?!" Hilda yelled, with an accusatory point down at the shovel. But freeing her left hand to point, caused the shotgun to weave treacherously again in her right.

"PUT THAT SHOTGUN DOWN!" Joe yelled, blocking Lucy with his body. "BEFORE IT GOES OFF AGAIN!"

"It can't go off..."

"PUT IT *DOWN*!!!"

There was something in his tone that made Hilda obey, albeit contritely. "I only had one cartridge," she moaned. "And it wasn't my fault it went off."

"It *was* your fault," Joe asserted, "plus you hit yourself in the head with that gun so I don't trust you either way!"

"I did *not* hit myself in the head!" Hilda argued. "You hit me with the shovel. And she saw it!" she added, pointing at Lucy.

Lucy opened her mouth to state that no, she hadn't seen it, then decided that maybe she didn't want to let Hilda know that particular tidbit of information. She snapped her mouth closed.

Joe pointed down at the hole in the ground. "And none of this would've happened if you hadn't cut the tight line to my septic tank."

"It's *my* septic tank!" yelled Hilda. "It's on *my* property."

"And I have all the legal paperwork...." Joe started but Hilda jumped in again to cut him off.

"I'm calling the Sheriff, see what he has to say about your paperwork. Especially when he sees what you did to my head."

"You go right ahead. But you'd better be ready to explain why you shot at an unarmed man."

Hilda's jaw dropped, but the recovered quickly. "You weren't unarmed. You had a shovel!"

Joe laughed. "Yeah. The Sheriff's gonna find that very persuasive."

"Look at my head!" she snapped, holding one hand up towards her forehead.

Joe copied her move, holding his hand out over the hole in the ground. "Look at my septic tank!"

Hilda touched her wound then held her fingertips out for Joe to see as if expecting him to have pity on her. "I'm *bleeding*," she whined. "You need to call an ambulance."

Lucy barely contained a laugh. "It's only a tiny cut," she said.

Hilda stomped one foot, like a petulant child, and declared, "I need stitches!"

But Joe noticed that her response was lacking some of her earlier venom and he realized that Hilda was running out of steam. Maybe it was the cold of the morning air, robbing her of that internal heat needed to keep anger a-flame. Maybe it was because the rest of the world seemed to have lost interest in their altercation. The dogs had long since wandered back over to his property and he imagined they were sitting on the front porch, waiting for him to let them into the warm. Traffic was crawling by on the highway as people braved the roads to get to work and the sun was working its way through the clouds to melt the surface of the snow.

Joe saw Hilda bend forward, one hand out to pick up the shotgun as he started towards her. She bolted upright again, scared.

"I'm only picking it up so I can leave," she said. "I need to go to the emergency room."

Joe stopped limping her way and pointed at her feet. "I just want my shovel," he said.

Hilda humphed, snatched up the shotgun and swiveled around, hastening towards her house. Joe let her scurry a few feet away before he started towards his shovel again.

"You haven't heard the last of this!" Hilda yelled back over her shoulder.

Joe retrieved his shovel, his lips pressed flat together in muted anger. "And that," he said to Lucy when he turned back to look at her, "is the one true thing she's said so far today."

*****

Lucy held her breath as she kneeled down next to the hole and reached in to retrieve Joe's boot. She pinched the top of it and tugged it out of the mud, trying not to splash any of the residual brown water on herself. She carried it a good few feet away and exhaled, hoping not to ingest any of the pong when she inhaled again. She hadn't had her morning tea, after all.

"Were you able to repair it?" she asked, as she placed Joe's boot on the ground for him.

"The tight line?" he said. He was most of the way back to her, having used the shovel to level his step, but he was actively shivering when he jammed his foot back into the boot. Lucy nodded. "Nope. I need a part," he went on, reaching over to scoop up the pry bar. "But at least for now, I've fixed what caused everything to back up into the bathtub."

He had a bead of moisture from the frigid morning air on the end of his noise and he bumped it off with the back of his wrist, then drew his lips back in disgust. "God, that stinks!" he said, holding out his hand to examine his glove. It was the hand he'd used to unclog the exposed section of tight line. The glove was saturated with brown water. He slapped it back down at his side, exasperated. "Come on," he said to Lucy. "Let's get inside. I'm freezing."

They started towards the fence together, the dogs looking across at them from the front porch. "Are you limping?!" Joe exclaimed as Lucy favored the side with the stabbing pains.

She nodded. "I banged myself up a bit coming across the fence."

"That damn Hilda!" snapped Joe. "I oughta call the Sheriff on *her*, for what she's done to us." He pushed the barbed wire almost to the ground with the shovel and the pry bar.

Lucy stepped over it, cringing at the pain in her hip. "Was it the shovel that nicked her in the head, do you think?"

"I have no idea," Joe replied, stepping over the barbed wire after her. "I had my face smashed down in the snow. But if it was," he went on, holding the shovel out like proud parent in front of him. "I'm getting it mounted."

Lucy laughed.

Joe veered right as they approached the side steps to the porch of the house. "I'll go put these tools back in the shed then I'm going to take a shower."

"We can do that now?"

"Uh huh. We just shouldn't flush the toilet until I get the tight line put back together."

"All right," said Lucy, climbing the steps. Maggie's tail began to thump on the porch. "Maybe leave those gloves out in the shed too," she suggested.

"You don't want odeur de poo in the house?" Joe teased.

"I'm likely to get plenty of that if we can't flush the toilet for a while."

Lucy was glad Joe could still be funny at a time like this. If she'd been the one out there, ankle deep in freezing cold, shitty water, the last thing she'd want to do was joke about it. Lucy slipped inside the house, the dogs close behind her, and she sighed happily at the welcome warmth. She quickly shed her jacket and boots and scooted over to the kitchen to finish making the tea.

She lit the gas under the kettle again, hearing her mother's voice in her head that the water needed to be boiling to make a decent cuppa, then turned on the tap in the sink to wash the abrasions on the palms of her hands. The tepid water stung against the raw rips but Lucy made herself leave them under the flow, looking out the window to take her mind off the pain.

It was strange, she thought, that a detail like the temperature of tea water was fixed in her brain, yet growing up in the city in England hadn't stopped her from quickly getting used to this pastoral view. The massive cedar tree, in the center of Hilda's field, impressed her every day with the way its full base billowed spherically, plumped out by thickly verdant branches. She thought that the lush shape, with no trunk visible, came from the fact that the branches arced down, then back up, like a ballerina's arms, creating a kind of fringe around the bottom.

Joe explained, however, that when the tree was younger, the swooping branches touched the ground and set roots around the base. So what looked like a single, mighty tree was really a circle of many, growing around the original, ballooning the base like petticoats under an Elizabethan gown. Lucy wondered how long that trompe d'oeil could go on, with the girth expanding as every younger tree set its own roots around the perimeter. Could it eventually fill the field? Lucy sighed; not if Hilda subdivided the land, she thought.

"Is she back out there?" Joe asked, coming in through the sliding glass door on the other side of the room from Lucy. He sounded worried, like he thought Hilda might be messing with the tight line again.

"No, no," Lucy reassured him, turning off the taps and picking up a small towel that was draped over the handle of the oven. She gingerly patted her hands dry as she leaned into the corner of the counter by the sink. "I was just thinking how the view is going to change if Hilda's successful with her subdivision."

Joe left his boots outside the sliding glass door and padded across to Lucy, his wet socks leaving footprints on the wood floor behind him. "Yeah. I don't even want to think about that. What I don't understand is why she can't come off her existing driveway to access these other lots she's planning." He pointed out the window where Lucy had been looking, at the wide apron coming off the highway that led into the long, curved driveway going up to Hilda's house. "She could come off it where it turns, and head right up the pasture, then put the cul-de-sac where her land abuts Jimmy and Laura's. That would be way more discreet than putting a road in next to us and I would've thought that would be a selling point. Plus she'd avoid our septic tank *and* the water line that services all the houses below the highway."

Lucy was looking out the window again, where Joe had pointed. "But she'd have to take that cedar tree out if she put the road in there."

"No, she wouldn't. She could go up through the pasture on the other side of that tree. There's plenty of room."

Lucy felt her spirits lift. "That's a great idea!" she said. "Maybe we should suggest it to her."

"Yeah, like she'd listen!" he scoffed.

Lucy looked directly into Joe's hazel eyes, curious.

"Reason only works with reasonable people," he told her.

The kettle whistled to a boil and Lucy turned off the gas and wrapped a hot pad around the handle to pick it up. "I just don't understand why she has to be so vengeful," she said.

"Me either! I never had a problem with Hilda until recently."

"You're sure about that?" Lucy poured a little boiling water into the bottom of the teapot, sluiced it around and emptied it into the sink before filling it with water.

"Pretty sure," he said. "She was with Burns and I didn't like *him*. But while she was with him, he left me alone, so I never interacted with Hilda." He looked out the kitchen window and sighed. "I get that my septic tank on her side of the fence is an unwelcome gift from Burns that she wished she hadn't gotten, like some kind of STD, but that doesn't give her the right to cut the tight line! And bring a *shotgun* to me fixing it!!"

Something had been nagging at Lucy since Joe's statement to Hilda outside. She put the kettle down and whipped back around to face him. "*Did* she shoot at you? Because if she did we need to call the Sheriff."

He shrugged, a flash of anger passing across his face. "I don't know what happened. All I know is one minute she was coming towards me and the next she was falling on her ass and I heard the gun go off. So maybe she was *planning* to shoot me. I don't know. She had no business bringing that gun, that much I do know!"

Lucy scooped two tablespoons of loose-leaf tea into the ceramic strainer, and lowered it into the teapot. "Maybe she's taking out on you what Burns did to her."

"I don't care what her motivation is, if she even has one; she still had no business bringing that shotgun. She didn't know how to carry it, let alone use it."

Max groaned softly, stretching his back legs on the floor next to the woodstove and the sound of his contentment overrode some of the sharpness in Joe's tone. Lucy put the lid on the teapot and leaned into the corner of the counter again as she looked at her husband. He definitely looked the worse for wear right at this moment. "So what are we going to do now?" she asked.

"You don't want to get too close to me," Joe replied, one hand up in the air as if warning her to stay back. "I'm wet and I smell terrible."

Lucy chuckled. "Er, yes, I know," she teased, "and I didn't mean that. I meant, what are we going to do now about Hilda?"

Joe shrugged. "Nothing. I'm going to fix the tight line and hope that bump on the head knocked some sense into her. But first, I'm going to take a shower."

*****

Once Hilda got home, she stepped out of her wet boots and let the shotgun drop heavily back down onto the kitchen table. She marched down the hallway to the bathroom, yanking off her wet gloves and hat, and peered at her bloody face in the mirror above the sink. Yes, she was going to get stitches for that, no question! Plus turn Connors in to the Sheriff for assault.

She picked up a washcloth, to clean the blood off her face, then changed her mind. Maybe she could get the nurse at the ER to take a photograph. She marched back to the kitchen, grabbed her purse and the file she'd put together about her short plat plans and made straight for the door.

*****

The nurse in the emergency room looked at Hilda like she was missing something. "You can probably just put a Band-aid on that," she offered.

"I want stitches," demanded Hilda.

"But..."

"At least two!"

The nurse shrugged. "Alright," she said, and sent Hilda back to a room in the ER where another nurse put two small stitches in the simple cut.

Hilda looked at the wound in the bathroom mirror at the ER before she left. Yes, that would do nicely, she thought.

She drove to the Sheriff's office in Mount Vernon and started to fill out a complaint form. It was busy at reception, and she could tell the woman behind the glass wanted her to move on, but Hilda demanded to know when exactly they were going to go out and arrest Connors.

The young Sheriff's Deputy sighed. "We probably won't arrest him. Not for such a minor complaint," she said.

"Minor?!" argued Hilda. "You're not the one with the gash in your head."

Another young Deputy, kind of a Nazi look-alike, with a nametag that read Deputy Sigglin, walked in at exactly that moment and Hilda watched the Deputy she'd been dealing with go over and whisper something to him. He took the complaint form and motioned for Hilda to move to a door into the office. He held the door open for her and then led her to a desk with two chairs. They both sat. Sigglin pulled in close to her, holding a pen over the complaint form, ready to take down the details.

Hilda started again. The Deputy was serious, attentive, as he carefully wrote down that Hilda was on her land, trying to ask Connors politely to leave, when he came at her with a shovel and caused a cut that required two stitches. But once he got all the information down, he looked at Hilda and said that he agreed with his colleague. They wouldn't go arrest Connors for such a small matter.

Hilda let big tears well up in her blue eyes and run down her face, bowing her shoulders forward to make herself as small as possible. A small, helpless, old lady. Deputy Sigglin rushed to get her some tissues.

"What if….what if…what if he comes after me again tonight?" she sobbed.

She blew her nose noisily, and then put the balled up, soggy mess of tissues on the desk next to Sigglin. She noticed he shifted her paperwork a little further away.

"Unfortunately there's nothing I can do until he breaks the law," said Sigglin.

"Assaulting me is not breaking the law?" Hilda whimpered.

"Not the kind of minor abrasion you have no," said Sigglin. "This is more of a civil matter than a criminal one. Now if he'd put you in the hospital…"

"I was in the hospital," sobbed Hilda. "Where do you think I just came from?"

She could see him squirming, not sure what to say, so she used her best trick. She let her blue eyes fill with more tears and then she turned them on him. "Can't you at least go talk to him?"

"I could probably do that," agreed Sigglin, and Hilda got the impression that he was relieved she'd given him an out. She let him have that feeling. "As long as he lets me on the property," added the Deputy.

"I would sleep so much better knowing you'd warned him,"

Hilda said, with a few small sniffs of appreciation. And since she had the young Deputy's full and sympathetic attention, she added, "Because I'm going to go over now to the County Planning Department and file my short plat paperwork. Once Connors finds out, well there's no knowing what he might do."

*****

Joe cleaned himself up, had some breakfast and, revived and refreshed, took Lucy up to see the doors on the new kiln.

"So it's finished?" she said, nodding at the double igloo looking construction in front of her.

"Yep. The only thing I might still do is capture the outside edges of the chimney with some angled steel but I don't need to do that right away. I do need to find a damper for the chimney," he added, pointing to an empty, rectangular opening at the base of the chimney up against the second chamber. "I'm thinking I might use a piece of hard ceramic fiber."

"Not a kiln shelf?"

"Maybe a mullite kiln shelf, but those are expensive and we're out of cash so the rigid fiber will be fine for now." He moved over next to Lucy and slipped his arm around her waist, his hand swishing against the exterior of her down jacket, his eyes on the kiln. "We need to do something for Pete. What he did for me here is huge."

"I agree."

The dogs were down, sphinxlike, alongside Joe, but they must have heard something because they suddenly leapt up, barking, and ran out towards the garden. The mid-morning sun had already started to defrost the snow on the ground and their paws spattered the surface slush as they ran. Joe and Lucy turned their heads to follow them, curious, and saw Sonny coming around the corner of the outbuilding where Joe stored cedar shake mill waste for his firings. His breath clouded the air ahead of him.

"Hey, Sonny!" Joe called out.

"Hey," replied his friend. He stepped into the kiln shed. "I just had lunch at the Mount Baker café," he said.

"Oh yeah? D'you bring me anything?"

Sonny's eyeballs fluttered sideways. "Kinda," he said with a sly smile.

"A cinnamon roll?"

Sonny shook his head no again. "Uh uh. Hilda was there, with a big wad of gauze taped to her forehead, and she said you hit her in the face with a shovel."

"Oh I already had that, first thing this morning," said Joe, sounding disappointed. "What else was on the menu?"

Sonny's eyes stopped, mid-flutter, then moved directly to connect with Joe's. "So you *did* hit her?"

"'Course I didn't!"

"I'm surprised you believed it," said Lucy.

"Oh she didn't say it to me!" Sonny put in, defending himself. "I would've told her, that's bullshit!"

"She came at me with a shotgun," Joe started to explain.

"A shotgun?!"

Joe gave a decisive nod of his head. "Yeah. A vintage, Ithaca Model 37 by the looks of it."

"Which she fired," added Lucy.

"At you??" Sonny looked at Joe with genuine concern.

"I don't know. I was face down on the ground."

"How come?"

"My feet were stuck in a muck hole."

Sonny looked out of the kiln shed, bemused. "In this snow?"

"Yes, in this snow," Joe asserted. "I had to expose the tight line to my septic tank."

"Why?"

"'Cause Hilda cut it."

"No shit!"

"Oh there was plenty of shit," Joe informed his friend, "and I was ankle deep in it. Which reminds me, you don't happen to have a four-inch flexible coupling, do you?"

"Uh uh," said Sonny, shaking his head regretfully. "You have to go to the County for that."

Joe stepped back, shocked. "What's wrong with the hardware

store in Concrete?"

"Parts for water and septic are only sold at Public Works down in Mount Vernon. And they're expensive."

"Of course they are!" griped Joe, his fuse considerably shortened. "Because it can't be an easy fix!"

Sonny shrugged, like there was nothing he could do about it, and turned his attention to the new kiln. "You got the doors on."

"Yep. Yesterday. With Pete."

"When are you gonna fire it?"

"As soon as I get it loaded. I was hoping to start glazing pots today but I guess I'll have to put that on hold."

"Why's that?"

"I need to drive down valley, get this part for my septic."

"I have to go down later to look at a job. I'll pick it up for you, if you like."

"Would you?"

"Might cost you forty bucks though."

Joe looked across at Lucy. She stretched her mouth down, indicating this could be a problem. "Is there anything in the cash jar?" she asked.

Joe's face perked up. "As a matter of fact, there is. I put the check the judge's wife gave me yesterday in there."

"Yes, but I was going to pay the electric bill with that." Lucy rethought what she'd just said. "You know what, it doesn't matter. I can cash that check…."

A car horn beeped twice from down by the house and the dogs leapt into action once more.

"Saved by the bell!" declared Lucy, moving out of the kiln shed. "Think customer. Think forty dollars," she shouted, moving as fast as she dared on the slowly melting snow, her aching butt a reminder that it wouldn't be fun if she fell again.

Behind her as she rounded the corner by the kiln fuel shed, she heard Sonny ask, "So where did the shovel come into it?"

*****

Lucy was still hidden by the cherry tree alongside the house when she spied the telltale dark green and gold of a Skagit County Sheriff's vehicle. She slowed immediately. Why? *Why*? she groaned internally. Why couldn't it have been a customer to add to their finances? Why did it have to be someone from law enforcement? Again?! Her mind raced the possibilities behind the visit as she lingered by the cherry tree, her eyes drawn to the sparkle of a pendulous, quivering bead of water on the underside of one of the branches. The last time they were visited by a Sheriff's deputy, she thought, Pete sold a couple of mugs to the officer, so maybe this was a customer *and* someone from law enforcement? Could they get that lucky twice?

The dogs ran towards her, having already gone and checked out the visitor, and jostled against each other to nose her hand with their kisses. It gave her the lift she needed to continue on around the corner and deal with whoever was in the driveway.

Unfortunately it wasn't the female deputy that she'd been hoping for; it was a tall, pencil-headed guy, who looked like he was prepping for an audition that required him to look officious. His face was devoid of any warmth and his close set eyes shifted cagily from side to side. The only thing that would have made his look more complete was a pair of narrow, mirrored sunglasses but as Lucy squinted to read his nameplate, she saw a pair poking out of the top of his breast pocket. If it hadn't been for Joe's earlier altercation with Hilda and the fact that Hilda had obviously received some medical attention for her little cut AND been stirring the mud about Joe in town, Lucy may have laughed at the official posturing on the part of this Deputy. Instead she took it as forewarning that he was there to threaten her status quo. Lucy drew on every scintilla of her naturally acquired British reserve and prepared to make the Deputy work for any information he gleaned from her. She stepped up to him without a smile or a greeting.

"Mrs. Connors?" he asked.

"Deputy Sigglin."

He looked surprised that she knew his name and opened his mouth as if to ask how, but was fumbling to pull a notepad out of his breast pocket and when he looked down to facilitate this action, he must have caught site of his nameplate, because when he raised his head again, Lucy saw that his eyes had narrowed, as if he were trying to piece together what had just happened. It gave her an immediate impression of his intellect.

"I'm looking for your husband, Joe. Is he here?"

"Here?" Lucy asked, pointing down at her feet while sounding suitably surprised.

"Yes."

"Then no," she said.

Deputy Sigglin's brow folded and Lucy wondered if this conversation were going the way he'd planned it.

"Do you know when he'll be back?" he asked once he caught up.

"Here?" Lucy said again, with the same point down at her feet. She took his blank look as concurrence and said, with just a touch of sweetness, "No."

Sigglin made himself sound serious. "I need to talk to him."

"Oh I know that feeling," Lucy agreed. "But he's like a fish swimming off with the lure."

"Wha…?"

"We've only been married a week and he talked me into it by saying that communication is the essence of relationship but now, when I say, 'I need to talk to you,' he somehow gets busy. Do you have a card?" she went on without pause.

Sigglin didn't even think; he just reached into his breast pocket again. "I do, yes."

"Great! I'll make sure he gets it."

The Deputy held the card out but stopped before Lucy could take it. "No, I mean I *have* to talk to him."

"I'll make sure he calls you," Lucy replied, lifting the card gently from between his fingers.

"I can't leave without talking to him," Sigglin insisted.

"Well then you're in a bit of a pickle, aren't you?"

"What?"

"You can't talk to him if he's not here, and you can't leave if you don't talk to him. That's what my mother would call a bit of a pickle. I think over here you call it a jam." Lucy looked up, as if seeing something in the sky suddenly. "That's interesting, isn't it? That you use jam as a euphemism and we use pickles. Where d'you suppose that comes from?"

Deputy Sigglin shifted his eyes this way and that again, but this time it was more because he seemed uncomfortable that somebody might be overhearing this conversation. "Can you tell me where Mr. Connors is if he's not here?"

Lucy inspected his card closely. "I can," she said. "But you have to tell me why first."

"No I don't," he rebuked.

"Oh I think you do," said Lucy. She looked up and met Sigglin's eyes with a soft smile, knowing that he was expecting her to expand on this thought. She didn't oblige him.

"I'm here to warn Mr. Connors," the Deputy said, leaning towards Lucy in a way that suggested she should be scared.

"About what?" she answered, with macabre excitement, like he was sharing a secret. She leaned towards him as she said it, offering her left ear so he could share it without being overheard.

Deputy Sigglins bristled, leaning back to a full stand, and Lucy knew she'd turned his attempt at intimidation back on him. He flipped the pages of his notebook, and glanced down in a return to officiousness. "About an incident of assault against him that we're filing with the Skagit County Prosecuting Attorney's office."

"My husband's been assaulted?!" Lucy exclaimed. Now she acted scared.

Sigglin's eyes scooted left and right, like he was trying to determine where the information got tangled up. "No, he did the assaulting."

"Oh I think you'll find he didn't," Lucy assured the Deputy.

"Your neighbor, Hilda Hess, said he did."

"The lady who hit herself in the head with the shovel?"

."I can't comment on that."

"How can you not comment on it and yet you're here to talk to my husband about it? Isn't that an oxymoron?"

Lucy let him chew on this a second while she watched a snowplow go by on the highway. It triggered a memory for her of this morning. Didn't she hear a snowplow go by right around the time Hilda was rushing towards Joe carrying a shotgun? Maybe the driver saw something. And wasn't there a school bus going by at one point?

"An oxy-what?" Deputy Sigglin asked, once he'd swallowed what she'd said.

"Moron," Lucy replied, offering a disarming smile again. "You know, when opposite words or statements cancel each other out. Like living dead."

The Deputy's features hardened as he caught up with the fact that she was messing with him. He disregarded her grammar tutorial and reverted to his reason for being there. "Mr. Connors needs to know that we've filed this complaint with the Prosecuting Attorney's office and I'm here to warn him to stay off Ms. Hess' property until this gets resolved."

Lucy wasn't having that. "Unless he wants to work on his septic tank," she explained, "which he'll have to do because Hilda Hess sawed right through the tight line, which is why….."

But Sigglin silenced her with one hand up in the air. "I don't want to hear any arguments…." he decreed.

This really irked Lucy. "Then you certainly don't want to talk to my husband!" she shot back.

Her tone must have irked him right back because he became more pointed. "Just tell him to stay off Hilda Hess' property."

"No," argued Lucy, surprising herself with her insistence. She was usually a bit of a chicken when it came to facing down government officials but the fact that this Deputy didn't even want to hear their side of the story, got her blood boiling. "I can't do that because he needs to repair our septic system so we can use it. And he has a court order *stating* that he has the right to ingress and egress of that property to maintain the septic system."

"Then he should have shown that to Ms. Hess when she approached him this morning."

"If she'd've approached him unarmed, he would have."

Sigglin cocked an eyebrow. "She was armed?"

"Armed and firing!"

His hand shot up again. "I can't get in the middle of this!"

"Then you can't be here."

"I think I can."

"I think you can't! Not unless you came to arrest my husband."

The Deputy shuffled awkwardly in the hips, and Lucy got the impression he was squirming, as if she'd caught him in a lie. Out of the corner of her eye she saw a Green Range Rover slow down out on the highway, its left indicator flashing, and heard Max and Maggie begin to bark behind her. Lucy glanced past the Deputy and saw the vehicle turn in at the end of the driveway. A dark haired woman with shiny red lips waved excitedly at her from the passenger seat and, as the vehicle got closer, Lucy recognized Craig and Caroline Hazlehurst, with their two big Boxers. She waved back smiling, glad of the interruption, and stepped to the right, closer to Deputy Sigglin, to make sure they could pull past.

Sigglin gave the Range Rover a cursory look as it went around them, into the main driveway, then brought his attention back to Lucy. "In the interest of keeping the peace," he stated, his tone more conciliatory than previously, "the reason for my visit was to *advise* Mr. Connors to stay off the property next door until this complaint gets resolved."

"Well unless you want to repair our septic system for us, that's advice we can't take," said Lucy. She looked over to where the Hazlehursts were parking in front of the silver fir trees on the property line, and noticed Max and Maggie running that way too, happily carrying a four foot length of frosted vine maple between them. This gave her an idea.

"In the interest of keeping the peace, you could always stand watch over my husband while he's knee-deep in wet poop repairing the thing," she suggested.

Deputy Sigglin shook his right hand back and forth in the air, his index finger pointing up, like this was a definite no. "I think the best protection your husband can get right now," he said, backing up to his vehicle, "is a good lawyer." With that, he climbed into the

Ford Explorer, slammed the door and backed down the driveway without looking at her again.

Lucy was amazed. Had she known that the mention of getting too close to some stinky shit would cause such a rapid retreat, she would have led with that. A car door banged shut and she swung around to see Caroline Hazelhurst already playing with the two canine greeters by tugging on the middle of their shared stick. "We came up hoping you had twelve teapots to sell us," she called out, as Lucy walked towards her.

"*Twelve* teapots?!"

"Yes. We've decided we want to give one each to our buyers at REI in Seattle."

"Well let's go and see," said Lucy, motioning towards the pottery shop, a definite bounce in her stride from the serendipity of such a sale. Maybe she'd end up with that forty dollars after all!

*****

"Have you thought any more about how we're going to handle this?" Joe asked later, stepping out of the bathroom in clean clothes, his hair wet from the shower. It was after 5:00 but he'd managed to get the flexible coupling on the tight line and the hole covered over before it got dark even though Sonny hadn't shown up with the part till almost 4 pm.

Lucy was sitting at the kitchen table with the various applications they needed to fill out spread in front of her. He could see, from where he was standing, that she was working on her application for permanent residency. He knew how anxious all this paperwork made her so he walked around behind her, lifted some of her golden locks, and gently kissed the back of her neck. She touched her free hand to the side of his face, but kept working. "I suppose," she said, and he watched her check the "no" box next to a question about whether she'd ever sold her body for sex, "we'll have to get a lawyer."

The house was filled with a spicy, tantalizing aroma coming from the venison chili bubbling on the stove in the kitchen. Joe padded over to it.

"If Hilda has indeed filed this complaint against you." Lucy added, still focused on her paperwork.

"You think there's a chance she hasn't?"

Lucy looked across at him stirring the chili with a wooden spoon. "I don't know," she said. "There was just something very off about the way the Sheriff's Deputy was acting when I asked him about arresting you, so I called Christine, Mary Lynn McEwan's daughter from the Tulip Festival…."

"Why'd you call her?" Joe asked. He banged the spoon on the rim of the pot and laid it back down between the burners on the stove.

"She's a Deputy in Mount Vernon."

"That's right!"

"And she told me that if it's not a criminal matter then Deputy Sigglin had no right to be here."

Joe walked behind her again, into the living room and picked up his sneakers from the hearth. He sat down in the rocking chair next to the woodstove and pushed his feet into them. "So you think he was lying when he said he'd passed Hilda's complaint along to the Prosecuting Attorney?" he asked, grunting a little from his diaphragm being compressed as he leaned forward to tie his sneakers.

"I don't know. But I got the distinct impression he wasn't telling me everything." She looked back down at her paperwork, pen poised.

"All Things Considered" was on the radio and they were talking about the popularity of some animated shorts on the "Tracey Ullman Show" that featured a dysfunctional family called "The Simpsons." Not having television Joe had never seen "The Tracey Ullman Show." He listened to the short clip they played of the animated characters interacting. "That sounds like Julie Kavner," he said, as he finished lacing his boots.

"Hmmmm?" said Lucy, then she smacked her tongue against the roof of her mouth. "Tch! Some of these question!"

"What?"

"They want to know if I'm a mental retard."

"For real?! It says that?"

"Uh huh. And have I had any 'attacks of insanity.'"

Joe sat upright, an eyebrow cocked. "Have you?"

"I married you, didn't I?"

He laughed, tipping backwards, his head thunking gently against the back of the rocking chair.

"What a thing to ask," he said when he settled back down. He stared out the picture window opposite, impressed with how dark it was for so early in the evening.

"They also want to know if I'm psychotic or have any mental disorders..." She flipped over the page on the form. "In fact mental illness comes up quite a bit." She stared down at the questions, bemused, then looked at Joe. "Don't they know there are wackos already in this country?"

"Yeah," he nodded. "But we don't want our wackos mixing with your wackos."

Now Lucy laughed.

Joe brought his eyes back to the window then on to the log wall beside it. The logs were flat sawn on three sides and he liked how their honeyed hue added warmth to the light inside the house. "You got any ideas on a lawyer for us?" he asked, still staring at the logs.

"You're not going to use the lawyer who helped you all those times when Burns was giving you grief over the septic tank?"

"Can't. He's retired."

"Oh. Well then I suggest my friend Gina's husband."

He felt her looking at him from across the room but he was intent on picking out the figure in the wood. "Gina?" he asked.

"Yes. Gina Klaassen. Didn't you meet her once when she came to the shop?"

Joe shook his head no although he knew it was possible he had met this new friend of Lucy's. He was just better at faces than names.

"Well anyway, her husband's a lawyer and, apparently, he doesn't take any crap."

"But our septic tank's full of crap."

"Oh ha ha," Lucy responded, dryly.

Trumpets heralded the "All Things Considered" theme music from across the room then Lucy added, her eyes fixed on her application, "They want to know if I was a member of the Nazi party from 1933-45."

"What??"

"I know!"

"And this is what I had to give a photograph of my left ear for?" Joe grumbled.

He wanted to get up and go over to the thermometer, see what the temperature was outside, but he was feeling pretty relaxed, sitting next to the woodstove. He stared through the window, not really seeing, just zoning, his elbows propped in the dip on the arm rests of the rocker, his hands hanging loose over his thighs. It must have been the half hour because they were giving the news headlines on the radio but he wasn't hearing them. He was wondering how many critters were out in that pitch dark, enjoying the absence of humans for a few brief hours.

"Good Lord," Lucy muttered.

"What?" he said, his eyes still blurred.

"They want to know if I'm a sexual deviant."

He flipped back to the present and looked over at her, amused. She made a slow, theatrical turn of her head his way, tipping her face down, her eyebrows raised, a slight taunt in her green eyes. Her hair made a frill of lazy curls against her cheek and he wanted to reach forward and sweep it gently over her shoulder but he was too far away. "What are you going to put?" he asked.

"No!" she snorted. "But I mean, it's ludicrous. Who gets to decide what that means?"

She focused once more on her paperwork and Joe used the interruption as impetus to lift himself out of the rocker and walk over to the thermometer. The outside temperature read 40 degrees; it wouldn't snow again tonight.

"Will you call your friend? See if we can talk to her husband about Hilda's complaint?" he asked, peering up at the sky through the window. All he saw was inky black, no stars, suggesting cloud cover.

"Why don't we just wait and see if there is a complaint?" said Lucy. "Maybe it'll all come to naught."

"Okay," he said. He turned away from the window and sidled up behind her again, resting his hands on her shoulders.

"A polygamist?" she scoffed.

He tried to see over her shoulder. "What's that?"

Lucy pointed to the question and read it to him. "Are you now or have you ever been a polygamist?" She twisted her head to look up at him. "They do know this is the United States I'm applying to, right?"

He laughed.

"I thought you were the ones that invented that."

"Now, now." He watched her make a neat check mark in the no box alongside the question. He rubbed his thumbs into the base of her neck and she let her head drop forward. He felt her lean back into the motion. "Are you nearly done?" he asked.

"Almost," she said. "I think I only have the questions about whether I'm a communist, an alcoholic, or have any communicable diseases left." She paused and he heard the tumble of a log inside the woodstove as the one below must have lost its structure. "Why? Are you hungry?" she asked.

He looked across at the pot of chili, thick and red with dark brownish beans suspended in the sauce. "Uh huh," he answered.

"Well we can eat."

"We can," he agreed slowly, like he wasn't sure. "But I was thinking…"

"Yes?"

"Maybe we should go find out if you're a sexual deviant first.'

He felt her chuckle under his hands.

Chapter 9

A week later Joe stood at the sliding glass door and settled the anxiety in his stomach with a long, slow breath. He rolled the door open and stepped out onto the back porch, ready to go unload the first firing in his new kiln. He tipped his face up to the sky, to see what the weather had in store, and felt tiny, droplets of moisture spit down onto his skin. It was snowing, but barely.

He dropped down the three steps from the porch to the grass and started up the path towards the studio and kiln shed. The dogs ran around from the front of the house to join him. Where had Lucy got to, Joe wondered. She was supposed to have been back an hour ago and he knew she wanted to be there when he cracked open the doors on this inaugural firing but he couldn't wait any longer. Not only was he anxious to find out whether his design had worked and he'd been able to get the pots – or at least most of them – up to temperature, but he'd just made his first appointment with the lawyer to discuss the summons he'd received from the Prosecuting Attorney's office, and he was anxious to find out if he could pay for it. He and Lucy planned to start the unloading at 2:00 and it was after 3:00 already. Maggie stopped at the end of the path and looked back down the driveway as if seeing something. Joe glanced over his shoulder, hoping that it was Lucy pulling in, but it was only the mail carrier, stopping at his mailbox to deliver his mail. He continued on up to the kiln, justifying his haste by telling himself he only had an hour and a half of daylight left.

The truth was he had to focus on something other than his ongoing septic tank saga. Who would have thought, he said to himself, a slight bitterness clawing at the back of his throat, that a mistake he'd made a dozen years ago would still be costing him so much. And it wasn't as if it he'd even made a felonious mistake. It was the mistake of believing in someone. He stopped at the end of the garden, lifting his eyes to the top of Sauk, but he couldn't see her because she was hiding behind a big, cottony, cumulus cloud. Yeah, he thought, it wasn't really believing in someone that had been his mistake; it was believing in the façade they'd presented. But what did he know about taking people at more than just face value? Shoot, at 24 years old he'd still been trying to fit with the world. He certainly didn't know anything about the ruses they were using to fit themselves.

He rounded the corner and strode over to the kiln shed, stopping at the edge of the concrete to lift the handle of the garden way cart he'd filled full of wooden boxes for the pottery. He backed it out onto the gravely ground, and set it down, then walked back around it into the kiln shed. Joe had built a simple pole building for his new kiln, with no walls, but it felt very quiet standing in the middle of it right now, as if it were cocooned from the rest of the world. Maybe he got that impression because this space had been so filled with noise two days ago, when he fired the kiln: wood snapping in the fire box as gases combusted, flames, thundering through the chambers on their way to the chimney, intermittent hammering, as he hit some of the larger ends of cedar on the concrete floor with an axe to break them up, and of course the radio, ever present, to keep him company with its loud music and busy news shows. He centered himself in the quiet today, holding one hand up in front of the 2 x 2 opening in the door of the first chamber, where he'd pulled a peephole brick so the heat could vent. He could still feel warmth wavering out onto his hand but not enough that he thought he shouldn't open the kiln. He looked at the tongue of soot, newly formed on the door above that peephole, then across at the bigger one over the stoke hole for the firebox. Yep, the kiln wasn't brand new any more. But hopefully he'd get about 15 years of service out of her.

He swung around and lifted a wrench off one of the shelves he'd built opposite the kiln. Now for the moment of truth, he told himself. Not that he wasn't used to disappointments. A kiln firing, like life, always had elements that didn't turn out the way he'd hoped they would turn out, no matter how well he tried to navigate the variables. The thing to do, he'd found, to ride out those disappointments, was to follow the love.

He stepped up onto the 1 x 12 board he'd placed on two upturned milk crates at the base of the first chamber and slid the wrench over the nut holding the doors shut with a steel plate. As he unscrewed the nut, he reflected on how he and Lucy had talked about going someplace new to build their life together, but he couldn't find a way in his mind to leave these mountains. Or these five acres. And he'd taken some hard knocks here. He'd been defrauded at the outset over the property line, had his house burn down around him, nearly lost his life – twice – and, the grand finale, a culmination of all the previous knocks, like a wrecking ball that hits just the right place to make the whole works collapse, his wife, Erica, left him, taking their baby daughter with her. At the time, it had made him want to pound his head against a wall over and over, screaming – *you idiot*! – but for reasons he couldn't quite explain, it had never made him want to leave. Because each blow from the wrecking ball had not only crushed realities he thought he wanted, it had opened up the path he needed to follow, like a cloud break in the sky.

It had revealed these mountains, not just as a background to his life, but as place of rejuvenation and inspiration. It had cleared the way to building a home instead of a shelter and it had sharpened his focus on the one thing he knew he could do, make pottery. And now, more recently, it had brought him Lucy. The nut came loose in his hand and he looked down at it, thinking about all he would have missed if he'd moved away from the Upper Skagit when life had beaten him down. Yeah, he thought, wrapping his fingers around the hexagon of steel. Hilda could drag every government agency she wanted into his life; he'd followed the love right back to this little piece of heaven again and again, and he wasn't going anywhere.

He jumped down off the board and put the wrench and the nut on the shelf then slapped his sooty hands against the sides of his jeans. Outside the kiln shed he saw the dogs, who'd been chasing each other this way and that around a fir tree, suddenly race up towards the playground. Probably headed to the creek to get a drink of water, he thought. He climbed back onto the board and pulled the steel plate towards him, causing the chamber doors to sigh away from their arches, releasing a band of warmth into the cold air around him.

"You couldn't wait, huh?" came Lucy's voice from behind him.

He swung around, startled by the voice in the quiet, then beamed his joy at seeing her. He pushed the bolt and plate away from him, back into the dip between the outside of the two chambers, and a loud, echoing clang filled the shed.

"That's my girl!" he yelled over the noise. "Right on cue."

"I'm sorry I'm late," she said.

But Joe had already moved on to the excitement of her being there and now he couldn't wait to find out what was inside the kiln. He stepped down off the plank and put one hand on the steel framework of the door. "You ready?" he asked, and walked the heavy door open all the way to the firebox.

*****

The colors were much better than he'd hoped for in his mind's eye. Vibrant reds, blues and greens created by the clear glaze getting just slightly too hot so that it gleamed on the outside of the pots. The copper green glaze, which always turned turquoise, was less garish in this new kiln, more muted and warm. And the matte white glaze had gone pink in many places, as he was used to, but on some of the pots it had progressed to a satin finish, which was both elegant and inviting. Lucy was taking the pots from Joe and putting them in the boxes and every time he handed her one with this satin finish she couldn't help but run her thumb gently over the surface, it felt so soft.

"That's different, isn't it?" she said.

"Yeah. I'm wondering if that's from those pruned limbs from the King David apple tree I burned this time. I've never had a satin finish on the pots before." He took the pitcher back he'd just handed her and ran his finger over it again. "I keep thinking this is the matte white but, you know, it could be one of the clear glazes." He passed it back to her. "Whatever it is," he said, "I like it."

She slipped it in the corner of a box. He handed her a teapot, after he checked the lid and the basket strainer inside it, and she put it into a box with four other teapots. "I need to keep all five of these," she told him. "Plus two more if you have it,"

"How come?"

"Because there weren't enough for Caroline Hazlehurst, remember? She took the five that we had and said she'd come to the pottery party in Seattle next Saturday to pick up the rest."

Joe chucked his head to one side. "That was a lot of assumption on your part, that this firing would turn out."

"Faith. Not assumption."

He growled low in his throat, like he wasn't buying it. "You could have been very disappointed."

Lucy just let it go by. She knew she was taking a risk promising something that hadn't come out of the kiln yet, but she also knew that Caroline and Craig were savvy businesspeople and good friends, who would have settled for something else if there hadn't been enough teapots.

"Where are we going to put all this?" Lucy asked. The kiln shed was stacked with boxes of fresh-fired pottery - on the boards over the sawhorses, in the garden way cart, on the cement floor - and Joe hadn't even started unloading the second chamber yet.

He pulled the last lidded casserole out of the bottom of the first chamber and tugged on the lid to get it off. When it didn't come off, he flipped the pot over and tapped on the bottom with a piece of broken kiln shelf. The lid popped off into his hand on the other side.

He handed it up to her, a squat, wide mouthed bean baking pot with trees drawn around the outside edge and across the lid, and then bounced up to a stand from where he'd been sitting astride the 1 x 12 board in front of the first chamber.

"Let's take them into the studio, then you can price them in the warm when we get that far."

Lucy nodded and immediately slid a box filled with cereal bowls towards her from the planks on the sawhorses, grabbing a firm hold of the bottom with both hands as she balanced the weight up against her torso. Joe did the same with a box full of mugs and he led the way out of the kiln shed, down the short path in the grass to the studio. The dogs jumped up from where they'd been chewing sticks on the ground outside the kiln shed and trotted ahead of Joe. "Get out of the way," he grunted as he approached the ramp up to the porch of the studio. The dogs wheeled right, across some cobblestone bricks half buried in the ground between the studio and the old kiln shed.

A loud rumbling punctuated by the jack-hammer sound of a jake brake drifted up towards them from the highway and Lucy saw the dogs perk their heads, curious, from where they were sniffing the gravel out in front of the studio. When the rumbling gave way to the reedy bellow of air brakes being pumped the dogs took off running, their loud barks competing with the growling idle of what sounded like a log truck.

"Sounds like somebody's here," Lucy said as she stepped over the gap between the porch and the floor of the studio that was usually filled with the rolling barn door.

"Could've been Walt, turning down Sauk Store Road. It's the end of the work day for log truck drivers."

Lucy pushed her box onto the glazing table, alongside the mugs. "Should I go and check?"

Joe was already on his way down the ramp from the porch again. "If you want," he said.

Lucy hurried away from the studio but she didn't have to go far before she noticed an older, barrel-chested, bearded man walking up towards her, the dogs at his heels. Beyond him she could see the orange cab of a short load logging truck, parked across the mouth of their driveway.

"Joe here?" the man asked before Lucy could greet him. His lower lip bulged under his beard and Lucy noticed that it barely moved when he clipped out his question.

Joe had a number of friends from the logging community and Lucy assumed this fellow was one of them. Especially since one side of the red suspenders he was wearing over his cream and brown wool shirt said Skagit and the other said Logger. She nodded. "He's unloading the kiln."

The guy spat a gob of brown liquid down onto the ground and both dogs slammed to a halt to investigate it. "'S'okay if I say hi?"

"Of course," said Lucy. She led the visitor up the hill and around the wood shed to the kiln. Joe had his hands on a box of small items – butter dishes, creamer sugar sets, candleholders – to move it down to the studio but he relaxed at the sight of the visitor. "Eddie Eldridge!" he called out, pleased to see the log truck driver. "What brings you this way?"

Eddie acknowledged Joe with a tacit nod and the hint of a smile. "I thought I'd better stop, make sure you was still with us."

"Why wouldn't I be?" asked Joe. He stepped out of the way to let Lucy grab another box of pottery to take down to the studio.

"I saw that woman coming at you with a shotgun yesterday and I figured she got close enough not to miss."

"You saw that?!" Joe and Lucy asked in unison. They glanced at each other and Lucy put the box of pots back down on the sawhorses.

Eddie nodded again. "I was behind that snowplow, watching her wave that gun around. I remember thinking - that Joe Connors, he better duck!" He spoke with a rich Tar Heel twang and Lucy noticed again that it didn't involve much movement of his lips.

Joe was excited by the implications of what Eddie had just said.

"Did you see her shoot?" he asked.

"Nope. But I sure did hear it! Made *me* duck, even though I was past your place." His eyes traveled up and down Joe, as if he were checking all the parts were still there. "How come she was gunning for you?" he asked.

"She cut the tight line to my septic system and didn't want me going over there to fix it. That's why I was doing it so early in the morning. I thought she might not be up yet."

Eddie Eldridge shook his head from side to side. "I told Clarence Burns it didn't make no sense to put that septic where he put it if he wasn't gonna let someone use it. But I guess he had other ideas. Now I know why he never sold this place to Deputy Wrenn."

Joe's eyes popped. He was aware that a lot of people in the Upper Skagit knew about the feud over his septic tank, especially the old timers, like Eddie Eldridge, but he'd never before heard this tidbit of information. "Doug Wrenn wanted to buy this property?"

Eldridge nodded. "Walked around with a blank check in his pocket for better part a two years. Told Burns – 'just name your price' - but Burns never would."

"*Now* the truth comes out!" said Joe, looking across at Lucy. "Burns was plotting all along."

"That devious old devil," she huffed.

"Ye-ah, that wouldn't be what *I'd* call him," said Joe.

Eddie Eldridge chortled. "Me either." He stepped outside the kiln shed and spat snooze juice down on the ground again.

Joe decided to take the bull by the horns. "But now I've got Hilda dragging me into court…."

"Over what?" countered Eddie. "You didn't have a shotgun that I saw."

Joe pouted like a petulant child and wah-wahed, "She says my shovel bit her in the forehead."

Eddie rolled his eyes and went and spat on the ground again.

"So would you help me out by saying in court what you saw the other day if I need you to?" asked Joe.

"'Course," Eddie replied.

Joe threw his hands up in the air. "Thank you," he cheered. "You just became my new best friend!"

Eddie's eyes slid from Joe to Lucy, then back to Joe. "You mean I wasn't before?"

Joe laughed out loud, then crossed his hands over his heart and joked, “You know I’ve always loved you, Eddie.”

“Just not as much as some pretty English girl, huh?” and his eyes slid back to Lucy.

She smiled shyly at him.

“Sorry,” said Joe, extending one hand in Lucy’s direction and the other towards Eddie. “I don’t think you’ve met each other. Eddie this is my wife, Lucy. Lucy this is Eddie Eldridge. If ever I need a log truck load of wood moved, Eddie’s the man I go to.”

“How do you do,” said Lucy, picking up the box of pottery she’d been intending to move at the start of their conversation. As she walked around the sawhorses, she leaned towards Eddie and made a show of whispering, “Between you and me, I’m still below Magnolia when it comes to his love.” She nodded across at Maggie, who was sitting patiently at Joe’s feet.

Joe looked down at his aging Chesapeake mutt and cooed, “Are you my girl, Maggie?”

Maggie’s tail swished left and right across the concrete floor, moving particles of cedar and wood ash into the air.

As Lucy moved away Eddie got drawn in to the kiln. “This where you fire the pots?” he asked Joe.

“Yep.”

Eddie was staring at the first chamber, which was now full of empty shelves, with just a few objects on the top shelf that Joe had put there to be refired. “It’s big,” said Eddie, impressed.

“And that’s only the first chamber,” said Joe. “We’re about to unload the second.” He was holding the angled steel handle on the door of the second chamber, preparing to walk that door open. “You wanna see.”

Eddie gave a terse nod of his head. Lucy walked back into the kiln shed and stood beside him. Joe turned his back on them both and walked the door open all the way to the chimney.

The pots tinkled as the cold air hit their warm surfaces. Lucy and Eddie stood, transfixed by what they were seeing. “Look at all that purple,” gasped Lucy.

Joe said nothing. He liked what he saw in the front of the chamber, top to bottom, but he knew better than to assume that kind of quality made it all the way through to the back. That was the nature of wood heat; it could be very uneven. But boy, he'd take more of those purple and lavender hues if he could get them!

"'S a lot a pottery," Eddie remarked, staring at all the shelves of pots in the chamber.

"And I had about the same number in this first chamber," said Joe, shifting the milk crates and 1 x 12 board over to the second chamber. Once he got them in place, he stepped up on top of the board, and touched the surface of a lamp base on the top shelf. He pulled his hand back and gave it a quick shake. "Yeah, that's still too hot. Pass me those gloves, would you?" he said to Lucy, motioning at some blue and black welders' gloves sitting behind her on one of the shelves.

"How long d'you have to let it cool down?" Eddie asked.

"Two days."

"And they're still too hot to touch?"

Joe took the gloves from Lucy. "At the top they are. Probably not down lower."

He lifted a fairly tall, plump jar in rich raspberry tones off the top shelf and pulled on the lid. It popped cleanly away from the base. He put it back on and held the jar out in front of him, for inspection. Satisfied, he passed it to Lucy, who'd also slipped on a pair of gloves. She swiveled around and put the pot in an empty box on the sawhorses.

Eddie's eyes never left the jar. "What's that?" he asked, stepping closer to the sawhorses so he could see it better. "Like a cookie jar?"

"Could be," Joe answered, peering towards the back of the chamber now that the jar had left an opening. He saw some glazes that looked like they hadn't quite made it to temperature, just as he suspected. "Could be anything you want it to be," he added, bringing his focus back to the front and picking up the lamp base.

"Can I touch it?" asked Eddie.

"What?"

"The cookie jar."

"Oh. Sure." Joe passed Lucy the lamp base and without seeming to, watched the log truck driver reach forward and dust the surface of the cookie jar with his thick fingers.

"That's warm," Eddie remarked, like he hadn't quite believed it when Joe had said it. He continued to stare at the jar as Joe and Lucy got into a rhythm of passing and receiving objects from the top shelf. Lucy placed them in a second empty box, so as not to be in Eddie's way. "Wife might like that," he muttered at one point. Lucy looked at him, wondering if he was talking to her, but when he didn't make eye contact, she went back to work.

"How much?" he asked when Lucy swung around again to put a tall, narrow pitcher, with dark purple – almost eggplant – columbines drawn on it into the box. She looked up at him, not quite understanding his question.

"The cookie jar," he said. "How much?"

Lucy stopped and looked more closely at the jar. It was a very pretty red and red was hard to achieve in the wood firing kiln. "Fifty dollars," she said.

Eddie gave a curt nod. "You gift wrap?" he asked.

Lucy raised her eyebrows and bounced her eyes around their sockets, thinking. "In the funny pages of the newspaper," she offered finally.

"All right then," Eddie declared, pulling his wallet out of his back pocket. "Wrap that up for me." He looked up at Joe. "I'm glad that neighbor of yours couldn't aim that shotgun," he said. "My wife would been outta Christmas present."

*****

The law office was in a small, nondescript building on the other side of a parking lot from the Skagit County Superior Court. "Makes it convenient," Joe remarked to Doris, the rotund, friendly-faced lady, who was working the front desk. The only desk, as a matter of fact, in the tight quarters of the reception area. There was Doris's desk, two plain, hard-backed chairs and a coffee table.

"He's on the phone right now," Doris indicated, pointing at the hollow core door behind her, "but he shouldn't be long." She motioned to the seats and Lucy and Joe walked noiselessly over the industrial, blue-grey carpet, enjoying the feel of the cool air from outside that they still carried with them in the artificially warm indoors.

They turned at the same time and sat, the door they'd come in through in front of them and the only window in the space to their left. Lucy was closest to the window and she watched the traffic going by on Kincaid Street as Joe fished through a basket of well-thumbed magazines between their seats, looking for something to read. He nudged her in the arm as he pulled out *Guns and Ammo*.

"My kinda guy," he said, flashing the magazine cover at her. Before he could open it though, the door to Kurt Klaassen's office opened and a Marlon Brando look-alike came out; tall, broad shouldered, square jawed with wide-set, clear blue eyes. He welcomed them with a simple lift of his eyebrows before disappearing back into his office, leaving the door wide open. Joe and Lucy looked at Doris, for direction, and she nodded her head, yes.

"Take a seat," Klaassen said as they walked in, his hand open towards two seats in front of his desk. Stacks of heavy books sat on a narrow cabinet behind his desk and there was a mostly full shelf unit of encyclopedic law books on the wall to the left of the desk. Klaassen walked around and dropped into his chair, immediately pushing on the backrest so it was angled away from his desk, a movement that seemed as practiced as it was comfortable. He clasped his hands behind his head and looked at Joe and Lucy with a face devoid of emotion. "What brings you to the big bad wolf today?" he asked, his voice soft, gravelly.

"Is that what you are?" Joe responded. "A big, bad wolf?"

Klaassen's face remained impassive. "Is that what you want me to be?"

"Well sure," said Joe.

"Okay then, that's what I am."

Joe looked at Lucy, who looked back at him, both of them caught a little off-guard. "In that case," said Lucy, making eye contact with the lawyer, "we want you to huff and puff and blow our neighbor's house down."

"All right!" said Klaassen, like this was the answer he'd been hoping for. He sprang forward, the backrest of the office chair pinging to upright behind him, and grabbed a legal pad and pen off his desk. He leaned back in the chair again, propped his right knee on the edge of the desk and balanced the legal pad on his thigh.

"Tell me why I should blow your neighbor's house down," he said, pen poised.

Joe and Lucy stumbled through the explanation together of what had happened out at the septic tank, handing over copies of Joe's court paperwork, entitling him to use and maintain the septic system and the summons from the Prosecuting Attorney's office. They finished with a brief mention of Hilda's spying and the visit from the County inspector.

Kurt Klaassen took copious notes as they talked and when they stopped, he dropped the tablet back on his desk with the pen and asked, "What did you do to her to piss her off?"

"Nothing!" Joe argued but Lucy laid a hand on his forearm, seeing the glint in the lawyer's eyes.

Klaassen's face became more serious as Lucy and Joe focused on him, both on edge about what he might tell them. "Here's what we're going to do," he said, his tone very serious. "I'm going to start by sending a letter to your neighbor that says - Fuck You. Stern letter to follow."

Joe tipped his head back in his chair and roared with laughter. "How much is that gonna cost me?" he asked.

"I don't know," said Klaassen. "Got any guns you want to trade?"

Joe winced, sucking air noisily between his teeth and tipping one side of his face down, so it would be obvious this was an idea that didn't appeal to him.

Now it was Kurt Klaassen's turn to laugh. "Gotcha!" he said. He pulled the summons towards him on the desk and glanced at it as he said, "I don't know how much any of this is going to cost but I doubt it will get too involved. I'll look more into why Deputy Sigglin –" He made eye contact with Joe. "- not one of my favorite Deputies –

why he took the complaint in the first place and maybe I'll talk to your witness. But I think this'll get thrown out before it even goes to court."

He sat back in his chair again and folded his hands over his stomach. "And if I can't get that done because it's based on bullshit, then I've got a favor coming to me from one of the Prosecuting Attorneys. Her teenage son had an interesting side business going in their garage and I scared him out of it." He nodded his chin toward the summons. "I think she can make this go away."

"That's great!" said Joe, smiling broadly. He looked at Lucy, who was also smiling, and took a hold of her hand. "That's really great."

"You're a potter, right?" asked the lawyer.

"I am," said Joe.

Kurt Klaassen sprang forward again, getting down to business. "I fixed up an outbuilding for my wife to use as a writing studio. Maybe you could make something for it?"

The way he said it suggested he had something in mind and Joe sat forward in his chair, spreading his hands out in the air, palms up.

"Tell me," he said.

*****

Hilda was up at the little white church in Rockport when she heard the news. She wasn't a regular church goer but every year, on the third Sunday in December, this church had a carol singing service, with a potluck feast of cookies and cake, warm spiced cider and hot chocolate downstairs afterwards.

The church was a small, wood-frame building with only about a dozen pews facing a simple table, that acted as an altar. Behind that sat three tall windows, narrowing at the top to form a peaked arch. And through the windows was a picture perfect view across the fields of Star Route Farm, up the glacial green of the Skagit River to the snow-covered mountains that formed Boston Basin.

A storm was blowing through the valley when Hilda slipped into the almost full church, and long threads of rain angled across the windows, obscuring that view but adding a level of coziness to the hundred-year-old timbers of the building. Hilda had slung a long, tan raincoat over her red velvet dress and she held onto the lapels and shook it, standing just inside the door, shedding rainwater on the mat below her feet.

People were chatting in the pews, waiting for the service to begin. Hilda noticed that the local librarian and part-time pianist, Betty Loiselle, had taken her place at the old, upright just inside the door. Betty must have sensed Hilda's eyes on her because she turned around, grinned and mouthed "Hi" at Hilda. Hilda lifted her hand in a semblance of a wave, then walked down between the pews and found an opening. The couple sitting at the end of the pew angled their legs inwards and Hilda edged past them, trying not to touch either of them with her legs. Then she sat down in the opening on the wooden pew.

It was when she leaned forward to collect the insert in the hymnal, listing the carols they would be singing, that she heard the English accent. She stopped, her hand on the hymnal, and peeked up, without moving her shoulders. Lucy was sitting in the pew in front of her. Hilda bristled at the thought that her one moment of seasonal peace should be violated by the presence of the enemy. Then curiosity bumped her irritation sideways.

There was something about the furtive way Lucy was communicating with her neighbor that stirred Hilda's inclination to snoop. She sat back and made a show of sliding first one arm, then the other out of her raincoat. This allowed her to see that the person Lucy was whispering to was Brenda Mackey, a retired, psychiatric social worker who lived part-time in the Upper Skagit. Connors' five-year-old daughter, Maddie, was on the other side of Lucy. The child was yakking and giggling with another little girl but the way Lucy's head was bowed towards Brenda's suggested to Hilda that Lucy didn't want the child overhearing.

Hilda let her raincoat slip down, then lifted it out from under her, folding it on the empty section of pew to her left mostly so she could scoot right and remain safely hidden from Lucy. She bowed forward again, and pulled the narrow tongue of paper out of the hymnal. She stayed forward, staring down at the list of carols inside a motif of holly, pretending to read while really listening to Lucy's hurried conversation.

"We found out yesterday, when Erica brought her to the pottery party. The news really put a damper on that event, I'll tell you!"

"Oh I'm sure it did."

"The funny thing is, Joe had been talking about wanting us to move to Montana."

Hilda's heart lifted. Connors was moving to Montana? She might be in luck this holiday season after all.

"And now he's got a reason?"

"I hope not! I told him he can move there, but he'll have to do it without me."

"You don't like the idea of moving to Montana?"

"I don't like the idea of living anywhere where it gets colder in the winter and hotter in the summer. I'm a temperate climate kind of girl."

"What did Joe say to that?"

There was amusement in Lucy's voice when she answered. "Well he's not moving if that's what you mean."

Hilda's spirits deflated as Brenda chuckled. Then she heard Lucy's voice again.

"No, he said he's glad I know that about myself."

"So what's he going to do?"

"About Maddie?" There was a moment of silence and Hilda wondered if Lucy were checking over her shoulder, to make sure the little girl wasn't listening. By the amount of girlish squealing Hilda could hear, she wasn't, but Lucy lowered her voice anyway.

"There's not much he can do. Except hope that this lawyer we're talking to can put together a parenting plan that allows for long visits."

"You're talking to a lawyer now?"

"Because of our neighbor we are. Yes."

"How's that going?"

"How's what going?"

"The problem with your neighbor?"

"Oh."

Hilda heard a rustle. She lowered her head further, hoping that if anyone were watching, they'd take her bow as an indication she was praying. When Lucy spoke again, she wasn't whispering, which surprised Hilda a little. "It's a bit of a non-issue at this point."

Hilda frowned. What did she mean?

"You solved the retail sales problem?"

"No, not quite. We filed the paperwork and now we've just got to wait for the public hearing. But I'm sure we'll get it because the main thing the County wanted to know was the environmental impact of the business. And since we're only applying for the right to make sales, the questions boiled down to our impact on traffic, which, of course, is negligible."

They wanted to know about environmental impact, thought Hilda. She could tell them about environmental impact. She'd seen the smoke coming out of the chimney to the kiln! The County should know about that. She heard Lucy speak again.

"But when you asked about how it was going with our neighbor, I thought you meant the assault charge. *That's* the part that's a non-issue."

Hilda's head popped up, she was so surprised by this news. Fortunately both Lucy and Brenda were facing front. She stayed leaning forward but she didn't bow her head again.

"Your neighbor retracted the complaint?"

"No. The Prosecuting Attorney's office threw it out."

Hilda gasped, then slapped the carol list insert over her mouth to stop any other reactions from popping out. But Lucy must not have heard her, because she turned to Brenda and said, for the whole world to hear, "They said it wasn't a criminal matter."

Hilda's mouth dropped open.

"Can she take it up in Civil Court?" Brenda asked.

Betty Mackey played some introductory chords on the piano and people shuffled in their seats. "Let's hope not," Lucy whispered as she and Brenda and everyone else in the church stood, singing, *"J-oy to the World...."*

Everyone except Hilda.

*****

The wind had died down but it was still raining steadily when Lucy pulled in the driveway after the carol singing. Joe was sliding two parts of an extension ladder back together out in front of the house and pottery shop and Lucy could see, even though he was bent over the ladder on the ground, that he was scowling. She put the ladder and his scowl together and wondered if the storm had caused a leak in the roof for his mood to have soured so but when she peered up at the twin gables on the house, she saw that he'd strung Christmas lights back and forth up into the peaks. That was one of his favorite things to do, put up Christmas lights, so why the bad mood? She couldn't see any lights twinkling on the electrical cords so maybe he'd gone to all that trouble and risk, climbing 30 feet up in the air when he didn't like heights, only to discover the lights didn't work.

She waited patiently in the driveway, while Maddie and her friend, Harper, giggle-sang "We Wish You A Merry Christmas" in the backseat. She kept waiting for Joe to look up, so she might sweeten his mood with a smile, but once he had the ladder back together, he yanked it up off the ground onto his shoulder and marched around to the side of the house with no glance in Lucy's direction. She navigated cautiously past the dogs, who were circling the Pinto ready to greet her, and parked next to Joe's truck.

The girls stopped singing and began fussing with their seatbelts, to get free, while trying not to drop the paper plates full of cookies that they'd brought back from the potluck.

"Do you want me to take you home?" Lucy asked Harper, looking at the 7-year old in the rear view mirror. Harper was Jimmy and Laura's daughter so she only lived across the pasture, behind Hilda's house.

"My mom said she'd come get me," Harper informed Lucy.

Joe appeared on the passenger side of the car, and Lucy knew he'd seen them when they pulled in but wanted to put the ladder away on the side of the house before joining them. He opened the passenger side door and flipped the seat forward. He leaned in to help Maddie with her seat belt.

"I've got it, daddy," said the little redhead, who was pulling her arms out of the belt that she had, indeed, undone by herself. She thrust the paper plate up towards Joe. "Look what I got for you."

"Cookies!!" he exclaimed. "D'you want me to hold them while you climb out of the car."

"No, I'm fine," she chirruped.

Maddie stood up, clutching the small paper plate of cookies, and Joe reached in and lifted her out of the vehicle. Then he did the same for Harper. Lucy climbed out of the driver's side, closed the door and turned around in time to see both girls lift their plates high into the air, squealing, as the dogs showed up next to them, very interested in what they were carrying.

"No!" yelled Maddie.

"No!" yelled Harper.

Both girls ran up the front steps, trying to get away from the dogs, who just trotted along beside them, enjoying the race. Once on the porch, the girls burst through the front door, slamming it shut behind them, leaving the dogs on the outside, looking in.

As soon as they were inside, Joe turned to Lucy and exploded.

"Get a load of this!" he said, his right hand out in the air, horizontal. "Erica calls, while you were out, to talk to Maddie. I tell her she's not home, I'll have her call back later, but while I have you on the phone, what's the best time for you to meet Maddie at the airport in Billings? And you know what she says?" He took a breath, his eyes fixed on Lucy's, glaring through the rain which wasn't making a dent in his fiery mood. "She says, Maddie's not flying to Billings. *I'm* going to drive her."

He jabbed his upper chest with his index finger to be sure Lucy knew who he meant when he said, "*I'm.*" She knew better than to say anything at this point. That would be like trying to put a finger on a lit firework to stop it from rocketing into the sky. She'd surely get burned.

"I say, what're you crazy?! I ain't driving her to Billings."

"How far is that?" Lucy was still trying to come to terms with how the vastness of the USA.

"A thousand miles or better. And in the worst of conditions, with all the mountain passes and snowfall in Idaho and Montana! I told her there's no way I can afford to take a week off work or however long it's going to take me to drive all the way to Billings! Plus my truck gets shitty gas mileage and on top of that we're going to have to stay in motels 'cause I can't make Maddie do day and night in a truck in the middle of winter and where am I s'posed to get the money for that? I tell her, it's not an option. Period. Don't even go there! So she starts with the tears and the – oh but you can't, oh but it's not safe, oh but I'm scared – *bull*shit, and I tell her, that's fine, then she can stay here, 'cause I never wanted her to move to Billings in the first place!"

This was the crux of it, Lucy thought to herself. He just really didn't want his little girl to move so far away. What had he told her? That it was a father's job to protect his children and he couldn't protect her if she was so far away.

"So then she starts in with the - You'd better not keep her there. I'll have you arrested – threats and I told her, fine, if you want her driven from here to Billings then *you* come and get her."

"What did she say to that?"

"I don't remember. Some blah blah blah about how she didn't have to let Maddie come and visit me. Makes me real glad we're talking to a lawyer. Maybe if we get a parenting plan on record, it'll put an end to the threats of me not being able to see my kid again." The minute the words were out of his mouth he threw his hands up into the air and turned a half circle then back, exasperated.

"Why would I even think that?! Look at all the legal paperwork I've got on my septic tank and it's not worth diddly squat when my neighbor decides to vandalize it."

Lucy really wanted to reach out and soothe away his worries but they were way too big to mollify with a rub on the arm. And they were justified. Court orders might give him some rights but if the other party chose to ignore those rights, there wasn't much he could do about it, short of taking them back to court. And who had the money to keep running in and out of court?

No, the best he could hope for was that Erica *wanted* him to spend time with Maddie, which so far seemed to be the case but there was always something. Something that made it not easy. Lucy sighed. She watched her neighbor, Laura, wishing Harper's dad would spend more time with his daughter and she watched Joe wishing he could be allowed more time with Maddie, and she wondered why there had to be these inequities. But then she supposed if the couples involved could work out their differences, they never would have broken up in the first place.

Her thoughts were interrupted by the sound of a car, out on the highway, smacking into a big puddle of rainwater. Lucy watched a long wave spray up into the air then hit the guardrail on its way down. The car kept moving but slower than before. Lucy peered at the vehicle; it looked like Hilda's. She'd noticed Hilda hiding behind her up at the church but then lost sight of her at the potluck.

"The thing that gets my goat," yelled Joe, pulling Lucy back to him. "Is how last minute all this has to be. She must've known she was moving to Montana long before we even planned this Christmas visit with Maddie but did she tell me? No-oo. She's gotta ruin my good time with my daughter by blindsiding me with the news last minute, so I'll spend my time agonizing over when I might see her again. And just so I don't get it in my head that maybe, *maybe* we can make this work, she has to drop the bombshell that the quickest and easiest way for us to get to each other isn't a possibility. Plus," he threw out, his hands springing apart in the air, like he'd just been struck by this idea, "she's not giving me time at the end of our two weeks to drive her back. No-oo! She wants her back by January 3rd, as agreed, so I'm gonna spend half our visit on the road." He looked down at the ground, his jaw clenched, and Lucy could see the muscles in his checks flex as he gritted his teeth. When he looked up at her his eyes were filled with a mix of bitterness and sorrow. "I think this whole thing is a ploy," he said, "to make sure I won't *want* to see Maddie again. And the worst part is, the way I feel right now, maybe I won't!"

Lucy opened her mouth to speak but he vibrated a warning hand in the air. "Don't! Don't even go there," he said. "'Cause you don't know how painful it is." But she did, she wanted to tell him. She surely did. Only he didn't give her a chance to say anything. Instead, she watched his shoulders open up and his body begin to turn, an indication that he was coming into his final word on the subject. "Painful and *expensive*!" he snapped. "I'm glad I've only got the one kid 'cause I sure can't afford any more."

Lucy felt like she'd been slapped. She wanted to argue that he was good at second chances and why not allow himself that opportunity with another child but his anger was like the rolling storm clouds; she just had to wait it out. She watched him march away, the gravel on the ground crunching under the weight of his displeasure.

"Where're you going?" she asked.

"To light the sauna," he barked, and rounded the corner by the side of the house, then disappeared.

*****

Hilda drove as fast as she dared given how much water was on the highway. At first she'd been shocked that the Prosecuting Attorney's office hadn't seen fit to let *her* know that they weren't moving forward with her case against Connors, but as the carol singing around her melded into white noise in her head, she realized that she'd been so busy looking for a road builder over the last few days that she hadn't gone through her mail. She'd picked it up from her post office box in Concrete but it was such a pile of Christmas catalogues and bills that she'd dumped it on her kitchen table without paying too much attention. She visualized the envelopes that she'd leafed through briefly before deciding they could wait; was there one that said Skagit County Prosecuting Attorney on the return address? Or Skagit County Sheriff's Office? She got a flicker of something with a bunch of letters above the address, something that she hadn't really paid that much attention to because she'd been distracted by a fluffy pair of moccasins on the front of one of the catalogues. Maybe that was something from the Prosecuting Attorney.

She found that possibility nagging at her as she sipped warm apple cider and nibbled on a reindeer-decorated cookie, dodging eye contact with Lucy by putting herself in the midst of some ladies from her knitting group and pretending to take part in their conversation.

Hilda was eager to get home and go through that stack of mail but she was so determined not to bump into her neighbor's new wife that she waited until she saw Lucy head out, a rug rat at each elbow. Hilda watched the clock on the back wall of the church basement as she smiled and nodded at the ladies around her. She wanted to give it ten minutes, so as to avoid running into Lucy in the parking area, but that just seemed to make the clock slow down. She waited as the minutes ticked excruciatingly by and once they hit the ten-minute mark she fluttered out as quickly as she could.

But now that Hilda was on the road, she wondered if she shouldn't have waited a little longer. The road from the church let out onto Highway 20 in a section that was just a few feet from the Skagit River and not only was the river high because of the non-stop rain, but there were numerous creeks overtopping their banks, making rivulets across the highway. Hilda was worried that one of them might pick up her aging Honda Civic and flush it – and her - into the river, but she couldn't stop now. The rain might keep coming till it trapped her up in Rockport, and the last thing she wanted was to get trapped. Instead she held her breath every time she drove through one of the crosscurrents, startling herself with the bump her car made when it hit the water and the rooster-tails it sprayed up into the air on both sides of the vehicle.

Then Highway 20 curved around to the right, away from its parallel with the river and in toward Rockport State Park. The road was still wet, but not nearly as dangerous, and Hilda picked up speed heading home. She got up to 50 mph between the tall, old growth trees of the State Park, noticing how they shrouded the highway, making the afternoon seem even darker than it already was from the rainstorm, and then she let her speedometer climb to 60 as she rounded the corner to head down the hill towards her place.

As she sailed down past the pottery, her eye was caught by the sight of Connors out in his driveway, railing at his new wife. Hilda rubber-necked until her car slammed into a patch of standing water and briefly hydroplaned. First she felt terror then immediate relief as the Civic stayed in the grooves of the well-traveled highway. She braked, and pulled into her driveway.

Still driving a little too fast in her eagerness to get to her mail, she bumped the Civic through the many potholes in the gravel driveway, splashing rainwater towards the fir trees on both sides of her, and pulled up in front of the small cabin that used to be a logging bunkhouse. She climbed out and looked up before closing her door, realizing that the rain had finally subsided.

It sounded strangely quiet now that nothing was pouring down from the sky, hitting against the branches of the trees before splashing down to the ground. And the air looked lighter, less dreary, now that the clouds had past through the valley. She slammed the door to the Honda Civic and marched towards her front door, being careful to avoid stepping in the bigger puddles on the ground. She had her good shoes on, after all; she didn't want to get those wet.

Once inside, Hilda made a beeline for the kitchen table and grabbed up the mail that she'd left there. She flipped each piece towards her, looking for something, anything, that might reveal what she'd overheard at the church, and stopped when she saw the gold Sheriff's star up in the left hand corner of an envelope. She dropped the rest of the mail back onto the table and ripped it open. She didn't have to read far before she caught the thrust of it; they weren't going to prosecute Connors for assault. It was a civil matter not a criminal matter.

Hilda thought about this as she dropped the letter back down onto the table and looked across the pasture at Connors' house. She still had an option to take him to court and maybe she would, but she'd prefer somebody else to have to incur the cost. She ruminated on this as she stared at his cedar shake roof, angling into the sky. Who could she get to pursue him now, if not the Sheriff? Her eyes drifted up, to the smoke coming from his chimney, and she watched it submit gently to the residual low pressure and move forward over the top of the gables. She stared for a moment, lost in wondering what she was going to do, then turned to stoke up her own woodstove.

As she turned, she noticed another plume of smoke, coming from the back of Connors' property. She watched it float horizontal above the property line then disappear behind the big cedar tree in the center of her pasture. Her eyes switched right, expecting to see it reemerge on the downhill side of the cedar. When it didn't, she assumed the smoke had dissipated into the environment.

And that assumption gave her an idea.

*****

The storm had let up, both inside and out, and Joe and Lucy sat wrapped in towels, on the porch of the sauna, zoning on the moisture-laden trees in front of them. It was cold, and steam from their bodies wafted up past the flickering lights of the candle lanterns hanging from the log beam above their heads. The dogs sat on either side of them, their noses occasionally bumping the air above them in the interminable quest for passing scents.

Lucy was lost in the drip, drip, dripping of accumulated rainwater coming from a thick patch of spongy moss on the trunk of a burly maple tree, while Joe was focused on the sporadic splashes from saturated lichen on a leaning length of vine maple. It wasn't that they were seeing what they were staring at in the candlelit dusk of the evening, so much as hearing it. And in their post-sauna, meditative states, it sounded like a rainforest rhapsody, with the gush of the creek to their right like brushes on cymbals, and the popping of firewood burning in the sauna stove adding the occasional drumbeat.

Joe spoke first, the sauna having quelled the storm inside him too. "That took the starch out of me," he said.

"Mmmm hmmm."

They fell silent again and both watched a leaf on a salal bush, overheavy with accumulate raindrops, tip so the water trickled down onto the ground.

"If only I could keep my life in this kind of balance, I'd be all set."

"What kind of balance? From the sauna you mean?"

"No, I mean nature's balance. Look at that," he exclaimed, pulling his right arm out of his towel and arcing his hand, palm up, towards all that was in front of them. "All that rainfall and it just gets sucked right up by the earth."

The thought made Lucy smile. "That always amazes me. You know that ditch at the side of the road, between here and the State Park?"

"Farmer Mike's place?" asked Joe. "Where the hang gliders land coming down from Sauk?"

"That's it. That was full to the brim with water earlier when I drove past it. But I know if I go back there an hour from now, it will all be gone."

"And that's what I want," Joe stated, with a definitive nod. "I want all the problems in my life to be gone. At the same time. None of this, I solve one problem – like with Hilda – only to have another rear its ugly head. But I can never seem to get that balance working for me."

Lucy chuckled as she remembered something. "We had this macro-economics professor at NYU who told us once that the economy is like a stainless steel bowl with a ball bearing inside it. And the ball bearing's moving back and forth and side to side." She drew her right arm out of her towel and showed the motion of the ball bearing with her index finger in the air.

"And economic theory is all about trying to find the steady state. But it's a misnomer because there really is no such thing as a steady state. Not only is the bowl curved, so it's hard to find a spot for the ball bearing to settle, but even if it manages to hold steady for a moment, something inevitably comes along and jogs the bowl, starting the motion all over again." She slipped her arm back inside the towel, to keep it from getting cold. "I thought that was a pretty good analogy for life."

"So what you're saying is I might never get my shit together."

Lucy smiled without looking at him. "Something like that."

Joe stood up, letting his towel drop to the slatted cedar under their feet. He stepped on it and began to get dressed.

"And to be honest," Lucy went on, still staring out in front of her. "I think we do better when we have something to struggle against."

"You and me?"

"No humans in general. You look at the things some people have to overcome to live their lives, and all you can see is their will to succeed. It's inspiring." She pulled the towel tighter around her. "I think people tend to languish if life is too easy."

"I wouldn't mind a little of that languishing."

Now Lucy laughed out loud. "You'd hate it. You're a worker bee if I ever met one! And I bet what's out there," she pointed at the woods in front of the sauna, "is major chaos right now. We just don't know it because nature doesn't get loud about it the way we do."

She stood up and started dressing, too.

"Yeah, I got pretty loud earlier," he admitted ruefully.

Lucy knew this was as close as he was going to get to an apology. "As long as you feel better, I suppose." She didn't want to start an argument, not after such a rejuvenating sauna, but she did want to suggest that his venting was better for him than for her. She buttoned the front of her 501s and added, "I was thinking, maybe there's a compromise to be had with Erica."

"Like what?" Joe was dressed now and sat back down on the bench to tie his bootlaces.

"Like maybe she can drive part way and meet you, so you don't have to do the full distance."

He nodded, still leaning over his knees. "That's a possibility, I s'pose."

"Or," said Lucy, pushing her arms into her sweatshirt. "Is there a train from here to Billings?"

Joe twisted his face to look at her. "Now that's a good idea."

"Then you wouldn't have to drive."

"And Maddie wouldn't have to fly."

"And it would be a lot quicker than driving."

Joe slapped his hands on his knees and stood up, revived. "I'll call Amtrak tomorrow, see what they say." He walked around the small porch of the sauna, and threw another piece of wood into the stove for Pete, who was down at the house, watching the girls.

Lucy was dressed now too and she picked up her towel and threw it around her neck, enjoying the feel of it against her still slightly damp skin. That had become one of her favorite things to do, put her towel around her neck after a sauna. She heard Joe close the door on the sauna woodstove and then he was in front of her.

"You ready?" he asked.

*****

They wandered down the narrow trail side by side, shoulders and hips bumping against each other, until it opened up at the top of the grassy, quarter acre Joe liked to call the playground. It was dark now and the night air felt crisp against the warm skin on their faces. They passed under an overhanging cedar tree growing out of a downed log, and could smell the rich, loamy aroma of the duff under their feet. When they emerged, down by the garden, the night sky opened up above them, with a smattering of stars and a half-moon, soft-focused by a delicate overlay of mist. They walked down past the studio and veered right by the loafing shed, headed for the back porch of the house. Joe stopped and turned to Lucy.

"Want to go look at the Christmas lights?" he said.

"Sure."

He took her hand in his and scooted her out past the cherry tree and down the driveway almost to the highway before he spun her around to face the house. Lucy gazed up at the fairy lights of red and green and pink and yellow zigzagging in the gables to look like two Christmas trees suspended in the sky. "Whaddya think?" he asked.

"I think I married a very creative fellow," Lucy replied.

An owl hooted in a tree nearby, and they both turned towards the clear, echoic sound, hoping to hear it again. In the distance a siren seemed to answer the call and they both turned again, this time in the opposite direction.

"Is that a fire truck?" asked Joe as they watched the flashing red lights rise over the brow of the hill. The big lumbering vehicle surfaced amid the lights and Lucy and Joe stared at it, like a compulsion, waiting for it to pass. But as it got closer to their driveway it veered hard towards them.

They both stepped back in surprise.

*****

The white fire truck with the overly large bumper filled with orange caution cones came to a stop alongside them, dieseling loudly. A swarm of yellow-clad firefighters in hard hats dropped from both sides and started to span out across the front yard. Joe knew each member of the volunteer crew, from their day jobs in the community, but he could tell by the way they were moving that this was not a social call.

"You got the kiln going?" Charlie Vangilder, the local fire chief, yelled over the noise of the truck.

Joe shook his head no.

Then random yells: "D'you see it?"

"Look for the flames."

"Check behind the house."

"Why can't we smell it?"

Joe watched them, baffled. What were they…?

As the crew jogged this way and that around the house, Vangilder trotted back over to Joe. "An anonymous female caller said you were burning tires here at your place, maybe in the kiln."

"Goddamn Hilda!" snapped Joe. "Why would she even say something like that when it's so easy to disprove?! I'm not burning any tires!"

Some of the crew had stopped jogging and were wandering back towards Vangilder.

"Yeah, I think we know that now," the fire chief told Joe. "Have you got *any* fires burning on your place right now?"

"Just the woodstove in the house." It was too dark to see the smoke coming out of the chimney but Joe pointed anyway.

"And the sauna stove," added Lucy, looking at Joe.

"Oh yep, there is that one. At the back of the property," he informed Vangilder, as he pointed again. "Straight up this driveway to the creek."

"Go check it out," the fire chief ordered two of the crew and they trotted away, their big rubber boots plunking on the gravel driveway and squelching through the puddles.

"Got any dinner for us?" Vangilder asked with a smile. "Mine's getting cold at home."

Joe threw his hands out at his sides, genuinely upset for them. "I'm sorry, guys."

"That's okay," said Vangilder pleasantly. "It's what we do. Good luck tomorrow though."

"Tomorrow? Why, what's happening tomorrow?"

"The woman said she left a message on the Air Pollution Agency's hotline before she called us, turning you in for the kiln. I expect they'll be out here first thing."

Joe sucked one side of his mouth into his cheek and rolled his eyes and his head in a circle of craziness. Then he looked directly across at Hilda's house in the distance.

"Well Merry fucking Christmas to me!" he yelled.

Spring

Chapter 10

It had been three months since Lucy submitted her application for permanent residency to the INS and she was beginning to worry. She'd already bought the tickets to go to England with Joe in May and if she didn't get her green card in time, she'd be stuck for an answer. She opened the top drawer in one of the filing cabinets holding up her fir plank desk and rummaged around in the back for the large brown envelope. She'd carefully kept all the immigration paperwork in this one envelope and was pretty sure that somewhere, in among the instructions, were suggested times for how long she'd have to wait for each step. She heard Joe downstairs, walking his breakfast dishes to the sink in the kitchen, and assumed it must be close to 8 am already.

She found the envelope and pulled it out, letting everything slide into her left hand as she drew it towards her. Without thinking about it, she dropped the empty envelope down onto the open drawer, then the copy of her completed application along with a copy of the money order she'd made out to the INS, and found herself staring down at the instructions. Her eyes scanned them, looking for the section that talked about dates. She turned the page, hearing the radio theme song play out the top of the hour downstairs, and found the section she'd been looking for; When Can You Expect to Hear from the INS?

Underneath she read the words, *You should receive a date for your interview with an Immigration officer approximately eight weeks after you submit your application.* Eight weeks, she said out loud. That's what she remembered. She lifted her head from the paperwork, and let her mind turn the problem as she stared out at the mist covering Jackman Ridge. The sky was dark for so early in the morning, presaging another dreary March day.

"I'm going over to work now," Joe called up the stairs and Lucy knew he was picking up a wool shirt from one of the hooks to wear on the short journey from the house to the studio.

"Okay," she said absently, her focus really on her completed application. She looked at the date she'd put on it – 12/12/87 - so then why the delay? Was there a problem with her physical? The technician at the hospital said her chest x-ray looked fine and her blood tests came back negative for HIV/AIDS so then what could be wrong? Unless that doctor made a problem for her.

He was a gaunt redhead with freckles and glasses, about ten years her senior, she guessed, and he'd been kind of brusque with her. She assumed it was because he didn't prefer to do the INS physicals, maybe because there were so many of them, at least by the looks of the waiting room, or maybe because he could only charge $50 as stipulated by the INS. Lucy didn't have much experience with the medical profession in the US but from all she'd heard, $50 wasn't much to pay for a visit with a doctor. So she let him poke and prod her in his cold, officious way, thinking he probably wanted to get it over with just as much as she did, right up until the moment when he told her to bend over so he could give her an internal. Lucy bristled. He was going to give her an internal examination without a nurse present? Not if she could help it. "My husband's out in the waiting room," she informed the doctor.

"We don't need him in here," the doc replied, in a tone that suggested he didn't want to discuss it.

Lucy bristled again. She was pretty sure that the recognized standard of care dictated that a male doctor have a female chaperone when giving a woman an intimate examination. But this doctor was holding the file to her future in America and giving her a look that said she'd better not try to hold him to any standards. She bent over, reluctantly, all the while asking herself how this would feel, say, to a young virgin from India, who wasn't supposed to be touched by men outside her caste.

Now Lucy wondered if her mere intimation to the doctor that there should be somebody else present while he gave her a gynecological examination had caused him to write something in her medical file that would stop her from becoming a permanent resident? But then why wouldn't the INS notify her of this? She looked at the instructions again and found a number to call.

She headed downstairs, picked up the phone, dialed the number and sat down in the rocker, preparing to wait. But someone picked up after the third ring. Lucy was pleasantly surprised; maybe calling early in the morning was the way to do it, she thought to herself. "I need to talk to someone about why I haven't received a date for my interview yet," she explained immediately to the woman on the phone.

"What's it an application for?" the woman asked.

"Permanent residency."

"Okay what's your name and date of birth."

Lucy gave her the information then waited while the woman put her on hold and looked. She came back saying, "You haven't received your interview date because you haven't had your physical, so we can't process your application."

"But I have had my physical," Lucy countered.

"Then you need to call the doctor's office where you had it and ask that they send your file on to us because they haven't done that."

"All right," said Lucy, feeling an edge of irritation that her suspicion had been right. "Will it still be eight weeks before I hear from you with an interview date?" she asked. "I want to go to England in May."

"No, you should be able to make that," the woman told her. "As soon as we get your physical you'll be approved for an interview."

"Thanks," said Lucy and hung up. She sat back in the rocking chair and stared up to the ceiling above her. She was pretty sure she had a receipt somewhere for her trip to the doctor's office but where? The ceiling was made out of thick, tongue-and-groove cedar that Joe had reclaimed from a church that was being torn down. He'd left it out on the ground outside, uncovered, before he installed it and it got rained on, which had darkened the overall look of the cedar and left water stains in places. Every time Joe put his feet up on the couch and looked at the ceiling he talked about wanting to paint the cedar, or stain it with something that would lighten the watermarks. But Lucy kept thinking she wanted to sand it. Be a pretty big job, she said to herself, looking at the lengths of cedar between the cross beams. But it would so much prettier to expose the honey browns of the cedar and it would probably make the ceiling lighter if the wood were sanded. She didn't have another show coming up in the short term; just the one she was negotiating with the college in Mount Vernon for next fall. The Tulip Festival wasn't for another month and the shop was slow right now so she needed something to occupy her time. Maybe this was it. Although it would probably be better to sand the cedar in the summer months, when she could leave the doors open to vent the sawdust.

While she was thinking all this, another part of her brain was running through the places she might have left the receipt from her physical and settled on the visual of it being in that big brown envelope with all the rest of her immigration paperwork. She jumped up, and headed back upstairs. She picked up the envelope, opened the top of it with her fingers and tipped it upside down. Sure enough a paper receipt dropped out. She picked it up and saw the name, address and phone number of the doctor's office.

Downstairs she went again, thinking they'd probably be open this early in the morning. She dialed the number and a receptionist answered. Lucy explained her problem.

"Well the person that deals with that isn't in the office today. But I'll tell her when she comes in and if you leave me your number she'll call you back tomorrow."

Lucy obliged and hung up the phone again. She heard Max and Maggie barking outside and looked out the sliding glass door to see them running down from the studio towards the front of the house. Somebody must be here, she thought. She got up and looked through the panes of glass in the front door. It was Sonny, come for his morning chat with Joe. Lucy headed into the bathroom for her shower.

*****

Joe was doing a low relief drawing on a piece of slab work when he spotted Sonny's baseball cap through the window in the rolling barn door to his studio. He pulled a bead of clay off the end of the pointed dental tool he was using to draw with and motioned for Sonny to come in. Sonny rolled the door open and stepped over the threshold, his red baseball shorts contrasting boldly with the gingery hair on his legs, a fact that registered in Joe's artistic brain. "How's it going?" Sonny said his voice nasal, breathy, as he walked across the studio towards the wedging table where Joe was working.

"Pretty good. I thought you were pouring concrete today?" Joe replied, squinting across at the clock in the corner above the clay mixer. He wasn't at his usual drawing station, at the end of the wedging table, but standing in the middle of one side, facing the door, a faded, pink and white butcher's apron tied around his waist.

Sonny plopped down in the chair at the drawing station, so he was facing Joe, and propped his right ankle on his left knee. "I hurt my leg," he said to explain his absence from work.

"You did?" Joe questioned, then glanced across at Sonny's leg and saw a long, wide, angry gash that ran from his knee down to the top of his white, athletic socks. "Oh, you sure did!" he exclaimed, thinking how the dark brownish red of the wound made yet another color variation on a theme. "How'd you do that?!"

"Dropped a beam on it."

"Ouch."

"It's okay," shrugged Sonny. "Looks worse than it is."

Joe cleaned the clay off his drawing tool again with a glance back at Sonny's leg. "Looks terrible."

Sonny avoided further discussion by nodding at Joe's project.

"Whacha you doing?"

"Making a wall piece for my lawyer's wife's writing studio."

"Oh."

Joe could feel Sonny staring at him but their relationship was so easy, it didn't feel intrusive. It just felt normal. He decided to explain what he had laid out in front of him. "She does stained glass as well as writes so I shaped it like a stained glass window in a church and now I'm carving panes into it, with a view out to the mountains."

"What's that curved bit across the panes?" Sonny asked, his neck stretched up so he could see the slab Joe was drawing on.

"That?" asked Joe, pointing at the rectangle he'd carved with curls at both ends. "That's a scroll. You know, a writing scroll? And then here," he pointed to the right of the area that looked like a section of parchment paper. "I'm going to draw a quill." He moved his hands back and forth over the clay, to suggest the image wasn't definite yet. "The lawyer wanted to hang her a shingle that defined her space, so that's what I'm trying for."

"Oh." Sonny relaxed his neck back down. "How's that going?"

"I only just started."

"No, I meant with the lawyer."

"Fine, I guess." Joe said, bending forward to draw the quill. "We've got an appointment with him this week, to go over this civil suit Hilda's filed."

"Is he going to talk to Eddie Eldridge?"

Joe glanced up. "Klaassen?"

Sonny nodded.

Joe looked back down at the quill he was outlining in the clay. "I think he did already. He wanted to hear what Eddie saw before he responded to Hilda's attorney." His speech slowed as he became more intent on his drawing, making steady, confident grooves in the clay. "That's maybe one of the things he wants to tells us when we see him." He straightened up, looking at the quill, then bent over again and drew evenly spaced lines away from the center, to make it look like a feather. He straightened up again and switched out the pointed dental tool for one in which he'd created a 90-degree bend at the point. "Plus he wants me to sign the parenting plan."

"How'd that turn out?"

"Don't ask," grumbled Joe. He bent forward again and used the flat end of the dental tool to carve the clay away around his drawing, to leave it in relief. "He just kept telling me to roll over and give Erica what she wanted. You can imagine how I felt about *that*! But I did it." Joe shook his head slowly side to side, his teeth clenched in a tight smile, like he was under duress, then added, "Like a good boy. So I can see my daughter."

There was a moment of quiet between them, filled by the gentle sounds of an acoustic guitar and a fiddle playing some toe-tapping bluegrass on the radio. Joe continued to cut away from the clay for a smooth, clean background, pulling the excess off the tool and dropping it into a bucket on the floor next to him, while Sonny looked around the 20 x 24 space. "Boy, you've got a lot of pots in here," he said after he'd seen everything.

"Yeah." Joe stood up, and let the dental tool clatter down with the others on the Formica surface in front of Sonny. "I'm beginning to trip over them. I guess I hadn't really thought about that when I built the new kiln." He walked over to his pottery wheel and picked up two of the gallon plastic tubs that were sitting on one of his circular bats, a round of flat wood that spun like a lazy Susan.

"Thought about what?" asked Sonny, as Joe walked back to the wedging table.

"That I need a space that holds 400 pots if it takes me that many to fill it."

"What are you thinking? That you'll build an addition?"

"Well I wasn't," said Joe, his eyes wide as he put the buckets of slip next to sculpture. "But I am now."

"I'll help," Sonny offered.

"Honestly I'm not there yet," said Joe. He chose a flat hake brush, half-inch wide from the jelly jar of brushes on the center of the table and dipped it in the blue slip. "I want to get this kiln half-way figured out first."

"I thought you said it was doing good."

Joe bent forward and silently filled the negative space around the quill with blue slip, then the space around the scroll. As soon as he finished, he stood back up and he looked up at his friend. "It was," he said. "Except there was a lot of underfiring in the second chamber."

"What's that?"

"Pots that don't quite make it to temperature." He laid the brush down and picked out another for the green slip. "So the glazes aren't melted completely."

"What happens to those?" Sonny asked.

Joe began painting parts of the diamond shape panes he'd made inside the window with green slip. "I fire them again," he said.

"You can do that?"

Joe switched back to the brush with blue slip on it and painted some of that in the windowpanes above the green. "Sure. Sometimes it's even good for the pots to get fired twice, 'cause the glazes get more glassy and wood-ashed. But it's hard on sales." He straightened up and dipped the brush in the blue slip again. "There was maybe two-thirds of the second chamber that was underfired. That's a lot."

"Oh," said Sonny. He sat forward in the chair. "Hey, d'you hear any more from the EPA guys?"

"Uh uh," said Joe, starting to paint some letters across the bottom of the window. He tried to space them evenly so they'd be easy to read. "The last thing they told me," he said, not taking his eyes off his work. "Was they were going to check and see if the kiln constituted an appliance, which would mean I'd need a permit to run it." He paused, focusing, straightened up and dipped his brush in the blue slip again, then bent forward to finish what he was writing. "But they haven't gotten back to me so I'm guessing the answer was no. I could tell the kiln stopped being a big deal to them though when I said I was only going to fire it about once every couple of months."

"They thought they could regulate it?"

"Hoped, more like." Joe bushed on the last letter, then stood up to look at it. Chez Gina, it said. He nodded; that ought to do. He lifted the 18-inch round of plywood that was holding the art piece and moved it to a ware board to dry.

"You done?" asked Sonny.

"For now. Tomorrow I'll set it between some sheet rock so it dries without warping."

"No, I meant are you done making pottery?"

"Oh. Yeah. That's all I had to work on this morning." He walked over to a bucket of water on the floor by the woodstove and sank his hands down into it to wash them off. "Which gives me time to go scratch my head over the bag wall in that second chamber."

"What's that?"

"The bag wall?"

"Uh huh."

"That's the wall of bricks on the inside of the chamber, next to the entry flue. You've seen it I'm sure."

Sonny made a face like maybe he had but he didn't remember.

"The bag wall directs the flames up when they come in through the flue, otherwise they'd take the path of least resistance across the bottom before heading out the chimney. So the pots at the top won't get to temperature. Capiche?" Joe asked, looking over his shoulder at his friend.

Sonny nodded; yes, he understood.

"But how tall to make the bag wall is all about trial and error and since I've had two firings now, both with a lot of underfired pots in the second chamber, I guess I'm still trying." He dried his hands on a towel hanging on the end of the wedging table. "I have to look at it again, see if maybe I should make it shorter. Or make part of it shorter," he mused, looking up at the ceiling. "That might distribute the heat more evenly."

"So these guys from the EPA aren't going to close down the kiln?"

"I doubt it. It was pretty obvious they didn't know what they were looking at. I told them, you created more pollution driving your vehicle the 50 miles up here to talk to me than my kiln could create in 20 years."

"Whad'they say to that?"

"Something about it not being illegal to drive a car. I said, my kiln's not illegal either, and they didn't disagree." He hung his apron with the towel on the end of the wedging table and lifted his wool shirt off the deer horn he used for a coat hook on the log post. "They said they want me to call them next time I fire it so they can come up and see for themselves what it looks like." He walked over to the door and put his hand over the light switch, ready to turn it off.

"You gonna call them?" Sonny asked, standing up to follow him out.

"Probably not."

"Yeah. I wouldn't either."

*****

Hilda had two piles of paperwork on her kitchen table; one was about her short plat and the other, her dispute with Connors. In between, she had some maps laid out. The kitchen window in front of the table showed it to be another miserable March day, but Hilda was warm in her flannel pajamas, with a fire in the woodstove behind her. She'd woken early, eager to get to all the new paperwork she'd unearthed yesterday at the County Assessor and County Clerk's office, and she nibbled on a piece of whole wheat toast and sipped on her coffee as she stared at the maps.

In front of her was a black and white copy of her own short plat map to the County, which showed the property line she shared with Connors as having that strange, three-sided parallelogram in it that Hilda knew all about. The property line went up between the two parcels of land from the highway, then jogged left at kind of a 45-degree angle, went straight again, then jogged right, at the same 45-degree angle before straightening out for the remainder of their properties. She wasn't sure exactly where the starting point was down at the highway easement, whether it was on her side of the big apple tree or on Connors's side, but the parallelogram sat above the septic tank, for sure, putting it squarely on Hilda's property.

Next to this map she had laid out what she found at the County Assessor's office yesterday, which was a map from 1975, the year Clarence sold the five acres to Connors. This map showed a straight line between the two properties and when Hilda saw that, she wondered when the parallelogram chunk out of her land became fact? She remembered Clarence griping constantly about Connors "stealing" his septic tank, but he'd never said a word about a change in the configuration of the property line.

Intrigued, Hilda went to the County Clerk's office to see if there were any transcripts from all the times her ex had gone to court with Connors over the stupid septic tank and found, to her horror, that a judge had drawn a big circle around the septic tank and told Connors to take as much of that land as he wanted to secure his septic system. For whatever reason, Connors and his ex had chosen a portion of that circle which didn't include the septic system, so Hilda was beginning to think he'd been hoist by his own petard.

She'd been furious that her criminal assault action against Connors had come to naught but since then, she'd found a great lawyer in Seattle, who'd agreed that a judge might rule in her favor on the assault in a civil suit against Connors. It was more expensive to do it that way but if the result was Connors getting slapped with an assault conviction, it would be worth it. And now Hilda was thinking she could tag onto her civil suit an argument that Connors chose *not* to make the septic tank his, so by default it was hers. And she could build her road over it. Just as soon as she found someone to build her road.

Hilda sipped a little of her hot, black coffee, feeling the warmth slide into the contentment she was experiencing. Gus had been right to suggest she go and look up the Court and County records. Now she had all the ammunition she needed for her lawyer to go in blazing.

*****

While Hilda was looking at her maps of the property line, Lucy was looking at the same maps on her kitchen table a few hundred yards away. Joe and Sonny came down from the kiln shed and found Lucy and Pete poring over the maps, trying to decipher some of the lines.

"What are you looking at?" asked Joe, closing the sliding glass door behind Sonny and leaving the dogs outside on the back porch, looking in plaintively.

"We're looking at Hilda's short plat plans," said Lucy. She was standing with her back to him and Pete was at the end of the table, sideways on to Joe.

Joe strode eagerly across the living room. "Where'd you get those?" he asked, coming up to stand beside Lucy.

She pointed across him at Pete, who was leaning on his hands on the table, one knee on a chair. Pete pulled off his reading glasses, to look at Joe, and said. "I've been getting friendly with a lady from the Planning Department and I asked her if I could get a copy, figuring they might help you fight this lawsuit."

"Thanks!" said Joe. "That was very thoughtful."

Pete gave him a boyish grin. "Well I did get a second coffee date out of the deal."

"Ahh," said the potter, like the truth was out. He leaned forward and touched the copy of the short plat. "Four lots!" he exclaimed.

"I know," sighed Lucy.

"It'll be different alright," said Sonny, who'd come up to the table on the other side of Lucy.

Joe snapped away and Lucy knew it was because he was frustrated by the thought of going from one neighbor plus Daisy the cow, to four neighbors. Or more. He walked over to the woodstove behind her and she heard him lift the steaming kettle. Then he carried it over to the kitchen.

"How come your property line has this jag in it?" Pete asked, his index finger on the parallelogram.

Joe didn't even look at the drawing as he set the kettle down on the kitchen counter. Lucy watched him put yesterday's coffee filter in the compost and slip a new one in the top of his coffee pot. "In one of the many times I ended up in court with Burns over my septic tank," he explained. "The judge offered us a chunk of land in the shape of a pie, and said, "Take as much of that pie as you want to put your septic tank on your property." And, Erica and I didn't want to hurt this old guy next door to us, so we took just a small piece. And missed our septic tank altogether."

Lucy saw Pete's mouth drop open and Joe turn and do a double take while spooning ground coffee into the filter. "Why didn't you take the whole pie?" Pete asked, incredulous.

Joe gave him a tight smile. "I was trying to be *reas*-on-able," he said, dragging out the word to make a point. "I hadn't learned at that point that reason only works with reasonable people, which Mr. Burns was not." He poured hot water from the kettle to the top of the coffee filter. "Plus we didn't want to be greedy. We just wanted our septic tank. But at that point, we didn't even know where it was - and Burns wasn't telling us – so Erica and I measured 10 feet behind the house, 10 feet in front and then joined the two." He nodded his chin towards the short plat map. "That parallelogram is those measurements."

"You should've got it surveyed," grumbled Sonny.

"I should've done a lot of things," Joe barked. "Starting with making payments instead of cashing Burns out. Then we'd've had some recourse. But we were young and naïve and we trusted him."

"So what did you gain in the piece of pie you did select?" asked Pete, looking down at the map again, his reading glasses propped on the end of his nose.

"It put all of the concrete slab on our property."

"But your property line runs in a straight line now from the end of the concrete slab to the highway," said Sonny, who had walked over to the front door and was looking through the panes at Joe's front yard.

"No it doesn't," Joe countered, filling the coffee filter for a second time with hot water. "Burns put up that barbed wire fence in a straight line when he lived next door to me but he kept dumping soil from his property over the fence into my front yard, so I'd know it was his. Then after he ran out on Hilda, she started sucking up to me - so I'd testify against him in court - and I took the opportunity to ask if I could move all that dirt in my front yard back onto her property. She said yes. In fact, she wanted it, she said, 'cause it was topsoil, so it'd be good for her vegetable garden." He set the kettle on the counter next to the sink and turned back to look at them again. "She didn't have to tell me twice. I loaded that mess in the back of my pick-up and took it over to her garden spot, in front of her house.

Then I cleaned up my front yard and started parking my truck there. But in reality there's a property corner right below our front steps."

"Is there?" asked Lucy, shocked.

Joe bounced from the kitchen to the table and pointed at the lower line of the parallelogram. "Yeah, see where this comes back, that's where it is." He walked over to stand next to Sonny, by the front door. Lucy and Pete followed and Sonny shifted left, to give them all space.

Joe pointed through the glass panes in the door. "The property line goes along the end of the concrete slab, then comes back in, at an angle, to the right of those silver firs I planted, up to the bottom of the front steps."

"So those silver fir trees are on Hilda's property," asked Lucy, disappointed. She loved those little trees.

"I think," said Joe. "Yes."

"What about the apple tree?" asked Pete.

"No, that's ours," said Joe. "The property line goes down to the highway at an angle, leaving the apple tree on our land." He shrugged, before starting back towards the kitchen. "I'm pretty sure anyway"

The others stared out through the front door, a few more moments.

Sonny turned first and ambled back towards the maps. "She's gonna put the road in right alongside your property line," he said, his attention fully focused on the short plat drawing. "She'll probably mess with you then and put a turn around or something right in your front yard."

Lucy's stomach tightened; could Hilda really do that?

"She can't," said Joe, as if he'd heard her. "There's not enough room in that little triangle for a turnaround."

"You get your truck in it," said Sonny, like this was proof.

"Yeah and I bet if we measured it, I get the cab of my truck in it. Nothing more."

"So? Somebody could pull forward then pull back," Sonny insisted.

"Why d'you have to be so negative?" Joe complained.

"I'm just saying," mumbled Sonny.

"The thing is," said Pete, coming in over them as he reached for one of the mugs hanging on nails over Joe's kitchen counter. All of them had defects right out of the kiln but they were still lovely. Pete picked a small, blue and brown mug, with glue covering the foot. "You need to start being proactive with Hilda instead of always being re-active."

"How?" argued Joe, refilling the kettle with water from the faucet.

"I'd see if I couldn't get the rest of the pie," said Pete.

"I already asked Klaassen that," said Joe. He walked the kettle back to the wood stove. "He said, not unless Hilda brings it up first. And then it won't do me any good unless the new judge is as sympathetic to me as the previous one." He set the kettle down with a clatter, and Lucy watched a yellow finch flutter out of the elderberry bush behind the house. "The truth is, I had my chance and I missed it. End of story."

"You know what I'd do?" said Sonny, drawing them all to look at him.

"No. What?' said Joe.

"I'd talk to Lou."

"Acosta?"

"Uh huh."

Sonny had built many houses for the local Realtor, Luigi Acosta, and Lucy had heard him talking about how the man was a skilled negotiator when it came to property disputes.

"I bet he could find a way for you to offer Hilda something where she could still put in her road and have her short plat but you'd get your front yard and septic system."

"Now that's not a bad idea," agreed Joe. "You want coffee?" he asked his friend, as he walked past him back into the kitchen.

"No, thanks."

"And that would be something that's proactive," said Pete.

"Yeah," agreed Joe. "Of course, we don't have any money..."

"My parents might help," Lucy put in. She'd never asked her parents for money before but she suspected they wouldn't be averse to giving her a loan, especially if it put an end to this years-long property line dispute.

Sonny walked over to the couch and lowered himself onto it, sprawling out immediately to get comfortable. "Maybe see Lou before you see Klaassen," he said. "Might give him something to work with."

Joe nodded. He sipped his hot, black coffee and sat in the rocking chair, diagonally opposite Sonny, the kitchen table to his left.

"Be good to get some kind of visual measure of how much land we're talking about," said Pete from the kitchen.

"If I can't afford to buy the land I certainly can't afford to survey that little piece," Joe said across to him.

"Doesn't have to be that involved," Pete countered. "You know where the property markers were – maybe still are if the surveyors sunk rebar down into the ground. You could draw a line between those markers in chalk -"

"Not if it's raining," muttered Sonny.

"Okay, not if it's raining," conceded Pete, "and take photographs."

"Hey," Sonny exclaimed, like he'd just had an idea. "You could ask Matt Chandler to fly you in his plane. Take some aerial photos."

"Now that's a *real* good idea," said Joe, his face filled with enthusiasm.

"Would that help?' asked Lucy.

"I don't know," shrugged Joe. "But it'd be fun to take photos from above. And Matt's been after me to fly in his little, red puddle jumper for months now. This'd be a great way for me to say yes."

"Plus it would show just how tiny this piece of land is," Pete said to Lucy. Then he looked at Joe. "It's what? A fifth of an acre?"

"Probably not even that much."

"See," Pete said to Lucy. "Hardly justifies all this animosity."

Lucy couldn't really visualize what a fifth of an acre might look like but it did seem that for all the vastness of the land around her, there'd been a lot of fighting over very little. But then, she thought, some people liked to fight. Maybe she should put that into a play.

"I'm going upstairs to write," she told Joe, leaning over the rocker and cupping her hands around his chin. He tipped his head back and she kissed him lightly on the lips, before scampering over to the stairs.

"D'you know Luigi's number?" she heard Joe ask Sonny before she lost herself in some characters, fighting for the sake of fighting.

*****

Three days later Lucy realized that nobody had rung her back yet from the doctor's office in Seattle, about her immigration physical. The clock was ticking as far as getting her paperwork in order before she left for England so even though she didn't usually prefer to push, she picked up the telephone to ring again. The DJ on the radio said sunny skies and Lucy looked out the picture window as she stood on the tile hearth, listening to the phone ring in her ear. Not here, she thought. The receptionist answered and Lucy explained why she was calling once again.

"Well the woman you need to speak to isn't here again, unfortunately," said the pleasant, female voice at the other end of the line, and then her tone became more curious. "But I gave your message to her yesterday and she said there's no record of you having a physical here, so she thinks you've got the wrong doctor's office."

"Actually I did have my physical there," said Lucy, winding her fingers irritably into the loops of the cord on the beige, Trimline phone. "And I have the receipt to prove it."

"Okay," said the receptionist, sounding like she believed Lucy. "I'll leave her another message and have her call you back."

"Please do. Because this is holding up my immigration interview," insisted Lucy.

"I'll make sure she knows that," said the receptionist.

Lucy hung the phone up on the wall and walked around the corner to grab her rain jacket. "Bloody cheek!" she muttering angrily as she jammed her arms into the thin, noisy, nylon jacket. "As if I wouldn't know where I had my physical!" And she marched across the living room and out the back door.

*****

Joe saw Lucy come up to the fuel shed and start moving armloads of cedar waste wood into a garden cart, ready for his next firing, but she didn't see him. He was in the kiln shed, up against the second chamber, taking some of the bricks off the top of the bag wall and replacing them with smaller ones.

Hopefully that'll do the trick, he thought, as he replaced the last brick, although he wouldn't find out until he opened the kiln after the next firing. It could have been how he stacked the pots inside the chamber that had made such a difference last time around. Heck, it could also have been the apple wood that he'd used in the first firing and didn't have for the second firing. The only way to find out was to change one of the variables. Slightly. He stood up from where he was kneeling over to reach into the chamber and slapped the soot off his hands. Firing with wood was nothing if not an exercise in patience.

The dogs were playing chase around a big maple tree at the back end of the studio and Joe decided to leave them to it. They'd catch up with him when they tired of their game. He'd go bug Lucy instead.

He walked over to where she was working and stood behind the garden cart. It was standing on end, and Joe stepped in between the two big bicycle wheels and angled his elbows in the open end of the cart, under the metal handle. Then he bent forward and rested his chin on his hands, the toe of his right foot propped on the arch of his left foot. The cedar shake mill waste was stacked in long, shoulder-high rows and Lucy was taking from two mostly empty rows to load the cart. Joe wanted to help but the space was narrow and there wasn't room for two people to pass in it. He'd only be in the way. She had her back to him and was bent over, filling the crook of her left arm with 24-inch lengths of aromatic kindling. When she had a full armload, she spun around, to walk to the cart, and jumped at the sight of him. "You scared me!"

"I was just admiring the view," he teased and saw the edges of her mouth flicker with a smile.

"I thought you were glazing pots," she said as she threw the wood into the cart.

Joe instinctively moved back, to avoid getting hit, and heard the wood thud against the plywood bed of the cart and clatter loudly as it tumbled into place. Lucy set to straightening some of the lengths of cedar to make full use of the space. "No, I was *making* glazes," he corrected, folding his fingers over the open end of the cart where he'd been leaning. The wheels of the cart spun on either side of him, shaken into life by the load dumped in the cart. "I did that, and now they need time to slake. I also counted the number of pots I drew tulips on for this next firing, then I switched to working on the bag wall in the second chamber."

"How many were there?"

"Tulip pots? 25." He winced. "We're going to get stuck with those if they don't sell at the Tulip Festival."

Lucy paused, enjoying the feel of the cool, damp air. She'd worked up a sweat already, moving the cedar. She watched the dogs take turns lapping water out of a defective bowl lying on the ground while she reflected on Joe's comment. She couldn't really know how well the tulip pieces would sell since this was the first time they'd been invited to participate officially in the 21-day festival. She blinked, pulling herself back to the present, and said, "I wouldn't worry about it, if I were you."

Joe followed her eyes to the dogs and saw that Max had a hunk of wood sitting next to him. "You're probably right," he agreed, walking over to retrieve the stick. He lifted it high into the air and tossed it into the raspberry vines at the top of his garden. Moisture sprayed in all direction from the wood as it turned in the air and Max took off running. Joe walked back over to the garden cart. "What time are we heading downriver?"

Lucy made a face like she didn't know. "Our appointment with Klaassen's at three and Luigi Acosta said we could stop by anytime after one so," -she shrugged- "maybe after lunch?"

Joe nodded. "Works for me." Max dropped the wood at his feet and Joe threw it a second time.

Lucy started back down between the rows of cedar to get the next armload.

"You can come get me once you get the cart full, if you like," said Joe.

Lucy stopped and turned to look at him. "Why? Where are you going?"

"Down to the house. I want to dig out the file with all the documents from the court cases with Burns, so I can take it to Lou."

"Okay. Add those maps from the other day, would you?"

"Uh huh, I was thinking the same thing. When does Tulip Festival start again?"

"April the 1st."

"And what's the date now?"

Lucy puffed a stray curl away from in front of her eyes as she looked for the date in her mind. "March the 18th," she remembered.

"Good," said Joe. Max dropped the stick at his feet again and Joe bent to retrieve it. "I still have a week or so."

He walked away, around the small, post-and-beam shed, and hurled the stick, then followed the dogs down towards the house.

*****

A few hours later they were on their way down to Klaassen's office, holding a very reasonable suggestion from Lou Acosta; one that hadn't taken the real estate mogul any time to come up with.

"This is what I'd do," he said, when they stopped in at his office overlooking the Skagit on their way through Concrete. The sunny skies Lucy had heard about on the radio had finally reached the Upper Valley and splashes of bright white danced on the surface of the river, making tiny rainbows of color on the Realtor's desk as it came through his spacious windows, adding whimsy to the dark wood.

"I'd offer to buy a stretch of land that puts all the easements on your property instead of on Hess'. So right now, your septic tank exists on her land plus a water line, correct?"

"That's correct," said Joe.

"A hundred-year old water line?"

"Uh huh."

"She won't want to hurt that if she can help it," murmured the tall, lantern-jawed Realtor.

"No," agreed the potter. "'Specially since the Department of Transportation put in that water line in to service a dozen houses below the highway."

"And it goes from Thompson Creek, at the back of your property, down across this little section of land here in the front that belongs to Hess, then under the highway?"

"Exactly right."

Acosta used a pencil to make a mark on Hilda's short plat map. "This is where it crosses the property line from your place to Hilda's?"

Joe twisted his head around, so he wasn't looking at the map upside down. "Above my garden site, yes. Towards the back of my property."

Acosta nodded. "Okay," he said. He started to draw a line on the map. "If I were you, I'd offer to buy a section of land that lies two feet into Hilda's property from this water line, all the way down to the highway. She'd have to leave that much separation anyway, between her road and the water line, and since it's too small a piece to put any other improvements on legally, she may as well sell it to you."

Joe and Lucy stared down at what he'd drawn.

"That's a great idea!" said Joe, marveling at its simplicity.

"It just tidies everything up between you," said Acosta, shading the area on Joe's side of the line that he'd drawn."

"How much do you think we should offer?" asked Lucy.

Acosta pulled down both sides of his mouth, bouncing his head on his neck, as if considering. "I'd start at three thousand dollars. But be prepared to go to maybe five."

Joe didn't hold back his shock. "You're kidding! I only paid $10,000 for the entire five acres when I bought it."

"But that was how many years ago?" asked Acosta.

Joe heard frequently from Sonny that he was clueless when it came to land values in the Upper Skagit so he was expecting the same from Acosta. "'Bout 15," he replied.

Acosta nodded. "Well now, in 1988, that five acres you bought would probably cost you anywhere from fifty to a hundred thousand dollars. Property's a lot more expensive now than it was in the seventies."

"Well I know that," Joe insisted. "But we're talking less than a quarter acre!"

The phone rang on the desk beside the Realtor and he put his hand on top of the receiver, ready to answer it. His demeanor was calm, his face neutral, pleasant, but there was something in his bearing that suggested they could take his advice, or leave it; but he wasn't going to get drawn into a discussion of its value. "You want to make it worth her while," he finished, before picking up the phone.

*****

Joe looked pensive as they turned back out onto the highway to make the 45-minute journey down to Klaassen's.

"Are you all right?" Lucy asked.

"I just can't figure out what I'm s'posed to learn from all this," he answered, his shoulders tight with agitation. "I made *one* mistake," he went on, sticking his index finger up in the air to emphasize the one. "And not even a bad mistake. Just something that hurt me, not anybody else." He made a nod of concession with his head. "Well, me and Erica." He turned to face Lucy and she saw anger, frustration, confusion. "And I'm *still* paying the price. Why? What am I missing here?"

Lucy didn't have an answer for him. She'd never met Clarence Burns and hadn't experienced the agony of the repetitive trips to court to try to settle the matter, but the actress in her was curious about the personalities behind the struggle. And now that she'd started writing a short play using characters based on these personalities, she was even more curious.

"What happened with Burns after Hilda moved in?" she asked.

"What do you mean?"

"I mean, did he stop bothering you?"

Joe thought about this for a second. "I guess." He nodded. "Yes."

"Even the dumping of stuff over the fence?"

"Did he stop dumping stuff over the fence?" Joe repeated, trying to recall the last time he'd seen Burns on his tractor on the other side of the fence line. He couldn't. Not since Hilda. "You know, I think he did," he said. "Why?"

"Because I'm beginning to think that Burns was all about the trap."

Joe's face pivoted toward Lucy, like she'd struck a chord. "Oh he *loved* trapping. Beavers, muskrats, bobcats, coyotes, whatever he could get. For the pelts. I think he told me that was the main reason he moved up here. Only the regulations changed and the market fell out for the pelts."

"So he turned to the humans around him, and lay traps in the property lines – for you, for Jimmy and Laura – and once he snared you, he enjoyed watching you squirm. He probably really loved the wild thing in you that kept snapping at him when he tried to retrieve the trap. Brought out the savage in him."

"He did like to fight."

"And then Hilda came along and distracted him because she was much bigger prey than you. I suspect it took all his mental energy plotting where to lay her trap and how to camouflage it. And I bet the camouflage involved him paying her a *lot* of attention because I think that's what Hilda's all about. "

"So what are you saying? That I have to pay Hilda a lot of attention? Because that ain't happening?"

"I know. But I think that means she won't accept *any* offer we make to buy that land because what she likes is the attention fighting with you about it gives her."

"That doesn't help me! That makes it sound like I'm stuck for the rest of my life, wrangling with that harridan."

Lucy eased the Pinto around the curve in the road leading up to

Hurn's field. "Not if you get more strategic and refocus her neediness you're not."

Joe sat up higher in the passenger seat and looked across Lucy for the elk. "You mean put some other poor sap in her path so she can torture them instead? I won't do that."

"I'm not suggesting…"

"Oh look!" he exclaimed, changing the subject and pointing across Lucy to the big field where elk would come out from behind the tree line and graze on the lush grass.

Even in the afternoon sunshine the field looked pallid from the winter die off, lacking that emerald glint it would get when spring refreshed the landscape, but when Lucy turned to look where Joe was pointing, she was electrified by the sight of twenty or so elk, running alongside her car, on the field side of the fence. The haunches of the huge, tan and brown animals, rippled with musculature as they ran, the bulls keeping their heads high, as if to protect their massive, wide-spread antlers from getting jostled. "They're beautiful, aren't they?" she whispered to Joe.

"Um hm," he muttered, deep in his chest. "But not to be trifled with."

Lucy glanced in the rear view mirror. There was a logging truck behind her and people stopped at the side of the road, watching the elk, in front of her. She had to have eyes everywhere, in case the elk suddenly turned, to head across the road. She'd seen what an elk could do to a motor vehicle and certainly wanted to avoid that if she could.

The Pinto pulled past all the sightseers and Joe twisted around to view the elk till they were out of sight. "Well that was worth the journey," he said, flopping back in his seat to face front, a happy smile on his face.

But Lucy hadn't lost sight of the subject they'd been discussing. "You know what you could do?" she said, with a small, wicked smile.

"Fill the freezer with one of those elk during hunting season?"

"No, I'm talking about Hilda again now."

"I know," said Joe with a sigh. "Live a happy life?" he

suggested. "That's what Jimmy from next door told me was the best revenge."

"I know and I think we should do that too, because that irks her more than anything. But I think you should try to find Clarence Burns."

Joe balked. "What good would that do me?! He's not gonna tell Hess to sell me that land!"

"I don't mean find him to interact with him. I mean find him to let Hilda know where he is. Didn't you tell me she asked you about that when you were talking to her about moving the dirt? That if you ever found out where Burns was, to let her know?"

Joe didn't remember. He was very good at moving on to the next thing in his mind and since the next thing had never been Clarence Burns, he hadn't had cause to revisit Hilda's request. But it sounded about right. "Could be," he said.

"And once she finds him, she'll need to spend all her time trying to devise ways to get her money back out of him. Or at least deprive him of enjoying it somehow."

"I wouldn't even know where to start looking for Burns."

"What about that customer, June something? Isn't her husband a private investigator?"

"You mean Steve Victor?"

"The one that sometimes stops and asks if you've heard of this or that person, or where a certain address may be?"

"Yeah, but I don't know that I'd want to ask him to find Burns."

"Why not?"

Joe shrugged. "I don't know. It doesn't feel right. I've never done him any favors."

"It wouldn't have to be a favor. We could pay him."

"With what?"

"His wife likes your pottery."

"Hmmm." Joe chewed on this for a moment, staring off out the window as they drove past the Ranger Station housing, hoping to see more elk in the field beyond the railroad tracks. But there were none there. "Yeah, no, I'm not doing it," he said finally. "Even if Steve Victor does find Burns, there's no guarantee Hilda the Horrible will take the information from me."

"You don't have to give it to her directly."

"I'm not doing it!" repeated Joe, getting heated. "I'm already spending more time than I want to on Hilda's crap. I'm not going to spend any time chasing down that cheat, Burns."

"I think that's the problem," said Lucy, knowing she was treading on touchy ground. "You don't want to spend any time on this and Hilda has nothing *but* time for it. You've got to find a way to redress that balance otherwise Hilda's likely to win."

"Win what?" snapped Joe. He threw his hands up in the air, palms up. "I don't have any more of me to give her."

He'd rue those words if he weren't careful, Lucy thought to herself, with a slight shake of her head. She looked out the window next to her rather than face Joe. She wasn't going to say any more on this subject. Because he could be very hardheaded when it came to anything that stepped between him and time at the potter's wheel. Very hardheaded.

*****

Klaassen breezed into the room behind Lucy and Joe and dropped some manila file folders on his desk as he went around it. "Take a seat, please," he told them, motioning to the chairs in front of his desk as he shrugged out of his suit jacket and draped it over the back of his seat. He dropped down into the office chair, put his elbows on his desk and drew himself in closer, then lifted a file from a stack to his right and opened it "Here's what we've got," he said. Lucy and Joe sat forward in their chairs.

"Hilda is bringing a civil action against you for assault and she's tagged onto it a part about you giving up your right to ingress and egress over the septic tank because you didn't take the land around it when it was offered to you."

"*What*?!" said Joe, immediately outraged.

"But," Klaassen continued over him, one hand in the air suggesting let me finish. "Since she brought it up, we can now counter with your request to take everything that was previously offered you."

The room suddenly became quiet. Lucy looked across at Joe, thinking this was the break they'd been hoping for but he didn't look convinced. If anything, he looked embarrassed.

"Well I don't need *everything*," he voiced. "I just want my septic tank and maybe the stretch of land beside it that goes down to the highway because that's what I thought I was buying in the first place."

"Doesn't matter what you thought you were buying," said Klaassen. "It only matters what the legal survey shows for the property line. If you want my opinion you got lucky with that judge, that he let his emotions come into play when he offered you the land that you thought you bought to secure your septic system. He didn't have to do that."

"I think he figured out pretty quick that I'd been defrauded," Joe defended.

"I'm sure he did. It probably wasn't his first time coming face to face with Burns over a property line dispute. Either that, or he'd heard all the local talk about this young potter who'd been taken for his septic tank. This is a small community, after all. Word travels fast."

"I know," Joe agreed. "Hess has been trying to find someone to build her road and I've heard a number of people have turned her down already."

"Mmmmm, I'm not sure that's true anymore," said Lucy and both the men turned to look at her, curious. "I heard Ulrich has taken the job."

"Marty Ulrich?" said Klaassen.

Lucy nodded as Joe asked the lawyer, "You know him?"

"Uh huh. I won a big settlement against him. A *big* settlement." Klaassen looked at them both, a twinkle in his eyes. "When Ulrich comes out to start the job why don't you ask that he give your lawyer a call." He picked something out of a small metal box on the table and handed it across to Joe. "Here's one of my cards to give him."

Joe smiled. "Tric-ky!"

"And in the meantime," Klaassen went on, "I'll come up with a response to this latest filing by Hess. Her lawyer's out of town for the next three weeks then I'll be gone for a week but that works in our favor because when's your public hearing for the amendment to your special use permit?"

"April 22nd," said Lucy.

"Right. So that should be decided before we potentially go to court over this," said Klaassen, spearing Hilda's legal documents with the tip of his index finger. "So the outcome can't prejudice your public hearing. Although, I should tell you, I'm pretty sure the assault part won't get to court because I have a witness who saw her coming at you with a shotgun and then heard it go off. She might get your septic tank but she's not getting you for assault. Not if I have anything to do with it."

Joe's stomach tensed. "Can she get my septic tank?" he asked, his mind whirring the fact that all the money he'd spent defending it so far would be for naught. Plus what if the County wouldn't issue him a permit for another? Then what would he do?

"Anything's possible," said Klaassen, his tone neutral, impassive. "Which is why I think you should let me put together a proposal asking that the judge reinstate the original offer for you to take as much land as necessary to secure your septic system. And this time, you should take everything that's offered."

Joe looked across at Lucy. She shrugged her eyebrows at him; Klaassen was the lawyer, not her.

"Okay but…"

"Take everything," Klaassen repeated.

"I heard you," Joe argued, "but we've also come up with an offer to buy a strip of land from Hess that will probably include all of the pie I was originally offered and then some."

"Show me." The lawyer's hands reached out, indicating the piece of paper Joe was holding.

Joe bounced forward in his seat and laid the short plat map down on the desk in front of Klaassen. Then he explained the shaded area drawn by Luigi Acosta.

"How much of this shaded area is the original pie you were offered?" asked Klaassen.

Lucy was watching the lawyer and noticed that his blue eyes had become steely. Hard. She moved her focus to Joe and saw that the question had him flummoxed.

"I don't know," he replied, after a long hesitation.

Klaassen nodded, studying the map. "So what you have to decide," he said, raising his eyes to meet Joe's again. "Is whether you want to offer to buy this section of land or have me argue that the judge should award it to you at no cost."

"Why can't I do both?"

"What do you mean?"

"Why can't I offer to buy it and then if that doesn't work, ask the judge to give me the pie again?"

"Because if you offer to buy it, you're implying that it's not yours. So if Hess decides she doesn't want to sell it to you, you can't turn around and argue that it was yours in the first place therefore she should be compelled to *give* it to you."

"But what if the judge doesn't award me the land? Can I then offer to buy it from Hilda?"

Klaassen bobbed his head this way and that, his lips pushed up, like this might be a possibility. Then he said, "How likely d'you think she'd be to sell it to you? For any amount?"

Joe looked across at Lucy. She was facing forward, biting her tongue, trying not to say, I told you so!

"I'm screwed either way, is what you're telling me," argued Joe.

"No. I'm telling you you've got to place your bet." There was a long, slow moment of silence as Klaassen kept his eyes down on the short plat map. He finally looked up at Joe's again. "So which is it going to be? What do you want?"

Joe answered flailing his arms around to show his agitation. "What I want is not to have to waste my time on this nonsense anymore. It doesn't interest me. I just want it to be over with so I can get back to making pots, which *does* interest me. That's what I want!"

"Well isn't that what we all want, Joe," Kurt Klaassen said without humor. "And when you find a way to do that, come get me, so I can do it too." He paused, his words ending the discussion like a ‘caution; do not cross’ ribbon in the air. When he went back to speaking, his voice was soft, immutable. “This mistake isn’t going away until you grab it by the forelocks and face it down. How you do that is up to you.”

There was quiet in the room again while Joe thought about this. Then he looked at Lucy.

“Maybe that’s what you have to learn,” she said softly.

“What do you want to do?” he asked.

Lucy shrugged again. “I want to follow our lawyer’s advice.”

“Which is?” Joe asked, looking back at Klaassen.

“You didn’t catch that the first and second time I said it?”

Joe did a double take at Lucy; did he miss something?

Klaassen leaned forward on the desk and said it a third time: “Take. Everything.”

Something inside Joe slumped; the weight of thinking he’d appear grasping if he asked for too much. Maybe they were right, he thought to himself; this is what he needed to learn. But he certainly didn’t like the way it felt. “Can I think about it?” he asked.

Klaassen nodded. “Sure,” he said. He closed the file folder and replacing it on the stack. Then he lifted another from the pile to his left. “Now for the parenting plan.”

And Joe slumped further.

Chapter 11

Lucy walked down to the mailbox at the end of their driveway and pulled out a stack of letters rubber banded inside Joe's ceramics magazine. She'd been up at her desk, writing, when she'd seen the mail carrier's white jeep pull up and it felt like a good reason to stop and change the picture in her brain. The cool March air tingled against her skin as she wandered slowly back up the driveway, leafing through the missives. There were a couple of bills, something from Klaassen – hopefully the final draft of the parenting plan because Joe really wanted a summer visit with Maddie – and then four - no five! - letters from customers responding to her outreach for testimonials to use at the public hearing. So far she and Joe had received 38 handwritten letters supporting their right to make retails sales, and every one made a warm curl of delight inside Lucy when she read them.

People said such things as this was their "favorite stop" on their journey through the North Cascades, that they looked at the pottery pieces they'd bought every day and remembered their time in Washington, that "locally made" was something to support, not close down. She looked at the return addresses on these new ones: Oklahoma, New York, North Carolina. Lucy knew from Joe that

North Carolina had a very well known tradition of wood-fired pottery so he was always impressed when people from that area bought pots from him.

She flipped past the last of the letters from customers and found what she'd been waiting for; a letter from the INS. She stopped, next to the fir tree growing alongside the big wooden, *Cascade Mountain Pottery* sign, and ripped across the top of the envelope. She didn't have to get the letter all the way out before she saw the date for her interview; Tuesday, April 19th. Finally! That hold-up at with the doctor's office hadn't delayed her interview past the time she would need it to get her green card together before going to England. It still irritated her, the way they'd treated her at the doctor's office.

She'd had to ring them a third time, since the woman she needed to speak to never did bother to ring her back, but fortunately this time, she was there. "Hold on and I'll put you through," said the same receptionist Lucy had spoken with the first and second times.

The woman blustered on the line, mid-sentence: "…and I already made it clear that you *didn't* have your physical here!" Her tone suggested Lucy should go away and stop bothering her.

"Yes I did," Lucy said as calmly as she could, "on January 25th. And as I told your receptionist, I still have the receipt for the $50 I paid."

The other end of the line went quiet, so quiet that Lucy wondered if the woman were still there. She waited and then suddenly, the woman spoke again, this time her tone filled with embarrassment. "Oh I'm so sorry," she said, with a nervous laugh. "You're never going to believe this but…. well it turns out I have your file right on my desk. Right in front of me. I can't imagine how I missed it."

Yes, Lucy thought to herself. I wonder how many immigrants you've cheated out of their $50 because they didn't have the language skills to defend themselves? She took a breath, to keep herself calm, and said, "Please send it on immediately to the INS."

"Absolutely," agreed the woman, and Lucy hung up, feeling angry that people were so cavalier in the way they took advantage of others.

Now she just felt ashamed that she hadn't reported this doctor's office to the INS. She was sure they wouldn't condone this kind of behavior. She looked down at the date again on her paperwork; maybe she'd find a way to tell them at the interview.

She stuffed the letter back down into the envelope and walked over to the daffodils blooming around the bottom of the King David apple tree down by the highway. It was amazing how that little splash of color could transform the still bleak March landscape. Spring was on its way, and Lucy could feel it in the air, like a vibration, as if the land were teeming with new life, humming below the surface, just waiting to burst forth. She bobbed down, tucking the mail between her knees so her hands were free to pick a few of the daffodils to put on her kitchen table, and noticed for the first time that the gnarly, old apple tree had two trunks, growing away from each other, to form a sprawling umbrella of branches over her head. Branches that she could see would soon be covered in a myriad of exquisite pink and white blossoms.

She snapped the stems on half a dozen daffodils, retrieved the mail and headed towards the house. On her way past the silver fir trees on the property line, she stopped, troubled by how insipid the smallest of the three trees looked in comparison to the other two. She stepped in closer and saw blackberry vines snaking through and around every inch of the little sapling. Choking it, she thought. Maybe that explained why it was so much smaller than its verdant, bristly counterparts. Lucy didn't like to garden but she couldn't bear the thought of this little tree being overrun by such an invasive weed.

Behind her, she heard the front door to the house swing open. She turned to see the dogs barreling down the front steps towards her and Joe standing on the porch, holding a mug of coffee. "Watcha doing?" he asked.

"I was wondering if I should cut these blackberries off this little tree."

"It would probably benefit a lot from that," he replied, coming down the steps towards her. "And it's a good time to do it since the vines are all dried up, so maybe they won't send out new shoots when you pull them, although I doubt it," he said, running everything together like one thought.

Lucy had imagined herself clipping them rather than pulling them, but she did know that blackberries were tenacious so if she didn't do something drastic to these vines, they'd just grow right back. "Do we have any pruning shears?" she asked.

Joe nodded. "In the green loafing shed."

Lucy looked up at the sky then back down to the tree. "Well maybe I'll do it while it's not raining."

"Chuck all the debris in a wheelbarrow, and I'll take it over to my burn pile. That'll stop them from re-rooting."

Lucy looked at him, curious. "Would they do that?"

"Given half a chance, you bet." He nodded at the flowers in her hand. "You picked yourself some daffodils, huh?"

"I couldn't resist," said Lucy. She looked down at the cheery yellow flowers. then remembered the mail. "And I got the interview date for my green card."

"Is it before we go to England"

Lucy nodded. "April the 19th."

"That's after Tulip Festival, right?" Joe said before taking another swig of his coffee.

"Yes. That ends on the 17th. It's going to be a busy week because our public hearing's on the 22nd."

"Earth Day," mused Joe. "Maybe that'll work in our favor with the Hearing Examiner." He smiled at her, a glint in his eye. "You know, a public hearing about the right to sell something made from the earth on the same day chosen to honor the earth."

"Oh very clever," she agreed, smiling back at him.

He slipped his arm around her waist and pulled her in close, his voice vibrating against her ear as he said, "Maybe if we do good at the Festival, I'll take you out to dinner after the interview in Seattle."

She giggled because it tickled and he kissed her on the cheek. Then they broke apart and started wandering up towards the house together.

"You smell like cedar," she remarked, having noticed the tangy scent in his hair. "Did you get the kiln loaded?"

"Uh huh. I think I'll fire it tomorrow night."

This was different. "Why at night?"

"Because this kiln takes longer to fire than my old one and I don't want to run out of daylight before I get to the end of the firing. Last time I was 13 hours from start to finish so I figured if I start at 4 in the afternoon, I should catch the height of the firing during daylight hours." He bumped his shoulder against hers, like he was sharing a secret. "Plus this way there's less chance Hilda will be up to call the pollution people."

"Oh. I thought we were going to let them know when you were firing the kiln."

"You can. I'm not," Joe stated.

Lucy laughed. "They probably wouldn't come anyway," she said. "Not on a Saturday evening."

"Wouldn't matter if they did. There's nothing to see in the evening. All the action's going to be early Sunday morning."

"How early?"

"Probably 5 am-ish."

Lucy eyebrows popped up as she climbed the steps towards the porch. "Yeah, they definitely won't be up for that."

*****

In the wee hours of Sunday morning Joe pulled the brick out of the peephole in the top of the second chamber and flames shot out and flicked up towards the top of the door. He waited for the backpressure to die down and then peered into the red heat to see if the pyrometric cones were bent. Cone six was flat and cone seven was well on its way, so he'd got it to 2200 degrees Fahrenheit up here. But he'd just checked the cones in the middle and bottom of the chamber and neither of them showed a flat cone six. So were the cones lying to him at the top or was it fired out here but not in the rest of the chamber? Maybe he'd check the draw ring.

In one fluid movement, Joe pushed the peep hole back into place, climbed down the two wooden steps, grabbed a long, metal hook he had hanging next to the shelves for the kiln posts and climbed back up the steps so he could reach the top peephole. He pulled the brick out a second time and now that the flames had died down, could see the shadowy outlines of pots, ghost-like in the red heat. He threaded his metal hook through the peep hole and carefully looped the draw ring, a simple circle of clay dipped in glaze, that was in the front of the chamber, next to the pyrometric cones.

Once he was sure he had a hold of the draw ring, Joe pulled it out, put the brick back in the peep hole and dipped the draw ring down into some cold water he had sitting in a small, cereal bowl on the step by his feet. The ceramic sizzled and trembled in the water as it cooled rapidly. Joe waited for it to clear.

He had the radio tuned to BBC World News on the boom box behind him and they were talking about the horrifying effects of a new drug called crack cocaine. Joe shook his head as he watched the draw ring turn from glowing red to matte brown and blue; he was glad he kept his world small so he didn't have to face some of the more unpleasant aspects of human nature.

He gently lifted the draw ring out of the water and held it up in front of his face. The glaze looked good and melted, clear and glassy on the surface of the clay. Maybe this top section *was* fired out. Which left him with the conundrum of how much longer to keep stoking for temperature increase in the middle and bottom of the chamber. He unhooked the draw ring onto the steel cross bar in the doorframe, jumped down off the steps again and hung the metal hook back on the nail where it lived. Then he switched gears back to stoking. He pulled the brick out of the mouth of the firebox, grabbed enough cedar to fill both his hands, and pushed it through the stoke hole, hearing it crackle and snap into flame as soon as it hit the fire. If the top got too much hotter, he thought, grabbing a second load of cedar, the glazes would start to run. He could end up with a lot of pots stuck to the shelves up there if he weren't careful. He glanced over at the clock next to his boom box: 4:20 am. He'd stoke for another twenty minutes then he'd check the cones again.

*****

Hilda couldn't sleep. She'd been staring up at the dark ceiling in her small bedroom, trying to figure out why Marty Ulrich, the one road builder who'd come out to look at her project, had stopped returning her phone calls. He'd seemed so eager when they'd looked at the plans together. Then he'd gone over to the site to "start marking the boundaries," so he could know what kind of equipment to bring in. She'd watched from her kitchen window and had tensed up when she'd seen Connors come out to talk with the road builder, but they both looked relaxed and easy. Friendly even. And when Ulrich walked back to his truck, he hadn't seemed agitated, not as far as she could tell. So then why was he ducking her calls now?

Hilda peered at the clock beside her bed and sighed. It was 4:30 in the morning; no way was she getting back to sleep. She threw her legs out of bed, pushed her feet into her slippers and padded out to the kitchen. There were still coals in the woodstove so she threw in another piece of firewood and stood in front of the hearth, thinking. She had really wanted this to work out with Ulrich because she'd promised Gus, that as soon as she had a road builder lined out, she'd fly to Hawaii and they'd celebrate. Last night, she'd had to tell him on the phone that she thought Ulrich might have backed away from the project. She heard Gus suck in air sharply and got the impression he thought she was lying to him. And she didn't know what to do to convince him otherwise.

Ulrich hadn't been Hilda's first choice. In fact he'd been pretty far down her list of recommendations because people said he didn't always do what he'd been paid to do. But Hilda was willing to take that chance. Especially since all the heavy equipment operators she'd called ahead of Ulrich had turned her down when she mentioned where she lived and where she wanted the road built. There was too much local scuttlebutt over the septic tank dispute and some of them came right out and told her they didn't want to take on a job that might end up in Court.

But Marty Ulrich, a local logger and ex-Marine, assured her that he'd known Joe Connors for years and "he won't mess with me." When Ulrich showed up at Hilda's house, she saw why. Ulrich was built like a tank and carried that 'don't-mess-with-me-I'm-a-Marine' attitude right out in front, where everyone could see it. Hilda had been very encouraged. So what in the heck could have spooked him?

Her legs began to feel too warm standing so close to the stove so she turned around and walked over to the kitchen table. Night was beginning to soften into day and Hilda bobbed down to see what she could see in the sky. Nothing. It was probably filled with rain clouds, she thought, for yet another dreary March day. Something caught the edge of her peripheral vision to her left and she scooted forward, curious. A quiver of red and gold, in the distance behind Connors' house. Hilda stared at it some more, wondering if he had a chimney fire. Then she lifted the binoculars up to her eyes and saw the flame. Her eyes narrowed as she lowered the binoculars back down to the table. She knew what that was. And she knew what she was going to do about it.

*****

Lucy was still in bed when a truck dieseled loudly into the end of the driveway. Maggie barked her way to the front door from by the woodstove downstairs setting off Max, who jumped up from the floor beside the bed and charged down the stairs, full speed, barking over Maggie's barking. Lucy peeked out the front window of the bedroom. It was a fire engine! But it hadn't arrived with lights or siren. So what was it…..?

She quickly pulled on her sweat pants and top, ran down the stairs, stuffed her feet into her Sorel boots, grabbed one of Joe's wool shirts and threw open the front door, her eyes squinting against the early morning sunlight. The dogs bounded out ahead of her and chased around the house after the fire chief, Vangilder, who was following the flame from the chimney of the kiln. Lucy slowed when she saw the vehicle wasn't going with him but instead Hank Throssel, one of the owners of the grocery store in town, was standing beside it, easy in his sweat pants and top. She walked towards him, a question on her face.

"It's the kiln, isn't it?" he said in his quiet voice.

Lucy's face was still quizzical as she replied. "The kiln's going, yes, but....?"

"It's your neighbor, isn't it?" Throssel went on.

"What is?"

"Somebody made an anonymous call from the payphone up at the park reporting a fire on this property."

"Again?!" Lucy squawked, as a few of the other crew members dropped from the truck, more to stretch their legs, it seemed, than to go in search of a fire. "You should've rung me. I would've spared you the trip."

Throssel shook his head no. "We can't do that. We have to come check it out."

"Next time I'll lay on some doughnuts," said Lucy, feeling sorry for them. It was Sunday morning after all. They were probably all wishing they were still in bed.

"I'm going to talk to your neighbor next time she comes into the store," said Throssel, looking off into the distance. "Remind her that we're all volunteers."

Lucy followed his lead and stared off at the house across the pasture. She pictured Hilda watching them through a window, her lip curled wickedly at her deviousness. Somehow Lucy doubted that appealing to her better nature would make any difference at all.

Chapter 12

March went out like a lion and the morning of April 1st there was a new coating of fluffy white snow on the landscape around the pottery. Lucy woke early, earlier than usual, and lay in bed wondering if the sun gently streaming through the big window behind their bed had woken her, or if she was just excited for the start of Tulip Festival. Last year she'd only worked the Festival a couple of days, towards the end, but the flowers - the flowers were intoxicating. Broad, voluptuous petals so smooth and velvety, they looked almost like skin, and in colors of such boldness that they called the eye, like the Pied Piper, and lifted the spirit with their show of spring. Lucy couldn't wait to see what an entire season of tulips would look like.

It was warm under the covers and sunlight or no sunlight Lucy noticed how cold the room felt. She definitely wasn't ready to get up and face the day. She rolled over, to snuggle closer to Joe, and saw the dusting of snow on the branches of the apple tree behind the house. "What the…..?" she muttered to herself, lifting her head to take a better look. Maybe it was just apple blossoms, she thought. But no, she could definitely see a thin lines of snow cradled in the crooks of the branches up against the tree trunk.

She rolled over the other way and looked at the cherry tree through the side window. That had snow on it too. She climbed out of bed and tiptoed the length of the room to look at the used, K-car station wagon she and Joe had bought two days ago and filled with boxes of pottery yesterday. She looked down through the small, mullioned windows, at the driveway out front; sure enough, the K-car had patches of snow on it too. "Oh no," she whispered.

"What's the matter?" Joe called across from the bed.

"It snowed last night."

"Did it? Maybe that means it'll be a good Festival."

"Maybe," said Lucy, not persuaded. "Or maybe it means I should borrow your thermal long johns."

"That too." Joe lifted his head just slightly so he could see her. "You've still got time before you have to get up, don't you?"

"Yes. It's only about a quarter past five."

"Allllllllll *right*," he crowed. "Then get over here and keep me warm."

And Lucy bounded the length of the room and sprang into bed next to him.

*****

Lyle and Ingeborg Pfeiffer set the tone for the Tulip Festival. At least in Lucy's mind they did. Despite the cold and the wind, which came whistling in from the Pacific Ocean and gathered momentum over the flat, agricultural land, they showed up early on the first day, "Because," explained Ingeborg, "two of my favorite things: tulips and pottery." The judge's wife was motioning with her right hand to the pieces Lucy had put on the counter of her booth, when her eye suddenly caught the pitcher in the far corner. The one which the bulb farmer, Julia Van Daveer, had filled with fresh cut tulips. "Oh look!" Ingeborg exclaimed. "The potter put them both together! I didn't know he drew tulips on his pieces."

"He drew them on a teapot last year," Lucy told her. "And it got a lot of looks, but it didn't sell."

"Well I think you might be selling this one today," Ingeborg said with assurance. "Hopefully it is for sale, even though it has tulips in it?"

"Oh yes. The tulip grower just likes filling the pottery with fresh flowers. She says it'll sell faster that way." Lucy pointed at the cut flower booth to her left. "Plus, the ladies selling flowers can show their customers what certain varieties look like when they're open, by pointing at them in my vases."

The two ladies selling at the cut flower stand, their noses red from the cold, waved and smiled at her. Then one of them pointed out in front of the flower booth. She was wearing fingerless gloves, and as soon as she pointed, she wrapped that hand inside the other, to rewarm her fingertips. Lucy looked where she'd pointed and saw Julia Van Daveer carrying over one of Joe's casserole dishes full of yellow, red and white tulips.

"Ohhhhhh," sighed Ingeborg, her gaze fixed on what the rosy-cheeked farmer had in her hands. "Look at that." The tulips sprayed like a rainbow in all directions over the top of the shallow casserole dish. Ingeborg peered down inside the pot as Julia set it down on Lucy's counter. "How did you do that?" she asked.

"I soaked a piece of oasis – you know, that green florist's foam? -" Ingeborg nodded. "- and I put it in the bottom of the baking dish. Then I pushed the cut tulips into it." She looked down at her handiwork. "It's a perfect pot for a tulip arrangement."

"I'll say," agreed Ingeborg. "And it's gorgeous too." She was leaning over to see the red tulips carved around the side of the casserole.

"Do you have the lid?" Lucy asked Julia.

The farmer grinned and pulled the wide, casserole lid out of the pocket of her work apron and placed it on the counter next to the base. "Sell the pot with the flowers in it," she told Lucy "No charge." She rapped on the edge of the counter twice with her fingers and added, "I'm guessing somebody will want it for their Easter table."

"I think that somebody might be me," Ingeborg confided to Lucy as she watched Julia jog away. "Lyle," Ingeborg called out to her husband, who was getting himself a cup of coffee from the next booth down. There were just four booths set up at the side of the field: the cut flower booth; Lucy's pottery booth; Friendship House, which sold hot drinks and cookies to benefit the homeless, and a booth selling film for people's cameras. They all faced the wide, triangular field that the Van Daveers had rented for their tulips this season and Lucy felt like she had a seat at one of nature's best shows. This early in the season there were only two varieties blooming, the red and the yellow double ruffle tulips, but that was enough to get Lucy excited to see the others flowers enter the stage, like a chorus line of color building towards a grand, painterly finale.

Lyle Pfeiffer nodded at his wife, lifted his coffee off the stand and walked towards them.

"Isn't this casserole dish lovely?" Ingeborg said, pointing at the object.

"It's a casserole dish?" Lyle asked, surprised. "Looks like a flower holder to me."

"Well it's got flowers in it right now, but you can use it to cook," Ingeborg told him. Then she looked at Lucy. "Can't you?"

"Yes, of course. It's really for baking in the oven."

"Baking what kinds of things?" asked Lyle. He sipped his coffee as he listened to her reply.

"Pot roasts, beans, chicken and rice. I use mine a lot for shepherd's pie."

"I'm hungry already," Lyle said, smiling at his wife.

"So what do you think?" she asked. "Do you like it?"

"Yes. Very nice," the judge replied in his gruff voice.

"I was thinking of getting the casserole and this pitcher here. See, they both have tulips on them," she added, as if to persuade him. "Red tulips."

Lyle Pfeiffer gave Lucy a sly wink and a one-sided grin, which she took as a 'watch this' signal. "Do you have the money to pay for them?" he asked his wife.

"I do," she replied. "It's in your checkbook."

"How can it be *your* money if it's in *my* checkbook?"

"Well watch, and I'll show you."

Lucy smiled. Between the flowers and the banter, the huge flock of pure white snow geese she'd passed on her way down to the field and the camaraderie between the vendors, she was in for a great Tulip Festival.

*****

Joe stopped at the grocery store in Concrete before heading out to the airport. He wanted to pick up some noodles to go with the spaghetti sauce he'd made for dinner. As he turned off the engine in his truck, he saw Hilda across the parking lot, hustling towards the store, her head down like she didn't want to be seen. Damn, he thought.

He threw open the door to his truck and stepped out. He wasn't going to be put off going inside just because of her. He stepped around in front of his truck and heard a voice he recognized call out, "So they let you come into town now, do they?"

Joe swung around and saw his old friend and former boss, Buck Vorhees, stopped in the middle of the parking lot, leaning his weight on a cane he had positioned in front of his legs. Joe had never seen Buck with a cane before but he knew the ex-logger and mill owner had to be his dad's age because he was a World War II vet. Maybe he was getting a little unsteady on his feet.

"Buck!" he called out, walking towards the old timer. "It's good to see you."

"It's good to see you too," agreed Buck. "In fact, I'm glad to run into you because just the other day I was admiring your house."

"You were?" said Joe. "You should have stopped in."

"Well I was with my brother and he had some place to be," Buck tossed out, like this was a normal state of affairs. He began to ease forward, towards the grocery store. Joe edged along beside him. "But I wanted to tell you that you built yourself a mighty fine house there."

"Why, thank you," said Joe, tipping his head down to cover his embarrassment. Then he leaned towards his old friend and whispered out the side of his mouth, "But, you know, I got some mighty fine wood from my old boss to help me build that house."

Buck chuckled. "I do remember making sure you got a few good lengths of lumber to take home with you."

"A few?" Joe scoffed. "You were a lot more generous than that. Seemed like every time I turned around you were finding some wood and telling me, 'Add that to the pile for your house.'"

Buck chuckled again. "Well, you were a good worker," he said, too modest to take the credit for his good deed.

Joe wanted to throw an arm around this gentle teddy bear of a man, to give him a hug of appreciation, but Buck seemed a little fragile with his cautious gait. "Are you okay?" he asked, looking down at Buck's legs. That's when he noticed the limp.

"Yep," Buck replied. "Just need a new hip is all."

"Oh I'm sorry. Are they gonna give you one?"

Buck nodded. "This summer."

"Well that's good. I want you to be able to enjoy your retirement," Joe said, smiling across at his friend.

"Semi-retirement," Buck corrected.

"How's that?'

"My brother's got me doing odd jobs with some of his heavy equipment. A little land clearing, stump pulling, road building."

Joe's interest perked right up. "Is that right?" he said.

*****

Hilda was trying not to be seen. She was still mad about the dressing down Hank Throssel had given her about making the fire department go out for no reason to the pottery. He hadn't even given her time to deny it; just told her not to do it again.

She rounded the corner by the frozen foods and saw Marty Ulrich getting himself some ice cream. "I thought you were supposed to be building me a road," she said, coming up on him from behind.

"That was my plan," said Ulrich, tossing his chocolate ice cream in his cart like he didn't give two hoots that she'd finally tracked him down. "But then I found out who Connors has for a lawyer." He let the door on the ice cream freezer slam shut and leaned into Hilda, his brow tight with anger. "And I don't want to go head-to-head with that pit-bull ever again!"

*****

Perspective was everything, Joe realized, as he peered down from Matt Chandler's single engine, Aeronca plane to see his house and property below. It was a gloriously sunny, mid-April day and the lines he'd drawn on the ground in powdered silica made the disputed section of land look tiny, inconsequential in this vast, swooping valley of the Skagit River. Joe took the lens cap off his Pentax 35 mm camera and started taking photographs of the zigzag lines around his house. From his aerial vantage point, the line that angled up, then back away, from his front steps looked almost like he'd drawn a pointer that said "enter here." Joe found himself smiling, enjoying that concept. Maybe he should make it permanent, as if he'd planned it that way to encourage people towards his shop.

The potter took three photographs in quick succession before Matt circled around to give him a second chance. He couldn't quite capture the line down by the highway because it was being obscured by the sprawling branches of the King David apple tree, which apparently didn't recognize boundaries imposed by humans. Instead, the tree was busy unfurling the leaves around its buds so the world would be able to see its springtime collection of exquisite white blossoms. Joe photographed his marks on the ground as best he could and then watched them get even smaller as Matt pushed the small plane forward, into the North Cascades. Joe relaxed back into his seat and watched the teal green of the river sparkle in the sunlight as they rattled through the sky above it at 80 mph. He felt Matt pull the plane up over a ridge, only to be lifted higher in the sky on the other side by the prevailing winds. Joe's stomach lurched but Matt pointed down to their right and Joe leaned forward again to see a cirque lake under a thick blanket of snow. He shifted forward and yelled at the back of Matt's head, "Is that Marten Lake?"

The pilot nodded and tipped the plane gently towards the steep, thickly forested slope on one side of the lake where Lucy had gotten lost the previous summer. Joe squeezed Matt's shoulder, acknowledging the gesture. The plane leveled out and rose up over another ridge straight into the welcoming sun. Once on the other side of this ridge, the wind sucked the Aeronca downwards and Joe felt his stomach lurch again. The plane was definitely moving in concert with the weather, he thought, rather than being in control of it.

Matt flew them over Jordan Lake and the Illabot Creek drainage where the canyons were still recovering from a devastating forest fire. Joe remembered sitting in his truck on the Illabot Creek Road after hiking in to fish Jordan Lake and seeing a huge billow of black smoke roiling up the canyon. It was 4 pm and he was worried there might still be loggers working on the landing where they pulled the fresh fell trees, so he drove out that way to check. He could see the landing was deserted once he reached a certain point on the road and stopped, rather than go any further, watching flames scream up the canyon from somewhere down below. Flames that mirrored the height of the logging tower, at 60 or 70 feet tall. Joe remembered his stomach lurching then too, not so much because he was scared he might get trapped by the fire, but because it gave him renewed respect for all those who fought forest fires. And he knew he never wanted to be one of them.

The plane rose again, over the ridge towards Arrow Creek and Joe marveled at the acres and acres of wilderness where the land was too steep to do anything but grow trees. Some of his favorite haunts were in this wilderness and while he always knew there was risk involved in putting himself in this country, he felt more at ease taking that risk than he did bickering over a few feet of land along a property line.

Matt flew them over Boulder Lake and the Dogbone Lake, both of which Joe enjoyed hiking into for the fishing, and then he tipped the plane gently sideways and glided them around, like an eagle on the wing, to head back downriver to the airport in Concrete. As they pulled away Joe's mind stayed on one of the logging roads, where he could look across the canyon at the wide expanse of trees and know that he'd just climbed that to get to the lake on the other side. He compared that to the few feet of land he'd outlined in white as they passed over his house once more and marveled that he could have thought himself greedy for wanting it. Especially since he could make it worth Hilda's while, by recommending her plots of land to visitors to his shop, who were looking to buy real estate in the area.

He put the lens cap back on his camera and wound the shoulder harness around it feeling a weight lift off his shoulders; he'd made a decision about his property line dispute. And as he slipped his camera back into its case he knew he would call Klaassen to tell him as soon as he got home.

*****

Lucy had her hand in the air and was answering the questions, which she'd already answered on the forms, as if by rote.

"Are you an alcoholic?" said the tall, dark-haired, mild-mannered Immigration official.

"No," said Lucy.

"Are you a psychotic?"

"No."

Lucy kept on with her monosyllabic responses but the truth was her mind was far away, thinking of little Maddie. Erica had surprised them with an unplanned visit with Joe's daughter at the end of Tulip Festival. "I have to fly to Washington to finish up some business," she told Joe on the telephone. "So I thought I'd bring Maddie with me. That way you get a little more time with her and I can introduce her to the flight between Billings and Seattle."

This led to a lovely, stress-free few days with Maddie. Joe brought her down to see the tulips and let her take a pony ride around the field. Then they both took her to the Woodland Park Zoo in Seattle the next day and went out for a Mexican meal in the evening.

It was a moment at the Mexican restaurant that kept resonating with Lucy. At one point in the meal Joe was joking around with Maddie who laughed and laughed at her dad. Then she rubbed her head against his forearm affectionately and blurted, "Oh daddy, I love you so much. I wish I could cut myself in two."

Joe looked at his little girl, surprised. "Why?" he asked.

But Lucy knew. She knew it was because Maddie wished she could spend as much time with her daddy as she did with her mother. She watched Maddie look away, playfully shaking her head to avoid answering the question.

"Just because," she said finally.

And Lucy's heart broke a little that at the tender age of five, Maddie already knew how to be diplomatic around grown ups.

The Immigration Official drew Lucy's attention back with what she knew was the last question. "Have you committed or have you been convicted of a crime involving moral turpitude?"

"No," she answered.

"Okay. Please sign and put the date here," said the agent, pointing down at the form with his pen. "And then take the form out front to get your temporary green card. Your permanent card should arrive within the next month," he went on, sounding like he'd said this a million times already today. "But you're good to travel before that with the temporary card. Do you have any questions before you sign?"

"I do," said Joe.

"Go ahead," said the INS agent.

"What if she's lying?"

Lucy almost kicked him under the table! Didn't he know these people didn't appreciate jokes? The agent had probably just pushed a buzzer underneath his desk that would cause three heavily armed individuals to storm into the room and handcuff her to the next plane out of here.

But the immigration officer didn't seem surprised in the least. He just looked at Joe and replied, "Well, if we catch her, we can deport her without due process."

"My advice," joked Joe in a whisper, as they walked out of the room. "Is don't get caught."

*****

Hilda tilted her head to one side and stared at her lawyer, Gerald Huntsinger. So Connors had a witness who'd seen her running at him with the shotgun? What difference did that make?

"I'm thinking," Huntsinger went on, seemingly oblivious to the genteel incredulity she was trying to project. "That it's probably not a good idea for us to proceed with the assault."

"I had the shotgun to defend myself," Hilda informed him, in an attempt to persuade him otherwise. "Any judge should be able to see that."

"Yes, but Connors was unarmed," Huntsinger went on.

"We don't know that," Hilda countered. "I've seen rifles in his truck and I was worried he'd have one of those with him."

The lawyer let this go by without a reply. Instead, he raised his right index finger and his eyebrows, as if he also had good news. "But," he said, and Hilda straightened her head on her neck. "His lawyer has an offer for us concerning the septic tank and the land around it and wants to discuss it with me as soon as he gets back into the office."

Hilda nearly pumped the air with excitement; now they were getting somewhere. Maybe Connors' lawyer being a hard nose had worked in her favor and he'd counseled the potter to make things right with his neighbor. "When will that be?" she asked.

Huntsinger glanced at the letter again, then at the calendar on his desk. "He says he'll be back first thing tomorrow. So as long as I can get a hold of him…"

Hilda's spirits lifted. "Should I come back tomorrow so we can go over the details?"

"Oh no, there's no need. I know this is a long drive for you."

It was true; Seattle was a long drive for Hilda. But she could spend the night down in a hotel in the city if it meant she could start planning her next move against Connors. She opened her mouth to say as much but Huntsinger was already on his feet, coming around the desk towards her.

"I'll let you know as soon as I find out what they're proposing," he said. And with one hand gently on her shoulder, he led her out the door and back towards reception.

The brevity of the visit just meant Hilda had more time to enjoy the beautiful spring day and as she drove north on the freeway towards the Skagit Valley, she couldn't help but play out in her mind how things would go down with Connors. She imagined he'd offer her a lot of money, enough that it might even pay for her road to be built; but she'd have to say no because her lawyer would require 40% of whatever he offered, and then there were filing fees with the County, and maybe title fees. It just wouldn't be worth it. So instead, she'd encourage him to spend his money putting in another septic system, this time on his property. And as an act of good neighborliness, she'd throw in the tiny triangle in his front yard to straighten out their mutual property line. And then, Hilda thought, a buzz of excitement shooting through her, then she'd build her road right up against it.

It was early enough that she decided she'd stop in Mount Vernon on her way home, and confirm her ticket to Hawaii with her travel agent. After all, she'd finally secured a road builder, who'd told her he expected to break ground on July 1st, so she had no reason not to go. She got another thrill when she realized she could get home and call Gus not only with some good news about her dispute with Connors but also her flight details to Oahu.

Hilda was feeling so good about the day that when she got to the Conway exit off I5, she decided to take it and drive the back way into Mount Vernon, past the tulip fields. The festival was over, so she'd be spared the gnarly traffic, but she knew the tulips often bloomed well past the festival, Maybe she'd catch some color in the fields.

She tootled her little Honda Civic along Best Road, past a flock of snow geese and up over the small, cobblestone bridge crossing the south fork of the Skagit River. Then the road straightened out for a while, dipping up and down between large farmhouses with interesting, angled rooflines, their barns full of equipment and livestock. Hilda's mother had been fond of telling her that these houses were Sears kit homes from the early 1900s and as ornate as they were, they were considered affordable housing back then. Very different from the mobile homes that were becoming increasingly popular as affordable housing in Skagit County, her mother used to say.

Best Road dipped down another incline and around a tight bend heading for the turn off towards La Conner, which used to be the little fishing village but was now a tourist destination town. As soon as Hilda passed the turn off she saw a blanket of vibrantly red tulips in a field that stretched as far as she could see under a picture perfect backdrop of Mount Baker. She didn't have her camera with her so she decided to pull off at the side of the road and take a long, slow, mental photograph with her eyes.

Hilda felt her spirit fill with the stunning sight as she committed it to memory and she drove away feeling renewed and invigorated. She stopped, further down the road, at her favorite nursery and treated herself to two bouquets of fresh cut tulips: one red, to remind her of the field, and one lavender with light cream edging on the petals. She laid them on the empty passenger seat beside her and headed for the travel agent, where the sense of positivism she'd picked up from the flowers, caused her not only to confirm her ticket to Hawaii, but pay for it too. She got back in the Civic and followed the craggy top of Sauk back home.

As she pulled up to get the newspaper from the box at the end of her driveway, she couldn't help but noticed the apple tree at the edge of her property, alongside the highway. It was covered in pink and white apple blossoms. She pulled forward a little, to admire it from closer, and noticed Connors, sitting in his front yard, painting it. Or was he drawing it? Hilda couldn't tell for sure. But he was definitely making art from the tree. She bristled, reminding herself that he was sitting on her property to make that art but then she relaxed again. She was feeling too good to go there in her mind today. Instead she sat and watched him lifting his head up and down as he looked at the tree then drew what he'd seen, thoroughly focused. She would have loved to do something like that at the side of the tulip field today but she didn't have the skills. Or patience. She could be patient with her knitting but that was busy work. Work that allowed her mind the freedom to think while her fingers kept the yarn moving over the needles. She wondered if Connors was thinking about something right now? Something unrelated to the magnificence of the apple tree in full bloom.

Then she noticed the tall, white haired man standing just behind him. It jogged a memory in her that she couldn't quite bring to mind. Had she seen this man before? He was very attractive with his tan skin and lean shape. If she weren't involved with Gus, he might be someone she'd like to get to know better. Hilda lifted her gaze from his long torso back up to his face and noticed the man was smiling at her. A warm, gently flirtatious, come hither smile that made Hilda blush, from her face all the way down to the tips of her toes. And before she knew what she was doing, Hilda realized she was smiling back.

*****

Joe was sitting on a lawn chair in the front yard with a piece of quarter inch plywood balanced across the arms, drawing the blooming apple tree on some stoneware clay that he'd shaped into a platter. He had covered the top of the platter with white slip, so he could etch the lines for the blossoms into it, then remove the excess white around them. That would be easier and more effective than trying to fill the tiny blossoms with colored clay after the fact. But now that he was here, he decided that all he needed to do was add blue slip to the white around the blossoms, to make the color of the sky that he could see through the tree. That would give a more painterly effect to the platter. He nodded to himself; he liked that idea.

He drew strong, confident lines in the clay for the trunk of the tree while his geologist friend, Sol, stood beside him, regaling him with stories of the millions and millions of gallons of oil he had on the land that he owned down in South America. Periodically, Sol would stop his narrative to bend forward and pick up a stick Max kept bringing back to him. Sol would toss the stick into the blackberry bushes and return to his story of how the oil would make them all rich, just as soon as he could find investors for the drilling.

It was all very entertaining to Joe, who hadn't seen his old friend for almost four months. Not since his wedding to Lucy, in fact, because Sol had been down in Peru for the winter, staying with one of his seven sons. But the retired geologist had flown back a couple of weeks early so he could attend the public hearing and, as he told Joe and Lucy when they picked him up at the airport after Lucy's immigration interview, "Give that Hearing Examiner a piece of my mind!"

Joe also found Sol's storytelling helpful because it allowed him to switch off his own internal monologue, so his brain could focus on replicating the complex apple blossoms on the clay with simple grooves from a pointed dental tool. The highway was quiet, since it was too early for summer visitors and too late for winter sports up in the high country. A tiny, red fox sparrow landed on one of the branches of the apple tree and Joe stopped drawing to watch it. The little brown bird with the white and brown belly had a lovely rosy hue to the tips of his feathers that picked up the pink edging on the mostly white apple blossoms.

Sol paused his monologue and Joe wondered if he were watching the little bird too.

"D'you see him?" the potter whispered to his friend.

"I do," Sol whispered back. "Makes me wish you could add a little pink to the blossoms on your platter there."

"Well I'm hoping they'll get a blush of pink from the kiln when I fire it," Joe explained. "Of course, I can't guarantee that."

"Like the apple tree," mused Sol.

"How's that?" asked Joe.

"Well she goes to all this effort to blossom……"

"He," interrupted Joe.

"What?"

"The tree's a he."

Sol shot him an inquisitive look. "How d'you know?"

"'Cause it's a King David."

"A King *David*?" repeated Sol, mystified.

Joe nodded up at his friend and saw that his face was filled with boyish wonder.

"I don't think I've ever heard of a King David apple tree."

"It's an old variety," conceded Joe, "so it's not that well known. But the apples taste great." He furrowed his brow, trying to remember something. "Didn't you eat some last fall?"

"I did. They were *delicious*."

Sol stopped talking and a pleasant, natural silence hung between them. Joe looked at his drawing as he cleaned a bead of excess clay off the point of his dental tool, waiting for Sol to return to his original thought. When that didn't happen, he prompted him.

"And?"

"And what?" asked Sol.

"You were comparing the vagaries of my firing results with the apple tree?"

"Oh yes." Sol swung back to his point like they'd never digressed. "So the tree goes to all this effort to make flowers, expending a mammoth, a *colossal* amount of energy, and he has no guarantee that fruit will result."

Joe nodded his agreement as he drew a fourth branch on the platter. "It all depends on the temperature," he mumbled.

"Exactly!" agreed Sol. "And your pottery is dependent on the temperature inside your kiln."

"Temperature and atmospheric conditions, yes," said Joe. He stopped working and looked up at his friend, right hand over his heart, teasing. "I'm touched that you would think to compare my work to that of an apple tree."

Sol scrunched up his face, lobbing the tease right back at the potter.

"No, actually I am," said Joe, returning to seriousness. He motioned towards the King David. "I mean who wouldn't want to be compared to this glorious feat of nature." He bent his head to his drawing again. "Except I wouldn't say that I expend as much energy creating my pottery as the tree does blooming."

"Maybe not on the individual pieces," Sol granted. "But when you consider all that you have invested in building and equipping your clay studio, the kiln and your shop, where people can come and pollinate future pottery pieces by buying what you have, then yes, you've expended a great deal of energy."

"A colossal amount?" Joe teased again.

"*Gargantuan*!" declared Sol. "And *that's* why the County should give you your permit!"

Max exploded out of the blackberry bushes right at that moment, as if he were seconding Sol, and ran to drop his stick at the geologist's feet again. Sol acquiesced by tossing the stick for his persistent buddy and Joe pecked away at the clay in front of him. Silence hung between them like so much peaceful synergy until Maggie, who was lying on the ground to the right of Joe, perked her head and nosed an alert towards the highway.

"I think we have company, Maestro," Sol muttered, as if he were sharing a secret that he didn't want overheard.

"What's that?" said Joe.

"A certain neighbor lady seems to be watching us from her car. Down by the highway."

Joe had his right arm wrapped around the top of the platter, coming at the details in the center top of the tree from above. "Oh," he remarked without taking his eyes off his work. "Then smile at her, I guess."

"Think I should?"

"I don't see why not. Lucy says Hilda needs a distraction."

"So I should *flirt* with her," said Sol, with the thrill of a schoolboy playing a prank. "I can do that."

And then he was quiet, and Joe could hear songbirds, enjoying the spring day, and Max rustling frantically in the bushes. He added some final grooves around the apple blossoms, to give them that multi-petal dimension, then cleaned the end of the dental tool again. "Did it work?" he asked, without looking up.

"She smiled back," said Sol.

"Good for you."

"Now it's your turn."

"To do what?"

"Smile at her. Break down her resistance before the hearing on Friday."

Joe winced but looked over at the Honda Civic anyway. He

couldn't quite bring himself to smile at Hilda, not after all the headache she was causing him, but he fanned his left hand in the air, side to side, letting her know he'd seen her.

The Civic promptly backed up, swung forward, and disappeared between the sentinel firs lining Hilda's driveway.

Chapter 13

They parked up by the revetment overlooking the river down in Mount Vernon the day of the public hearing and hustled away from the car towards the hearing rooms by the courthouse. It was only 1:30 pm and the hearing didn't start until 2:00 so they didn't need to rush, but adrenaline made them push the pace. Lucy and Joe were both very nervous. Plus it was raining. A fine soft rain like the one they'd had on their wedding day. Lucy found herself wondering what this might mean for their public hearing. She could believe that it was bad news or she could tell herself that if rainy marriage meant happy marriage, as Délphine said, maybe the same was true of a public hearing. Or she could stop overthinking it and just keep moving forward.

Sol was with them. They all three walked in a straight line down Kincaid Street, where the traffic came off the freeway, towards downtown Mount Vernon. Then they turned left down South 3rd. The county offices were on their left and the courthouse on their right. They dodged behind the courthouse and under the concrete stairs, which made a bridge between the two spaces. As soon as they turned towards the hearing rooms, they saw the crowd beginning to form outside.

“Is that for us?” Joe asked, his shock echoing off the concrete tunnel under the stairs.

There were already a half a dozen people huddled outside hearing room B, where they were supposed to have their hearing. Lucy saw Connie and her new husband, who’d hosted their pottery party in Seattle; Stan and Bobby Joe; a person she recognized but couldn’t name; and Julia Van Daveer, the tulip bulb grower. Lucy felt her face break out into a big smile.

The rain had been a good sign after all.

*****

Hilda decided on the red blouse with her black dress pants because she liked the way they looked on her. She tipped her head down, looking at herself in the mirror. She imagined it would just be Connors at the hearing with her, maybe his wife, too, but just in case they brought that flirty guy with them, she wanted to look her best. And the red did look good on her. She shimmied a little, from side to side, then tossed her head back up, and forced herself to think more practically. Red and black were both power colors, a point in her favor at the Hearing, and the two together made her look elegant yet professional. Yes, this was what she was wearing.

She glanced at her watch. It was still only 12:20. Time enough for her to stop and pick up her mail before making the hour’s drive down to Mount Vernon. She should leave a moment to find a place to park too, she imagined, since the county lot by the hearing rooms was small and filled up fast. She didn’t want to look too eager by being the first to arrive but she also didn’t want to be late. She dabbed some powder on her nose, fluffed her gray curls and slipped into her black pumps. Then she hurried out of her bedroom and down the hallway towards the front door, feeling a little buzz of excitement.

Show time!

*****

"He-ey! How are *you*?!" Joe called out, as Craig and Caroline Hazlehurst sauntered towards the hearing room. "Thanks for coming."

"Of course," said Caroline. "We couldn't let our favorite potter lose his place to sell on the highway."

"Yeah," laughed her husband. "Where else would we stop to let the dogs go pee?"

Dave, from upriver, leaned towards Lucy and said, "I feel like a groupie, waiting outside the stage door to get an autograph with all the other Joe Connors' fans."

Lucy laughed but inside herself she was warmed by all the friendly faces that had come to speak on their behalf. The area under the stairs was filling up with people from Seattle, Mount Vernon, Rockport, Marblemount, Bellingham. And their friend, Twyla, herself a business owner, had driven all the way over from Omak.

"I'm flattered," Lucy heard Joe tell Stan and Bobby Joe. "I had no idea so many people would show up." He pointed across at her. "And Lucy says we got 80 some letters from across the country in support of this amendment."

"So you're saying I should go get myself some coffee 'cause you don't need me?" joked Mario, Katie's husband, over the heads of some of the upriver attendees.

"No, no," laughed Joe. "I think I need all the support I can get."

****

Hilda couldn't believe the words in front of her eyes! She'd found the large, manila envelope from her lawyer curled into her mailbox and had pulled it out with alacrity. Just what she'd been hoping for; news of the offer from Connors before she went down to the hearing. She took it back to her car to open, for privacy, and sat tall in her seat. She ripped open the top of the envelope. She reached inside and pulled out the cover letter, propping it on the envelope against the steering wheel so she could read it. But as she read, her mouth dropped open and her head began to pound with her rising blood pressure. The tone told her from the outset that this was not going to be the news she'd been expecting and she was so shocked, so completely aghast, she couldn't focus on anything other than the key phrases. "...advise you not to proceed...," ".... impeding his right to work on his septic tank...," "...asking for all the land....," "...$1,500..."

Her head flipped up at this last, like an angry horse, bucking against its rider, and she felt like she wanted to spit, she was so mad. $1,500! *$1,500*!! That's what Connors was offering?! Not to purchase the land but - what did it say? Hilda looked down at the letter again and read – "....in the interest of good neighborliness..." She snorted. Good neighborliness! Connors was proposing she grant him everything that he'd previously been offered in court, i.e., all the land around his septic system, so he could work on it without further impediment, but, in the interest of "good neighborliness," he'd throw in $1,500?? Hilda thought not. Not as long as she was alive on this green earth!

She went to toss the letter and envelope on the passenger seat beside her when she noticed the mention of an attachment under her lawyer's signature. She pried the top of the envelope open with her fingers and peered down inside. There were some 8 by 10 photographs in there. She pulled them out and laid them on top of the letter in front of her.

These were aerial shots of Connors' front yard and her adjacent property, with lines of white on the ground. Stuck onto the photographs were arrows pointing to the lines, with descriptions. Hilda read the descriptions. The zigzag line around and in front of Connors' house was described as the existing property line; the straight line, to the west, was described as the proposed property line. Hilda snatched the letter out from under the photographs and looked for an explanation. She found it in the third paragraph. This was the section of land Connors proposed she give up in the interests of "good neighborliness" and fifteen hundred bucks. Well he could propose all he wanted; she wasn't doing it!

She stared at the white outline on the ground. It looked like a parody of something the police would draw around a dead body, except it was shaped more like a one-sided lightning bolt than a human. Hilda felt a dark, cheerless resentment, like slow boiling tar, begin to foment inside her; Connors was sitting inside that outline the other day, like he already owned it, drawing the apple tree. She squinted, trying to see where the line went under the apple tree, but it was hidden by the sprawling branches. She took her index finger and drew an imaginary line out towards the highway from where the chalk disappeared. It looked like that tree was on her property.

And Connors had the gall to use it for art?!

*****

A smiley, dark-haired woman with glasses came and unlocked the door to Hearing Room B and stepped back to let everyone in. Joe counted 20 people pass ahead of him into the brightly lit room and was very pleased that he knew every one of them. He didn't know all their names but knew he'd seen them in his shop at one time or another and assumed they must have signed the guest book, which is how come they were here. They'd received one of the letters Lucy had sent out, and had come to say their piece on his behalf.

At least he assumed they'd speak on his behalf although for sure he'd find out once they got to the microphone, in the center of the room. Joe's biggest hope was that he wouldn't have to say anything himself. His plan was to keep his head down and speak only if spoken to. Let Lucy do the talking for him.

He counted four rows of six plastic chairs on both sides of a common aisle, so 48 seats in all, although he imagined they could bring in more if needed. Plus there was a seat behind the simple, wooden desk for the Hearing Examiner. The chairs were brown, the carpet dark blue and the walls white, with no art on them. It was a pretty bland space and Joe almost wished he'd brought a book, to have something to look at while he was listening to people speak. But he'd tough it out.

His inclination was to sit towards the back but Stan from Seattle stopped him again, to ask what was running in the Skagit River, and when Joe turned around Lucy was already sitting in a seat on the aisle in the middle of the room. She was chatting with their neighbor,

Laura, who was sitting on the other side of the aisle from her, but as soon as Lucy saw him looking around the room she caught his eye and patted the empty seat beside her.

"Man, I can't believe how many people have showed up for this," he whispered when he sat down between her and Sol, who was fully engaged in a conversation with Brenda Mackey. His eyes scanned the entire room but he still didn't see Hilda anywhere.

"I know," Lucy whispered back. "I hope you're flattered."

"I am."

"And it's not even time yet so there might be more coming."

As soon as Lucy said this Joe saw Sonny slip into the room, his eyes sliding over the crowd, nodding at those he recognized. Most of the Upper Skagit contingent was sitting on the left side of the room. Sonny trotted that way, giving a high sign of recognition to Joe on his way by. Then Pete sidled in, threw him a wave, and edged down a row of seats to sit in the midst of three attractive young women.

Joe recognized the women but couldn't put names to them. "Who are those women Pete's sitting with?" he asked Lucy.

Lucy moved her head closer to him, so she could see between Craig and Caroline Hazlehurst. "Isn't the one on his left a Sheriff's Deputy?"

"That's right!" he agreed. "Deputy Porteous." Then he realized why she looked different. "She lost some weight."

"No, she's just not wearing that puffy uniform with all the gear on her hips that makes her look bulky," Lucy told him.

Joe conceded with a lift of his eyebrows. "Makes sense."

"The one to the right of Pete is a midwife. And I think that's her girlfriend next to her."

Joe turned to face her. "How do you know a midwife?"

She met his eye speaking low, so as not to be overheard. "From the shop of course. Why?"

"No reason," he shrugged, like it didn't matter. "I just thought you might be keeping something from me."

Lucy looked surprised. "Like what?"

Joe held his palm out towards the woman, to indicate it should be obvious. "She's a midwife."

"Ohhhh," Lucy responded, getting it. "Wouldn't *that* make your day!"

Joe didn't rise to her sarcasm. Instead he slid his hand over the top of her chair, pulled her closer to him, and whispered in her ear, "I wouldn't mind actually."

She spun towards him, their faces almost touching. "Really?!"

He knew he was blowing her mind after all he'd said about not wanting another child, but there'd been something so special about the impromptu visit with Maddie they'd just experienced. Something relaxed and comfortable. As if not knowing it was going to happen freed it of expectations, which made it easier for him and Maddie to be at home with each other. And home had turned out to be a place Joe wanted to revisit. "As long as you can work it for us to buy health insurance then I'm all for it," he said.

Lucy's green eyes darted back and forth as she looked deep into his eyes, trying to ascertain whether he was serious or not. For a second it felt like they were all alone, locked in a moment of intimate complicity.

Then he heard the door open again and turned to see Kenny stride into the room, his bearing tall and upright, just like the Navy had taught him.

"All right," announced his friend and customer, a big grin for all to see under his bristly moustache. "Let's get this party started!"

*****

Hilda parked at the library and scampered, as fast as she could, her heels clicking furiously on the sidewalk. She'd wasted too much time on that pointless, hateful letter from her lawyer and if she didn't hurry she'd be late. She didn't want to miss her chance to speak in front of the Hearing Examiner. She didn't want to miss that at all.

She blew across the intersection at Kincaid before the light could change against her and glanced at her watch as she approached the corner of the one block of county buildings. Good, it was only 1:55. She still had five minutes. She slowed, feeling heat in her chest from walking so fast, and lowered the collar on her raincoat. She'd be under cover of the stairs between the buildings next and wouldn't need the protection from the rain. She took a big, calming breath and walked more sedately, head high, around the corner onto the little cobblestone throughway leading to the hearing room. That's when she nearly ran right into Jimmy and Laura, her other neighbors. They were very involved with each other, as Jimmy held the door open to Hearing Room B for his wife, so they didn't see her; but the sight of them brought Hilda to an immediate halt. She hadn't expected *them* to turn up!

Her eyes pinballed this way and that as she reflected on the implications of their presence. Did she even want to go in now that she knew Jimmy and Laura were here? What if they mentioned some of the things she did to them when they were in the midst of their property line dispute. The thought made Hilda feel suddenly quite queasy.

She started edging towards the door to the hearing room again just as a postal worker that Hilda recognized from Concrete arrived from the other direction, her arm linked through her husband's. The woman acknowledged Hilda with a polite, "Hi!" but the husband only grunted tersely. Hilda was pretty sure the husband was one of Connors' hunting buddies. Her queasiness increased when she saw them open the door to the hearing room and disappear inside. This was not looking good for her.

She stopped moving, a couple of feet away from the door, and knew she had to make a decision and make it now, before somebody else that she knew showed up and opened the door for her to go in.

There were windows on either side of the door to the hearing room, tall, narrow windows that would give her a view of the room but probably obscure her face from the people inside. Hilda checked her perimeter and then sidled up to the closest window. She put her face up against the brushed glass and let her eyes roam the room.

She was stunned to see it was almost full. And there were a bunch of people she knew from the Upper Skagit. As her eyes drifted over the faces she could see, she realized about half of them didn't like her. She'd never been able to figure out why she drew such hostility from others but if these non-fans of hers were in that room, it was probably to speak on behalf of Connors. She clamped one hand over her mouth, fearing she might be sick, she was so nervous. She scanned the room for Connors. There he was, right in the middle of the throng, laughing and joking like he hadn't a care in the world. Hilda wanted to go in and wipe that smirk right off his face but she wasn't sure about facing all those people. What should she do?

She took another deep, calming breath and felt the waves of nausea begin to subside in her stomach. She wasn't doing anything wrong. She had a right to protect her residential neighborhood from light industry and she knew that most of the people from the Upper Valley would agree with that. Plus there had to be *someone* in there who'd come to speak against Connors. Because she was sure not everybody liked him.

She took a big gulp of courage and reached towards the door handle when a big, burly guy, who'd stood up to take off his tan and brown wool shirt, turned so she could see his face. Damn! It was Eddie Eldridge.

Hilda flipped 90 degrees and flattened herself against the wall, hiding. She still owed Eldridge for a log truck load of firewood. *Now* what was she going to do? She couldn't even try sitting someplace where he wouldn't see her because as soon as she got up to speak he'd be onto her. Damn, damn, damn!

A black cloud of anger hovered in front of her eyes. She didn't come all this way for nothing! Maybe, since it was so close, she'd go over to the Air Pollution Agency instead. See how far those guys had gotten in closing down Connors' kiln.

She turned, hearing a sound to her left and saw Pete rounding the corner towards her.

Hilda bolted.

*****

The Hearing Examiner was a chubby, round-faced man with round glasses and not much hair. "He looks friendly," Lucy whispered to Joe. He gave his name and announced what they were there for and then pointed at the microphone in the center of the aisle opposite him and welcomed anyone who wanted to come up and speak to do so.

Lucy stood, feeling a responsibility to get things started. "My name's Lucy Connors," she said, once she got to the mic, "And I don't think I really need to go over the reasons why our business, *Cascade Mountain Pottery*, qualifies for this amendment to its special use permit, because that's all detailed in our completed application form." She pointed forward at the file in front of the Hearing Examiner, assuming their application was in it. "But I do want to say that I think my husband had a very clever idea, when he came up with our home-based business. Not only did he build something very attractive – and we get a lot of people stop just to take a photograph of the house – but by putting the retail shop in the same location as his pottery studio, he made a place for visitors to be part of the whole experience. And, as I'm sure you read in some of the many letters written in favor of us getting this amendment," she said, wanting to remind the Hearing Examiner of the 80 plus letters written on their behalf. "Seeing the studio and the kiln before buying some of the pottery to take home, makes our business a favorite stop on the North Cascades Highway. I imagine anything that makes visitors feel welcome to the Skagit Valley has got to be good for other businesses, too. So I'm hoping that you'll give us all a break, by granting us this amendment. Thank you."

A trim, older gentleman from the left side of the room stood up as she walked away, and when she sat back down next to Joe, who had his head bowed like he was in church, praying, the fellow started talking at the microphone. Joe's left hand came out and patted her on the knee but he kept his head down, listening.

"The first time my wife and I pulled into the *Cascade Mountain Pottery*, Mr. Connors was still in the process of building his house," said the man, his manner relaxed, easy. "And there was no one there except a big, friendly, brown dog, lying under a blue tarp strung between an apple tree and a Douglas fir." His hands moved in the air in front of him as he described what it looked like. "There were four tables under the tarp along with the dog, all of them made out of rounds of wood on upside down tree stumps, and they were covered with pottery. And in the center of one, was a coffee cup, with a sign in front of it that said - Leave Money Here. I've never forgotten the sense of trust that I got when I saw that coffee cup. I think we picked out a mug each, and a small serving bowl – is that right?" he asked, looking across at his wife. She nodded. "And put our money in the coffee can. And we haven't stopped going back since. That little pottery shop is a great reason for a drive up the valley and, for my money, I hope it'll always be there."

The next person at the microphone was Erik, an upriver resident who was usually only comfortable in front of people when he had a guitar in his hands. "Yeah, hi," he said, bending down so his mouth would be close to the microphone, his face turning red. "I'm a neighbor of Joe Connors and his wife, played at their wedding in fact, and I'd like to say I hope you keep letting him make sales from his shop because otherwise where am I going to find a place to buy my sister a Christmas gift at 11 pm on Christmas eve?"

The whole room laughed and Lucy felt the tension she'd been holding inside, start to decompress. She looked at Joe; he still had his head down.

Julia Van Daveer stepped up to speak. "I'm a bulb farmer in Skagit County," she told the Hearing Examiner, "and I know the value of being able to farm your own land. I agree with Lucy that Joe's dream of having a little shop attached to his home where people can visit the studio and see where the pots are made, is a great concept. I think there are more people that wish they could do business that way. I know I look forward to being able to farm my own land and invite people onto it during the Tulip Festival. It's hard when you have to rent somewhere to do your work. It cuts into the profit margin and requires all sorts of time for set up and take down. Plus with pottery I imagine there's the breakage factor if Joe and Lucy have to take their work elsewhere to sell it. No, I'm in favor of leaving him his little shop in the mountains. Just as long as his wife keeps bringing the pots down to my tulip field every April," she said, breaking into a gentle, musical laugh that made Lucy smile. "Because I like filling them full of flowers."

Gary Cunningham, Joe's erstwhile hunting partner, was next and Lucy sat up in her seat. Gary wasn't much for speaking in general, let alone public speaking, and she was touched that he'd showed up to this hearing. "I'm a huntin' buddy of Joe's," he said in his tight, Tar heel twang. "And he's a great guy and makes nice pottery. Especially the chicken bricks 'cause they cook an elk roast so it don't dry out. My wife loves hers and does grouse in it sometimes and even uses it to bake bread so you should look for one of those at his shop if you ever get up that way. Only don't go in October 'cause I plan on taking him deer hunting up at Three Lakes then."

Then Pete took his place at the microphone and changed the feeling in the room with his blunt, angry words. "This is bullshit!" he told the Hearing Examiner, without preamble. "In Japan, this man would be revered!" He pointed across the room at Joe. "And if we had any sense we'd revere him here, instead of hounding him with red tape. That way he might stay around, and fill the whole damn valley with his beautiful, wood-fired pottery."

People around the room started to clap as Joe's shoulders rocked with laughter.

*****

The guy at the Air Pollution Agency had been very unhelpful, giving Hilda some nonsense about how his research had shown two minutes worth of a 747 flying overhead was more harmful to the environment than 20 years of firing a wood-firing kiln.

"But what about the smoke?" she said. "Isn't that illegal?"

"Well within certain parameters," he said. "But we have to prove those parameters and so far, we haven't been able to coordinate it to have someone present at one of the firings."

"Then give *me* the parameters and I'll tell you how he's breaking them!" Hilda snapped.

At which point the sloppily dressed, jowly jackass really made her mad her by lowering his voice, like he was talking to a child, or, or an *old* person, and saying, "I'm sure you would, but we can't just take someone's word for it if we're to file a complaint against Mr. Connors. We need proof."

Hilda was so angry she stormed out of his office without thinking to ask if he could at least walk across to the public hearing, and say that he was investigating Connors' kiln. She stood on the street between the two venues wanting to kick herself for not doing that. He could have been her cover. She looked at her watch again; twenty-five minutes had gone by. Maybe some of those people would have left the hearing by now.

She went back to the window she'd peered in before, hoping to see Eldridge gone. Maybe Jimmy and Laura too. Or, at the very least, a feisty debate that she could slide right into and not get noticed so much.

But when she looked in through the window, the first person she saw was the Hearing Examiner. He was listening to someone at the microphone in the center of the room and smiling. *Smiling*!

Hilda marched back to her car fit to burst.

*****

Three of the ladies from the cut flower booth next to Lucy in the tulip field were huddled around the microphone, like back-up singers, talking one on top of the other.

"What we're concerned about," said the first.

"If you don't let Joe sell his pottery out of his shop in the mountains," the second went on.

"Is that he'll be forced to sell in other places," explained the third.

"Like at the Tulip Festival."

"And take it from us...."

"He's not someone you want standing in the booth next to you..."

"...like a caged animal..."

"...growling at the customers..."

"*Buy it or leave me alone!*"

"He was great when it came to helping people park their cars in the wet mud at the side of the road," explained the first.

"Even when they sprayed rooster tails of mud up and down his clothes…."

"And then complained because they got some on their car…"

"He was pleasant and cheerful in that situation."

"But you don't want to trap him in a booth," cautioned the one, with a sad shake of her head.

"Definitely don't want to do that," agreed another.

"'Cause he's grouchy when he's trapped," they all ended together.

The clock over the Hearing Examiner's head showed 3:30 already but everyone had presented such different takes on the same subject that it felt like no time has passed at all. Some talked about how they enjoyed having the shop in the Upper Skagit because it made a nice day trip for them with visiting friends and relatives, others talked about how much they enjoyed the pottery they'd bought at that shop and a teacher from Sedro-Woolley stood up and described taking her third graders on a field trip to a place where they could see all the steps involved in making art, from start to finish. Jimmy and Laura stood and talked about Joe's little shop being a saving grace for them, providing them with some revenue for their artwork when they had nowhere else to sell.

"The only thing we regret," Jimmy said into the microphone. "Is that we didn't get to own the land right next to Joe and Lucy. 'Cause we would have built a retail shop right alongside them and not have to drive all the way to the Pike Place Market in Seattle to sell our artwork."

There was a moment of silence and the Hearing Examiner looked around the room, to see if anyone else wanted to speak. That's when Sonny stood up and shyly sidled over to the microphone. But once he got there, Lucy noticed his posture became upright, bold. "I'm with Julia Van Daveer," he started, loud and clear, without any room for argument in his tone. "I think Joe's real lucky to have a place to make his work and sell it because he can keep his overhead down and, that way, the price of his pottery, too. I can't see how it's not a win-win for everyone involved. Heck if I could, I'd work from home and I suspect you would, too," he said, nodding at the Hearing Examiner, who smiled beatifically back at him. Sonny threw his right arm out towards the rest of the people in the room. "Everyone would. Which has gotta be good for the environment because then people aren't driving everywhere. Plus anyone that goes to Joe's studio is gonna want to buy one of his pots, so you may as well make it legal cause who's going to turn away someone offering to give them money? I know I wouldn't." He turned, not waiting for an answer to his question, and marched back to his seat.

"Can I ask which one of you is Joe Connors?" asked the Hearing Examiner, once he determined that the public comment part of the Hearing was over.

Joe raised his head and his right hand but kept his mouth shut.

"I've never," said the Hearing Examiner, his eyes totally on Joe, "in all my 30 years of doing this job, had such a positive crowd at a public hearing. I don't think I *dare* do anything except grant you this amendment to your special use permit. Do you have any questions?"

Now Joe spoke. "Can I get my money back?" he asked, tongue-in-cheek.

"Oh no," said the Hearing Examiner dryly. "This is County government. We don't give money back."

And with that, he hit his gavel on the sound block to announce that the hearing was over.

*****

It was on the drive back upriver that all the anger and frustration and feelings of humiliation merged into that one, smug wave Connors had given her from his seat in front of the apple tree the other day. How dare he?! How dare he think that he could taunt her with his casual enjoyment of her property. He wanted to act like it all belonged to him? Well, he could think again.

She didn't care if the County wouldn't help her, or the Air Pollution, or the Sheriff's office, or even her wuss of a lawyer, because Hilda knew now what she had to do to prove to Connors that it all belonged to her.

And his days of enjoying it were over.

*****

Joe and Lucy dropped Sol at the train station in Mount Vernon, so he could head back to Seattle and take the ferry to Gig Harbor, to be with his son, Pedro. Then they were alone, floating on all the positive energy they'd received in the hearing room. It was as if they'd been forced to jump out of a plane only to find they had parachutes, which not only saved their lives, but made the journey down breathtakingly beautiful. So much so that it even made sense of why they had to jump in the first place.

"What are you thinking?" Joe asked, as they pulled onto the freeway to head for the agricultural fields of Cook Road and then on to the Upper Skagit.

"I was just thinking that it ended up being a good thing that we had to go through this hearing," replied Lucy.

"I know!" agreed Joe.

"All those people, taking time out of their busy lives. And they said such lovely things about you and your pottery." She looked across at him. "You've got to be feeling like a million dollars."

Joe was looking down at his hands, not really knowing where to put himself he was so humbled by the outpouring of love. "I am," he admitted. He lifted his head and looked out the passenger side window at Burlington Hill. Sonny had told him there were plans to put a housing development way up high on that hill and Joe could see where they were logging it already. He snapped back to the present, not wanting to lose the feel-good buzz he had going on inside himself. "And Jeff Martinez –"

"The fellow that builds high-end, log cabins up in Marblemount?"

"That's the one – he walked up to me after the hearing and said, 'I thought for a moment there that I was at your funeral, people were saying such nice things about you.'"

They both laughed.

"It certainly had that feel to it," said Lucy, pulling the K-car towards the exit.

"And no Hilda," mused Joe.

"No Hilda."

"I wonder why she never showed up?"

"I wondered that too. But then I thought, "Oh, what a bitter thing it is to look into happiness through another man's eyes.""

"Is that Shakespeare?"

"Uh huh. Some people just want to suck you into their misery. Look at all the times Hilda has had to do something that involved a lot of noise right along the fence line when we had company. It's as if she can't stand to see us enjoying ourselves."

"Well she would have seen us enjoying ourselves today, that's for sure. I didn't have to say a word the whole time. I loved that."

Lucy nodded. "I wouldn't be surprised to find out she did turn up but when she saw all the people in that room," - she looked across at him - " and she had to recognize a lot of them as allies of yours from upriver," – she went back to focusing on the road – "she bagged it."

"You think?"

Lucy bobbed her head right and left, like she was weighing his question. "Would you have wanted to go in if the room had been full of her cronies?"

Joe shrugged. "I doubt I'd've cared" Then he looked across at her again. "Does she have any cronies?"

"Probably not," conceded Lucy. "And I think that somehow proves my point."

*****

Hilda dropped the chain saw and her work gloves in the back of the Honda Civic and slammed the tailgate closed. She marched around to the driver's side door and threw herself into the vehicle. She turned the key in the ignition and it whirred angrily at her. She looked down at the dash. She'd been so eager to change out of her clothes and get this thing done that she hadn't even switched off the engine when she pulled in.

She bumped the Civic as fast as she dared down to the entrance to her driveway and left it there, remembering to switch off the engine this time. She rolled out, opened the tailgate and slipped on her gloves. Then she grabbed the chain saw and marched away with the tailgate wide open. She wasn't going to be here that long.

Connors' dogs started barking at her from his front porch but Hilda didn't care. Propelled by her spleen, she strode the few hundred feet along the highway easement and stopped in front of the apple tree, her back to the highway. The dogs leapt off the porch and down the front yard, stopping at the end of Connors' pick-up truck, about 20 feet from the apple tree, without missing a beat in their barking.

"Oh, LAY *DOWN*!" Hilda yelled, not really expecting them to obey but not being in the mood to be threatened by some mutts today. Both dogs surprised her by dropping to their bellies under the tailgate of the pick up. The one white-headed dog back-talked her with a loud, prolonged moan, but Hilda gave him a hard stare, forcing him to lower his head onto his front paws and shut up.

Then she focused on the apple tree. Gus had told her to make a wedge cut on one side of the trunk if she wanted the tree to fall in a certain direction and Hilda wanted it to fall towards her pasture. But the trunk wasn't that big around and she didn't want to waste time finessing the cut.

The rain had stopped and the blue sky was filled with warm sunlight again but Hilda wasn't interested in the weather. She jerked the starter rope on the chain saw and, first try, it roared to life. Things were definitely moving in her favor now.

She touched the bar to the left side of the trunk, underneath where it forked in two, and golden chips of newly splintered wood flew out into air, dispersing over the grassy ground. Hilda had the bar on the saw angled down, figuring the physics of the angle, and the weight of the second trunk, leaning to the left, would make the tree fall towards her pasture. But three quarters of the way down through the trunk the tree decided to fight back. It thunked down onto the cut, and trapped the bar of the saw under its weight. Hilda was out of business.

She was so pumped with malice she didn't miss a beat. She left the chain saw suspended in the tree and marched across Connors' front yard, towards the small, green loafing shed that Clarence had built for his cow back when he owned this land. The dogs jumped up to follow her but Hilda pointed at them and yelled, "STAY!" They lowered themselves back to the ground and stayed.

Hilda got to the shed and yanked open the sheet metal door. She peered into the dark, cobwebby interior, looking for an axe. Sure enough, there was one, leaning up against a rake and a pry bar. She grabbed it.

She marched it back down to the tree, and without pausing to think about it, swung at the right side of the trunk, just above where the chain saw bar was trapped, like a woman possessed. Connors wanted to make art out of her apple tree? Well let him make art out of this! And this! And this!

Hilda heard a loud crack and looked up to see if the tree was on its way down when a limb, shaken into action by her hammering, dropped from above and hit her square in the center of her forehead. The dogs took off for the shelter of the porch again as Hilda dropped the axe and stumbled backwards in a daze, feeling her legs totter underneath her like a drunk at a party. She clutched the sides of her head with her hands, to stop the spinning, and to protect her skull from cracking if she fell. But both the wooziness and her double vision cleared when she stopped moving and as soon as her breathing slowed, Hilda realized the blow had startled her more than damaged her. She looked down and saw her attacker, a limb about the size of a cucumber, poking upright out of the ground. She kicked it, in punishment, but it just twanged in place, sending a jolt of pain from her toe all the way up to her forehead.

Hilda grabbed up the axe again and with all the might of a bear that's been poked, hurled it against the apple tree. This time the blade met the trapped bar and the apple tree surrendered with a whooshing, reverberating thud down onto the ground.

Hilda stomped back to her car, satisfied.

*****

An hour later, Joe and Lucy came riding over the crest of the hill, eager to get home and enjoy the sun that was streaming in through the front window of the car. Lucy had plans to take the dogs for a walk in the State Park and Joe wanted to start some tomato seeds under the south facing window in the bedroom. They'd be gone for much of May but Sonny had agreed to water the plants and take care of the dogs. Since the season for growing tomatoes was short in the Upper Skagit, Joe wanted to get an early start.

"Maybe we should take a celebratory sauna when we get home," said Lucy, as Joe stared out the window at two deer, browsing the grass at the side of the highway.

"I wouldn't mind that," he said. "And it's nice enough out that I could light the barbecue and grill those elk steaks Gary gave us."

"Oo, I wouldn't mind that," agreed Lucy, taking her foot off the gas as they neared the pottery. "Especially since I didn't….."

"WHAT THE…..?!!!!!!" yelled Joe, sitting bolt upright in his seat, a look of complete horror on his face. "I DON'T BELIEVE IT! I DON'T FUCKING BELIEVE IT!!!"

Lucy gave him a double take then hit the brake, thinking maybe one of the dogs was dead in the highway to have provoked such a sudden change in mood. "What's the matter?" she questioned, her eyes sliding this way and that over the asphalt, in search of a carcass.

But Joe was fixated on whatever it was he was seeing and Lucy felt his head turn towards her, then around behind her, as she slowed the station wagon to turn left into their place.

"SHE CUT DOWN OUR KING DAVID APPLE TREE!" Joe bellowed.

But as he said the words, Lucy saw it, to her left, from the driveway. The beautiful, old, King David apple tree, lying on the ground, its blossom rich branches reaching up into the air, like a dying plea; please don't kill me.

Joe had the door on his side open and was already half way out so Lucy stopped and threw the car into park in the middle of the driveway. Anguish welled up inside her as she watched the dogs slink down from the porch, picking up immediately on the boss' raging grief, their heads and tails low as if they should somehow have prevented this. As Joe burst across the grass, howling in anguish for the tree, they skittered forward and slid under his hands, hoping to console him.

"Why would she *do* this?" Joe cried as she stepped out of the car and stumbled towards him.

Lucy had no answer.

"There's something seriously disturbed about that woman, that's what this tells me," Joe decreed as he circled the tree slowly, his hands out, like he was imploring it to come to life again. "I mean, what had this tree ever done to her except make oxygen and beautify her world? And look," he said, bending over and picking up the axe. "She botched how she killed it and had to go get my axe to retrieve her saw."

Lucy watched the color in his face go from ashen to pink to red and she knew that his grief was coalescing into anger.

He looked across at her, his eyes hard, the line of his top lip flat. "If this is her warped way of getting more attention, then guess what? She succeeded. Because now," he said, pointing down at the tree, like this was the reason. "Now, I take *EVERYTHING*!"

Interlude

Chapter 14

It was early afternoon when the sooty green train creaked its way between the platforms in Bridgwater, Somerset. It was an older train, with blue and cream patterned upholstery seats that had lost their bounce over the years and wood trimmed windows and doors. Joe peered out the fingerprint smudged window at the brick station house then hefted the backpack on his shoulder that Colin had lent them for this part of their holiday.

"Be awkward, wouldn't it," his brother-in-law told him, "traipsing around the English countryside lugging suitcases?"

"I wouldn't know," said Joe. "Never having gone to the English countryside."

"Trust me," said Colin. "Our villages may not be big, but they can be hilly. Particularly down in the west. You'll be much more comfortable with a backpack." They were in the downstairs hallway of Lucy's parents' house in Southend, a commuter town on the tip of the Thames Estuary, and Colin stopped with his hand on the door to the front living room. "Where are you going exactly?"

"I want to take him to Bath," Lucy said.

Colin made a face. "Are you sure? That'll be packed at this time of year."

Lucy had only been to Bath once, when she was a teenager, but she could still remember the crescent-shaped street with the old, white façade rowhouses and how appealing they were. She really wanted to take Joe to see that street too but she knew how much he disliked crowds. She looked across at him. "Should we just see if we can find John Leach's place instead?" she asked.

"Where's that?" asked Colin.

"It's in Somerset too, not far from Bath. In the village of Muchelney."

"And who's John Leach?"

"He's a wood-firing potter," Joe explained. "And from what I've read, he's got a shop next to his home and his studio and kiln all right there on his property, like me, so I wanted to check it out if we had time."

"Do you want to meet this potter?"

Joe shrugged. "If I could, sure."

"Then you should make an appointment."

"You think?"

"Definitely. I'll give him a ring and set it up for you."

"Thanks, Colin."

"Of course. Are you spending the night in Muchelney?"

"No, we're just popping in before we go down to St Ives," said Lucy, "to see Bernard Leach's pottery studio."

"A relative?" questioned Colin.

"John's grandfather. Well, late grandfather. He's dead now," said Joe.

Colin stopped, his hand on the door to the living room at Lucy's parents house. "Why does he still have a pottery studio if he's dead?"

"Oh. They preserved it, like a museum, because Bernard Leach was so influential in bringing back interest in the handmade object in the 1950s. He was a very, very famous wood-firing potter. Still is, really."

They stepped into the front room and found three small boys tearing around the furniture, leaping on and off the sofa and armchairs, pow-powing each other with finger guns, while Lucy and

Colin's brother-in-law, sat in the midst of them, trying not to look like he was loving it.

"Who's in charge here?" Colin asked, tight-lipped, of Michael, the brother-in-law.

"Apparently not me," chuckled Michael. "I told my son to settle down," he added, pointing at the 3-year old who belonged to him, "but your sons wouldn't let him."

"You know what Granddad's going to do," Colin warned his two young sons, "if he catches you jumping on his sofa!"

The boys ignored him as they raced around his legs, bounded one after the other up onto a seat of the couch then dive-bombed the chair opposite.

"Right," said Colin, putting a son under each arm and then transferring them to his lap as he lowered himself into the armchair in the center of the mayhem. He looked up at Joe, his face deadpan. "Which one of these are you taking with you?" he asked.

*****

A gentle-eyed stationmaster at Bridgwater told them it was the better part of ten miles to Langport and the weather was supposed to turn nasty, so perhaps they ought to take the bus. From there they could walk the mile into the village of Muchelney. His words sounded round and stretchy, like bubble gum in his mouth, with a pirate's burr to the Rs and Lucy told Joe later, "That's a Somerset accent."

The fellow was right about the weather, they decided, because when they got off the bus and started down the winding country lane towards Muchelney, they noticed that it was warm, sultry even, as if a rainstorm were headed their way. They'd been on the train and the bus for a long time it seemed like and it felt good to stretch out walking. Especially along this quiet length of country road where it was just them and the birds chirruping in the hedges alongside them. Joe let his head swing from side to side as he took in the views of the rolling greens fields broken only occasionally by the presence of hedgerows and drystone walls. "Looks like their ground was as rocky as my garden before they planted it," he mused out loud. "If the length of that stone wall's anything to go by."

Lucy was lost in a play she was envisioning, where a woman, ironing center stage, heard an emergency broadcast announcement on the radio about the end of the world coming in ten minutes. She'd just decided she would call it *The End,* when she heard Joe say something about a wall. She looked at him, wondering what he was talking about, then followed his eyes to the right, to a meandering stonewall that they'd just passed. It had never occurred to her that these walls were built from all the rocks farmers found in their fields. But then, these walls had been such an intrinsic part of her childhood, she doubted she'd ever considered how they were built. She could see that would be something that fascinated Joe, however.

He stopped, to study the wall some more. "That's a work of art," he said, snapping a quick photo with his Nikon. "Makes me want to go home and build one at the end of the concrete slab with some of that rock I've collected for Sol."

"Oh that would be lovely," Lucy agreed, thinking immediately about this little piece of England being reflected on their property in the Skagit.

"Of course, I'd have to break the rock up," Joe went on. "Because part of the appeal is how they make all the pieces fit together so the wall's tight." He let his camera hang down around his neck again and came in close to her, slipping his right hand up her back to her neck and gently turning her so they were both facing the hedge.

Lucy felt the nape of her neck tingle with his touch. She was glad to have this time alone with him. A time when they weren't distracted by the constant need to make a living and the never-ending round of chores. When they were momentarily protected from all the extraneous difficulties being lobbed their way, like tennis balls over a net. Difficulties that neither of them had planned on when they'd tied the knot. But then, she thought, nobody could plan what was thrown at them in life. And if they could, they'd probably be bored to tears. People needed things to test their mettle against, she thought, as if to calibrate their fight or flight response.

That was something that fascinated *her*.

Joe pointed across her line of sight with his left hand. "See there are smaller rocks slipped in the cracks between the bigger ones," he said, and she felt a momentary thrill at the deep resonance of his voice so close to her cheek. "Some are horizontal, some vertical, some ninety degrees to the field, some parallel." His hand moved this way and that in the air with his words. Then he paused, and she knew he was figuring out the geometry of it all. "That was part of the plan so it didn't fall over," he said. "Like stacking firewood. And I'll bet that wall's been there for hundreds of years. Hundreds," he reiterated, his tone thick with admiration.

"Thou wall, O wall! O sweet and lovely wall!" said Lucy, amused. No wonder Shakespeare made a character out of a wall. Maybe he was into the mechanics of them, like Joe.

"*Midsummer Night's Dream*, right?"

"Uh-huh," said Lucy. She slipped her hand in his and led him back out into the center of the lane. This was a little bit of a turnaround in their relationship. Usually it was *him* introducing *her* to something new, but here, she was the one making the introductions. And loving his reactions to them.

A black Range Rover broke their solitude as it barreled around the blind curve in the road ahead of them. Joe pulled Lucy back in to the hedge and the vehicle whipped past them like it was being chased.

"Un-believable," he muttered, shaking his head.

"What?" said Lucy moving forward again.

"The speed people drive at on these tiny roads. And in *both* directions! With hedges blocking visibility!! How do they not run into each other, that's what I want to know?!"

"Lane discipline," Lucy stated.

"Yeah, that's what your dad said when I asked him."

"I'm sure," said Lucy. "He taught me, don't forget." She let go of his hand and skipped ahead of him, turning to walk backwards so she could look at him as they chatted. "Maybe that's why we have hedges at the side of the road though rather than drystone walls. So cars will have a softer place to land if they can't make the turn."

"No, I imagine they don't have stone walls alongside the roads because the days of slave labor were long gone by the time they paved these footpaths."

"They're not footpaths," chided Lucy. "They're lanes."

"Yeah, well whatever they are I'm glad I'm not driving them. And if anyone flattens us against the hedge again, I'm liable to throw a rock from one of the walls at their rig."

"You didn't like being flattened against the hedge with me?" asked Lucy, flirting a little with him.

He smiled roguishly. "I would rather have been flattened *under* the hedge with you," he said.

"Well come on then, catch up," Lucy teased, "and maybe that can be arranged."

She turned and started running down the lane. Joe didn't hesitate. He chased right after her, one hand clutching his camera while the pack bounced up and down on his back.

*****

There was an ironmonger's on the way into town and Joe stopped to look. "This place might have a brick chisel," he said.

"What do you need a brick chisel for?"

"If I want to build a drystone wall at home. Well, not a *dry*stone wall. I need to use cement otherwise it'll get overrun by moss and weeds where we live."

The ironmonger's was on the corner of the street, a brick building with a slate roof with a tiny door right on the angle of the corner. It was small enough that Joe was worried he wouldn't get through it with his backpack but he managed. Inside he found a maze of small aisles, packed from floor to ceiling with hardware. He could have spent hours in there, looking at all the things for sale, except it was stuffy with trapped heat and he had very little room to move wearing the backpack. He was about to walk out when he looked around a tight corner, and saw a wall covered with hinges. Black, cast iron, hinges many 12 inches long with fleur de lys on the ends of them.

“Look at this, Lucy,” he whispered because the closeness of the space made it seem appropriate to whisper. “This is exactly what we’ve been looking for.”

Joe wanted to build doors for all the rooms in their house out of knotty pine and use this kind of hinge to give it that country look. But he also wanted the hinges to add structural integrity to the doors by reinforcing the connection between the tongue and groove. Back in the States the hinges they’d found were all stamped metal and he wasn’t sure they would be sturdy enough to hold the weight of the wood. But these cast iron hinges were extremely sturdy, and not any more expensive than the flimsier stamped ones in the States. “I wonder why they have so many?” he voiced to Lucy.

“Well it’s the Tudor look, isn’t it?” she said. “To go with all the old beams and low ceilings in the houses people restore over here. Like in the pubs.”

“Do we have enough money to buy some of these?”

“How many do you want?”

“Well two for each interior door, so 8. But we should probably take 10 or a dozen, just in case.”

“Aren’t they heavy?”

“Yeah. That’s why I like them.”

“But you’ve got to carry them. And not just today. When we go on, down to Cornwall, and then over to France. That’s a lot of extra weight for you to be trekking around.”

“Maybe I’ll make you carry them,” he teased.

“Then no, we don’t have enough money,” Lucy teased right back.

He chuckled but then got serious again. “The thing is these are exactly what we’ve been looking for.”

“Yes, but I bet my mum knows where to find the same thing in Southend.”

“You think?”

Lucy nodded. “And I bet she can tell you where they’re the best price, too. She might even come along and negotiate a cash deal for you.”

A bulky Englishman with a pronounced beer belly and patchy

red skin tried to ease past them with a quick, "'Scuse me," but there was no room for the belly and the backpack in the narrow aisle. He and Joe did a clumsy contra dance until there was just enough room for the fellow's girth to push past. Then Joe nodded at Lucy with his eyebrows. "Let's get out of here," he said.

*****

The sign for Muchelney Pottery was set in a brick planter right in front of a cottage with a thatched roof, but the shop where the pottery was sold was in an outbuilding set back from the road. An expanse of small, mullioned windows, like the ones in Joe's pottery shop back home, showed a variety of handmade objects and a sign above the entry door read, Pottery Shop.

Lucy gazed in through the windows, at the small bowls and pitchers sitting on the sills inside, while she waited for Joe to slip off his backpack and mop his brow with a red and white bandana from the back pocket of his jeans. There was a definite design to the pottery here. The pieces looked like what Joe described as standard ware. They were all thrown similarly, and had just a touch of darkish green glaze up around the lip, leaving the rest of the item to be bronzed by the kiln.

"You think I should leave my backpack out here?" Joe asked.

Lucy swung around to see him propping his glasses back on his nose and shoving the bandana back into his pocket. "I'm sorry?" she said.

The door to the shop opened and Joe grabbed his pack and backed up a few feet to let two ladies come out.

"Hi there," he said, as the visitors smiled and nodded at him, closing the door behind them. He walked around the small, ornamental tree growing in front of the shop, to where Lucy was standing, as the ladies headed down the driveway towards the road.

"I'm wondering what I should do with the backpack," he said again.

Lucy had seen an orange and white, older style, VW bus, Like Pete's, and two other cars parked out by the sign so she cupped her hands around her eyes and looked deeper into the shop, to see how many customers were in there. She spotted only two, edging around the tables of pottery but it was a small space, and it had lot of pottery in it. "I'd leave it out here if I were you. I doubt anyone's going to bother it."

"Maybe I can tuck it in behind this tree," said Joe.

The door to the shop jingled open and a friendly-faced, older woman with a broad smile and a pageboy cut to her blondish hair, popped her head out. "Can I help you with anything?" she asked with a welcoming lilt to her question.

"I'm worried about bringing my backpack in," said Joe, pointing down at the offending item.

The lady flapped her hand in the air. "Oh no, don't worry about that," she said and Lucy heard the Somerset brogue again in the long, flattening out of the vowels. "I've got just the spot for it."

She motioned with her fingers for them to follow her.

*****

Joe set the backpack down behind the sales counter, where the assistant showed him, and then inhaled a big, keen breath as he took in the whole shop with his eyes. Wood shelves built into the walls held tidy rows of pitchers and sugar jars, mugs, teapots and casseroles, all in John Leach's signature style; minimally glazed around the lip with golden to deep brown flashing by the flame on the unglazed bodies. The walls behind the pottery were white, which accented the flashing on each piece, and gave them an inviting allure, like a warm amber light in a window on a dark night.

Joe stepped forward, to one of the long, narrow trestle tables in the center of the room, where Lucy was looking at butter dishes.

"What time is it?" he whispered.

Before Lucy could answer, the sales assistant called out, "Are you by any chance the potter from America who has an appointment with John?"

"At 3:15, yes," said Joe. "Yes, I am."

"Oh good," beamed the woman. "I'll let him know you're here."

"Do I have time to look around the shop first?'

"Of course," she said with great enthusiasm. "I wouldn't want to stand in the way of anyone and their shopping."

Lucy smiled across at her; she knew that song. Then she told Joe, "It's five to three."

"I'll help these customers," said the sales assistant, reaching her hands out towards the young couple approaching the counter with a teapot and some mugs. "And then I'll let John know."

Joe turned back to the table and slowly walked away from Lucy. The long slab of knotty wood, oak he guessed, was covered in groups of kitchen items: salt pigs, spoon rests, garlic jars, plates. He picked up a 10-inch diameter plate that was glazed in the center and had a small, unglazed rim. He flipped it over to examine the bottom. "Nice dinner plates," he muttered.

"Supper plates," said Lucy.

"What's that?" he asked, surprised by her reply.

"They're called supper plates," Lucy reiterated, walking towards him. She pointed to some labels on the table. "See. Supper plates and tea plates. You should make some this size," she said, motioning to the smaller plates. "They'd be handy."

Joe put down the supper plate and gently slipped his fingers under the rim of a tea plate to lift it up. "They are nice," he agreed. He flipped it over, to look at the bottom again. "But I'd call this a sandwich plate."

"Well sandwiches are part of tea," said Lucy, walking towards the other end of the table.

"If you say so." Joe put down the tea plate and moved further down the table. He stopped and slipped his thumb down into the pouring spout of a mixing bowl. Where the glaze met the unglazed clay was smooth, seamless. Very accomplished. There were three sizes of mixing bowls nesting neatly inside each other. That was one of the benefits of making standard ware, he thought. Throwing objects the same size again and again meant you could trust that they would fit where you wanted them to fit. Joe didn't make standard ware. His hands always drifted towards a variation on a theme. He didn't know why. It's just what he was comfortable doing.

He moved over to a shelf holding large, lidded jars with wide mouths that narrowed to a smaller diameter foot. Bread crocks, the label in front of them said, but Joe called them old English bread jars. He'd read about them in his ceramic's magazine a few months back; about how the English used to store their finished bread in jars like these. While the function didn't interest him that much, the shape did, to demonstrate his wood-firing. The jar was big enough that he could do a drawing in the top half, then leave the bottom half unglazed, for flashing by the flame.

He had immediately made a prototype, with mountains colored a bronzy green by the local clay under a clear glaze in the top quadrant, and an unglazed lower section. When it came out of the kiln, the clear glaze had run down the mountains in purple streaks, like purple waterfalls, and the bottom was flashed a golden brown. Lucy loved it. Joe gave it to her and came into the house later to find it sitting on the bookshelf in their living room, filled with sewing stuff.

These bread crocks by John Leach had no glaze on them, other than what the kiln gave them naturally in flashing by the flame, and Joe slipped his hand up around the shoulder of the pot, enjoying the texture of the clay against his skin. He moved on to a shelf holding pitchers and spied, just down below it, two shelves labeled "seconds." He crouched down and started looking through the marked-down pots. Most of them were there because they hadn't been flashed by the flame, leaving the clay a pale biscuit color instead of the bronzed, almost gold finish so prevalent on most of John's pottery. But there was a pitcher in the back that did look well wood-ashed.

Joe reached past the pots in the front, and pulled the pitcher towards him, wondering why it was a second. He flipped it over, to look at the bottom, and heard the door to the shop jingle open.

"Joe?" said a male voice.

"Here I am," said Joe. He quickly replaced the pitcher and corkscrewed to a stand facing the door.

There he saw a man, leaning in through the open door; a man with a thick, brown beard and a mop of matching brown hair poking out from under a blue, cloth, bucket hat. It was John Leach and his face broke into a wide, cheery smile as he acknowledged Joe with a lift of his hand before backing out of the door again.

Joe strode around the display tables with a nod to Lucy to follow.

"We'll be back," he said to the friendly sales assistant before stepping outside, into the lemony sunlight, and stretching his hand out towards John in greeting.

*****

Lucy saw the slight touch of grey around John's temples and in his beard and guessed that he was about ten years older than Joe. He had a firm handshake and his arms, what she could see of them below the rolled-up sleeves of his lightly checked, cotton shirt, were very muscular. Like Joe, she suspected he had strong upper body strength, from all the years of wedging clay. They'd make a great pair of rugby players, she thought.

John greeted her warmly and then looked back at Joe and pointed off to the right. "We're about to have tea and biscuits in the garden," he said. "Would you like to join us?"

"We'd love to," said Joe. And then he stood back to let John lead the way.

*****

The garden was surrounded by hedges so even though it wasn't far from the country road that brought people in and out of Muchelney, it was very peaceful and private. Joe and John sat down next to each other on lawn chairs and launched immediately into rapid-fire conversation. A young woman, who may have been a studio assistant, Lucy guessed, by the clay splatters on her jeans, handed them each a mug of tea but Lucy noticed that the rest of the people in the garden were helping themselves from a small picnic table. She followed their lead and poured herself a mug of hot tea with a splash of milk, then picked up a digestive biscuit to go with it.

That was one thing Lucy missed, living in the States; digestive biscuits. Americans didn't have anything even close to this sweet biscuit that was a simple combination of plain and whole-wheat flour. And neutral enough in flavor that you could put a slice of cheese on top of it and turn it into a savory snack.

She hovered by the table and watched the others hustle over to lawn chairs with their tea and biscuits and fall quickly into conversation with whoever sat next to them. This must be a timed tea break, she thought. She found an empty chair and sat down in it, wondering what the protocol was for dipping a digestive biscuit? That's how she'd usually eat it but it wasn't always considered seemly in public. She glanced around. The women next to her didn't seem to be dipping but across the grass, she saw a tall, skinny fellow on John's left, dunk his digestive without a care in the world. That was all the permission Lucy needed.

She lifted her biscuit and moved it to the mouth of her mug and then got stymied by the fact that it wouldn't fit. Now what was she going to do? She lifted the mug and looked at it, then looked across at the one the skinny fellow was using. His was wider in the mouth. She should have thought about that when she chose her mug at the table.

She placed the biscuit on her knee, deciding she'd come back to that later, and took a sip of her tea. It was good and strong, just the way she liked it. Across from her, Joe and John were completely engrossed in their back and forth, like two foreigners, thirsty to converse with someone who spoke the same language.

She sipped her tea again, enjoying the sound of a mourning dove cooing close by. That particular sound always made Lucy think of England, probably because it was the accompaniment to many moments spent in her back garden as a child. There were plenty of other birdcalls around her in John Leach's sun-dappled, grassy garden, with its borders of pink and red rhododendrons, bowing blue bells and budding rose bushes, but it was the gentle, full-throated coo of the mourning dove that captivated her.

She looked down at the mug in her hand again, wondering why she'd chosen this particular one. Mugs were very personal, she'd come to realize selling Joe's pottery. They had to be just the right size, shape and color and they had to feel right in a person's hand. This one appealed to Lucy because it had a plump roundness to it rather than being straight-sided, and felt the way a tea mug should feel in her opinion. She lifted it into the air and saw the unmistakable Muchelney stamp on the bottom but it was different than the ones she'd seen in the shop in that it was glazed a soft, sage green, almost to the foot. Everything was right about it, except the mouth was too small for her digestive biscuit. Well, she thought, there was always a solution for that.

She snapped the biscuit in two on her knee, hearing the women next to her get more vocal about Margaret Thatcher's proposed poll tax. She took half the biscuit and lowered it gingerly into her tea. The trick was to moisten it just enough to soften it, but not so much that it would fall apart and splash down into the liquid. This was a learned art that she suspected most English people had perfected, given the national regard for digestive biscuits. She was just about to pull the biscuit out when a voice in her left ear said, "What do you think?" startling her away from her mission.

Lucy's head whipped left. "Sorry?" she said, then remembered the biscuit. She turned back to her mug, lifted the digestive and watched as the soggy section broke away and sank out of sight. "Bugger it," she muttered.

"My sentiments exactly," seconded the woman.

Lucy didn't know if she was referring to the biscuit or the poll tax but she went with the latter, mostly to cover her embarrassment over having been caught dunking. "It sounds like it's going to be much worse for the poor than it is for the rich," said Lucy. She set the remainder of her broken digestive back on her knee. "Because isn't it based on how many people live in a house instead of on the value of the property?"

"Yes!" said the woman, clearly offended by this fact. "So a family of five living in a small house is going to end up paying more than a wealthy couple living in a mansion."

"It's not right," said the young woman to her left, shaking her head from side to side.

"My parents are pretty upset about it," said Lucy, "even though it's only the two of them living in their big house now."

"Well you don't overtax the poor, do you?" said the woman next to her. "That's not what England's based on."

"Is it certain that it'll go through?" asked Lucy.

"What, the poll tax? Oh yes! Thatcher's already signed it into being, although we won't have to pay it for a year or so. But some of us are talking about taking to the streets, we're so upset."

Lucy was surprised. She'd seen any number of street riots, protesting matters political, in France when she lived there, but she'd never witnessed the English get up in arms about anything. She was about to ask when these street protests might happen when everyone in the garden started moving, an indication that tea break was over.

Lucy looked left and right, to see if anyone was watching, and then crammed the rest of her broken digestive in her mouth and took the last, big swallow of tea, avoiding the dregs of the chunk that fell in.

She sat back, savoring the taste while feeling satisfied that she'd been able to sneak it in. Then she hopped up to follow Joe and John.

*****

Joe paid attention to the gravel under his feet as John led them across the pottery yard, towards the kiln shed. He was impressed with how clean it looked. He wished the area in front of his studio and kiln shed looked this together but where they lived, nature grew through the gravel as soon as it got watered. And it got watered frequently in the Upper Skagit. Maybe if he laid some black plastic down before he graveled....?

"This is what we use to fire the kiln," he heard John say as they passed a big stack of eight-foot long bales of mill edgings. "For the most part it's larch," John continued. "Cut offs from the fencing and house siding they make at a mill about ten miles from here. I like the fact that we fire our kiln with a renewable resource."

"Do you mind if I take a photograph?"

"Please do," said John. He swiveled around to face Lucy while

Joe snapped photos, and pointed off into the distance. “We’re actually planning to plant about 4,500 hardwood trees next year in a nine acre field that we own. A bit of a plantation, to pay back what we use in firing the kiln.”

“I have a small plantation on our five acres too,” said Joe, putting the lens cap back on his camera. He looked at John again and added, “But it’s to help pay for my daughter’s college when she gets that far.”

“How old’s your daughter?” asked John as he walking them into the kiln shed.

“Five,” replied Joe.

“That should give you a bit of time at least to get the trees to a decent size,” laughed John. He pointed across at a willowy, blond teenager who was glazing pots at a station a few feet in front of the kiln. “And this is my daughter. She’s getting ready to go to college in September.”

“For pottery?” asked Joe.

“No, no,” said John as the young woman rhythmically dipped and turned the objects in her hands, then carefully placed them on a ware board next to her. She didn’t seem bothered by their presence or by the fact that they were talking about her. “Although she is going to study art. But she’s just helping us out today with the glazing.”

The teen turned to her dad and treated him to a wide, warm smile reminiscent of the sales assistant’s smile in the shop. Joe wondered if that had been Lizzie Leach helping him find a spot for his backpack.

The girl went back to glazing and Joe looked across at Lucy, who was watching John watch his daughter. He wondered if she found the idea of a child working in the family business as appealing as he did. Although he’d want the child to be wooed to the pottery the way he had been.

“Did you work for your father?” he asked John. “Or grandfather? Is that why you became a potter?”

“No, no,” mused the English potter with a gentle shake of his head. “It was almost more organic in me than that. Pottery had been such a huge part of my life, for as long as I can remember. Forever really. I was born in a room above the shop in my grandfather's pottery back in 1939, and then, everywhere I looked when I was growing up, there was pottery. So it just felt natural to me to become a potter. As natural as having the same accent as your parents." He smiled across at Lucy. "At least at first. And then sometimes you branch away, don't you? So I *studied* with my father and grandfather but then my wife, Lizzie, and I bought this condemned cottage and piggery back in 1964 and, a year later," -He stretched his hands out on both sides of him, to indicate everything around them- "Muchelney Pottery was born."

"So this used to be a pigsty?" asked Lucy, looking around.

Joe looked around too and glimpsed wide boards above their heads holding rows and rows of glazed pots waiting to be loaded into the kiln. That was one solution to not having enough space, he thought. He dropped his gaze back down to the double chamber kiln and got in position to take a photograph.

"No, we turned the pigsty into the shop where you were earlier," John answered Lucy. "And our pottery studio is in the building with the thatched roof, out by the road." He looked at Joe. "I'll show you if you're ready."

Joe nodded. "Ready as I can be," he said.

He followed John out of the kiln shed but glanced back in at the pots above John's daughter's head, wondering who had to climb up and down to get those pots when they were ready to fill the kiln.

*****

Inside the thick-walled pottery studio, Lucy recognized the skinny fellow she'd seen dunking his digestive biscuit and realized, from what Joe had told her, that it was Nick Ries, the other full time potter at Muchelney Pottery. She also saw the young woman with the clay splatters on her jeans, sitting at the wheel, throwing. It was a fairly spacious and well-lit space with thick, white plaster and lathe walls and low beams hanging down from the ceiling. Joe took some more photographs as John put on a long apron, tying it in the back, readying himself to work in the clay. Everywhere she looked there were pots in neutral off-white to silvery grey tones and she thought about how they'd get bronzed by the kiln. If they were lucky. There was always that element of unknown to wood-firing.

Joe took one last photograph and then stretched his hand out towards John. "Thank you," he said, his voice deeply appreciative. He gave a nod toward Nick and added. "Thank you both. This has been great."

Lucy could see he'd been fed by this visit. She smiled and nodded her agreement. "Yes, thank you," she added.

They stepped back out into the pottery yard and looked up at the rain clouds gathering in the sky. "Can we afford to buy a pot?" Joe asked her as he folded the strap around his camera then slipped it into its compartment in the black, nylon bag.

"We'll just make ourselves afford it," Lucy whispered. "Because I'd like a piece, too. Especially after all the time they gave us."

Joe nodded. He slung his camera bag over his shoulder and slipped his arm around her waist as they wandered back up the driveway towards the shop. "There's one in the seconds that looks like it would be perfect for us," he said.

*****

Joe shoved the backpack into the overhead rack and bounced down into the seat next to Lucy. They were alone in the train carriage and he slid one arm around her back and wrapped the other around her front until his hands were overlapping, and he was tucked in tight against her. "Thank you," he whispered into her hair before kissing the side of her head.

"What for?" she asked, surprised.

They were on their way to Portsmouth to take a hovercraft over to France.

"For letting me do all this pottery-related stuff. You never would have gone to St Ives to see Bernard Leach's studio if it hadn't been for me." He swayed his head from side to side, as if weighing another factor. "Or stopped in at John Leach's...."

Lucy pulled back from him a little, so she could look into his eyes. "Yes, but I enjoyed both, very much," she assured him. "And now that we're married what matters to you, matters to me. I mean, it did even before we were married but it just feels more so now. We're a team, aren't we?"

"We're a pack," he affirmed, smiling down into her green eyes. Then he caught the look on her face that suggested she didn't get it. "You know, like wolves. Or dogs. Where you go, I go. And hopefully our kids go too."

"Oh, so it's kids now, is it?"

Joe laughed. "No, I meant kids as in if we have one, plus Maddie. 'Cause Maddie's part of our pack, isn't she?"

"Definitely."

He pulled her close again and nuzzled her affectionately. "Whatever the reason, I'm grateful you let me visit some of the giants in the world of pottery. But now it's your turn."

"What do you mean?"

Joe shrugged one shoulder carelessly. "Well, we're visiting your friends in France so it'll be more about you than me over there."

"I doubt that," said Lucy. "I think Délphine's dad wants to share his sculpture studio with you and drive us up to the little house he owns in the French Pyrenees. That sounds like something you'd enjoy, doesn't it?"

"Allez a la montagne?" asked Joe, with an Americanized French accent.

"Yes, we're going to the mountains," said Lucy, looking out the window at the sign on the platform where the train was pulling in. Ashford, it said, so the next stop would be Folkestone.

A gaggle of noisy, effervescent schoolgirls, all in matching uniforms, suddenly appeared in the narrow corridor outside their carriage, jostling, each other forward to find places to sit. Joe and Lucy turned towards the noise just as a small group huddled around the door to their carriage, fiddling ineffectively with the handle. Joe leapt up and sprung the handle open, then moved back to take the seat opposite Lucy.

"Thanks," giggled a couple of the girls before they piled into the carriage and took all the remaining seats.

Joe smiled across at Lucy as the train swayed from side to side leaving the station. He leaned forward with his elbows on his knees so she could hear him over the run-on, high-pitched cacophony that had overtaken the carriage. She leaned forward too.

"You know what John Leach told me?" he said.

She shook her head no.

"He said that if I stagger the bag wall – checkering I think he called it – but if I stagger the bag wall," - He threw his hands up in the air vertically and set them apart as a visual aid - "So put gaps between the bricks on each layer, I'd get better movement of flames throughout the pots. Which might help with my underfiring problem in the second chamber." He nodded that he thought this was a good idea. "Plus," he went on. "He told me to pay attention to the bag walls in the second and third chamber of his grandfather's old kiln at St Ives. John said he was pretty sure they were shorter than the one in the first chamber."

"And were they?"

Joe nodded his assertion. "I took pictures," he said.

Lucy rolled her eyes.

"What?" said Joe.

"It only took 6,000 miles and a honeymoon to get you to talk to another potter."

"No," corrected Joe. "It only took 6,000 miles and a honeymoon to get me to talk to the *right* potter."

*****

It was about 9 am in the little village of Vilamos, high up in the French Pyrenees and Lucy was sitting on the deck outside the small stone house belonging to Délphine's family. Her eyes were fully involved in the richly verdant meadow below her that quickly dropped out of sight to reemerge, in the distance, as tree-cloaked mountains topped by an impressive array of snow-capped peaks. Her mind, however, was still on the small, bronze sculpture

Délphine's father, Laurent, had slipped her as a gift in Bordeaux. A sculpture he'd created of a mother and child curled together. "To bring you luck," said Laurent. "For…well, you know."

Lucy smiled. She liked Laurent's subtle way of promoting motherhood. She'd take the sculpture, which was small enough that she could cradle it in the palm of her hand, back to the Skagit and set it on her dresser. And maybe it would bring her luck.

The morning sun was heating up the deck around her already but Lucy's eyes rested comfortably on the layer of mist just below snow level on the mountains opposite. It was reminiscent of the view from the top of Sauk and yet different because the trees in the foreground were not indigenous. "That's why we try to protect the old growth in the forests back home," Joe told her as an aside. "So the generations of the future will be able to see the land the way it was meant to be seen." He was looking at the vista at the end of the cobblestone street that wound up through the white stucco and stone houses stepped into the side of the mountain when he said it. "Although this is lovely," he added appreciatively.

They'd driven up for the weekend from Bordeaux with Délphine, her husband, infant children, parents and most of her eight brothers and sisters. When Joe found out that Laurent was going to spend a couple of hours in the early morning refurbishing another stone house he'd just bought in the village, he quickly offered to help. That left Lucy time to spend with Délphine, an elegant, attractive Frenchwoman who had such a kindness about her that Lucy treasured the things she'd learned from her, like rare gems, to be taken out and appreciated often. Sometimes the two of them spoke in French, sometimes in English, and sometimes, because they'd both taught English as a foreign language in Strasbourg together, they spoke a mix of the two languages. Un mélange.

A sound behind her made Lucy turn, and she saw Délphine coming out of the house carrying two small cups rattling softly in their saucers.

"My brothers," chuckled Délphine.

"What?"

"*Ils font la gueule*," she said, as she set the cups of café au lait down on a bench in front of them and sat in the deck chair next to Lucy.

"They're upset?" said Lucy. "About what?"

"Joe."

"Really?!" The word went up and down like an arpeggio as it came out of Lucy's astonished mouth and she heard it echo in the meadow below.

"Because he's helping papa. They say he's making them look bad."

Lucy laughed. "Joe will love that." Then she got more serious. "The truth is, you'll never get Joe to sit around for too long. He likes being busy."

"You were always like that too."

"I still am," said Lucy.

"Are you? Because that's one thing I wanted to ask you," said Délphine in her perfect English, lifting her milky coffee and sipping it tentatively. "How do you fill your days, living so far out?"

"Oh I have a lot to do, selling Joe's pottery, trust me."

"But that's not really your thing, is it? I mean, you left France to go to America because of the theatre," Délphine went on. "Don't you miss it?"

"I still do theatre," said Lucy, anxious to reassure her friend. "I have an acting job lined up for this autumn, with a little directing, too." She picked up a sugar cube that was resting in the saucer below her coffee cup. "But it'll get more complicated if we have children," she admitted, "because we live so far from the city." She dipped the sugar cube into her café au lait and then popped it in her mouth. She let the sweet, warm coffee flavor melt on her tongue before she went on. "But you know," she confessed with a certain amount of humor. "I'm still on the stage in my head most of the time. I run dialogue that I'm making up, I create scenarios. That's why I've started writing plays more seriously. I told myself that way, I can play all the roles in my head and I don't even have to go to auditions."

Délphine bobbed her head gently side to side, as if she were weighing this answer while staring at the view in front of them. A burst of raucous laughter sprang from the house and Délphine winced. "I hope they don't wake the twins," she said.

"How long do they usually sleep?"

"Well they don't usually sleep now but their routine is... you know... *compromis*."

"Oh I hope it's not our fault they got disrupted."

"*Ah non*," Délphine reassured her. "*Ça va*." It's okay. "I just think," she said, her tone an indication they were going back to the subject, "that if you'd stayed in France you'd be on stage full time by now. Things were going well for you here, *non*?"

"Yes, but then I would never have met Joe." Lucy shared a smile with Délphine, then got more serious. "Plus," she said, "we don't get to create all the scenarios we participate in. Of course, you know that. We just get to accept or reject the roles we're offered in them. Sometimes I feel like you have to swallow your pride and accept a role that *isn't* what you had in mind, because it might lead to something that will take you on to the best role of your life."

"Is that your way of telling me you like being a wife and stepmother to Joe's daughter?"

"I do," said Lucy, reaching for her café au lait. "Even though I didn't think it was what I wanted."

"I know. I was going to ask you about that too," said Délphine. "What changed?"

The sound of Joe's voice drifted their way from the street behind them and Lucy felt a thrill chase through her heart.

"I did," she told her friend.

*****

"So are you ready to go back?" Colin asked, placing a glass of wine in front of Joe and a beer in front of Lucy. It was Sunday lunchtime and they were in a window nook of a pub that was being held together by 400-year old wood beams under a thatched roof with low, plaster and lath ceilings and a creaky oak floor.

"I am," said Joe.

"Me too," agreed Lucy. "Although we've had a wonderful time."

"Very inspiring," nodded Joe.

Colin swallowed the mouthful of beer he'd just taken and put his pint glass with the frothy, amber liquid back down on his beer mat. "In what way," he asked, his head cocked to one side in interest.

"Well I got a tip on how to reconfigure part of my kiln," said Joe, "and I'm going to do that as soon as I get back. Hopefully get a good firing out of it for the summer season."

"And I got an idea for a new play," said Lucy. She looked across at Joe ad added, "Plus we're talking about building a stonewall at our place like the ones we saw down in the southwest."

"Yes, mum said you bought some brick chisels at the ironmonger's the other day. And some hinges, apparently." Colin made a face, brow furrowed, one side of his upper lip cocked, like he didn't get it.

Joe threw his head back and laughed at his brother-in-law's antics. "Yeah, so I can build a door for the bathroom," he said when he came back towards the table. "So next time you come out, you can poop in private."

Colin looked horrified. "Joe! Please!" he hissed, glancing both sides of him to see if they were being overheard. Then he sat upright in his chair and lifted his beer in a kingly manner. "We don't talk about that kind of thing here."

Joe laughed again, shaking the table so some of Lucy's beer slopped onto the little round, cardboard mat advertising Watneys Pale Ale underneath it.

"Did you get your septic tank issue resolved?" asked Colin.

Lucy and Joe shook their heads in unison. "No," said Joe. "We've got that waiting for us when we get back."

Colin wrinkled his lips again in slight distaste. "Oh. So I can poop in private, just not on your property," he teased.

"Yeah. Don't remind me," countered Joe.

He and Lucy locked eyes in an unspoken accord consistent with members of the same pack. Then she broke away and looked at her brother.

"We should change the subject," she said. "Enjoy what little time we have left free of Hilda's shenanigans."

"You're exactly right," said Colin putting both hands on the edge of the table in front of him, preparing to get up and fight the crowd back to the bar. "Who'd like some crisps or peanuts before we go back to our roast beef lunch?"

Fall

Chapter 15

"Daddy, I'm hot," complained Maddie as they switchbacked slowly up, through a vast sloping meadow of wild blueberry bushes. The late September sun seemed to be following their ascension since they'd got an early start, warming the air around them and promising a fine day up in the high country. But they were all wearing long sleeved shirts and jeans, to protect themselves against the abundantly leafy, morning dewy, blueberry bushes and all beginning to feel a little overdressed for the day.

"Well pretty soon we'll be up at the lake and you can take off your boots and paddle in the water."

"They're sneakers, daddy. Not boots."

"Sneakers then."

"Can I swim in the lake?"

"Sure. If you want."

Lucy could hear their repartee but wasn't focused on it as she navigated the tight game trail between the wild blueberries, her eyes drinking in the deep, dark green forest blanketing the gentle contour of Betty's Pass in the distance. Suiattle Mountain and Illabot Peak were visible over the ridge and the entire picture made her think of a line from the play she'd seen recently in Seattle, about this being "God's country." Lucy missed the centuries old architecture of London and even France, where she'd lived for a spell, but she was definitely being wooed by the echoing peace of this untainted landscape. Was this what the playwright meant by the term God's country? She didn't know. But if there were ever a place where man had not been able to intercede it had to be here, in these too steep to conquer mountains.

It was strange, she thought as the trail loped down between her feet and made her stumble a little. She'd retained that one phrase and yet she hadn't liked the play at all. It was way too much of a docudrama for Lucy's taste, with the actors stepping forward and delivering their lines to the audience as if to make a point. Lucy liked theatre that was more physical, directed in a way that made the audience feel like they were part of the story, and not just viewers. She remembered going to see "The Cherry Orchard" directed by Peter Brook at a theater in Paris called Les Bouffes du Nord. The theatre had a very small orchestra with semi-circular balconies in ornate plaster rising above it, like a towering Elizabethan hairdo. The director used those balconies, having actors appear from behind the audience, calling their lines down to the characters on stage, which made Lucy feel like she was a family member, sitting on the couch in the living room with the story unfolding around her. Maybe it was all those years growing up watching Shakespeare. Stories that had to be played, not told, to the audience.

"You want some water?" Joe asked her as she emerged from between the knee-high bushes to an undulating grassy meadow interspersed with trees and taller blueberry bushes. He was holding the water bottle out in her direction but Lucy shook her head no. It hadn't been a very arduous hike and she could wait. She smiled at Maddie, who'd taken her outer shirt off and was tying it around her waist, and realized that she was hot now too.

Joe tucked the water bottle into the side pocket of his backpack and smiled across at her. "Ready?" he asked.

She nodded and they moved forward, closer together now that they were on flat ground with space around them. Down at the house the grass was already getting covered with the orange and gold leaves of fall but here it was still that bright, summery green. They came around a patch of young fir trees and were stopped by the sight of a black bear just a few feet away from them, feeding on some blueberries. The sheen on the bear's black fur rippled like shiny metal but then Lucy noticed the blonde tips, like frosting on the fur. Joe had mentioned that black bears had the greatest number of variations in coat color of any bear but she'd never expected one to look like this. It was beautiful.

Joe's hand dropped to the pistol on his hip but Lucy reached forward and touched his arm lightly to stop him. She knew he was just getting ready, in case he needed to fire a warning shot into the air, but she was bewitched by the animal's beauty and couldn't imagine scaring it.

Fortunately, the bear had already scented them and turned in one fluid, rolling move, its fur bouncing sunlight like a fiber optic wand, and ran for the woods. Joe beamed at her. "That was worth the price of admission!" he whooped.

"I'm glad we left the dogs at home with Sol," Lucy remarked. She hadn't wanted to, for precisely this reason, thinking if they ran into a bear in the woods, the dogs would offer her protection. But Sol really wanted the company, while he watched the shop for them, and Joe wasn't about to argue. So the dogs stayed.

And now, amazingly, Lucy discovered that the one thing she'd been scared of since moving to the Skagit – running into a bear – had actually filled her with awe. She knew it was stupid, to be scared of bears. She'd lived in Manhattan for two years and walked home from the subway, to the loft apartment she shared with Skye's mother, at all hours of the night, and *that* didn't scare her! She knew there was probably way more danger from human beings in Manhattan than there ever would be from a bear in the woods. But bears were outside Lucy's comfort zone so she'd been having trouble getting her mind around her fear.

"Yeah, the dogs would have been after that bear like flies on a bad smell," said Joe, looking at Lucy, his eyes bright with enthusiasm. "Did you see the frosting on its fur?"

"I did!" marveled Lucy. "Is that what you mean when you talk about color phase bears."

"Yep. I've seen cinnamon colored black bears and ones that are almost blond, but I've never seen that kind of highlight on a black bear's fur." He smiled. "It looked like it had been to the hairdresser, didn't it?"

"My grandma, Janet, gets her hair done like that," Maddie piped up.

"Is that right?" said Joe, turning to lead them into the meadow and on towards the lake

"Can I get my hair done like that, daddy?"

"Only when you can afford to pay for it."

*****

It had been too quiet for Hilda's taste for too long. She'd obeyed her lawyer's advice that she stay away from Connors' septic tank until they came to a definitive decision about who owned what and where, but now, if she weren't careful, she'd lose her chance to break ground on her road before the weather changed.

Connors had marked his septic system with some kind a birdbath, it looked like, and Hilda was thinking she'd go over and measure 30-feet from that to where the edge of her road could start. She trained her binoculars on the sign for his business; it said CLOSED. She'd seen him leave in his pick-up, about 45 minutes ago, with Lucy and the kid, and she was hoping to measure before they got back. Then she'd head down to the Commissioners' office in Mount Vernon. Maybe stop by the Air Pollution Agency again; find out why they hadn't come out to investigate Connors's kiln when he fired it yesterday. She wasn't going to let them get away with that much longer.

Hilda put down the binoculars and slipped a yellow, expanding tape measure into the pocket of her red down vest. She pushed her feet into her muck boots and went out the front door, crossing the gravel in front of her house quickly, intent on her mission.

She stepped onto the grass at the edge of her pasture. It was still dewy and she saw moisture flick up over the toes of her olive green muck boot. She passed in front of the big cedar tree, her eyes on the birdbath and not anywhere else. The truth was, she didn't want to look at the stump of the apple tree. She'd been having strange dreams recently, where people were chasing her. Only they weren't people so much as silvery ghosts, and they moved awkwardly, like their limbs were rigid. The closer they got, the more Hilda could see that their limbs were branches; pocked, gnarly, weathered-gray, wood branches. She couldn't understand why. Then one of the branch people held something up in front of Hilda. She thought it was a candle but her eyes were fuzzy because her head hurt. So she squinted and when she squinted she saw what it was. It was the little limb that had fallen out of the tree and hit her. The mouths on the branch people were wide open and round, like knots in a tree. And they were screaming.

*****

Sol walked out onto Joe's front porch, meaning to walk down to the entrance to the driveway and put the sign to open, when his head turned towards Jackman. There was a refreshing nip to the morning air that made him hunt for signs of fall among the trees up there. And as he hunted, envisioning the millions of years of geological layers under those trees, he drifted the length of the porch and down the side steps, to graze on the ripe, evergreen blackberries. Max and Maggie followed him the length of the porch and stood watching, right up until he lifted one of the berries to his mouth. Then they trotted down the two steps and over to him. Maggie sat at his feet while Max sniffed the berries on the low vines and delicately pulled the occasional one off between his lips and ate it.

Sol had his eyes half shuttered down, like Maggie, dreaming about all the petroleum the trees on Jackman could make if left to rot back down into the ground, when something moved, under his line of sight, to the left of the big cedar tree in the pasture. He dropped his chin to detect the movement and saw Joe's neighbor hurrying across the pasture towards him. Immediately he spun on his toes and sat on the ground, his back to the blackberries and the pasture, pulling his knees in towards his chest, to make himself small. The dogs were watching him, their heads cocked, wondering what kind of new game this was. Sol put his index finger to his lips and motioned with his other hand for them to lie down. They obeyed.

A raven leapt out of the elderberry bush behind Joe's house, caw caw cawing his way up into the sky and Sol cringed, thinking he'd given himself away. He looked up to see a red tailed hawk wheeling over his head and then dive bomb away in the direction of Sauk as the raven came close enough to threaten him. Sol held his breath, waiting for the birds to have revealed his presence, but nothing happened. Nothing other than the return to quiet all around him.

Sol sat in the quiet talking himself through what he should do if the neighbor was walking this way with destruction on her mind. Joe had asked Sol to keep an eye out for Hilda while he watched the shop and the dogs, and he *specifically* requested that Sol not let her get near his septic tank.

"But what should I do if she does go near it?" Sol asked.

"Call the cops!" ordered Joe. "Just call the cops."

*****

Hilda kept her eyes down as she veered towards the birdbath, hoping not to make eye contact with what was left of the tree. It wasn't her fault. She couldn't have known it wasn't on her land. And it was only a stupid apple tree. She got to the birdbath and even though she knew she was overreacting, kept her back to the King David. She lifted the ceramic bowl that Connors must have made, and hooked the tongue of the tape measure over the edge of the metal stand under the bowl. But when she lowered the bowl back down a chunk came off in her hand.

"Augh!!!" she cried out in frustration. She'd barely touched the thing!

Immediately she knew, she *knew* what had caused the bowl to break. Hilda spun to face the remains of the apple tree, pointed an accusatory finger at it, and yelled, "That's *enough*!"

*****

Sol was still waiting to see where Hilda would end up when Max's head popped up, his eyes trying to see over the blackberries like he'd heard something. Sol quickly put his hand out in the air, palm down, the way he'd seen Joe do, and Max lowered his head back down onto his front paws with a soft grunt. Slowly, Sol rolled his head 90 degrees, and peered through the blackberries. Sure enough, Hilda was there, right up against the stoneware bowl Joe had set out on a metal stand to mark the top of his septic tank.

Sol put his hands, palms down, on the concrete slab, thinking he'd lift himself into a crouch and crab walk over to the front porch, then dash in to call the cops.

But before he could push up, he heard a yell, "That's *enough*!" and the dogs launched themselves towards the sound, barking like they were going to tear the speaker limb from limb.

*****

Joe peeled the pale green lichen off the short length of vine maple that someone had left at the rocky fire pit next to the lake and threw it into the small campfire he'd built. He wanted to keep the bugs at bay. Lucy was grateful for the fire, too. She was attempting to dry out Maddie's sneakers, which the little girl had got wet almost as soon as they arrived at the lake. The lichen popped and fizzed tiny white sparks, like a spinning firework, and Maddie squealed with joy and clapped her hands together.

"Do it again, daddy," she begged.

"Not right now. I'm going to finish my sandwich first," Joe said, leaning into the smoke to keep the mosquitoes off his face while he ate his cheese sandwich.

"Can I go back to the water then?" asked Maddie.

"Did you finish eating?"

"Yeppers."

"Then yes you can."

Joe and Lucy sat in the warm noontime sun, munching on their sandwiches. Joe had one eye on Maddie, dancing in and out of the water a few feet away from them and the other on the surface of the lake, hoping for rises. "Did you have fun, poking at the fire while I fished?" he asked Lucy.

"I did," she told him. It's restful, watching the flames."

"Mmm, hmmm. I've always been a bit of a fire nut myself."

"Is that why you fire your kiln with wood?"

"That comes into it, sure. But think of how much money we save by using that waste wood. I bet if we had to come up with the money to fire with propane every time I need it, we wouldn't be able to do it."

Lucy squinted through the smoke from the fire and the sunshine in her eyes to smile at him. "You're a pretty good business man for an artist, you know that?"

"Except I don't like doing the business part. That's what I've got you for."

"I don't like doing it either. I like helping you making your business work but I want to be creative too.'

"And you are. With your playwriting."

Lucy popped the last of her sandwich in her mouth, nodding.

She did like creating characters and playing the roles in her head. "But what if nobody wants to watch my plays?" she said, after she swallowed her bite.

"They will. You watch. You'll keep working the material until one day, something will break for you and then they'll want everything you've written."

His belief in her filled her all the way to the tips of her toes and she found herself smiling. How different it was to hear she could, instead of she couldn't, something that had been the norm in her childhood in England.

"Talking of making your business work," she said, scrunching the tin foil she'd wrapped around her sandwich into a ball and pushing it back into her daypack. "I want to make a suggestion."

"Uh oh."

Lucy poked at the fire with a long stick, flipping the last piece of wood so it would get consumed before they left. She propped the stick against the rock circle and leaned forward, resting her forearms on her knees. She'd thought about this quite a bit but it would come out of the blue to Joe so she wanted his full attention.

He blinked across at her.

"I think you should stop selling so much firewood in the winter," she said.

His face creased in surprise. "Why?"

"Because we went weeks this summer without mugs or cereal bowls, or teapots, coffee pots, a lot of stuff really, in the shop, yet we had plenty of visitors to buy them. And there's more profit in your pottery than in the firewood. So if you spend the winter stocking up, I think we'd be better off financially."

"But would we be able to make our bills in the winter without the cash flow from the firewood?"

"Maybe not the first winter. But if we do sell pottery to all those people that stop in during the summer months, instead of sending them away empty handed, I should be able to save enough for us to pay the bills the following winter."

He let his eyes drift back out to the lake but he was obviously thinking about what she'd said. "I do like cutting firewood though."

"I know. And you can still do that. But instead of having to be at the beck and call of every ne're-do-well who rings you in the middle of winter, having just put their last stick of wood on the fire, you could sell just to your regulars."

He nodded, agreeing. "Yeah, and most of them think ahead," he added, still looking off at the lake. There was a moment of silence, while he thought about this, then he pulled his eyes off the lake with a noisy inhale, like he was bringing himself back to life. "Well you're the one with the degree in economics," he said, "so I'll defer to you."

Lucy smelled a little something acrid, like burning rubber, as she watched him fold the foil from his sandwich into a small square. Her peripheral vision caught what it was and she launched forward, grabbed Maddie's sneakers and smacked them on the bare earth around the fire pit to put them out.

"Oh crikey!" she said. "I burned her sneakers."

"You burned my *sneakers*?" Maddie sing-songed on her way back up from the water's edge. She didn't seem mad so much as curious about what they looked like.

Lucy had them upside down and was peering at the underside of the toes, where they'd caught fire.

"Did it burn through," asked Joe.

"No. But they're pretty badly charred."

Joe came around the fire pit and took the sneakers out of Lucy's hands. "They'll still wear," he proclaimed.

"They were brand new, daddy!" argued Maddie.

"I'll buy you another new pair," Lucy told her, sitting the little redhead down on the log next to her and wiping her wet feet with one of Joe's bandanas.

"Can you get me a pair the same as these? I like the purple bears on them."

Lucy tipped her forehead down and raised her eyebrows, a

cautionary look into Maddie's brown eyes. "I'll get you whatever they have in the Department store in Concrete," she said.

*****

"I wasn't doing anything!" Hilda screamed as Sol followed the dogs over to the birdbath.

"No, no, I'm sure you weren't," said Sol calming the dogs by patting them both on the head. They were only barking to be friendly, after all. As he bent to pat them, he noticed a shard from the bowl, lying on the ground. He picked it up and looked across to see a large chip out of the lip of the bowl. He slotted the shard into it, like he was completing a jigsaw puzzle.

"I didn't do that!" Hilda defended immediately.

Joe had pointed out the crack in the lip of the bowl when Sol complained that he shouldn't use such a magnificent item for a birdbath. "Look, see, right there," said Joe, showing him the thin dark line from the lip down into the wall of the bowl.

"Well then surely it won't hold water," argued Sol.

"It'll hold enough for the birds. They only need a little in the bottom and this crack is up by the rim."

"You could dab some glue on that crack and I'd use it for my fruit," Sol persisted.

"And deny the birds a place to bathe?"

Sol stuck his dentures out to show his aggrievement, but let it go with the potter. He wasn't going to let Hilda off so lightly.

He turned his piercing blue eyes on her, hoping to make her feel like a deer in the headlights. She squirmed. He cupped the palm of his left hand towards her. "Blackberry?" he asked. And she squirmed again. This time more coyly. Now he had her exactly where he wanted her.

"Tell me about your short plat," he cooed.

*****

"What time is it now?" Joe asked, as they came off the Grade Creek Road and back onto Highway 530, headed for home.

Lucy swiveled her watch on her wrist rather than move her arm to see the face. She didn't want to wake Maddie, whose head had lolled against her when she nodded off in the Chevy. "It's a quarter past two," said Lucy.

"And what time did you tell people to show up tomorrow?"

"For the kiln opening? 10:00. But I'm not sure if anyone's coming."

Lucy had taken a suggestion from Ingeborg Pfeiffer that she and Joe invite a small group of people to come and see the pots coming out of the kiln after they were fired. "'I'll even bring my gloves," said the judge's wife. "So I can help. And maybe a bottle of wine, to celebrate."

Lucy took the suggestion to Joe.

"Sure," he agreed. "We can do that. Although I'm not going to guarantee there'll be anything to celebrate."

"Hmmm," mused Lucy. "Maybe we'll drink it to commiserate then."

The real difficulty was that Joe only told Lucy on Tuesday that he was going to fire Wednesday through Thursday, which meant by the time she wrote and mailed the postcards to those invited, they only got a day's warning that it was going to happen. And she suspected some of them would already have plans.

"Well we still have to open the kiln, whether anyone comes or not. So I think once we get back, I'll go up and pull one of the peep holes, so the kiln can vent, and sweep the kiln shed."

"And I'll head straight into Concrete with Maddie and hopefully find her an acceptable pair of sneakers."

*****

The pain was excruciating. It came on suddenly, when Hilda

was driving down to the Commissioners' office, and it made her want to rip one side of her face off. She went and filled out the paperwork anyway, embarrassed that she might be slurring her words because the clerk was obviously having trouble understanding her. Maybe her tongue was swollen. Her cheek too, by the looks she was getting. By the time she signed and dated the appeal the right side of her face was so painful, she couldn't even be bothered to ask how long this would take. Instead she got right back in her car and drove directly to her dentist's office, worried she was in sudden need of a root canal.

But Dr. Wang poked and prodded, bent over her open mouth, and surfaced saying, "No, I think you have something stuck between your molars in the bottom right."

"Can you get it out?" Hilda begged.

"I think so," replied the dentist. Then bent forward again. "Okay, hold still," she instructed.

She didn't give Hilda a sedative or anything to numb her teeth; she just pulled and pulled on whatever it was that was stuck. It hurt so much that Hilda's eyes filled with watery tears and she wanted to snatch at the dentist's arm and order her to stop. But the pain in her jaw from whatever was in her teeth was worse, so she suffered it.

After what seemed like an eternity, Hilda felt something give and the pain lessen slightly. Dr. Wang held something up above her face, turning it this way and that in the pincers she'd used to pull it.

"It's a seed from an apple," she declared, a smile in her voice, like she was proud of her discovery.

Hilda tsked, glad that the worst was over with. The strange thing was, she thought as she climbed out of the dentist's chair, she couldn't remember the last time she ate an apple.

Chapter 16

Buck Voorhees backed the Caterpillar tractor down off the low boy trailer attached to the dump truck and then signaled his brother, Bruce, that he was good to go. Bruce let out the brake on the dump truck and slowly pulled back out onto the highway, headed west, as Buck drove the CAT into the end of Hilda's driveway. He turned off the noisy yellow machine and slowly climbed down.

Hilda watched all this with growing impatience. Her vision was bothering her again today and making her feel light-headed so all she really wanted to do was get back to her house and sit at her kitchen table. The sooner she could get Buck lined out to start on her road, the better.

She watched him step cautiously down onto the asphalt at the end of her driveway, moving his blocky, slightly overweight, seventy-something body like he wanted to protect it. Buck Voorhees wasn't Hilda's type but she did find herself drawn to the gentle, cherubic look of his plump, rosy cheeks. He was a man who'd run a small sawmill up here in the valley all his working life but after his wife died, he quit, preferring to do occasional, local land clearing with his brother's heavy equipment.

He moved haltingly towards Hilda, his hand outstretched. "Well I made it!" he announced, smiling. "And I'm sorry it's taken me so long to get to this. First my brother insisted we drive to Oklahoma this summer to visit relatives I've never even met. And then I got back and had to have one of my hips replaced, if you can believe it. The things they can do with modern medicine! I asked 'em, can you take the curmudgeon out of my brother but they said no-oo. They're not that far advanced, I guess." He chortled but when Hilda didn't enjoy the joke with him he became serious again. "Anyway, I'm back on my feet now and ready to get started. Where am I going in again for this road?" he asked, looking down the highway towards the pottery.

Hilda held out the short plat map she'd brought down the driveway with her but found she had to take a moment to steady herself, wait for the lines on the map to clear, so she could see them. When that happened – finally – she didn't waste any time. She pointed down at the road. "You hug my property line down by the highway and then move in toward my pasture."

Buck wasn't looking at what she was showing him. He was patting the breast pockets of his shirt and glancing over at his pick-up truck, which he'd left on the hard shoulder of the highway. "I can't see that without my glasses," he told her. "Just give me a minute."

Hilda waited as he walked with excruciating deliberateness over to his truck. She felt her impatience growing, which made her head spin even more. Which made her nauseous. She smacked her lips together, watching him open the passenger door, lean in and then proudly hold up a pair of cheater glasses for her to see. Then she had to wait for him to make the return journey back to her.

"Show me again, would you?" he asked once he was beside her with his glasses on.

She obliged, somewhat testily, but Buck didn't seem to pick up on her irritation. Instead he nodded, like he knew what she was talking about, and then asked, "Is there a marker for your property corner down by the highway?"

Hilda had been hoping he wouldn't get into that. She swallowed before she answered. "Just.....stay to the left of that old tree stump," she blurted.

Buck looked down the highway easement and then back at Hilda. "D'you mind if we walk down there together."

Hilda panicked and everything started to turn. The next thing she knew, Buck had a gentle hold of both her elbows. "Whoa there," he said, his voice warm, soothing. "Are you okay?"

Hilda blinked repeatedly, wondering why there was two of him. "I'm fine," she whispered. "Just light headed is all."

"Did you eat breakfast?" she heard him ask.

She blinked again, wanting to see the source of such tenderness. As her vision narrowed from two to one, Hilda found herself staring at the very image of an apple.

*****

Lucy followed the eclectic group of people up to the kiln feeling a secret thrill. She really liked the subtle diversity of the Upper Skagit, with its loggers and hippies, pagans and Christians, naturists and developers all being drawn to coexist in the magic of the Skagit, but she wasn't sure it was a truly representative slice of the world's diversity. So she worried that children raised here wouldn't have a sense of the greater picture. But today they had Judge Pfeiffer and his wife, a couple of citrus orchardists from Jerusalem, who'd stopped in the shop yesterday afternoon because the wife was a part-time potter and Joe had invited them back for the kiln opening, Sol, a man who grew up in Montana yet spent his working life in Peru as a petroleum geologist and a young, native Hawaiian woman who lived in Skagit County and worked for the Federal Park. She had also brought her two young sons along to the opening.

"Where'd they go?" said Joe, looking down on both sides of him for the boys as he led the group up to the kiln.

"Maddie took them the back way around the studio to go and play in the woods above the creek," said Lucy.

"Is that okay with you, Kayla," Joe asked, and then looked over the top of his glasses at the friendly young mother. "Did I say your name right?"

She smiled. "It's Kah ee lah for the i in the center. Kaila," she repeated. "But don't worry. A lot of people call me Kayla. And yes, it's great that my boys are out in the woods. As long as you don't mind them leading your daughter up some trees, because I know they'll do that."

"She'll love it," Joe assured her, stepping ahead and threading his way past the garden cart he'd put in the entrance to the kiln shed. Kaila and Sol followed him but Lucy led the Pfeiffers and the people from Jerusalem around the rain barrel at the corner of the shed to come in from the side.

*****

"I had a slice of toast," Hilda snapped, throwing both hands up in the air, to rid herself of Buck's gentle clasp on her elbows. What was *wrong* with her, seeing his face as an apple? She was obsessed! But at least she felt a little better.

"I suspect you're hungry," he said. "How about I park the CAT on your land and then take you out to breakfast."

Hilda wasn't listening. Another car had just pulled into the pottery and she watched it stop in front of the house and a young couple get out. The female took off immediately, around the house, up towards Connors' studio and kiln. Hilda's eyes narrowed; what was he doing over there?

"I'll just come in from here," Buck was saying.

Hilda was aware of his right arm pointing, along the highway easement, but she was watching the young man who'd got out of the car. Why was he staring at her?

"And I'll drive the CAT up towards where you want the cul-de-sac, then leave it there while we go get a bite to eat."

Buck stopped speaking, leaving a void, which jarred Hilda into focusing on him again. "What?" she said.

"Breakfast," Buck reiterated.

"What about it?"

"I think it might do you some good."

But Hilda was getting her pep back. She didn't like this young man looking over at her and she didn't like the sounds of laughter drifting down from Connors' kiln area. She had a plan. "Where did you say you were going to park the CAT?"

Buck pointed to the right of the big cedar tree in Hilda's pasture. "Up where the map has the cul-de-sac."

"No," said Hilda, pointing down at her short plat map again. "Take it beyond the cul-de-sac to where it runs alongside the property line. You'll see a ten foot stretch of sheet metal fencing. Park it there."

Buck looked askance. "It's pretty brushy that far in," he cautioned. "I might end up knocking down some of the small trees."

"That's okay," Hilda replied, feigning sadness. "They have to come down sometime."

She pictured all the people up by Connors' kiln that would be affected by the noise and was secretly glad that time would be now.

*****

Joe jumped up onto a milk crate and unbolted the metal plate keeping the door closed, while Lyle put a lens on his camera and Ingeborg pulled on her gloves to help move pots around.

Lucy shifted right, to stand in front of the boxes on the sawhorses, where she would put the pots, and the people from Jerusalem followed her. "I'm Lucy by the way," she said to the sweet-faced older woman.

"I'm Tilly," replied the lady, shaking Lucy's hand. "And this is my husband, Peter."

"And you're from Jerusalem?" asked Lucy. "Because you sound like you're from South Africa."

"Well that's where we grew up," confirmed Peter. "But we moved to Jerusalem, what?" - he looked at his wife – "twenty-five years ago?"

Tilly nodded without taking her eyes off the kiln as Joe walked the door to the first chamber open. A gentle wave of warmth blew towards them, drawing everyone forward just a little as if to bask in it.

This was the sixth firing in this new kiln and Lucy was beginning to be able to tell, at first glance, whether the heat had given the glazes just the right "scald" to transport them from dull to luminescent. Today she saw sheens reminiscent of the first firing.

"Nice satiny look to some of the glazes," she said to Joe.

"Yeah," he agreed, lifting out a small dream jar with a soft, ivory coat over rose tones. He held it out in front of him, examining the glaze.

Lucy peered over his shoulder. "Is that a clear glaze? Or the matte white?"

"I'm pretty sure it's the clear," he said, with a certain amount of question in his voice. "And you know, I think it's that apple wood. Remember how this happened in the first firing?" He looked down, as he handed the jar off to Lucy, and his glasses slipped down his nose. He pushed them back up irritably. I really ought to get these adjusted, he thought.

"You use apple wood to fire your kiln?" asked Peter.

"Not usually, no. I use cedar." He popped the lid off the top of a garden lantern and passed it to Lucy who walked it to the cart. "But my neighbor cut down my apple tree so I burned the wood in the kiln."

"Why did your neighbor cut down your apple tree?" asked Tilly.

"You'd have to ask her," grunted Joe.

"Is that the neighbor that's been giving you problems?" Lyle chimed in.

"You got it."

Joe passed Ingeborg a garden lantern too and she followed Lucy's lead and put it in the back of the garden cart.

"What kind of tree was it?"

"A King David." Joe stopped working for a moment to look at Peter. "Are you familiar with that kind?"

"I am," nodded the citrus orchardist. "It's an old variety."

"And the apple has a dense, kind of grainy flesh?" his wife asked, rubbing her thumb over her fingertips as she looked from Peter to Joe.

"That's it," said Joe.

The sound of air brakes followed by the beep beep beep of a large vehicle backing up drew his eye towards the highway.

Lyle looked at the couple from Jerusalem and said, "His neighbor is a nasty piece of work."

"Sounds it. If she cut down his apple tree," said Tilly.

"It might grow back," her husband suggested. "When did she cut it down?"

"April," said Lucy, taking a tall vase off Joe. "When it was thick with apple blossoms." She placed the vase in a box and pointed back at the potter. "He drew it on a platter."

"I think that may have been why she cut the tree down," Sol added, from his spot against the door of the chamber. "Joe was enjoying it too much."

"The platter came out good though," Joe acknowledged, grinding the bottom of a tall jar with a small piece of silica carbide kiln shelf.

"Do you still have it?" asked Tilly, her eyes hopeful.

"No," he replied, and then handed off the jar to Ingeborg. "We sold it."

"Well I think your neighbor made a big mistake, cutting that tree down when it was blossoming," said Peter, a mournful look on his long, craggy face.

"Why?" asked Joe. "Not that I don't agree with you, because I do. But, what are you thinking?"

Peter lifted his shoulders. "Apples are full of symbolism and mythical power. And – well, I'm not a religious man but I know my bible – a tree that was named for a shepherd who slew a giant? That's got to come back and bite her."

"And don't forget that in Greek mythology," said a voice from outside the kiln shed, "an apple led to the fall of Troy."

Lucy peered around the boxes on the sawhorses to see a beautiful, curvy black woman with a wide, happy smile.

"Oh hi there!" Joe called out to the woman.

Lucy looked up at him, wondering who this new arrival was. He handed her two mugs from the second shelf down. "Those are sold," he said. Then nodded his forehead towards the newcomer and added, "This is the woman I was telling you about who teaches Gamelan music at the University of Washington."

"Hi. I'm Naomie," said the young woman with a small wave to Lucy.

"I'm Lucy," she smiled back.

"And my boyfriend's here too. He's just watching the heavy equipment get unloaded off the semi."

"What heavy equipment?" asked Joe.

As if on cue, the loud, dieseling growl of a massive yellow caterpillar tractor came crashing, snapping, crunching and small tree falling it's way slowly up through the brush on the other side of the fence.

*****

Lucy was staring down at the mugs that Joe had given her to put in the sold box and barely noticed the arrival of the CAT. They were a generous size, narrowing in the neck before widening again at the lip, and the glaze felt smooth and inviting against her fingers when she touched it.

In the background she heard Joe asking, "Ten points for anyone who knows what Gamelan music is."

"I know," said Ingeborg, reaching forward to take two more mugs off Joe that looked like the one Lucy was holding.

"Those are sold too," Joe told her.

"At least I think I do," continued Ingeborg, turning to look at Naomie. "Isn't it traditional Indonesian music made with gongs and metallophones?"

Naomie nodded.

Lucy put the mug in the sold box next to its "match" just as Buck switched off the CAT and the sudden quiet compared to what had been in her mind drew her attention. She looked across and saw a big piece of equipment on the other side of the garden fence. Her heart sank; the road next door was about to become a reality. She turned to Joe, to see if he'd noticed, but he was reaching into the back of the second shelf down while looking at Naomie.

"Some stringed instruments too, right?" he asked.

"Rebabs, yes," said the Gamelan music professor.

"Is that what we call a spike fiddle? Three strings on a small, round drum three stringed face with a long spike on the bottom?" asked Kaila.

"Yep," nodded Naomie.

Ingeborg passed the mugs Joe had given her over to Lucy and asked him, "Can I spend my ten points on a new mug?"

"Yes, get one of these," her husband called out. He was bending over the box on the bench seat where Lucy had put the first two mugs, snapping photos of them.

"I can't," said his wife. "Those are sold."

"But they are lovely," agreed Lucy.

She held one of the mugs Ingeborg had given her on the palm of her hand, for everyone to see, and Lyle swung around with his camera. Joe had left the bottom half of the mug unglazed and the clay body was toasted. In the top half there were two, overlapping glazes; deep turquoise and azure blue, and where they met were shades of lavender and rose. The effect made Lucy think of waves on a sundrenched beach and somehow, also, the hippie art of the sixties. She'd been too young to really notice the sixties but as a student in London, she'd seen many reflections of them. These mugs reminded her of airbrushed LP covers, bubble letters, tie-dye and streaky, sun bleached jeans. And she really wanted them.

"There's two more," said Joe, reaching past Tilly with the last two of the set. "They came out pretty well," he added.

"I'd buy all six of them," said Naomie.

"Me too," said Lucy. "But they're for a customer in Florida."

Naomie pointed between Ingeborg and Tilly, at the center of the first chamber. "Well I'll take that jug there then," she declared.

"The cider jug that has the same blues as the mugs?" asked Ingeborg. She didn't wait for an answer, going on with a question to Joe. "Is that a cider jug?"

He leaned back from the chamber to see what she was pointing at. "Could be for cider," he said. "Or something stronger."

Lucy saw his eyes flick over to the CAT on the other side of the fence, without seeming to be bothered by it.

"Or beer," said Naomie.

"Well I have my eye on that jug," Ingeborg said, looking at Naomie as she leaned forward to place two cereal bowls Joe had handed her into a box.

A rhythm was establishing itself around the kiln; a rhythm of reaching in and passing out, of placing and turning for more; a rhythm that involved Lucy and Ingeborg, sometimes Tilly, and a box at Joe's feet where he was placing mugs not pre-ordered. The banter went on over the rhythm.

Joe interrupted the conversation between Naomie and Ingeborg with, "Who are you?" and Lucy turned to see a young, fellow with coloring similar to Kaila's, standing at the end of the garden cart, outside the kiln shed.

"I'm James," said the young man. He pointed at Naomie, smiling, and said, "I'm with her."

"That's my boyfriend," Naomie explained. "And he makes

beer," she added, as if to justify her need for the jug to Ingeborg.

"So does my husband," Ingeborg shot back. Then she looked over her glasses at Naomie, like a school marm, chiding a student. "And you came late."

Naomie threw her head back and peeled out laughter.

"Is that what you do for a living, James," Joe asked, pulling the lid off a small jar. "Make beer."

"No, I'm a gunsmith," said James.

Joe's face lit right up.

*****

Buck climbed down from the CAT and crunched through the broken lengths of vines, twigs and sundry other brush around the back of the machine. He stepped up to the rusty sheet metal fence, rested his forearms on it, and waited.

Joe handed off the sugar jar he'd been holding to Ingeborg and glanced over at the fence again. There was his friend, Buck, leaning on it, looking across in that placid, ever-easy manner of his. "Would you excuse me a sec?" he said to everyone at the kiln and climbed down off the 4 x 12 he was standing on to unload the top of the chamber. He moved between Ingeborg and Sol, gently touching Lucy's forearms with his fingers as he edged past her to head over to the garden.

"Are you okay?" she asked softly.

"I'll be right back," he said. He edged around the garden cart and pointed at James. "Don't go anywhere."

James raised his eyebrows, as if curious what he meant by this, then smiled down at the ground. "All right," he said.

Everyone at the kiln watched Joe stride away from them, towards his garden. Then they all turned back in one synchronized movement and looked at what they could see of the pottery still waiting to come out of the first chamber.

Joe went past the end of the cedar fence and crossed the width of the garden at the open end, on ground that previously held his green beans this season. The dirt was surface dry after so many days of sunshine, but still soft and spongy from aerations by the rototiller. Joe felt himself gently sink and rise, sink and rise, with each step until he reached the narrow, grassy path alongside the fence. Then he was on solid ground again. It took five steps for him to get to Buck and when he did, he turned, his back to the kiln, and rested his forearms on the fence alongside his former boss and mentor.

There was an ease between the two men, born out of mutual respect and affection. Joe would always have a soft spot for Buck because of the work he gave him when he was a newly arrived hippie in the Upper Skagit, fairly green in everything except making pottery. And because he let Joe work the winter months at the sawmill, then quit to make pots in the summer. But he knew Buck did it because he appreciated Joe's work ethic and drive and wanted him to make it as a potter.

"How's your hip?" he asked the older man, whose wide, well-mapped face struck Joe as a portrait of peace.

"I'm still breaking it in but it's better than the old one," replied Buck with a big smile. He nodded towards Joe's kiln shed. "And you look like business is booming."

"I don't know about that," Joe rebuffed. "I'm unloading my kiln with an audience for the first time."

"How's that feel?"

"Pretty nerve-wracking," laughed Joe. "I have no idea what the pots will look like till I get them out, so it's got lots of potential for embarrassment."

Buck nodded once more towards the kiln. "Your audience looks like they're loving it."

"Yeah, they're a great group," Joe said, with a quick glance back towards the kiln shed. He leaned a little closer to Buck and whispered. "But I don't do embarrassment well."

Buck chuckled.

Joe bumped his forehead towards the CAT. "So you're doing it, huh?"

"Looks like."

"I've been dreading this."

Buck shook his head gently from side to side. "No need."

There was a moment of silence, then Joe confessed, "I don't do change well either."

"Most of us don't, son. Then you get to my age and look back and think – well I guess I handled it after all."

Joe grunted, not persuaded. "She's gonna change the whole look of the neighborhood."

"Uh huh. And you changed the look when you moved here. And the next person'll change it even more."

Joe half closed one eye and smiled. "When did you get so wise?'

Buck looked somber. "I fought in a war. I know what happens when people can't think things through."

Joe couldn't dispute this. Buck had served with the 82nd Airborne in World War II and fought for five days in Normandy, just managing to keep alive by staying one step ahead of the enemy.

He heard laughter coming from the kiln shed, as people amused themselves in his absence. He was going to head back but something about the CAT confused him. "Is the road even gonna come up this far?" he asked his old friend.

"Not according to the map. But I think she wanted me to make a start on punching in the section that goes to the back lot." He paused and Joe noticed a slight twinkle in his eyes when he added, "Either that, or she wanted me to make a whole lot of noise and interfere with your gathering."

Joe smiled. "She tried to slide that past you, huh?"

"I'm guessing."

"Well, we're not going to pay any attention to you so I wouldn't worry about it."

"I'm not. Because as it turns out, I'm not going to work the machine yet. I'm going to take your neighbor out to breakfast instead."

"Hilda?!" exclaimed Joe. "Why would you want to do that?"

"Diversionary tactics," whispered Buck.

The sun sliced through the morning mist and Joe recalled another fact about Buck. He had been captured after five days of fighting in Normandy, and spent the better part of a year as a POW. But he didn't try to escape, he told Joe, because his commanding officer gave him orders *not* to escape. Instead his job was to distract the enemy any way possible.

He smiled into Buck's eyes. "You tricky dog, you!"

"Hey. all war's deception," Buck reasoned, his hands raised. "And when the cause is right...."

Joe looked up at Jackman Ridge, emerging green and gold from under the morning fog. ""We few, we happy few, we band of brothers,"" he quoted.

"Shakespeare's *Henry V*," Buck added.

"Gets me every time," said Joe, punching the center of his chest with a fist. He smiled at his mentor. "Thanks, Buck."

The older man bowed his head in acknowledgement. "Anything for the king."

"King Henry?" questioned Joe, mystified.

"No-o," scoffed Buck, lightening their dialogue with his tone. "The King *David*. That's what your apple tree was, am I right?"

"You are! I'm surprised you remember that!"

"I remember the delicious cider you gave me from its apples one year."

Joe sighed. "They were great apples."

"Mmm hmmm." Buck got serious again. "Will breakfast give you time to finish?"

"Should do," Joe remarked.

There was another, louder burst of laughter from the kiln shed and Joe whipped his head around to see what was going on.

"You'd better get back to the party," said Buck.

"Yeah," agreed Joe, as he started to move away. "I think my

wife's telling lies about me again."

.

*****

"Okay, where were we?" Joe asked as he trotted back across grassy gravel towards the kiln shed.

"You had me not going anywhere," said James.

"That's right." Joe slipped past the cart, in between Tilly and Peter and climbed back up onto the 4 x 12. "Because I have a question for you."

"About beer?"

Joe didn't answer. He had his right arm all the way up to his shoulder into the second chamber, trying to pry a small pitcher off a shelf in the back. It finally gave and he pulled it out and examined the bottom for glaze defect. He looked at Lucy. "Did I give you a sugar bowl before I went and talked to Buck?"

"No, you gave it to me," Ingeborg answered.

"Okay, this goes with it," said Joe and handed her the cream pitcher. He reached back into the kiln and put his fingers on the lip of a wide shallow bowl. "No," he said in reply to James's question. "It's about guns."

"That I might be able to answer."

"I seem to be having trouble getting the trigger on my .308 to function correctly. I had a big, three point deer in my sights last season and I got all set up to take the shot. When I went to pull the trigger it wouldn't go off and wouldn't go off and wouldn't go off until, when it finally did, it fired to the right of the deer. And I thought it was maybe me but then I did some target practice with the gun and the same thing happened."

He was taking lovelights out of the kiln and Lucy was filling a box with them but he stopped, to hold one up in front of him and turn it around. The stars and moon cut outs on the luminary were wrapped in reds and white and a soft, sage green that Joe had never seen before. He couldn't tell if maybe he'd changed something in the formula of the green slip or if, again, it had something to do with the apple wood. As he passed it over to Lucy, he asked, "Would you put this on a shelf in the studio instead of in a box? I'd like to look at it again."

"I don't blame you," she said, admiring the object, too. She saw Naomie follow it with her eyes, wantonly, as she slipped past her, heading for the studio. Lucy stopped to show it to her.

"Yeah, don't tease me," said the beautiful young woman, with a deep, inviting laugh. "Just show me one that I *can* buy!"

"Oh don't worry," said Lucy, heading down the path to the studio. "There's a whole second chamber full of pots still to come."

"Who manufactured your .308?" James asked across the crowd.

"Remington," said Joe.

"That's what I thought," replied James. He launched into an explanation. "Remington, among many gun manufacturer's at one point, were worried they'd get sued if their triggers were light enough that somebody could put their gun down on the table and it would accidentally go off. So they increased the poundage of their triggers, which makes them harder to pull."

"I've read about this," said Lyle.

"And I have a Ruger with the same kind of problem," said Peter

"What caliber?" asked Joe.

"A .270."

"Nice," Naomie piped up.

Joe pulled out a shallow serving bowl filled with night-sky blue and tiny explosions of gold, like stars, dotted about the center. He dipped it down for Sol to see and said, "Wood ash."

Sol moved, as if to take the bowl, but another pair of hands beat him to it.

"Can I see that?" said Kaila.

"I can put you in an after market adjustable trigger that will have a clean, crisp break without being hair trigger if you like," said James.

"What kind would you use?" asked Joe, ignoring Sol's pout as he gave Kaila the bowl.

"Probably a Timney trigger."

"He put one on my model 700 and I really like the trigger pull now," Naomie said.

"Any chance I can test drive it?" asked Joe.

"My model 700? Sure. Do you have a place to shoot?"

But before Joe could answer, Maddie burst onto the scene, her cheeks filled with the healthy glow of playing outside.

"Daddy, daddy, daddy," she squealed.

"What, what, what?" he replied.

"I got *dirt* all over my new Barbie sneakers!"

Joe's mouth dropped open, as he acted shocked. "Does that make her Mud Barbie?"

"*Dad*-dy!"

Lucy came back into the kiln shed and peered across the end of the garden cart to see Maddie's sneakers. "We can wash that off," she assured the little girl.

"Now?" asked Maddie.

"Well not right now, no. But before you leave to go back to your mum this afternoon."

"And look what I found," said Joe. He pulled his right arm out from between the shelves and showed her the small object she'd made during her summer visit.

Maddie's mouth popped open and she ran around the rain bucket, squeezed past Naomie, Lucy and Tilly and held her hand out for the object. It was a coil made basket with a vertical, looped handle, glazed a deep turquoise.

"May I take a photograph?" asked Lyle.

Maddie spun around to face him and everyone else at the kiln. She held the basket out on the palm of her left hand, and turned it by the handle, gently, slowly, with her right. Just like her daddy, thought Lucy.

Kaila's boys arrived in a gust of outdoor energy.

"See, I told you I'd beat you," boasted Maddie.

And before anyone could ask them if they needed anything, they were gone, and Joe was handing Lucy the basket, saying, "Put that somewhere safe, would you, please?"

*****

The short plat map was laid out on the table to one side of them, so they could both look at it. "The thing is," said Buck, setting his fork down on the plate and touching a napkin to his mouth. They were up at Honey's Eatery in Marblemount, and Hilda sipped mint tea and nibbled on one of Honey's famous, homemade cinnamon rolls while Buck polished off a ham omelet with hash brown potatoes. "I love the cinnamon rolls," he told Hilda, "But my doctor said I have to watch out for diabetes at my age."

Hilda wondered how old that might be. She was sure Buck was older than her, but maybe not by much. So maybe this double vision thing she was experiencing was just that she needed glasses, like him. He didn't seem to have any problem seeing the map as he stared down at it, yet she couldn't merge two into one to clean up the lines. If anything the lines kept moving, and she surreptitiously sniffed her tea to make sure there wasn't something stronger in it.

"The thing is," he repeated. "If I come in here with the CAT...."

Hilda looked at where he was pointing. She could see the highway and she could see her road but every time she tried to hone in on their connection, things got fuzzy. "Can I borrow those for a moment?" she said, pointing at the cheater glasses propped on the end of his nose.

"Your eyes giving you trouble?" he asked.

Hilda bristled, not wanting to be accused of anything related to age, but his face was so serene as he handed over his glasses that she felt herself get a little gooey inside. "Only recently," she admitted. "And only sometimes." She slipped on the glasses and the map got a whole lot bigger, but a whole lot blurrier too. She pulled them right back off, grimacing.

"That wasn't it?" Buck inquired with such genuine concern that Hilda felt herself lured into confessing.

"I've been having double vision," she blurted.

"That's not good," said Buck. "Have you been to the eye doctor?"

Hilda watched him put a forkful of omelet in his mouth as she shook her head no. "It's only been for the last few days."

"Well you should probably still go," said Buck, wiping his mouth with a napkin again. "Are you having any other symptoms? Any headaches?"

Hilda nodded miserably, picking at her cinnamon roll with her fork. She touched her forehead with her other hand and said, "Right here."

The door tinkled a little chime as somebody came in or went out. She turned to look; a middle-aged couple, full of smiles, inquiring about a table for breakfast. When she turned back, Buck's warm brown eyes were smiling solicitously at her.

"For how long?" he asked.

"What?"

"The headaches," he said, gesturing with his chin towards her forehead.

She thought about it as he laid down his fork and lifted a slice of apple off the side of his plate. "Since the summer," she said, feeling a sudden, inexplicable ache in the pit of her stomach. "Maybe a little longer."

"And you didn't bang your head, or sustain an injury?" asked Buck, shaking his head from side to side as he said it.

Her brow creased as she tried to remember.

Buck crunched down on his slice of apple and tiny droplets of juice sparked into the air around him. Immediately Hilda felt something stab at the center of her forehead.

"Oh!" she gasped, dropping her fork with a clatter and slapping her hand over her mouth. She hadn't thought about that piece of apple wood since it hit her last spring. Was that…?

"What is it?" asked Buck. "Are you okay?"

His kindness was almost overwhelming and Hilda felt tears sting the backs of her eyes. She wasn't going to cry, she told herself. She wasn't. And she certainly wasn't going to tell him what happened with that apple tree.

She bit back the emotions and lowered her hand from her mouth. "I think I'm tired," she whispered. "I haven't been sleeping well."

"Maybe you need a vacation," said Buck. "Stress can do strange things to us."

Hilda nodded and sipped her tea again. The idea of sunshine and walks on the beach with Gus did sound appealing. "I have tickets to Hawaii still," she told Buck. "From a trip I was supposed to make this spring that I had to cancel because my road builder fell through."

"Well you have your road builder now," Buck said, pointing at himself. He picked up his fork again and scooped up the last of his omelet. "Why don't you let me get to work while you're sunning yourself in Hawaii?"

Hilda thought about this for a moment while he finished his mouthful. She wouldn't mind being gone while the work was happening. Coming back to a fait accompli. No more arguments. And she knew Gus would be glad to see her.

"Don't I have to be here in case you need something while you're building the road?" she questioned.

"Like what?" he asked.

She opened her mouth then closed it, realizing she didn't want to suggest he might have trouble with Connors, or with Connors' lawyer.

But Buck was buttering a triangle of whole-wheat toast and didn't seem to have noticed her lack of reply. "As long as I can stay downriver of the water line," he said, looking up at her. " I won't need a thing."

Hilda was miffed that he knew about the water line and she must have shown it because Buck continued with an explanation of how.

"My uncle Glen used to own one of the houses down the hill," he said. "And I remember him showing me where the water line ran under the highway when we'd tromp up to the creek to work on the intake. That was a long time ago," he reflected. "Back when that land was more woods than pasture. Before Clarence Burns owned it."

"You knew Clarence?" Hilda asked.

"Uh huh," said Buck and popped the toast in his mouth.

Hilda waited for him to finish his mouthful and go on to say what a lowlife no good son-of-a-gun Clarence was. But he didn't. He just wiped his mouth with his napkin again and smiled across at her. "If you don't cross the water line," she told him. "You won't bring the road back towards that corner of my property like I want."

"I know," nodded Buck. "I see that on your short plat map. But you're going to sell that front lot."

"So?"

"D'you really want the new owner to have to take on the DOT if the water line breaks under the road?"

A pain began to radiate from the center of Hilda's forehead. "But that lot won't have access to the new road," she told Buck. "It's only for the back two lots."

"So you'll be the one fighting the DOT?" Buck threw out. He picked up his coffee and took a swallow.

The pain in Hilda's head began to pound as her mind grappled the implications of what he'd just said. "But if you stay to west of the water line," she moaned. "There'll be a section of land alongside the stump of that old apple tree that will be virtually useless to me. So why would I keep it?"

Buck placed his coffee cup carefully next to his plate. "Why indeed?" he asked.

Hilda narrowed her eyes, scrutinizing the man on the other side of the table from her. Why was it he seemed to know things they'd never discussed? Was he just insightful or had he participated in the ever-present rumor mill in the Upper Skagit? She wanted to suspect the latter but the way he avoided badmouthing her ex, made her doubt. She sighed, feeling his words slip into a part of her conscience that she usually ignored. It made the pain in her forehead lessen, turn to warmth even, and she began to feel it radiating throughout her. "I don't like Connors," she told him with a forthrightness that surprised her.

Buck leaned forward, like he was sharing a secret, and said, "All the more reason to make *him* pay the property taxes on that useless piece of land."

*****

Lucy sat on the top step of the porch, between the dogs, and waved as Joe pulled out of the driveway. They'd had to scramble, to get him out of the house on time to make his connection with Erica because quite a few of the people at the kiln opening had lingered, buying pots, having lunch and just chatting. But it had been a great opening. And Joe discovered that John Leach had been right; staggering the bag walls and making the one in the second chamber shorter than the one in the first, improved heat distribution dramatically. For the first time, almost all the pots in both chambers got to temperature.

Once the K-car was out of sight on the highway, Lucy let her gaze drift to the smallest of the three silver fir trees on the property line. It had really struggled after she freed it from the blackberries. In fact, she thought she'd killed it. Fortunately, now it seemed to be perking up. Its branches were more green, less yellow, and didn't seem to be sagging quite so much. It certainly gave her a lesson in co-dependency, that little tree. She hoped it would flourish, of course, now that it had overcome being released from the stranglehold by the invasive blackberries, but she'd have to wait and see.

She tipped her head back, letting her hair fall straight down behind her, and reveled in the warm, September sun on her face and neck. She could have gone down to Seattle with Joe and Maddie but it was Saturday, and she and Joe always tried to keep the shop open on Saturdays. Plus this would give her time to start pricing and organizing the new pots. Although she wouldn't mind getting a chance to go for a walk in the park with the dogs too. She debated that for a moment. Joe probably wouldn't be back before dinnertime, since it was two hours down to Seattle and two hours back, so maybe if she kept the shop open till 5:00 then went for a walk? Yes, that should work.

Max sniffed at her left ear, tickling it, and Lucy ducked out of his reach, giggling. Then she turned back and petted his soft, white head. He had such thick fur. "And such sensitive skin," she crooned, pulling his nose towards her and kissing him between his eyes. Maggie's tail thumped on the porch - *me too, me too, me too* – so Lucy let go of Max, swung around and ran her hand over Maggie's smoother, silkier, caramel colored coat. She heard a vehicle slow down out on the highway and flipped her head around to see a black and tan jeep pull up to the mailbox. Lucy was still intrigued by the long arched tins, like bread tins, that people put at the end of their driveways for their post here. And the fact that inside theirs was a tiny bowl that Joe had made.

"What's that for?" she asked him the first time she saw it.

"To put money in, for when I don't have a stamp for a letter. I put the letter inside the mailbox with small change and the mail carrier takes it to the Post Office for me."

Lucy thought that was incredibly accommodating on the part of the postal worker. In England, the postman just stuffed everything through the letterbox in the front door and scarpered, probably so he wouldn't *have* to take anything away with him. Although she grew up a big town and wondered if in the rural parts of England, postmen were more accommodating? She did miss the red, Royal Mail, post boxes on the corners of the street in England, though. So in deference to that, she painted their mailbox red, to remind her of England.

In the distance she heard the telltale tinny clank of the end being thrust closed on the mailbox, and then she watched the jeep pull away. Lucy stood up, brushed off the backs of her jeans, and walked down the gently sloping driveway. It really felt good to be out in the sunshine. She stretched out towards the sign for the business, feeling energized by the day, and then slowed down approaching the highway. She automatically ran the childhood mantra she'd learned from her mother through her head, "Right, left, right again," just so she could remember to do it the other way when looking down the road for oncoming traffic here. It might take her a few years to get that, she thought. There was no traffic coming west on the highway, so she stepped out in front of the mailbox and gathered up the mail.

Her return journey up the driveway was more sedate, even though the dogs were sitting up on the front porch, wondering where she was off to next. But Lucy did her usual things of leafing through the letters on her way back up to the house. There was one of Joe's dad's lengthy epistles in his beautiful, forward sloping cursive; a bill from the power company, which now they'd be able to pay thanks to the kiln opening, a postcard from her sister – Lucy flipped it over – from Gibraltar – and then one from the County Commissioners.

Wait. Who? she thought, her step faltering. What was this about? She ripped open the long, white, number 10 envelope, still stepping towards the house, and pulled out the letter. She unfolded the top, then the bottom, to reveal the words on the page. Notice of Appeal, it said in bold letters across the top. What? thought Lucy. She stopped now, in the middle of the driveway, to focus on the message. Max trotted down from the porch with his stick in his mouth and dropped it by her foot but Lucy didn't pay any attention. Her eyes were racing left to right, scarfing up the information. Hilda Hess had appealed the Hearing Examiner's decision, allowing them to make retail sales from their shop on Highway 20, and now they had to appear before the County Commissioners to restate their case.

Lucy slapped her hands down to her thighs in annoyance, a corner of the letter coming to rest on Max's ear. She heard the pock pock sound of his ear flicking against the paper as she looked across the pasture towards Hilda's house. You miserable old bitch! she thought. You just can't leave us alone, can you?!

She brought the letter back up in front of her, scanning it for the date of this appearance. There it was. Friday, November 4, 1988. What really irked her was that these commissioners were allowing someone who didn't even show up to the public hearing an appeal of its decision. She felt her teeth grit together as she imagined herself balling up the letter and shoving it down Hilda's throat.

But Lucy didn't like those kind of thoughts in herself, not after the way her dad had been. She stood for a moment, hearing her breath snort out of her like a bull in a pen. She didn't feel up to pricing pots now, not after this news. And there wasn't any mill waste to stack. Her mind ran over all the things that could keep her busy and give her an outlet for her anger. It settled on one.

She stomped back up to the house and in through the front door, leaving the dogs looking after her like they didn't understand what they'd missed. She threw the mail on the kitchen table and looked up at the ceiling, hands on her hips. "Okay," she announced, like a fencing teacher calling for the ready pose. "You're it."

Chapter 17

Almost a month later, Joe took his 30.06 and his new backpack out to his truck and put them both on the front seat. He closed the door, to go back into the house, but found himself staring across at the open wound on the land made by Hilda's road. It was early, barely daylight, and the shimmer of overnight frost on the surface of the raw, scraped dirt made it more bearable, but it was still way wider than anything he'd imagined. A sixty-foot wide gash of mutilated soil amid the lush, rainforest greens of the landscape around it. It made his skin crawl.

As he stood staring at it, he noticed movement alongside the big cedar tree. A flicker of light tan. He waited, knowing the light would even out to give him a better view if he were patient. The morning was cold, crisp, with enough humidity to make the air feel fresh. Birds peeped their early morning calls all around him. Long, uninterrupted, high-pitched whistles, like piccolos, trilling through the pastoral peace.

Then the doe moved, goose-stepping towards Hilda's road, her two fawns cavorting behind her. He watched her turn a studied eye in the direction of the highway, then swing her nose back around towards Sauk, and follow it with her hooves. She started up the road slowly, flicking her tan ears 180 degrees to make sure her offspring were following, then she bolted when a large bird, maybe an eagle or a blue heron, whump whumped in the sky above them. Joe watched the doe bound once, twice, three times up Hilda's road, and disappear into the brush with her twin fawns.

It was a glorious sight, one of the things he lived for, yet still he sighed, thinking how last year at this time, those deer would have been browsing the drops under his apple tree. Or browsing some of them on it, if he were to be honest. He came out many a morning to find numerous apples with one bite out of them, because they were too heavy for the deer to pull off the branch and just high enough to require the deer to stand on their back legs to reach them. Once tasted, if the apple didn't fall to the ground, the deer moved on to the next one.

Joe noticed the light quality softening and turned to see the sky above the highway filling with cotton candy whispers of baby pink. He watched, as the pink turned to peach and the peach to gold and then it was daylight.

His eyes dropped to the spot where the King David once stood, reaching for the sky this way and that with its sprawling branches. He felt a deep sadness for such loss due to an act of spite. He noticed a limb sticking up from the ground next to the stump. That'd be a good one for Max, he thought. He walked the half a dozen steps down to it, and bent to pull it out of the ground. But a quick tug showed him this stick wasn't coming out of the ground. He squatted down next to and ran his finger over the spiky, brown-red twigs emerging from the top. New growth, he said to himself.

Behind him the front door opened and closed and Joe rose to see Lucy, her thick curls mussed from sleep, standing on the porch in her sweats, holding a mug of tea. "Come here and look at this," he called out, as both dogs chased around the back of the truck to reach him.

She clomped down the steps in her oversized boots and came towards him, her hands wrapped tight around her mug.

"Look," he said when she came up alongside him. He touched the limb with the toe of his boot. "You know what this is?"

She looked at him like it was a trick question. "Ummmm. A stick?" she joked, and then raised her tea mug up to her lips.

"It's a limb, from the old apple tree," Joe said, ignoring her humor. "And it feels like it's rooted."

"The tree's growing back?" marveled Lucy.

"Looks like."

She smiled. "Nature rules," she sighed.

"Yeah." The dogs were sniffing along Hilda's road and Joe slipped his arm around Lucy's waist, gently turning her around to face the road, too. He pointed at it as he spoke. "And I'm guessing," he said, "that before we know it, that eyesore will get ruled by nature, too. There'll be all sort of green growth sprouting through the surface of it come springtime." They watched Maggie squat down and pee. "Especially if the dogs keep watering it," he added.

Lucy laughed. She turned to look at him. "Gary just rang to say don't drive down to his house. He'll come up here and get you."

As soon as she said it they heard a truck, rumbling up the hill towards them. They both looked over to see Joe's hunting buddy's white, Chevy one-ton come to a stop where the road met the highway. Joe leapt back to his truck, to get his gear, and Lucy followed, setting her tea down on the top of the bed.

"Will I see you before I leave for the theatre tonight?" she asked.

Joe's smile widened and he rocked his head roguishly from side to side. "Depends on whether I get lucky or not." He was pumped. Gary was taking him deer hunting at a series of high mountain lakes over on the Twin Sisters. "But I'm not familiar with that country so I don't know how involved it might get if we each get a deer. Might be well after dark before we get back. What time are you heading out?"

"Around 5:00."

He leaned forward and kissed her gently on the lips. "Well

break a leg," he said.

"You too," she replied. Then she pointed a caution at him. "Only not really in your case."

The Chevy rolled around onto the highway and pulled into their driveway. Joe strapped his rifle over his left shoulder and set his pack down on his toes. He threw his right arm out and Lucy stepped forward, slipping her arms around his waist, under his wool shirt. He cinched her in tighter to him and dropped his face down to nuzzle her neck, then he let her go, grabbed up his pack and strode across the driveway, a bounce in every step.

"See you when I see you," he yelled out as he stepped up into Gary's Chevy.

Then he and Gary headed off to their adventure.

*****

Buck had been right, thought Hilda, as she hung up the phone from talking with Luigi Acosta. The realtor had already found her a buyer for the front lot but the buyer said it was only a go if she sectioned out the road and everything east of it. "He apparently doesn't want to pay property taxes on something he can't use," Acosta told Hilda.

Hilda told Acosta she had to think about it but she really wanted this sale. Once she had that first money she could pay Buck to come in and finish the road up to the second and third lots, which would probably make them easier to sell. And then she should have all the money Burns robbed her of back and could make plans to sell this run down house he'd left her with and move on. Where, she wasn't sure.

It had been wonderful to spend three weeks on the Big Island of Hawaii this month with its constant sunshine and warm temperatures. Hilda hadn't missed the never-ending drizzle of the Upper Skagit and the chill it put in her bones. And she'd noticed after only a few days that her vision problems and headaches had gone completely. She wasn't pleased to find them creeping back on since her return.

The only problem was, she still wasn't sure about committing to Gus. Oh, he was a nice enough guy, and had more money than she'd originally thought, as a retired veterinarian. But he spent most days involved in his extensive garden over there in Kona. And when he wasn't in the garden, he was at the local farmers' market, selling his excess produce, making friend with all the locals. Hilda felt he wasn't paying enough attention to her, and she didn't like that. She didn't like that at all.

She looked out her kitchen window, at the fresh layer of snow on the top of Sauk. It was getting cold already here. Another season of trying to keep up with all her firewood needs and hoar frost, like chunks of fresh coconut, wrapped around sticks and branches down on the ground. She looked at the frost, skirting the ground around the base of her big cedar tree, and frowned. The greens and browns of the Pacific Northwest were all very well but it would be nice to wake up to warm weather and the bright, bold reds, purples and oranges of tropical flowers.

In the distance she could see the gables on Connors' house, and the tendril of smoke coming out of his chimney. She was ready to have that view be over with, that was for sure. Her eyes dropped to what she could see of her new road from this window. If she did what Buck and Acosta suggested, and took out the road and the contended ground that seemed determined to defy clear ownership beyond it, then pretty soon there'd be a house on this front lot, and she wouldn't have to look at Connors and his happy life anymore.

Hilda picked up the phone and dialed Acosta's number at the realty office. It was time to move on.

*****

The Pass was still open and people were making the most of their last hurrah with the fall colors in the high country by driving the highway. Lucy was busy all day hopping in and out of the shop to wait on customers and she finally put the sign to closed at 4 pm so she could touch up her tattoos before heading down to the theatre.

The character she played wore her life on her skin and Lucy loved having to apply the temporary tattoos to her arms and legs. Today she was sporting a swallow, a crab, a rose, a heart pierced with an arrow, a pair of die and then, her favorite, an eight-inch long, fire breathing dragon. They all needed some refresher dabs from the little pots of paint and the two-inch, fine paintbrush that came with the script.

She brought the dogs inside with her, and went into the bathroom. She slipped out of her jeans and sweatshirt and examined her tattoos in the long mirror she'd hung on the inside of the knotty pine door that Joe had built using some of the hinges they'd brought back from England. Yes, she thought; the dragon wrapped around her shin definitely needed more red and yellow added to it.

She filled a small tumbler with water and then went and sat on the couch, alongside the stove, to touch up her tattoos. With Joe gone, she had the radio turned off in the house, and while she painted, her mind mused dialogue between the characters in the play she was writing. The dogs slowly relaxed from a sit to a down to a sprawl in front of the stove. Lucy had hoped to write a scene in her play today but there'd been too many interruptions from the shop. Oh well, she thought, moving from the dragon to the swallow on her arm; maybe tomorrow. She certainly didn't resent the income those interruptions had brought.

When she finished touching up the swallow, she washed off the brush and dabbed it in the red. She glanced up at the clock over by the kitchen before starting on the rose on her upper arm, and was surprised to see half an hour had gone by already. She wouldn't have time to eat before she left, but that was okay. Tonight was closing night and there was a low key cast party planned in one of the local restaurants. She'd eat then. Although, she thought, washing off the brush again so she could mix a little red with the yellow and touch up the crab, maybe she should take a cheese and tomato sandwich with her. That way she wouldn't get *too* hungry before curtain.

Max and Maggie both cocked their heads up at the same time, and Lucy waited to see if she heard a car pulling in driveway. Just because the sign said closed, didn't mean people wouldn't pull in, especially since it was still light. When she didn't hear anyone, she went back to painting her crab, thinking maybe the dogs were tuning in to Joe, further down the highway, making his way home. These dogs tended to know he was arriving home long before she heard his truck on the highway. Although he wasn't in his truck today. But still. She moved her head back, to get a better view of the crab she'd just painted. Maybe, she thought, the character in her play that she wanted to hear things without them being said, maybe that should be a dog.

Both dogs let their heads flop back down onto the wood floor and Lucy put down the small paintbrush down in the lid of the metal tin holding the paints. Then she dabbed a dry brush in some white, sparkly powder and dusted the surfaces of all her newly painted tattoos, starting with the driest first.

Satisfied that they were the way she wanted them for the show, she pulled her jeans and sweatshirt back on and carried the little brush and the pot of water into the kitchen. She rinsed them off and made herself the sandwich. She wouldn't mind if Joe pulled in before she left because it was getting close to dark now and she'd like to know he was home, safe and sound. But maybe she'd call him from the theatre at intermission. She wrapped the sandwich in tin foil and fished in the porcelain jar on the counter for a tea bag. He might even want her to skip the cast party and come straight home after the show.

"And that would be okay with me," she told the dogs, as she walked towards them to throw one more piece of firewood in the stove. Once done, she tightened down the drafts, to keep the fire burning longer, went back to the kitchen to grab her sandwich, and then made for the door.

*****

"You need a ride somewhere?' the old guy called out when he pulled up alongside Joe. He was leaning on the steering wheel of his pick-up, talking across a kid who looked like he might be about ten years old. Maybe his grandson, thought Joe.

"Thanks!" Joe replied. "But it kind of depends on how far I need to go." He'd followed an old mining road out to this logging road and had started to see other vehicles and hunters; but he'd made a big loop away from the trailhead where he'd parted company with Gary and wasn't sure if this road would get him back faster than going back the way he'd come. "I'm trying to get to the bridge on Sulfur Creek Road that crosses the South Fork of the Nooksack. D'you know the one I mean?"

"I do. And that's a ways from here. This road dead-ends in an old Scott Paper clear-cut, just this side of Wanlick Creek. You'll see a trail, on the other side of where the creek crosses the Nooksack, and you can follow it upstream to the bridge. I could drop you at the clear cut."

Joe thought about his offer. It would put him in yet another place he didn't know but he got the sense that daylight was getting short and he'd prefer to get back to Gary's truck before dark if he could. "D'you know what time it is?" he asked the old fellow.

"Yeah," said the man, looking at his watch. "Almost 3:00."

"Okay then, yes. Please," said Joe.

Not that there was really a time limit on when he should get back to the truck. At least, not as far as he knew. But then Gary wasn't that much of a communicator. The two of them had made the hour and a half drive up the Baker Lake Highway, over Wanlick Pass and on down Sulfur Creek to the South Fork of the Nooksack, without saying much of anything to each other, let alone discuss details of where they'd hunt and for how long.

Gary drove them to the end of a short logging road once they crossed the South Fork of the Nooksack, and parked the Chevy. They climbed out, put on their packs, and slung their rifles over their shoulders. Then Gary pointed at an outcropping of rocks on the uphill side of the road.

"We're gonna go in from there," he said, without any kind of preamble. "There'll be chute pretty quick. You pull up through that chute to get to Three Lakes. I'm gonna break off and hunt Heart Lake."

Gary knew every inch of these mountains and he kind of had a way of believing everyone else knew them just as well, too. Joe didn't disillusion him because he'd spent most of his life out in the woods, even though some of those woods happened to be in the Adirondack Mountains of his childhood. But he knew how to follow his sign and was pretty sure he'd find his way back to the truck.

"Okay," he agreed. He and Gary often split up to hunt, so they wouldn't be huffing down each other's necks, but so far Joe had always been familiar with the terrain. This would be new for him.

"See you back here after a while," said Gary, with a tight nod of his head. He was in his early thirties, a year or so younger than Joe, with endless stamina, like him. There was a wealth of trust between them that they could help each other out of a jam if need be. Joe nodded back.

Five minutes later Gary broke off, to climb the ridge over to Heart Lake, and Joe scrambled up rocks and downed logs to get to the Three Lakes area of the Twin Sisters. He came out in the meadows Gary had told him about, that surrounded the three small lakes. The meadows were loaded with blueberry bushes and Joe thought immediately about bringing Lucy back next summer, when there would be berries to pick. And maybe also fish to catch. It was raining, and the heavy cloud cover socked everything in around him; but there was also a blissful peace to looking out at the mist while walking through the brushy meadows in search of deer sign.

He found a creek, emptying out of the third lake, and started to follow it, curious about where it went. It wasn't that far before the creek crossed an old gravel road and dropped over a hillside into a pristine, suspended, emerald valley. Big, old growth trees grew out of the hillside heading down to the basin and Joe saw that the gravel road he was on zigzagged down through these trees. He started down the road, switchbacking left and right, his eyes all the time looking through the trees, hoping he'd spot a deer grazing on the brush at the bottom of the basin.

He was still very much alone in the verdant mountain dell when he got to the bottom. He lingered a moment, enjoying the cool, expansive feel of the richly oxygenated air in his lungs, then decided to head straight up through the trees to get back to the top. He clambered through the undergrowth, using the trees to give him counterbalance so he could gain traction in the rugged dirt and made quick headway uphill. About half way up, he grabbed a hold of a mountain hemlock, pulling himself up to the left of the tree, and heard a sound immediately behind him, to the right. He whipped his head around in time to see a big, black bear, barreling down the hill the way he'd just come up. Joe's heart pumped with excitement as he realized they'd both passed the hemlock at exactly the same moment, on opposite sides. He watched, spellbound, as the bear found the zigzagging road and filled the silent glade with the sound of its claws, clicking against the gravel as it ran. Joe watched, until he could see the bear no more, then spun around to continue up, his whole being alive with the joy of that moment.

Back at the top, Joe decided to follow the old mining road out a ways, hoping to see a deer to make his day complete. The rain was getting heavier and Joe hunkered inside his thoughts, lured by the gentle downward motion of the road until, before he knew it, he was on the Scott Paper Mainline with this old fellow asking him if he needed a ride.

"Thank you kindly," he said, as the grandpa pulled up at the end of the road, by the clear cut, pointing forward to where Joe would find the trail alongside the Nooksack.

Joe stepped out and followed the old guy's directions until he came out by the river. The sky on all sides of him was dark with clouds and the temperature had dropped. If this kept up, Joe thought, it might snow before he got back to the truck. He hitched his pack higher on his back and started a steady pace down the rocky riverbank on the downhill side of the Nooksack.

He was watching his footing when he ran out of trail and looked up to see that the bank was steep right down to the water on this side of the canyon. He'd have to cross to the other side. The Nooksack wasn't very deep but the water still slapped back and forth, taking from the bank on one side to deposit it on the other, switching the position of the cut bank and the flood bank. Joe walked a log across the river, thinking he was probably going to have to switch back and forth across the water all the way up to the concrete bridge.

Sure enough, he walked another few hundred yards and had to cross again, this time using stepping-stone rocks, protruding from the water, to make it to the other side. The Nooksack was shallow so it didn't bother him to have to cross it again and again but it was going to add time to his journey. He pushed on, wanting to beat nightfall, and got to another cut bank about a quarter mile upstream. This time he was back on some logs, crisscrossing over the current, and further upstream still, he had to slop through the shallow water to get to the flood bank on the other side.

Now he was beginning to feel wet through and through, from precipitation on the outside and sweat on the inside of his wool pants and shirt. But he pumped on, reassured by the old guy's assertion that it wasn't but a couple of miles upstream to the bridge.

He got to the next cut bank and looked up, ruefully, at the tiny flakes of snow drifting down from the sky. He turned towards the river and swung his right foot forward onto a boulder, his face down, to see where he was going, and in one swift motion, his glasses slid down off his nose and into the Nooksack. "Goddammit!" yelled Joe, his frustration echoing in the canyon. He dropped to his knees on the boulder, pushing the butt of his rifle back to protect it, and reached his right hand down into the icy water, fumbling for his glasses. But there was nothing. He peered, hard, down into the riverbed, hoping they'd got caught against a rock. But between his blurry vision, the speed of the current and the onset of twilight, he knew, in the pit of his gut, that his glasses were gone.

And he knew that he wasn't getting back to Gary's truck tonight.

*****

Lucy bounced off the stage at intermission, exhilarated from performing, only to find her co-director waiting in the wings for her, his face very serious. For a moment she wondered if she'd made a mistake in her monologue but she hadn't flubbed her lines and she could feel the audience listening to her so she didn't think it was that.

"What's the matter?" she asked, immediately worried because Lawrence was usually so easy going. So why was he looking at her like that?

"You got an urgent phone, which came through to my office, while you were on stage. Joe's missing."

Lucy felt her smile fade. "What?" she said, as if she hadn't heard him. But really she was having trouble understanding what he'd said.

"I didn't catch the woman's name but she was somebody's wife. Somebody out with Joe. I got her number." He motioned with his left hand towards the short corridor backstage. "You can call from my phone." He looked apologetic now. "I guess Joe didn't make it back to the truck."

She saw him studying her face, for signs of a reaction, but she had none. What he was saying didn't make any sense. Then he did a quick about turn and led her to his office.

The corridor was narrow and Lawrence Green swayed left and right, almost touching the walls as he moved down it. His carriage was that of a young man but the silver tips to his dark, wavy curls and his silver moustache both suggested he was older. Lucy clipped along behind him in the stiletto heels she had to wear for her character and then passed in front of him when he stood back in the doorway to let her by.

He stepped back out into the corridor, pulling the door closed behind him. "Take whatever time you need," he told her.

Lucy dialed the number for Paulette and Gary, glad she had it memorized, and somebody answered on the first ring.

"Hello?"

"Paulette, it's Lucy."

"Oh thanks for calling back. I'm really sorry to tell you this but Joe didn't make it back to the truck today."

"What does that mean?" Lucy's mind still couldn't make sense of the information.

Paulette sounded very patient, concerned too, when she explained. "He and Gary were s'posed to meet back at the truck and Gary waited and waited till it was well after dark. Then he got worried."

"So where's Gary now?"

"He's here. He came back so he could switch to his work truck because that has a phone in it. He's planning to go back out with Tip, our brother-in-law, and hopefully Pete. He wants to leave Pete in the truck, down the road a ways where the phone can get reception, and he and Tip carry walkie-talkies. That way if Joe needs help when they find him, they can use the walkie-talkies to reach Pete and he can use the phone to call for medical help"

The thought that Joe might need medical help clutched at Lucy's heart and filled her mind with the image of him lying, bleeding somewhere. She snapped away from her fears, thinking practically. "You want me to try to reach Pete?"

"Please. And tell him to just to come right up if he's willing to go out."

"I'll call Sonny too, just in case."

"All right."

"And I'll call you right back as soon as I know," Lucy ended. She hung up by depressing the receiver buttons on the phone with her fingers, waited two seconds, then let them go to hear the dial tone again. She called Pete.

Pete picked up on the second ring and Lucy told him what was going on.

"I'll get my boots on," he said, his voice already filled with the urgency of the situation. "Then I'll head up to Gary's."

She hung up again and dialed Sonny and Sarah's number. She heard the phone ringing in her ear as her mind skittered to the possibility of Joe having a negative encounter with a bear. Again, she reined in her fears, knowing they wouldn't do her any good. Her eyes scanned Lawrence's office, looking for a clock. They ran over stack after towering stack of published play scripts, over a small table holding models of a set designs and Roman gladiator helmets, over laurel wreaths, bejeweled swords and shields, theatrical make-up and the odd set piece. It was all the stuff of Lucy's dreams. But right now, with the phone ringing in her ear, and the anxiety that Joe might be waiting for someone to come to his rescue, all she wanted to do was find the time. She finally looked behind her and found a clock on the wall, above her head. It was almost 8:20. Maybe Sonny and Sarah were at a football game at the school in Concrete, she thought. Lucy hung up and called Paulette back.

"Pete just pulled in," Paulette told her, without waiting to hear Lucy's end of it. "And I'm making coffee and sandwiches. When will you be home?"

"I'm supposed to stay through the second half but I'm going to see if I can leave now."

"Will you call me?"

"When I get home? Yes. Although what if I do have to stay till curtain? I won't be home before 10:30 if that's the case."

"Doesn't matter," said Paulette. "I won't sleep till Gary gets back with Joe."

The thought that Joe might not be back before that late sank deep into a place that Lucy hadn't gone yet. A cold, sick feeling rushed across her stomach. "Should I call Search and Rescue?" she asked. Paulette had a lot more experience waiting on a husband to come back from a hunting trip than Lucy did.

The line suddenly got very quiet. Then Paulette said, in a voice that was soft, gentle. "I would, if it were Gary."

Lucy hung up, feeling unprepared. She wanted to get out of her costume and make-up. She wanted to have a phone book in her hands so she could look up the number for Search and Rescue. She wanted to be at home without having to waste an hour driving there.

And, more than anything, she wanted Joe to walk in the front door and announce that he'd "just been a little late, is all."

*****

Joe found a logjam on the banks of the Nooksack and decided to hunker down inside it for the night. It was snowing pretty hard now and the tangle of mostly old growth firs, sticking up and out from the bank like spilled, oversized matchsticks, would give him certain amount of protection from the cold. He'd light a fire, eat the sandwich he'd made for his lunch and hopefully find a dry spot to sleep for the night.

He climbed inside the logjam, bent low because there wasn't enough room to stand, and propped his rifle against a log end. He pressed a hand on the ground, to see how damp it was, and felt moisture rise up between his fingers. Yeah, he wasn't lying down on that, he thought.

He stepped back out of the shelter, pulled off his pack, and reached inside for his flashlight and fire starter gear. But his hand landed in a pool of water. "What the....???" he said out loud. It was a brand new pack and supposed to be waterproof. He touched the outside of the pack; that was dry. Then why...?

"Argh, No!!" he cried out, when he figured out what was going on. The seams of the pack had soaked up rain like a thirsty sponge and seeped it through to the inside, which was *not* waterproof. Joe pulled out a sodden matchbook and remembered that he hadn't transferred his waterproof tube of matches into this pack yet. Nor his pitch wood, he realized, as he fumbled around the puddle in the bottom looking for it. In fact, now that he thought about it, much of his emergency overnight gear was still at home, in his old pack. He could have kicked himself.

He pulled out his flashlight and turned it on. The beam was faint, like he needed to change the batteries. But his back up batteries were.....back in his pack at home! "Dammit!!" he yelled.

He reached inside the pack again, hoping for something, anything, that might help him light a fire. His hand felt something soft and squishy. That would be his cheese sandwich, he thought. Then he felt a cylinder, metal and hard, with a handle and what felt like a spoon, rubber banded to the outside. Lucy must have slipped that thermos full of soup he'd rejected into his pack without him knowing.

Joe snatched it out, feeling a glimmer of hope in this dark and miserable night. He ran the beam of his flashlight around the inside the logjam and spied a jagged log end, protruding forward on one side. He crouched over to it and sat, putting the flashlight in the groove where his thighs met and the thermos between his knees. He pulled the spoon out of the rubber band, unscrewed the lid on the thermos and let his head drop forward to inhale the heavenly, much welcome aroma of warm chicken soup.

*****

Lawrence Green was adamant. "Don't even think about the curtain call," he told Lucy, with a dismissive flap of his hand. "Just go home. But call Search and Rescue first. The sooner they get on Joe's trail, the better. I have a phone book in my desk."

When Lucy did get home, she found three messages waiting for her on the answering machine. She hoped that at least one of them from Skagit Search and Rescue, with better news than they gave her when she spoke to them earlier.

She hit play and the machine beeped. "Hello, Mrs. Connors, this is Marsha from Skagit County Search and Rescue calling you back. I wanted to let you know that I did check, and the area where your husband is missing is on the border of Whatcom County, so it's not in our range. As I suspected. But I went ahead and called Whatcom County Search and Rescue and they should be contacting you about going out to find your husband."

Lucy stared at the answering machine. That wasn't what she wanted to hear. At. All. It beeped again and a deep baritone said, "Hi, this is Jacob. I'm with Whatcom County Search and Rescue and we just got a call from Marsha, at Skagit SAR. She wants us to go out on a search for your husband, in the Twin Sisters wilderness area, but like I told her, Three Lakes is in Skagit County, not Whatcom. The line between the two counties is kinda murky in that whole area but according to our map here, Three Lakes is definitely part of Skagit SAR. So my advice is you give them another call. Good luck."

Lucy couldn't believe this! What in the world did they think this was? Wimbledon tennis?? The machine beeped a third time. "Hi, Mrs. Connors, this is Marsha again with Skagit Search and Rescue. I don't know if Jacob, from Whatcom, got a hold of you yet but he did call me back and said that the area where your husband is missing might be in Skagit County. I'm still not sure that's right but I'm working on it. I'll be back in touch just as soon as we know for sure."

Lucy shook her head vigorously. She wished they would bloody well make up their minds! There might be a life at stake here! She snatched up the phone and dialed Paulette.

She answered on the first ring, sounding startled. "Hello?"

"It's Lucy. Did I wake you?"

"No, no. I'm mopping the floor. That's what I do when I'm worried. I clean."

"I'm worried too," agreed Lucy. "But not enough to clean the floor." And they both shared a little laugh. "To be honest," she went on. "Most of the time I'm *not* worried about what's happened to Joe. He'll be fine if he just had to spend the night in the woods. He really will." She paused, not wanting to give the thought credence by saying it out loud, then added, "It's only when I think he might be hurt that I worry."

Paulette immediately launched into a story. "One time Gary was out in the woods, dressing an elk, and he cut an artery in his left forearm. He tied it off with his bandana, finished gutting the elk, got it in his truck and drove home. And it was an hour – an *hour*," Paulette repeated like she still couldn't believe it. "Before he came inside and showed me what had happened. I tell you," she finished. "These mountain men are tough!"

That was exactly what Lucy needed to hear.

*****

Joe had a lighter in the pocket of his wool pants and messed around for a while, trying to get a fire started. But the wood was too wet and he didn't have anything flammable to set under it. If he had the little hunk of pitch wood he usually carried around, he said to himself, he'd soon have a fire going. Pitch was nature's petroleum; it lit right up. He slipped the lighter back in his pants pocket and crouched into the logjam, back over to where he'd been sitting to eat. He wrapped his arms tight around himself, clutching his forearms with his hands, and tried to picture Lucy, asleep in bed at home, sure in the knowledge that he'd make it out all right. But the thought of her worrying, waiting – hoping - for him to come walking through the door, overshadowed it. And he hated himself for doing this to her.

*****

Lucy opened the drafts on the woodstove and filled the firebox with wood. Paulette had told her the weather was awful up at Three Lakes, so Joe would surely appreciate a nice, warm house when he got home. She let the dogs back in from their quick trip outside and notice the gust of cold that followed them into the house. Maybe she'd sit downstairs for a while longer and make sure the woodstove stayed stoked. She plunked herself down on the couch and started scribbling new lines of dialogue for her play in a notebook, but her mind kept drifting places she didn't want it to drift, like a supermarket trolley with a dodgy wheel. What she really wanted was for the phone to ring, but apart from the cycling of the refrigerator, the sometimes hiss of the kettle on the woodstove and Maggie, twitching her paws against the wood floor as she dreamt of chasing squirrels, the house was incredibly quiet. She looked down at the page again, her pencil poised, and thought about Joe wrapped up in his silver foil emergency blanket inside his pop up tent somewhere by a lake. And she wished she were there with him, keeping him warm.

*****

The snow muted the constant roar of the Nooksack River, making the silence around Joe louder, yet softer, and giving his mind nowhere to hide but inside his own thoughts. And his thoughts took him back to the bear, going down the hill on one side of that hemlock while he was going up on the other, avoiding hurting each other with the help of a tree. Why couldn't he and Hilda get something like that going? He understood that it was a major pain in her butt that his septic system was on her side of the fence, but then he thought it was a major pain in *his* butt what she was doing to her land. But if they didn't work at not hurting each other, likely as not they'd both end up screwed.

He thought about the area of land, between Hilda's new road and his property, and how trashy Burns had made it look with all that debris he'd piled on it. He remembered looking down on the zigzag in his property line when he was up in Matt Chandler's plane and his mind skipped from there to the zigzagging road he'd been on earlier today, and how it must have led somewhere at one point. To a mining claim, he guessed, in the bottom of that basin. What must that have looked like when the miners were gouging at the ground, in search of hidden treasures? And yet the desecration had totally vanished, replaced with a Zen garden for the wildlife to enjoy.

One image slipped on top of the other and Joe began to visualize the land around his septic tank all prettied up with grass and shrubs. He'd love to make it look that way only he didn't really own it. Hilda didn't really own it either since, technically, Clarence Burns had sold it to him. It was as if they were borrowing it from each other and fighting over who had the bigger claim to it.

His mind drifted back to the bear heading down towards that lush grass. Nobody owned anything in the end, he thought. It's all just borrowed ground, claimed by humans for brief periods of time. Better to make it look nice in that time, he decided.

He looked out into the darkness and watched the snow flurry around the end of the logjam. If he did clean up that section of land, Hilda might be successful in selling her front lot. Then they'd have neighbors between them. Like the tree, between him and the bear.

*****

The phone rang again at 10:30 pm. Lucy jumped, hopefully, eagerly, only to be deflated by Marsha, from Search and Rescue, confirming that they wouldn't be going out after Joe because it was still unclear which side of the county line he was on. Lucy didn't argue. How could she? But she couldn't help but remark on the irony of them being stalled by yet another boundary line dispute.

She walked back over to the couch and sat, staring at the flames flickering behind the glass door of the woodstove, thinking about boundaries. Lines in the ground. What good did they do? Anyone could come along and move them if they had the right firepower. Look at Alsace; one minute it belonged to the Germans, the next to the French, and then back to the Germans, depending on the war. She'd heard stories, when she lived there, of people waking up in the morning to new passports and orders to speak that language. What could they do but obey? Until they came up with their own language and identity. Alsatian, a glorious mishmash of French and German. She wondered what would happen if people could go into any country, without the need for paperwork. Would populations naturally settle out and become more equitable? Maybe people would fight less if they weren't tethered by a passport. Like taking dogs off their leashes and seeing them suddenly get along instead of arguing about who was the boss. What was it Buck used to tell Joe? "You never really own anything; you're just keeping it warm till the next critter comes along that needs it." Lucy liked that. She hoped Joe was keeping warm up in the no man's land of Three Lakes.

*****

Joe shifted position, fighting the urge to yield to the trenchant cold creeping into his bones. He thought about Lucy, and how he believed his life was over when Erica left him, but it was really just the beginning of something more wonderful. Like the river, life had its cut banks and its flood banks, and he just had to dig deep and wait to find out where this cut bank he was in right now was going to come out.

Then he heard a gunshot.

****

At 3:15 am the phone rang again. It was Pete, to say they'd heard a gunshot. Gary had tracked Joe's sign to an old mining road and he'd fired his rifle – twice – then heard someone fire back. They were getting closer. It was the first time the tension in Lucy's stomach eased. She walked upstairs and climbed into bed, without even taking off her clothes. She pulled her knees in towards her chest and thought about her granddad, and how much he would have liked Joe if he'd lived long enough to meet him. Lucy remembered how small she was, standing next to his bed, watching his eyes watch her as he prepared to leave this world. When she thought of things spiritual, she thought of her granddad somewhere close, watching over her. And she fell asleep asking him to keep a watch out for Joe tonight.

*****

Joe waited, thinking he should hear another shot now that he'd fired his rifle. But there was nothing. He fired once more, into the big, wet snowflakes coming down from the sky, and waited again. But still nothing. He crawled back into his makeshift shelter, set his rifle down and folded himself onto the log again. He'd spent many Sundays in church since Erica left him but now, alone in the vast, uncompromising wilderness, he couldn't help but share the Native people's belief, that the spirits of his ancestors were roaming the woods around him. He leaned forward, his forearms resting on his thighs, his face almost touching his knees, and prayed that they'd make this night shorter for him. And find a way to tell Lucy that he was okay.

Chapter 18

At exactly 6 am Lucy's eyes popped open and she wondered immediately why Search and Rescue hadn't called her yet. She threw the covers off and headed downstairs, letting the dogs out on her way past the front door. She rounded the corner into the living room, planning to stoke the woodstove, but before she could get that far, the phone was in her hand and she'd dialed Skagit Search and Rescue.

It was still Marsha at the other end. "We have determined that your husband is in Skagit County," she told Lucy. "But now we've got the problem that our team of volunteers is still out rescuing a kayaker who got stranded off the San Juan Islands." Her voice was gentle, reassuring, but the words sounded harsh to Lucy. "They've been out all night on this rescue," explained Marsha, "although they do have the kayaker now so I'm expecting them back pretty soon. Once they're here, they'll turn right around and go back out for your husband."

"I think I'm going to call some friends," said Lucy. "And see if they can't go out sooner."

"You can do that," Marsha encouraged. "And maybe let us

know if you find anyone. But we'll still go out for Joe."

"Okay, thanks," said Lucy, a sense of despondency beginning to wash through her. She dialed Shana and Dave's number before it could get a grip on her.

Shana answered, sounding sleepy. "Hello."

"Shana, it's Lucy. I'm sorry if I woke you."

"Oh no, I wasn't sleeping," Shana yawned into the phone. "I was just lying here enjoying the thought that I don't have to get up because it's Sunday."

"Joe's missing," blurted Lucy.

"Joe is? Where?"

And Lucy let the whole story pour out of her.

*****

Joe grabbed his rifle by the barrel and stumbled his way out of the shelter at first light, prying his frozen body into a stand. It wasn't even first light, really; more like the suggestion of first light. But he was alive and more than ready to get moving. The cold had seeped all the way down to his marrow and he was having trouble keeping his body from trembling like a wet dog. But he was alive, he told himself again. And still able to move. So that's what he was gonna do.

He squinted upriver, trying to clear his vision enough to see further than ten feet out, but it wasn't happening. He looked downriver. At least that way he knew, and he might even be able to catch a ride again on the Scott Paper Mainline when he got that far. He peered, foggy-eyed, into the logjam, to make sure he had everything, and saw a patch of color on the ground, just inside the mouth. "Piece of shit!" he grumbled as he slung the pack onto his back.

He hoisted his 30.06 onto his left shoulder and began the long, slow, bleary march down the trail alongside the river, heading for the clear cut at Wanlick Creek.

*****

The dogs barked on the front porch; Maggie low, slow, repetitive, Max louder, more frantic. Lucy dropped her toothbrush in the bathroom sink and smacked a towel against her mouth to clean up the mint, foamy white. She really needed to rinse but maybe this was Joe.

She scrambled around the bathroom door and saw Sonny climbing the front steps, shushing the dogs, who were leaning towards him excitedly. Lucy opened the door and the dogs trotted inside.

"Why didn't you call me?" Sonny said first, before he even made it over the threshold.

"I did. You weren't home."

"You should've left a message. I would've met up with those guys and gone looking for Joe."

She could tell he was hurt that he hadn't had the chance to go out after his friend.

"Gary wanted to keep moving," she told him, as he lowered himself into the rocking chair next to the woodstove. She walked across the living room and sat on the couch across from him, one leg folded under her. "Dave and Shana are going out today though."

"I can't go today. I promised Mario I'd help him with a building project. I can't get out of it."

Lucy waved her hand at him not to worry.

"Did Search and Rescue go out?"

"Not yet. They said they would though." She was rigid in her pose, as if relaxing might somehow take her mind away from Joe. Max came over and laid his head on her thigh, his eyes tipped up towards her, worried. She ran her fingertips from his nose back past his ears to his neck, making a small groove in his thick fur.

"You know he's going to be okay, right?" said Sonny.

Lucy nodded again, without looking up at him.

"Joe's been spending nights out in the woods since he was ten years old. He's gonna be okay."

Maggie made a sudden, small ruff, with a toss of her head, and Lucy wondered if she'd heard something outside. But Max didn't move. She waited, to see if someone came to the front door, but there was no one. Lucy tipped her head sideways, looking at Maggie; maybe she'd just been agreeing with Sonny. After all, she'd been with Joe for ten years, a lot longer than Lucy.

"At least we have health insurance now," Lucy said, thinking the worst. "So if he's hurt I can take him to a hospital."

"He ain't hurt," scoffed Sonny, to reassure her she knew. "He's probably sitting by a campfire, cooking up some breakfast."

Lucy wanted to believe that. But somehow she couldn't picture it.

"Hey," Sonny went on and Lucy could tell a change of subject was coming. Something to occupy her mind so she wouldn't fret. "I saw Luigi Acosta at the football game in Concrete last night and he told me it looks like your neighbor sold that front lot."

"Well that's good," Lucy muttered, still making grooves in Max's fur with her fingertips. And then what Sonny had said registered and gave her a thought. "Maybe the new owner will make a deal with us for the land over the septic tank."

"I doubt it," said Sonny prompting Lucy to look up at him. "Acosta said the guy would only buy the front lot if Hess took out everything from the new road to your property line. And she bit."

Lucy pushed her lips up, resigned.

"What time is it?" asked Sonny, turning his head to look at the clock on the wall. "7:30," he said. "I gotta go." He put both hands on the arms of the rocking chair, to push himself up, but hesitated, looking at her from under his ginger eyebrows, his blue eyes full of kindness. "What are you going to do while you wait?"

"Finish brushing my teeth, then clean the bathroom."

"Nah," countered Sonny. "Leave that for Joe to do when he gets home."

*****

Hilda picked up the phone to call Buck Vorhees feeling pretty darned good. She'd had breakfast in Concrete, then gone by the realty office where Luigi Acosta had handed her the escrow check for the front lot. She had it right in her hand and felt as giddy as a kid the night before Christmas. Hopefully Buck would get right on building the rest of the road so Acosta could sell the back two lots for her. Then all she had to do was make a decision about the land alongside Connors. She glanced out her kitchen window, as the phone rang in her ear, and saw Connors' front yard filling with cars. Really, she thought, glancing back at the clock on her microwave. It was only 8:30 in the morning. And the Hearing Examiner thought the pottery shop didn't have an impact on this quiet, rural neighborhood? She blew an irritated puff of air from between her lips – phuch! – and pain began to radiate from the center of her forehead.

*****

Joe's whole body ached with cold and fatigue and part of him wanted to find a young hemlock, where the boughs came all the way down to the ground, and climb in underneath. It would be soft and dry and the branches would be like a blanket over him. He could rest a while. Let himself get warm. The tips of his fingers felt like a million pinpricks but he couldn't see to move them, to clear them of the sensation. His wet wool pants chafed against his thighs like coarse grit sand paper. If he rested he might be able to get up a head of steam for the long walk out of here, his mind whispered. But Joe just kept putting one foot in front of the other. He had way too much calling him home to stop and rest now. Way too much.

*****

Panic clutched at Lucy. "Why haven't they called yet?" she beseeched, her eyes on the phone.

Dave and Shana had turned up with Joe's artist friend, Luther, and a paramedic from the Bellingham fire department, Tom, who lived just down the hill from the pottery. Then Matt Chandler, who'd taken Joe up in his Aeronca plane, and his wife, Charmaine, pulled in shortly afterwards with a woman called Willow, who had come to sit with Lucy. Lucy didn't think she really needed anyone to sit with her but she wasn't going to argue. All these people in her front yard, geared up to face the weather, made her think of her wedding again, and how the community had thought of things Lucy hadn't even considered. They knew way more than she did about what it was going to take to track Joe and she felt a sudden rush of exhilaration for the gift they were giving her.

"Yeah," said Shana, as Charmaine spread a Forest Service topographical map of the Twin Sisters out on the hood of her truck. "For one second I contemplated staying in bed, 'cause it's Sunday. And then I thought, if it were me out there, Joe would be the first in line to go find me."

Lucy's eyes filled with tears.

"We'll find him," Luther said, stepping forward and wrapping her hand in his. His hand was warm and it was the first Lucy noticed that hers were cold.

"Tell Skagit Search and Rescue that we're going in from the Wanlick Creek side," Charmaine said, pointing down at the map. Petite and feisty, with a warm, giving heart, Charmaine had driven most of the Forest Service roads in the Mount Baker Wilderness for work, and hiked just as many for pleasure. Lucy felt very reassured by her presence in the group.

She felt very reassured by everyone in this group, truth be told, and once again, emotion overwhelmed her. This time pride, for the richness of her community. In front of her stood a fire chief and his fire crew wife, three EMTs, an ex-Park Service Hotshot, who'd fought forest fires, an ex-Search and Rescue volunteer, a Forest Service employee and a 911 dispatcher for the Park Service. Not only did they all work in these mountains, but they also spent their free time hiking and recreating in them. If anybody could find Joe, it would be these people.

But they'd been gone almost an hour now and they still hadn't called her.

"It takes an hour and a half to drive up to the trailhead," Willow told her.

Now Lucy understood the benefit of having somebody sit with her. And this somebody used to be a chorus lines dancer on Broadway, which gave them a shared knowledge of theatre to discuss so Lucy wouldn't fixate on Joe being missing. Plus now, Willow was a dispatcher for the National Park Service, so she knew exactly how long the roads were to all the trailheads in the area.

"How's your show going down at the college?" Willow asked.

Before Lucy could answer, the phone rang behind her head. She snatched it up and listened to the person on the other end, then hung up. "That was Skagit County Search and Rescue," she told Willow. "They're on their way up the Scott Paper Mainline now."

"That's good," Willow encouraged. "They'll run into the others up at Wanlick Creek that way. And they'll be in a Sheriff's rig, so they'll have a phone. Plus some emergency medical gear."

Lucy felt that sick fear shoot through her stomach again. "Now I'm getting really scared," she said.

"Joe will have toughed it out," Willow reassured her with a shake of her head, like there was no way this wasn't true, her long blonde hair swishing across her shoulders. Then she looked Lucy squarely in the eye and added, "He's coming home."

"He'd better," warned Lucy. She drew her brows together, concerned. "Because I'm pregnant."

*****

It was the thought of the baby, as well as Lucy, that kept Joe trudging back and forth across the Nooksack until he came out by Wanlick Creek. The rain and the snow had filled the creek banks and he was going to have to get wet all the way up to his knees crossing it. As if the rest of him weren't already that wet, he told himself. He stepped into the current and slushed through the water to the other side. He didn't even bother shaking off, his mind was so caught up in the rhythm of his forward march.

Now that he wasn't in danger of losing his footing, he lifted his head, his neck one big ache from having been stretched down for so long, and peered at the trees ahead of him, on the edge of the clear cut. He could see their shadowy outlines guiding him this way and that towards the open land. He squinted again, his eyes detecting something that wasn't a tree. Something that was smiling in a warm, familiar way. And out of the mirage that his tired mind seemed to be offering him, stepped Shana. She slipped her hand in his and he felt warmth encircle his numb fingers. "Hi Joe," she said. "How're you feeling?"

She fell in step beside him, her presence making him feel at home already. And then there was Tom, suddenly on the other side of him, holding out dry pants for him to change into. But Joe didn't want to change; he wanted to keep on moving, towards the group of familiar faces that were emerging as he got closer.

In the background he saw a woman he didn't know, raise her hand and shout, "Stop! And we'll come and rescue you."

"I ain't stopping for no-one," Joe declared, and marched, along with his friends, past the Search and Rescue workers and on to the Sheriff's vehicle idling at the end of the road.

*****

Lucy saw Pete's truck pull in the driveway and her heart stopped. He was crying. She waited, inside the front door, Willow standing behind her, as he got out and blew his nose on his bandana.

He stuffed the bandana in the back pocket of his jeans, and started for the house, looking grim.

"No," Lucy whispered. "No-oooo."

Willow stepped forward and opened the door for him.

"We couldn't find him," Pete choked out, his chin wobbling like he was about to cry again. "We just couldn't find him."

The phone rang before Lucy could even react to what he'd said and she grabbed it.

"Mrs. Connors?" said a voice she didn't recognize. "I have someone here who wants to talk to you."

She heard him pass the phone. And then,

"Hi, babe."

Chapter 19

Three days later, they were lying on the couch together, wrapped in each other's arms, looking up at the ceiling.

"I love how light it is," Joe remarked. "Really brings out the color of the cedar."

"Like honey and cocoa," she suggested, gazing up at the cedar tongue and groove she'd sanded. "Instead of black coffee and driftwood."

He laughed. "My wife the writer."

"Got to practice those images," she told him, dropping her gaze to look at him. She liked how familiar the lines in his face were becoming, like a map on her heart.

"You did a great job," he told her.

"Thanks. But you still haven't answered my question." She heard the dogs chasing each other on and off the back porch, making a circle from the front steps to the side steps, enjoying a game now that the rain had stopped and sun was peeking through the clouds. She glanced at them. They were panting plumes of white so it was still cold out.

"Question?" Joe teased.

She raised her eyebrows, in mock frustration. "What are we going to do about the letter from Klaassen?"

"Oh." He got more serious. "I think I want us to do it."

"Really?" She was surprised.

"If we can," he shrugged. He waited for her to discourage him but her green eyes just stared up into his, expecting more. "I had an epiphany, when I was hunkered down last Saturday night, that if I do what it takes to help her sell her lots, then we'll get a buffer between us. And maybe coexist without killing each other."

"You think accepting her offer will help her sell her lots?"

"I think me cleaning up that land will help her sell her lots. And if we own it, I'll clean it up."

Lucy nodded. The Beatles were playing on the radio. *"It's been a ha-ard da-ay's night."*

"I sort of had an epiphany too," she told him. "About how none of this really belongs to us anyway."

"Buck's saying, about us just keeping it warm?" Joe clarified.

"Uh huh."

"Well and it's true," he agreed. "I mean, when we die, this will all go away," he said, motioning to indicate what was around them. "Maybe not literally, but everything that's us on this five acres will go away."

"Unless the baby wants it," said Lucy, resting her hand on her belly.

He slipped his hand under hers, smiling. "How is the baby?"

"Feels fine," she said, smiling back at him. "We'll get to see it on Friday."

"Friday?"

"The ultrasound? Remember? Doctor Deb wants us to have one because she thinks it might be twins."

"Twins would be fun," he grinned.

"For you maybe." She was being sarcastic but she loved his enthusiasm.

"Don't we have something else on Friday?"

Lucy made a face, like she'd tasted something bad. "The appeal," she reminded him. "With the Commissioners."

"Fucking Hilda," griped Joe.

"Shush," whispered Lucy. And she covered her belly with her hand again. "Not in front of the baby."

He laughed, then got serious again. "That's the only thing that makes me *not* want to accept her offer."

"Really? I thought you'd resist giving her *any* money after the way she turned us down the first time."

"I did too," agreed Joe.

The music on the radio got jaunty. *"Sergeant Pep-per's lone-ly hearts. Club. Band."*

"But I got talking with Buck yesterday, after he'd finished for the day. He was walking back to his truck as I was coming up from the mailbox and I started ranting and raving about Hilda wanting to take the $1500 that we'd previously offered now that it suited her. And he said – "Well how much is she offering to sell you for that amount?" So I showed him Hilda's drawing, you know, in Klaassen's letter, and he said it was good that she included the road because that way, we could put in a semi-circular driveway."

Lucy's made a little o with her mouth. "That's a really good idea."

"That's what I thought. It'll make it so much easier for our customers."

"I like Buck. He's very insightful."

"Isn't he though?"

"I think we got *really* lucky that he ended up building Hilda's road," Lucy remarked. "I mean, what were the chances she'd run into Buck? He doesn't even advertise, does he?"

"Uh uh."

She saw something in his face. "Did you....?"

Joe looked away, feigning innocence. "I might have slipped his business card in her mailbox."

"You tricky dog, you."

"That's the same thing I told Buck."

"I'm sure. I learned it from you."

He got serious again. "Can we afford $1500?"

Lucy made a big nod, once up once down. "I just deposited my check from the college and between that and what I've saved from the pottery, yes we can."

The phone rang and Joe rolled off the couch to answer it. "Can I still give up cutting so much firewood if we use the savings?" But he had the phone in his hand before she could answer. "Hello?"

Lucy stared up at the ceiling as she listened to his end of the conversation.

"Yes, it is."

The Beatles sang out, *"Come together .... right now .... over me."* The DJ was having a Beatles extravaganza she thought.

"Are you kidding me?!"

She swung her legs off the couch and sat up, so she could see him.

"No, that's great. And there'll be a letter confirming this? Hot dog!" he whooped. "Thanks! You just made my day."

He listened a little, then laughed uproariously before hanging up.

"Yes, yes, yes, yes, yes, yes, yes!" he hollered, punching the air with his arms and legs, his hips gyrating like he was doing the twist.

The dogs barked and bounced on the back porch, steaming up the window of the sliding glass door with their shared enthusiasm.

"That was the clerk from the commissioner's office," Joe finally told Lucy. "Hilda cancelled the appeal."

Lucy's mouth dropped open. "A peace offering!" she declared. "And before we even agreed to pay her for the land."

"I know!" grinned Joe. "I'll take it."

"Maybe she had an epiphany too."

"Maybe." He laughed again. "And the clerk was a hoot. After she finished telling me about the cancellation, she got all officious and said – Now get back to work!" He pushed his forefinger through the air like he was being chivvied along. "'I want a baking dish like my sister's. Only blue.'"

*****

The day before Thanksgiving, Joe lifted the candle lantern down off the ware board in the studio where it had been sitting since the fall firing and set it on the wedging table in front of him. He'd looked at it long enough now. And it was time. He still wasn't sure of his motivation, whether he was putting a forever reminder of the King David in her hands or re-tending the olive branch she'd given him, but he was doing it.

He picked up the lid, with the stars and moon cut outs, and swirled it around in his fingers one more time, wondering if he'd ever get that satiny, sage green again. Then he wrapped it in some newspaper. He lifted the base and wrapped that in newspaper too. Maggie sat patiently beside him, watching. "What do you think, girl?" Joe cooed. "Think she'll like it?"

He flapped open the plain blue gift bag Lucy had given him for this purpose and slipped first the base down into it, then the lid. He picked the bag up by the handle and walked to the door before he could change his mind.

*****

Lucy watched Joe's truck through the kitchen window appear and disappear among the fir trees lining Hilda's driveway, then continue on to her house. She could see him in the distance, green and black checked wool shirt over jeans, climbing the few steps up to the front door. They'd both seen Hilda leave in her Honda Civic so they knew he wouldn't run into her, which was what he preferred.

The gesture was all his; Lucy had just agreed. She watched him bend over, set the blue gift bag down by the door, then head straight back to his truck.

There you go, Hilda, Lucy thought to herself. A piece of the valley, to light your way to Hawaii.

45897846R00237

Made in the USA
Middletown, DE
16 July 2017